Stephen Hughes studied Spanish and Portuguese Literature at Hull University. An unpredictable and wide-ranging career saw him as a TEFL teacher based in Spain, an equity research analyst in London, New York and Madrid, and as a TV producer creating and writing innovative content for the national broadcaster Antena 3 Neox, also in Spain. This is his debut novel. He currently lives and writes on the Wirral peninsula.

For my wife, Marcela.

Stephen Hughes

SURFACING GLITCH

AUSTIN MACAULEY PUBLISHERS™
LONDON * CAMBRIDGE * NEW YORK * SHARJAH

Copyright © Stephen Hughes 2024

The right of Stephen Hughes to be identified as author of this work has been asserted by the author in accordance with sections 77 and 78 of the Copyright, Designs and Patents Act 1988.

All rights reserved. No part of this publication may be reproduced, stored in a retrieval system, or transmitted in any form or by any means, electronic, mechanical, photocopying, recording, or otherwise, without the prior permission of the publishers.

Any person who commits any unauthorised act in relation to this publication may be liable to criminal prosecution and civil claims for damages.

This is a work of fiction. Names, characters, businesses, places, events, locales, and incidents are either the products of the author's imagination or used in a fictitious manner. Any resemblance to actual persons, living or dead, or actual events is purely coincidental.

A CIP catalogue record for this title is available from the British Library.

ISBN 9781398464391 (Paperback)
ISBN 9781398471184 (ePub e-book)

www.austinmacauley.co.uk

First Published 2024
Austin Macauley Publishers Ltd®
1 Canada Square
Canary Wharf
London
E14 5AA

Table of Contents

I: Surfacing	9
II: The Search for Emma	15
III: The Forge	23
IV: Reflections	36
V: The Royal Society	57
VI: On the Brink	76
VII: The Bell	93
VIII: 21:00:00	101
IX: Gryphon	121
X: Burnt Ash Lodge	147
XI: The Rise of Alves	179
XII: Lucie Alone	197
XIII: The Auction	213
XIV: Identity Matters	228
XV: Trial Run	241
XVI: Welsh Gold	256
XVII: Entangled	289
XVIII: Inside	304
Acknowledgements	327

I
Surfacing

Bidston Moss — 1865

Surfacing is both exhilarating and disturbing. He coughs, taking ragged gulps of air deep into his lungs. All the subconscious routines seem to have snapped back into place without interruption but even the simplest of these such as blinking or the chill breeze provoking a shiver of raised hairs across the skin can feel frightening and bizarre. They need more time to bed down, to ease into the background, to build a sense of belonging and familiarity. He wipes his forearm across his face, clearing the rain from his eyes.

He is crouched over, kneeling, his head collapsed on his chest. There is a wet earthy mud oozing halfway up around his ankles. He strains the muscles in his neck, raising his head a fraction. A desolate marsh stretches away from him, clumps of grasses and tall reeds growing out of the waterlogged ground. To one side, the quagmire extends an indeterminable distance to the horizon while behind him, not more than a mile or so away, a dense forest of tall cedar pines mixed with silver birches rises up, marking the inland edge of the bog, presumably. No people, which means no witnesses. Less complications. That in part must be why this location was selected. But it is so cold. The rain is mixed in with wet snow.

He presses the palms of his hands to each side of his head; an excruciating pulsating pain refuses to subside. No way could this have been part of the plan. He struggles to pull together all the randomly firing strands of thought into some recognisable order, but for some reason he cannot quite pinpoint, his mind keeps veering off track and any meaningful pattern eludes him. It is as though his mind were flickering in and out of sync, phasing into and out of coherence, just brief moments of lucidity followed by scrambled, disjointed confusion. He must have been out here far too long.

He steadies his breathing. Then he hoists himself to his feet and stumbles forward, wrenching one foot after the other out of the soggy gluey marshland towards the tree line. A couple of seagulls squawk loudly as they take flight irritated at his disturbance. After several gruelling minutes, he clambers up the last few feet out of the bog to a more well-trodden path which skirts the marsh and he follows it uphill to a rise which offers a better vantage point. He looks around slowly, making out in the distance a tangle of small houses with shining wet slate-tiled roofs huddled together in the shelter of an imposing wooded hillside with a bare sandstone ridge above. A church on a low mound above the houses with a solid-looking square tower commands the terrain surrounding the village. Still nobody visible.

In the murkiness and the unrelenting cold sleet, which combine to smother out almost all of what meagre late November daylight there is, he looks down at his sodden clothing: a stylish long dark overcoat, the lower half covered in mud and slime; elegant breeches soaked through, also filthy; ruined knee-length soft leather boots. He leans over and brushes away some of the muck and grass still clinging to his coat but as his wide lapels flap open he notices with much graver concern that his white shirt is drenched not just in rain and mud but in a profusion of blood.

He is stunned. This is beyond absurd. He is not injured, that much is obvious enough. He has some scratches on his hands and lower arms but no cuts which could have yielded such an amount of blood. And if it isn't his, then whose blood is it? There was no-one else with him when he surfaced or at least he hadn't seen anyone; he can offer no reasonable hypothesis as to the provenance of the blood.

He quickens his pace following the track which climbs gradually away from the marsh and widens the closer it gets to the edge of the village. By the time he reaches the first few cottages, the rain far from easing is falling much harder, collecting into rivulets of water flowing back past him down the muddy lane towards the marsh. Unsurprisingly, the dire weather is keeping everyone off the street. But even so, he is more wary now, more vigilant, taking his time before slinking from the shadow of one building to the next.

He had been anticipating clarity not only of mind but of purpose too, a powerful momentum driving towards identifiable objectives. But he has neither, he realises. He is wandering around blind and the longer he remains out here the more urgent his need to re-establish some sort of control. The stabbing pain behind his eyes is only intensifying and through the mist of his wider exhaustion from the surfacing ordeal itself, he can now identify alarming signs of an automatic response being triggered; non-essential functions are progressively being bypassed. Something is not right. It makes him feel as though he is becoming uncoupled from time itself, falling further and further behind as each second passes, perhaps now just moments away from winding down to a complete stop.

He enters the churchyard under a roofed lichgate and follows the cobbled footpath up through the cemetery with its neglected looking headstones, many leaning precariously close to collapse. He edges along the damp lichen-covered walls of the church until he reaches the main door. He turns the large ringed door handle but it is locked.

Surely he should have seen that coming, this was never going to be the sanctuary he was counting on. He sighs in resignation. The doorway offers little protection from the freezing sleet which up here on this low hill is being driven by the wind and bites into his face. He is starkly aware that he cannot allow any reset to happen out here, alone. He feels a hint of dizziness, most likely also part of his temporal and spatial disconnect.

Then, perhaps as the result of some subtle shift in the direction of the wind, he makes out for the first time the repeated clanking sound of metal striking metal. He leaves the churchyard and walks further up the lane closing in on the noise. He sees before him the glow of a real fire from a forge burning brightly in a large open-sided barn. He creeps forward and stops just outside, where the light cast by the flames struggles to pierce the dense gloom.

From here, though, he can feel the warmth on his face while he can keep out of the light, still enshrouded in the murk and wet. He is mesmerised by the fire burning in the forge. Its warmth holding him fixed to the spot. He is so cold. And not just physically but mentally too. It is like his brain is freezing over, congealing, getting clogged up in the simplest of operations. Then he flinches, recoiling back into full awareness of the risk he is taking standing out here. This is no minor surfacing complication; something has gone seriously wrong.

A young man no more than twenty-five years of age holds in one heavily gloved hand a pair of tongs gripping a red-hot iron rod which he is pounding savagely on an anvil with the hammer in his other hand, shaping it into what looks like a large meat hook. Such is the heat in the forge that the blacksmith has dispensed with a shirt and is wearing just an old and grimy leather smock to protect against the sparks sent flying by each blow of the hammer, the sweat down his back reflecting the glow from the fire roaring in the hearth behind him.

Perhaps it is the sound of the rain pelting down on the man's already soaked overcoat which alerts the blacksmith somehow to his unannounced presence. Whatever the reason, the blacksmith suddenly spins around, brandishing the smouldering iron hook as if it were a weapon.

"Christ Almighty, Duncan, you half-scared the living daylight out of me," he stutters in relief, instantly recognising the man. So, his name must be Duncan. Progress of a sort.

The shock the blacksmith has suffered on seeing Duncan seems real enough as, far from lowering the hook, he holds it there between them, aggressive and challenging, black smoke curling up from its glowing red-hot claw. He shouts out, peering into the gloom, "What the hell are you playing at, sneaking up on me?"

"Are you seriously going to attack me…with that?" Duncan nods towards the hook.

Only then does the blacksmith look down and notices with some surprise just how intimidating the hook must be and, with what looks more like annoyance than anything else, he drops it into a large bucket of water, sending a hissing cloud of steam to the rafters.

Duncan's eyes dart back and forth scouring the shadows for others who may be behind the blacksmith deeper inside the forge but he sees no-one, the blacksmith seems to be alone.

"What are you doing here?" the blacksmith barks back at him, nervy and combative.

"I saw your fire…I'm so cold."

"You want to come in here? That's a first. Why don't you go back up to your fancy mansion on the hill?" The blacksmith then adds, more to himself than in reply, affected by a clear tinge of sarcasm, "Unbelievable."

The openly rancorous tone underlying the blacksmith's sneered outburst shocks Duncan into silence. He is clearly much older than the blacksmith, ten years at least he would guess and the quality of his attire belies a social status vastly superior to that of a blacksmith but that on its own cannot justify such a bitter response. The two clearly have form.

Duncan knows he has to say something. He has to stand up for himself. The longer he remains silent, the more the blacksmith eyes him up and down, his annoyance intensifying and now seemingly laced also with ever-growing suspicion.

"Listen, I'm not sure…"

"Jesus!" the blacksmith shouts out, interrupting Duncan and taking a couple of steps towards him and pointing at his shirt. "Is that blood? You're covered in it. What the hell has happened to you?"

Duncan backs away, nervous, pulling his coat together almost guiltily.

"It's not mine," Duncan asserts but his words come out in a vague, less than convincing tone. His grip on things is drifting out of his reach.

"So whose is it?" There is an edge now in the blacksmith's voice. He moves to the entrance of the forge and looks quickly up and down the lane outside, trying to see if anyone is out there following Duncan or anyone who maybe could have noticed or overheard their exchange on his arrival at the forge.

"I can't say… I just need some time, that's all." Duncan can feel his voice now noticeably weaker, trembling. His tongue like dried leather in his mouth. His words are starting to slur into each other. "I just need to figure out some stuff."

"I'm sure you do," the blacksmith seems genuinely shocked at Duncan's muddled confusion.

Even Duncan's logic is now slipping away. He had expected some issues but it is clear to him now that this dazed state can only mean the reboot had failed in some way, some vital part of the code had perhaps been corrupted or the realignment interrupted in some way. He can come up with no other explanation as to why these procedures would not have happened earlier, during his surfacing.

As a direct consequence, his mind is shutting down. Right now. Forcing him to take some time out, to give the inlaid upper register of mental functions a chance to settle and to knit more profoundly within his newly reset subconscious systems. Duncan panics as he realises he cannot even say if his mind will return at all if it is forced into an uncontrolled shutdown.

"Look, you'd better come inside," says the blacksmith, with a look of concern at Duncan's bewilderment as he steps to one side. "Where's James?"

Duncan steps cautiously past the blacksmith and enters the barn. He is fading fast now, his vision blurring. It feels like a corrosive rust is fogging his thoughts, jamming all his senses.

"James?" he only just manages to utter the name in a deep throaty whisper as he lurches forward stretching for the support of the doorframe but fails to grasp it and he collapses to the ground and passes out.

II
The Search for Emma

Lisbon—Present Day

Heading to Lisbon is undoubtedly a hysterical overreaction, typical Lucie, but there is something about the voicemail which has frightened her. Logical explanations are easy to come up with, of course: most likely Emma's lost her phone, or dropped it, or maybe she has gone away for the weekend with new friends or colleagues to some place outside the city with zero mobile coverage and so she is oblivious to the gazillion calls Lucie has made. But since receiving that message on Wednesday night, Lucie has been unable to get in touch with her friend for love nor money.

There is nothing in the message itself that she can point to which suggests anything calamitous may have happened and certainly no justification for involving the police or the consulate, but deep down she fears Emma may be in danger. Irrational? Without a doubt. More a feeling, as is so often the case with Lucie, call it intuition or premonition, whatever, rather than anything you can put your finger on. It comes from some deeper level and she can do nothing other than to hear those inner voices constantly ringing out like alarm bells. By the weekend, she is frantic and so now, on Sunday evening, here she is seated on an EasyJet flight to Lisbon.

It was just three weeks ago that Lucie had accompanied Emma to Heathrow to see her off. Emma had been thrilled at her invitation to Lisbon to collaborate for the summer at the prestigious Bisset Science Institute. It was a massive achievement for her. Too good to be true, for something like that to have happened to her, Emma had said. But that is not actually the case at all. Emma somehow always lands on her feet even if the roadmap to things working out that way appears indecipherable. This posting though, could represent a whole step up in her career. This could really be life-changing.

Lucie had left Emma by the WH Smiths while she bought a bottle of water for the flight, even though Emma tried to explain that the Bisset Institute had stomped up for business class in spite of it being just a short haul flight to Lisbon. Up front they stretched to as much free water as you wanted or at least Emma imagined that was the case.

But as often happened, Lucie plunged on regardless and two minutes later came back out with the bottle in her hand, just in case. They decided that even their limited budget could stretch to a glass of Prosecco to say farewell in style before Emma would have to go and check out what it was that made a business lounge so sort after.

As they went up the escalator to the food court on the first floor Emma seemed fixated looking backwards down at a glitzy silver Jaguar on an exhibition stand on the lower level. Neither Lucie nor Emma had ever aspired to owning flash cars, or at least that was what they always told each other whenever they came face to face with one. But there was no denying this particular one's sleek looks, the interior unimaginably plush. Emma noticed Lucie's agonised and mocking roll of the eyes and they both burst into laughter. Ostentatious, attention-grabbing. Sure! They staggered into the bar still laughing.

They had hugged goodbye at the queue for security but then realised that business class passengers could use Fast Track, so no waiting for Emma and before Lucie could even think of preparing for it, Emma was gone.

"Hey Lucie, it's Emma here. Just wanted to talk. Something weird…No bother. I'll call later on. Love you."

That was it. But she didn't call later on and something weird…? What does that mean?

Emma is the closest thing Lucie has to actual family, and vice-versa. They had both grown up together at Carsphairn Hall on the shores of Loch Doon near the border between Dumfries and Galloway and East Ayrshire in the southern uplands of Scotland where both their mothers had sought refuge from very different but equally tragic crises back just before the turn of the millennium.

Carsphairn Hall is an elegant and substantial manor house set in an extremely isolated and unusual location for such a grand residence. Craggy peaks descend into forests of tall pines and lower down softer hills of grassy hummocks tumble out onto the stony shore of the long winding loch. The house itself is built on a large wooded promontory jutting out a good half a mile into the water. No other houses are visible anywhere on either side of the loch. It is a scenery of pure, wild beauty.

The original owner who had developed the property had gone bust—most said unsurprisingly—and was forced to sell out at a ridiculously low price to the only buyers interested: a large independent self-contained community. All the locals called them hippies but while they certainly shared some ideals with that movement like living sustainably off the land, they were not driven by mind-expanding drugs and free love, well not to the exclusion of all else at least.

There were at one point upwards of twenty people living there at any one time. Their income came initially from donations made by the residents themselves and, as those petered out, from selling agricultural produce such as free-range eggs and fruit and veg grown in the huge walled kitchen garden down the drive towards the main gate. But in a further push to supplement their revenues they also offered sheltered housing for women escaping domestic violence or in need of major crisis rehabilitation as a service provided for the local council.

Lucie was actually born at Carsphairn Hall itself, just. Her mother's passport reveals that she was from a village called Laforêt close to Vresse-sur-Semois in the Ardennes forest in eastern Belgium. Just how she ended up in Scotland remains a mystery to Lucie but from the social security records that Lucie looked into many years later, it is clear enough that her mother became pregnant by a shipyard worker in Glasgow.

Lucie's mother had a deep sense of being Catholic and wanted to have the child come what may, regardless of her father's insistence that he could not afford a child and suggesting she should have an abortion. He was an abusive alcoholic and became more and more violent the longer the pregnancy progressed, culminating in Lucie's mother having to leave her father after he hit her in a drunken brawl and threatened to kill both her and the unborn child.

She was driven to Carsphairn Hall by a social worker from Ayr in her own car. From Dalmellington, they turned off up to Loch Doon and followed the single file track for several miles around the loch. Amidst this bleak and empty countryside, you come across an unassuming entrance which leads up to a house of such unexpected style and grace as to be starkly at odds with the rest of the area. The social worker didn't even have time to turn her car around before Lucie's mother went into labour prematurely.

Lucie was born that night in one of the nine rooms in the main building with the help of the social worker herself and several of the women co-op dwellers. Emma who was eight years old at that time and who obviously was not allowed to be present at the birth, sat nonetheless right at the top of the stairs within earshot of the whole amazing incident, shocked but intrigued.

In fact, Emma is the one who has always been there, sitting on that top stair, so to speak, looking out for Lucie and now Lucie feels there is something not quite right about it being Emma who has disappeared, if indeed she has, and Lucie the one doing the finding. Especially as Emma herself had suffered a much deeper emotional disturbance even than Lucie and has struggled more than Lucie to accept and come to terms with it.

Emma had explained to Lucie that in some way she feels that she is paying the price for some previous wrong she must have committed, although she cannot figure out exactly what it could have been. A profound sense of guilt that she in some way is responsible for all the despair and misfortune that has befallen her family. A pain which although it has faded with the years, still haunts her today.

Her father had for a time been a successful investment banker in Edinburgh: a risk-taker, an achiever. But he never could face up to the humiliation of confessing that he had—as part of the latest corporate cost-saving drive and through no direct fault of his own—lost his job. He racked up massive debts to maintain the illusion that everything was unchanged but eventually more than a year later it all became too overwhelming for him to bear and he hanged himself when Emma was just seven years old.

Emma's mother never overcame the shock of her husband's suicide and perhaps more than that, the way he had deceived her over such a long period of time. She felt betrayed by his suicide. Then, in the aftermath, the family suffered the total loss of all their possessions: their home near Prestwick, even the minimal savings that Emma's mother had always kept to one side for emergencies.

It was then that Emma's mother was accepted into the Carsphairn Hall community. But she never recovered; she increasingly lost touch with reality. It was undoubtedly tough on Emma having lost her father and then having her mother withdraw into a place from which she was also excluded. Less than a year after Emma's arrival at Carsphairn Hall, Lucie arrived and Emma found a different focus for her life.

Lucie's mother never took to the role of motherhood and could not abide the petty bickering of the other residents and it was only a few months after Lucie was born that she had a massive fight with the community leader and she stormed off, abandoning Lucie, never to be heard of again. That same week, Emma's mother died of complications related to her medication which were never fully explained to Emma. And the two girls were alone.

Lucie had dozed off on the plane but awakens with a jolt as they touch down in Lisbon. She finds her way out of the airport and only then realises it is almost midnight, she doesn't know where Emma is staying and she has nowhere to sleep. Excellent, great advanced thinking, again typical Lucie. Too late for anything else, she takes a taxi into the centre of Lisbon, booking a room at a hotel near the Rossio square on route. Her credit card will have to suffer a bit over the next few days but what can you do?

The following morning, bright and early, sees Lucie walking through the park at the heart of which sits the Bisset Science Institute. The fact that this is where her friend came to work is the only lead Lucie has in her search for Emma, although disappointingly she admits she has no contact name, not even a department title. Something to do with physics about sums up Lucie's understanding of what Emma had been recruited to do here.

Of course, Emma would just march straight into the building demanding answers right, left and centre, but Lucie likes to think she adopts a more nuanced approach. Or perhaps she hesitates a moment due to the very palpable fear in her gut that she is about to make a massive fool of herself and of Emma too into the bargain. Emma will never believe or understand how Lucie has been so freaked out by a simple voicemail. But in the end, she has not come all this way for nothing and she takes the plunge.

The Institute itself is a modern concrete structure which blends into the parkland that surrounds it remarkably well. As Lucie approaches, the morning sunlight is sharp and crisp. It will be baking hot later on but now there is still some freshness in the air, only the lightest breeze and an intense sapphire blue sky, a deeper blue than any sky Lucie can remember. She walks up the wide steps and across a low bridge over a shallow pond dotted with small islands of tall grasses.

The entrance hall is beyond a concrete overhang which stretches several metres out from the building. The brightness renders it a black impenetrable rectangle which as Lucie walks into its shade suddenly reveals a massive atrium behind a glass facade. She enters the building and approaches the main reception desk which is dwarfed by the scale of the hall. The switch to an air-conditioned chill sends an unexpected shiver across her skin. At the same time, the rustling of the breeze outside is starkly replaced by Lucie's footsteps echoing tall into the space above.

Lucie asks after Emma who in theory should be working here, somewhere. The receptionist makes a brief call in Portuguese, and then politely asks Lucie to stand in front of an electronic camera, prints out an identity card with Lucie's name and photo stamped on it and invites Lucie to go up to the third floor, waving a hand towards a bank of lifts beyond the far end of the reception area.

Lucie is met by some sort of glum-looking secretary as the lift doors open on the third floor and she is shown in silence into a meeting room which looks out over the park to the Lisbon city skyline. Lucie stands by the full-length glass windows taking in the amazing view with her back to the room.

"Quite a view, wouldn't you agree?" says a man in his mid-forties in almost accent-less English as he enters the room brimming with confidence.

"I wish I were here sight-seeing," Lucie replies curtly.

"Lucie, isn't it? My name is Fernando Castro. I am head of the Bisset Science Institute." He offers his hand and they shake somewhat awkwardly. "You are looking for Emma?"

"I haven't been able to contact her since Wednesday of last week," Lucie explains. "This is so unlike Emma."

"You know her well, I take it?"

Lucie looks at Castro suspiciously. What sort of question is that? Isn't it obvious?

"I wouldn't have flown here from London to find her if I didn't," Lucie says a little more dryly than she had intended.

"You came from London to find Emma?" Castro sounds impressed and puzzled at the same time.

Lucie is losing her patience with this nonsensical chitchat, "Could you just tell me where she is and I won't disturb you any further."

"My apologies. But I am afraid I cannot help you, exactly."

"What do you mean?"

"Emma didn't come to the program on Friday," he affixes a false sounding emphasis to the word *'program'* which causes Lucie involuntarily to raise her eyebrows.

"She didn't?"

"She should have been leading a group session, but she didn't show up." There is a silence which extends an uncomfortable length.

"And you did…?" Lucie tries to prompt Castro to explain further.

"Well, we thought she must have been ill or something."

"So, nothing." Lucie allows her frustration to show.

"Hang on. This is not some school classroom we are running here, Lucie. If someone doesn't turn up, we assume there is a reasonable justification, at least the first time."

"There were other times?"

"No, not at all…Well, except for this morning. She hasn't come in yet this morning."

"…into the *program*?" Lucie says sourly, imitating Castro's pompous intonation.

Lucie notices him frown, his body language closing down. She really could have tried to make a bit more of an effort to be pleasant. She hasn't handled this well at all.

"Look, there is nothing I can do, honestly. Really you should check out the place where she is staying. I am sure that will clear all this up."

"I don't know where that is," Lucie confesses.

"You are so *close* and yet you don't know where your friend is living in Lisbon?"

Lucie shrugs, she keeps asking herself the same question and has no answer.

"Regulations do not permit me to give out personal details of staff," Castro says dryly, at the same time pulling the phone from the middle of the table towards him and dialling on speakerphone. This is going from bad to worse. He speaks to someone briefly, presses the hang-up button a little too aggressively for Lucie's liking and addresses her again coldly, "Security will escort you out of the building."

Her meeting is over and it could hardly be termed other than a disaster. The only thing she knows now is that Emma is indeed missing. But Lucie has no intention of allowing this first setback to discourage her. There is something about this smarmy individual, Castro, which doesn't sit well with Lucie.

She just has to regroup. But there is one thing she can be certain of, that she will have to get her act together if she is going to find Emma. She will have to come up with a strategy worthy of Emma herself, but without her input. That is going to be a serious challenge.

III
The Forge

Bidston Village—1865

This time, from the moment he regains consciousness, Duncan recognises that he is firmly back in command of his thought processes; several hours must have passed. He can hear the rain clattering against the corrugated iron roof of the forge, it clearly hasn't eased at all. He is still in the same wet clothes lying facedown on the floor in a corner, well away from the hearth.

He feels cold. His throat is dry. He notices a metallic, bitter taste in his mouth from the thick layer of charcoal dust and burnt iron flakes which cover the floor. The air is heavy with the acrid smelling fumes from the fire. His sensory perception, the interaction between the external physical environment and his mind is more coherent, more vivid, the definition so much sharper and more intense.

Thankfully the piercing headache has lessened too and he even dares to hope that perhaps those realignment issues—triggered by the interruption he now considers must have been the primary cause of the problems he suffered during his surfacing—may have been taken care of while he was unconscious, without his ever needing to become aware of it. After his embarrassing collapse, passing out right in front of the blacksmith earlier, he feels relieved that maybe he can get things back on track without any lasting consequences.

He hears two voices, both male. Straight off he recognises one of them as the blacksmith's with its distinctive local accent. His face is turned towards the back wall, so he cannot see who the other one may belong to. They must be several paces away, somewhere near the entrance to the forge. But he certainly doesn't want to risk moving his head as that may well reveal that he is no longer unconscious, which in turn could scupper any likelihood of his picking up what may prove crucially important information. He remains absolutely still, listening intently.

"You ask me, it's pretty clear cut."

"Come on, Kal."

The blacksmith's name must be Kal.

The second man continues, "We don't know for sure it was him. It's Duncan you're talking about, remember."

"So now you're an expert on Duncan, give me a break."

"I just mean…"

But Kal cuts him off, "Listen, I've never—and I mean never—seen Duncan like that. Didn't know where he was. Completely off his head. In shock, I'd say."

"But that doesn't mean he killed James though, does it?" Duncan just about smothers a choke of astonishment.

"Just look at him, Angus. All that blood; that's all the evidence I need."

Duncan is going to have to tread very gingerly here; so much for getting things back on track, so much for no consequences. Given his still at best sketchy grasp on how things actually work around here in terms of his standing in the community, he can only guess how much clout he may or may not possess, and from Kal's dismissive attitude and his eagerness to jump to conclusions, that may well not amount to much, at least in the blacksmith's eyes. From here, things could so easily swerve off into unpredictable and unacceptably perilous outcomes.

He concludes that it would be infinitely wiser just to slip away unnoticed right now before these two reach a verdict in their debate as to his guilt or innocence. But as he quietly tries to start to pull himself further into the shadows, he suddenly realises that his hands are tied in front of him securely with a stout rope.

In his dismay, he pulls hard against his tether which snaps taught, alerting the two men to the fact that he has come to. Both Kal and Angus spin around to face him. Duncan struggles to a sitting position, his exasperation mounting. The rope binding his wrists loops away in front of him and is fastened to a hook in one of the barn joists way up in the rafters.

"What's all this about?" Duncan challenges the blacksmith head on. "Let me loose, will you Kal?"

At least, Duncan doesn't seem to be having any difficulty in forming his words, all that unbecoming slurring mercifully gone.

"Oh yeah, right away, whatever you say, m'lud," Kal guffaws, winking at Angus with no attempt to hide his scorn from Duncan; releasing Duncan couldn't be further from his intentions. Kal seems to be positively relishing his moment in the spotlight.

The second lad, Angus, only gets to play the role of lieutenant here and a reluctant one at that; he seems much less sure of himself and, encouragingly, of Duncan's guilt. But Duncan also immediately sees that Angus is no more than seventeen or eighteen years old at most, a good five years younger than Kal and as such will no doubt go along with whatever Kal dictates. Angus too looks strong, not as much as Kal but certainly he would not be easily overcome either if push were to come to shove. But as things stand right now, Duncan disappointingly has to accept he is in no position to do anything along those lines.

Angus approaches Duncan and squats down on his haunches next to him and as if appealing to his better judgement says, "Listen, Duncan…You must tell us what happened out there. You can see that, right?"

"I wish I could, honestly. But it's all just a blank." What else can Duncan say? It is the truth, after all.

"Well, that's convenient, isn't it?" Kal, incensed, paces back and forth near the forge door.

"Give it a rest, can't you?" Duncan blurts out, losing his patience with this smug pretentious brat, no longer able to bite his tongue. But at the same moment he realises that in his current circumstances he has no other course of action than to try and keep the conversation alive to see if he can discover any more of the facts which have landed him in this predicament in the first place.

He continues in a calm but resolute voice, "Look, all I can tell you is that I came to out on the marsh and I made my way here."

"The marsh? It's the Moss. Who would ever call it the marsh? You see what I mean, Angus."

"He does seem a bit confused, I'll give you that."

"If you ask me, we should string him up right now," Kal grins at Duncan mocking him.

Duncan has no doubt that his threat is pure bluster, in no small way for the benefit of his underling but it is nonetheless concerning that even the possibility of his being lynched is being mentioned at all.

Kal laughs and continues, "Why wait for the police? They'll only cart him off and who knows if he will ever get his just deserts or not. That guy from Wallasey who killed his own kid brother, he got off scot-free."

"He had been carrying on with his missus, though."

"Well? So that makes it OK to stick a meat cleaver in his gut, does it?"

Angus nervously tries to lower the tone back down a notch, "Don't you think maybe it should be the police who decide how to handle this, not you or me."

"Yeah, right. Well, all I am saying is that we should make sure that the same doesn't happen here."

Having to listen passively to Kal's cruel taunts with no comeback available to him highlights to Duncan just how desperate his position has become: his memory only kicks in after the crime causing James's death had been committed; he doesn't even know the man he is being accused of murdering; he is tied up with no apparent escape route and even he would have to agree that on balance, with the evidence of all that blood down his shirt, he hardly looks the incarnation of innocence. Neither is Duncan in any way confident that the arrival of the police is going to improve his prospects.

Suddenly, a woman rushes into the forge from the now total darkness outside. She is elegantly although practically dressed in a white bodice modestly buttoned to the neck and a dark green full skirt to her ankles with a knee-length black satin over-jacket. As she lowers and shakes off her umbrella which has evidently provided scant shelter from the lashing rain, Duncan sees her face clearly for the first time and is shocked at how astonishingly attractive she is. He cannot take his eyes off her.

As she looks over at Duncan, he can see the distress evident on her face. She is in her mid-twenties, tallish. She has strawberry coloured hair tied back although the wind has dislodged a few loose strands which fall unheeded across her face. Her eyes are grey-greenish like the sea under an overcast sky. Her skin is beyond pale. She is hauntingly familiar to Duncan but how could that be? How could he possibly have any recollection of her at all? But there is no denying it; her face is there, etched somewhere inside his mind.

"What's going on here, Kal?" she demands.

"He's killed James," the blacksmith states with conviction.

"That's ridiculous," the woman retorts, taking a step towards Duncan.

"I don't think this is a good idea, Jules," Kal intervenes to stop her from approaching Duncan.

"You two…Out! Now!" Jules certainly has no problem commanding authority. Duncan is impressed. He also notices a delicate Irish tinge in her voice, not a full accent, just a suggestion of one, which he can't help but find enchanting.

"But we are keeping guard until the police arrive," Kal responds peevishly.

"Well you can do that outside, can't you? I must speak to Duncan, alone." Her tone is strict, like a schoolmistress allowing no room for any more childish nonsense.

"Yeah, all right, I suppose…So long as he stays tied up." The way Kal surrenders so sheepishly surprises Duncan; Kal appears to be incapable of defying Jules. He almost seems besotted with her himself.

Jules shooes the two guys out of the forge. They break into a trot to avoid getting soaked in the downpour, tip-toeing delicately around the puddles as they cross the muddy track which threads through the village. They take shelter under the wide eaves of the stables opposite, from where they can still keep tabs on what goes on inside the forge although they are definitely out of earshot. Jules then directs her attention to Duncan. She takes a couple of paces towards him until she is standing over him before she speaks.

"Why did you do it?…For God's sake, Duncan. Why?"

"I did not kill anyone," Duncan states in what he thinks must pass as an emphatic, convincing tone, but given the way Jules frowns knowingly, it may well have fallen short of that by some degree.

"So who did, then?"

"I don't know."

"You don't know? You don't bloody know? That's not good enough! Just tell me what happened."

"I truthfully don't remember…"

"Stop! Right now. This is madness. Don't you realise?" Jules looks terrified. "I won't let you ruin our lives. Do you hear me?"

"I must have blacked out, somehow, on the marsh…the Moss, I mean."

"Mother of God! Is that it? Is that the best you can come up with?"

Jules walks to the open door of the forge breathing deeply as though she is trying to bring her mind back from a brush with insanity. She looks out at the rain splashing into the mud outside before turning back to Duncan again.

She walks over and kneels down on the floor facing him and looking him straight in the eye continues, "You may try to hide behind that blacking out nonsense with those two out there, but it won't wash with me. Do you understand? We have been through far too much together for you to spout this sort of drivel at me."

So Duncan now knows that he and Jules are together, or were at some point. It just fits so well, even though he cannot remember anything of their time together. Duncan is elated. He feels so close to this woman. In spite of her sharp tongue, he is sure a deep understanding must have existed between them.

Duncan looks deep into Jules's eyes and says gently, "You know I am not capable…of killing anyone, don't you?"

"Do I? Really? Just take a look at your shirt. *That* is James's blood."

"Why would I want to kill James? Just tell me that." Duncan says with sudden heartfelt honesty.

Jules just stares at him looking genuinely perplexed at his claiming to be unaware of why he might want James dead. So it just could be that he actually did have a motive for murdering him, maybe even a pretty compelling one. Unfortunately though, rather than alleviating things for him, this realisation could well complicate his position, as it only makes him more likely to have been the killer. And if that motive were widely known, which from Jules's expression he cannot rule out, any attempt to try to deny his involvement with the police would become even more challenging.

Then quite suddenly Jules snaps into an altogether more clinical mindset, "Look, let's be brutally honest, shall we? We both know that James was a thieving bastard. Right?"

"But how does that help us? Please Jules, we don't have much time and I need something plausible to explain *this* away." He pulls his blood-stained shirt out towards Jules.

Jules continues undeterred, "I understand it's been difficult…*He* has been difficult. All the—what did you call it?—'skimming'. He has been ripping us off ever since you brought him back from Jamaica. There's your justification. He's been asking for trouble and now he's got it. It is over. Done."

"What are you suggesting? That I admit to his murder even when I know I didn't do it?"

"But you don't remember anything," Jules sneers. "How can you know if you killed him or not? Denying it is not going to help anyone, least of all you. You need to have your story clear for the Head Constable when he arrives. Otherwise, he will rip you to pieces."

"How come James sparks so much rage in you?"

"What is that supposed to mean?" Jules says, her anger making her voice tremble. Duncan senses that this James could have been the source of major friction between them in the past.

"What was it about James that got to you…personally?"

"It wasn't me. One way or another, James was set on destroying *us*. Not you or me individually, but both of us. He had been angling for that big bust up, like the one earlier today at the house, for ages. He just pushed and pushed. But it wasn't money he was after either. He wanted more. He wanted control…over everything."

"Even you? Did he want you?"

"Don't even go there, Duncan," Jules says dismissively.

The doubt settles across Duncan's mind. What is it she wants to hide from him? He recoils from an awareness of a sharp sense of jealousy bubbling up in his veins. Was there some intimacy or secret which James shared with Jules and she protects even after James is dead? But at the same time Duncan's rational freshly surfaced self is asking just how these emotions emanating from his previous existence could be flooding into his rebooted psyche at all.

Somehow, the interruption to his surfacing has not only caused the realignment issues which led to his collapse and his forced shut down but much more startlingly has left some subconscious emotional pathways intact when they should all have been purged, and with what other, as yet unseen, consequences may have been triggered he can hazard no guess. But right now, captivated by Jules's still shocked and indignant expression, those concerns seem nothing more than trivial as he feels his passion for this beautiful woman cascade ever deeper inside him.

At that moment, there is a rising clatter and splashing of hoofs on the mud-drenched lane outside the forge as a cart drawn by a pair of horses arrives in the village, followed by a commotion of shouting which reaches the barn only in parts through the wind and rain as the Head Constable clumsily dismounts issuing orders to his runner, a low-ranking junior officer who has accompanied him, for the horses to be kept ready. The Head Constable disappears briefly into the stables opposite the forge.

Kal and Angus take the opportunity to re-establish their position inside the forge, keen to make sure the Head Constable will notice their vital contribution in guarding the prisoner although Duncan imagines that of no lesser importance is their desire to secure the best possible vantage point from which to watch and maybe even to influence proceedings.

Jules leans forwards towards Duncan and takes his face tenderly in her two hands and, making sure that she cannot be heard by either Kal or Angus, whispers, "You have to say he went for you with a knife. Nobody will mourn his passing. It's your only chance."

"Now she swears undying love for him again. See?" Kal sneers, visibly distraught at seeing Jules lavish such tenderness on Duncan, "Shame about yesterday, mind."

By his own admission, Head Constable Whitely has attended the call out himself in spite of the lateness of the hour, due to the gravity of the crime and, above all else, who is involved.

"Knifings in Liverpool are commonplace enough…" he explains as he enters the forge, removing a waterproof mackintosh he had draped over his head for protection from the rain just for the few yards crossing from the stables and throws it over a wooden work bench to dry near the fire, "…and even in some parts of Birkenhead, around the docks. But Bidston Village, I could hardly believe my ears when your lad Davey rode up and told me what had happened."

The Head Constable's runner also enters the forge and takes up his position next to Kal and Angus near the entrance.

Head Constable Whitely is, Duncan thinks, in his late fifties or even older. He is mostly bald and is not even wearing a hat or cap despite the rain. He dries his face and neck with a rather soiled-looking handkerchief. He has a pock-marked, well-weathered face. He hasn't shaved in days.

His drink-induced paunch is putting noticeable strain on the fabric and buttons of what is his only allusion to uniform: a grubby dark blue tailcoat with faded triple piped arrows on the lower end of the right-hand sleeve and a diamond shaped metal plaque showing his force number sewn into the left collar. His shirt looks a shade off-white, not unlike the handkerchief and together with his limp unstarched collar, all suggest he must live alone. But what he lacks in physique, style and cleanliness, he makes up for in personality.

"And for you, Mr Chambers, to be involved…Well, we have always had an excellent understanding in the area of contraband measures on the docks, I am sure you would agree."

Duncan wonders just how far that understanding may have stretched but he elects to keep silent rather than provide further evidence of his memory failure.

"Indeed," the Head Constable continues after a long pause, "I have always held you in the highest esteem. So your involvement here requires the arm of the law to exercise no small degree of tact and delicacy." But that apparently doesn't extend as far as to suggest that Duncan should be untied.

The Head Constable changes tack, "I have just inspected the body of James Riley, lawyer and accountant to your own shipping line, which was found this afternoon out on the Moss, and with whom I hear you had some sort of altercation prior to his demise. And now I can see that you yourself have a good proportion of the blood he lost when dying on your clothing. Could you just elucidate for us what actually happened?"

"I remember very little…"

The Head Constable cuts Duncan off in mid-sentence, "Listen, Mr Chambers, shall we get something straight from the outset? Not remembering is not an option here, get it? To me that sounds like a straight confession of guilt." The Head Constable's eyes slowly follow the rope from Duncan's wrist up to the rafters above, a gesture Duncan feels could easily be construed as a veiled threat.

Kal certainly sees it in that way and as he approaches the Head Constable and in a softspoken tone, although deliberately loud enough to be audible to all those present, he suggests, "Should we not just finish this off here and now, so to speak?"

"Has he confessed to any crime?" asks the Head Constable although Duncan notices that he does not rule out a lynching, however.

"No, he certainly has not," Jules interjects quickly, "and there will be no lynching here, Kal. Do you understand?"

"He had been stealing from me for years," Duncan offers in his defence.

"So there's your motive," Kal is quick to add, smiling at Duncan.

"Shut up will you Kal, or get out," the Head Constable says, causing Kal to back away a couple of paces, suitably chastised. "What I want to know, Mr Chambers, is how he died, not why?"

Duncan looks fleetingly across at Jules who remains impassive. Hesitantly he says, "He had a knife…"

"Well, now we *are* making progress. Somebody certainly had a knife but on the evidence I have seen I'd hazard a guess that it wasn't James."

"He lunged at me and we fought. He must have been stabbed in the fight…Accidentally."

"Right, accidentally," the Head Constable concludes. "That's your story then, is it? The truth, so help you God?"

"It is," Duncan states, although increasingly he feels out of his depth.

"So, now you clearly remember the incident…That is good. But one thing deeply troubles me having just examined his body over there in the stables. Mr Chambers, just how did James…'accidentally' as you put it…end up with two stab wounds in his back and one in his neck which sliced through his jugular vein causing him to bleed to death in a matter of seconds?"

"No! It can't be!" Jules is appalled.

"This was a vicious killing," the Head Constable expands with apparent relish. "There was no honourable duel here. You stabbed him twice in the back and then slit his throat, like he was an animal."

"That could not have been me. I swear I did no harm to James," Duncan states almost as a reflex, his eyes darting fearfully back and forth from the Head Constable to Jules.

"Yeah, well, changing your story every other minute won't help your chances of convincing a jury of that either, but we may well get to see that put to the test. If we get that far, that is." Duncan again picks up on some vague ill-defined threat that matters could be dealt with here in a less than orthodox manner.

The Head Constable turns away from Duncan. "Kal, could you and Angus please help Constable Wainwright here put the prisoner on the back of the cart and make sure he is tied up securely."

As Duncan is led by his tether out to the open backed cart outside the forge, Kal seems to take particular enjoyment in goading him, suggesting he won't even make it to the lock-up cells, playing at the same time to the small crowd which has gathered outside. In spite of the rain still pouring down, most of the inhabitants of the village have pitched up, all desperate to get a view of Duncan being carted away by the police.

In spite of the mass of evidence building against him, Duncan remains absolutely certain that he could have had no part in James's brutal murder, not because he feels incapable of such an extreme level of violence, he is certainly capable of that. But rather that he cannot identify anything Duncan had to gain by it. Duncan would never have taken his revenge in this way. Surely, he would have confronted James about his corrupt behaviour or about his relationship with Jules in a more intelligent manner, where he would have something to show for it in the end. Not some frenzied attack implicating only himself.

But strangely, what is uppermost in his mind at this seemingly hopeless juncture, actually what absolutely fascinates him, is that his mind keeps drifting back to Jules. Kal ties the rope firmly to the hitch ring on the rear deck of the cart and Duncan sits cross-legged silently searching for Jules amongst the crowd, but doesn't spot her. Duncan recognises that he should now be setting a whole new agenda, it should be gnawing away unstoppably at his insides, while in fact he still feels trapped inside some emotional legacy unleashed from inside Duncan's past.

The whole idea of his surfacing was designed to offer a clean break from Duncan's previous existence but now he finds himself tethered to the back of a cart, accused of murder and in the minds of everyone involved already tried, found guilty and sentenced.

And right at that moment, as though his eye were being drawn by that same emotional link, he catches a glimpse of Jules standing in the background but no sooner than he has made eye contact with her, she looks down at her feet, turns and walks away up the lane at the back of the stables, rounds a corner and disappears from view. She has no intention of witnessing his downfall in person. She too has no doubt as to his guilt. Duncan bows his head in despair.

Kal and Angus then help the Head Constable's runner to haul the tarpaulin containing James's dead and mutilated body from the stables opposite and load it with some difficulty onto the cart next to Duncan. They are taking advantage of the ride to shift the corpse to the mortuary which is conveniently located adjacent to the lock-up cells.

Some minutes later the Head Constable takes his seat next to the runner up front, who cracks the reins lightly ushering the horses to walk on and the cart pulls out of the village on the track towards the town.

In the darkness at the back of the cart, Duncan unobserved carefully removes from his sleeve the meat hook which Kal had been fashioning in the smithy when he arrived hours earlier. Duncan could never really understand how nobody noticed that when he was paraded in front of the crowd and pushed up onto the cart, his overcoat was not hanging quite as comfortably as befits a garment of such style and cost.

It shows just how overconfident and arrogant his captors have been. The hook could by no means be considered sharp but its ragged unfinished edge should suffice to cut through the rope and release his hands if time is kind to him.

The Head Constable had made it clear as they set out, shouting over his shoulder at Duncan that he had heard all he needed from him. His guilt was beyond any reasonable doubt. So, they had travelled in silence for most of the time.

The closer they get to Birkenhead, the more Duncan convinces himself that the Head Constable is capable of brazenly turning a blind eye to his well-being in the lock-up cells. And if Duncan were to turn up dead the next morning, having taken his own life according to the inquest findings, the Head Constable would believe justice had been served just as efficiently or perhaps even more so than if he had been hauled through the legal niceties and sent to the gallows some weeks from now.

As they approach the first gas street lamps of Birkenhead, the horses' hoofs echoing back loudly off the tall wall that they have followed most of the way down the dock road, Duncan knows his time is running out and he must act now. He makes a final desperate effort to pull his wrists apart and succeeds in breaking the frayed rope tether he has been scraping against the hook edge ever since they set off. He bides his time for a few seconds so he can take advantage of the last pool of darkness before the deserted warehouses and empty dock buildings are transformed into dwellings, before they enter the town itself.

He rises to his feet, and in a single wide arcing motion, he swings the meat hook high in the air above him and brings it down with brutal force straight into the right-hand side of the runner's neck. The runner drops immediately to his knees, blood spurting from the wound where the hook remains firmly lodged in his neck.

With an aghast shocked look on his face, the runner makes a futile attempt to grab the hook but topples forward falling in between the two horses, which immediately rear up in panic, jolting the cart wildly, causing it to overturn and sending both the Head Constable and Duncan crashing to the ground. The horses run off down the dock road still attached to the reins.

Duncan is the quicker to react and before the Head Constable has realised fully what has happened Duncan has sprawled over him, pinning him down and has wrapped the remains of his rope tether around the Head Constable's neck and now he tightens it with all his strength.

Duncan presses his mouth close to the face of the Head Constable and utters with a bitter grimace, "How dare you threaten me. You just wouldn't listen, would you?"

The Head Constable flails at the rope but can do nothing to stop the attack and slowly his lips begin to turn a deathly blue and purple colour.

"I honestly cannot waste any more time here…" Duncan shows no mercy and squeezes the final breath out of his victim, "…I have so many things to do."

When it is over, he gasps, exhausted, and rolls onto his back. It has stopped raining. A few moments later, he slowly gets to his feet, contemplating dispassionately the carnage he has caused and then turns nonchalantly away and slips into the shadows.

IV
Reflections

Lisbon—Present Day

Lucie cycles skilfully to a skidded halt just outside the main entrance of the Bisset Science Institute. Her years of pedalling like crazy around Loch Doon on that abandoned wreck of a bike she and Emma had found and fixed up is finally paying some dividends.

She is dressed in bright multi-coloured lycra leggings and a clinging sports bra. A cycling helmet and a courier delivery backpack in garish reflective orange complete the look, all of which she purchased in the same store where she hired the bike.

Absolutely no-one, Lucie hopes, could recognise her as the same girl who only that morning had entered the building to see Fernando Castro. She locks the bike to a railing, adjusts her backpack, removing a large envelope which seems, given its size, to contain documents and with one last deep breath, she walks with conviction into the building.

"Sala de postagem?" she cries out towards reception. She has found out, thanks to Google translate, how you say *post room* in Portuguese although her atrocious accent most likely renders it close to unintelligible. She hoists the package aloft in the direction of the same receptionist who had greeted her earlier on, hoping that this might clarify her intention. This time she is waved down a side staircase without so much as a glance. Confidence, as they say, is the key to disguise.

As she descends the stairs, the natural light fades, replaced by a flickering neon underworld and the slick, stylish decor of the reception hall is progressively superseded by an ever more grubby, neglected functionality the deeper she goes. In the post room at the bottom, trolleys filled with packages of all shapes and sizes are littered across the whole space, with one even propping open the fire-doors all but blocking the emergency exit entirely, forcing her to turn sideways on to squeeze past.

A long counter stretches all the way down one side of the room, manned at its far end by a bored looking guy who Lucie thinks is far too young not to be in school. He perks up noticeably as she approaches, more interested in her lycra-clad physique than anything else, no doubt.

"Package for Emma Kelman," she says.

"Deixá-lo lá," the post room guy says making no effort at all to dissimulate his blatant staring at her breasts.

"I'm sorry?"

"Leave it over there," he surprises Lucie speaking in a remarkably good English accent.

"This is personal delivery only," Lucie counters.

The lad disinterestedly pulls the phone across the counter and checks for a number on his computer screen. He has a short conversation in Portuguese and then states, "She's not in the office today."

"This is the address I was given," Lucie says angrily. "What do I do now?"

The lad shrugs, "I can sign for it, if you like."

"No way. I can't hand this to anyone other than Ms Kelman. I need her home address."

"We are not allowed to give out personnel data," he quotes from the employee manual.

"Oh, give me a break, won't you? This is urgent. If I don't deliver this quick, I will get it in the neck."

"So why should I break the rules for you? What do I get out of it?"

"Look, I don't have money. I wouldn't be working as a courier if I did, would I?" Lucie is indignant that the post room guy wants a bribe of some description.

"You are quite something, you know? I don't believe a word of it. You're not a courier rider at all, are you?"

Lucie looks at the lad differently. She has been rumbled.

He lays it out for her, "A real courier would jump at the chance of me signing for the package. Delivery done, move on. What is your game?"

"How come you speak such good English?" Lucie has no real hope now that she will be able to turn this around. Genuine curiosity has fuelled her question.

"I spent a couple of years just outside Birmingham. A while back."

"Wow! Living the life, weren't you?" Lucie scoffs gently. "I mean…compared to Lisbon."

"I see you know Birmingham," the lad smiles.

"Some," Lucie admits.

"So how come you are here, stuck in this basement with me, pretending to be a courier?"

"My friend is missing. I didn't know how else to get her address. Can't you help me? Please."

"Well, that I can sort of relate to," Lucie's impassioned plea seems to have struck a chord with the lad.

"I have to find her. Somehow."

The lad appears in the end to have none of the issues with protocols that Fernando Castro had. He couldn't care less about the rules. "Listen, I shouldn't tell you her address, as such," he says while bringing up Emma's personnel file on screen and swivelling it towards Lucie "but there's nothing I can do to stop you seeing it by chance, I reckon."

All he needed was to be in on Lucie's playbook, rather than being the guy who gets duped by some phoney courier. And remarkably, with no fuss, his allegiances have flipped and he is firmly on the side of this rather cool-looking lycra-clad lady in distress. Lucie leans forward and notes down Emma's address.

"You've saved my life…" Lucie thanks him, realising that she doesn't know the lad's name.

"Ricardo," he prompts her. He looks well satisfied at his conspiracy with Lucie and wishes her luck in her search.

Lucie can, nevertheless, totally feel his ogling stare on her backside as she runs up the stairs but she has Emma's address and she bursts back out of the building in high spirits. That went rather well.

Less than an hour or so later, Lucie looks at her reflection in the windows of the shops as she walks up the street towards the Santa Justa lift tower which offers the quickest as well as the quirkiest way to climb the long and exhaustingly steep hill from the main square of Rossio up to the more residential and fun night life area of Bairro Alto which is where it seems Emma is staying, just a stone's throw from the Basilica da Estrela.

She is now back in her own drainpipe jeans and sleeveless tee-shirt. But she is more interested in how she looks in the pair of sunglasses she has just bought from a street vendor next to the rather grand steps leading up to Rossio station.

Hey, it is really bright in Lisbon, dazzling. Sunglasses are fully justified. Everyone wears them.

She tilts her head this way and that, checking out the style which, given her smile, seems not to displease her. But then that smile fades as she experiences a fleeting sensation on some subliminal level, like catching a glimpse of some pattern layered behind reality. Then it deepens into a feeling of unease which snags and pokes at the edges of her consciousness and finally crystallises around a figure she sees standing in the background behind her in the reflection, a figure she has seen before. She is being followed.

As a kid at Carsphairn Hall, as far back as she can remember, Lucie had always taken advantage of mirrored images, to scan for any other parallel information or meaning not apparent from the usual non-inverted perspective.

Back then, Emma was with Lucie most of the time, the two had become totally inseparable: more than sisters, more than friends. The community too seemed comfortable to let Emma take on this role. Perhaps they saw it as killing two birds with one stone: Lucie had a devoted carer, while for Emma it provided a sense of purpose which went some way to offset the difficulties she endured at school.

But despite that intimacy and attention, it was with some surprise that Emma noticed that from Lucie's favourite spot, the sun trap near the gate in the walled garden, Lucie, aged four or five, not more, would use the reflections in the glass panels in the greenhouse as an early warning system for any adults venturing into the garden. She knew all the angles, the scope and range of the reflected image, allowing her to gain a few seconds advantage, in which to decide whether to hide from them or not.

It was second nature to her, to identify things in a reversed version of reality. She became adept at finding out stuff about the adults who would come in to buy vegetables and fruit grown there, a way of spying on them without their knowledge. When in full view, they would shower her with kindness, almost adulation, but then, as Lucie grew older she began to see in those reflected images their sniggered criticisms or worse, their thinly veiled disgust at Carsphairn Hall's educational shortcomings at having the two girls out of school during term time. But what did they know? They came and went without seeing what really happened behind the closed doors of the community.

Before her father's death, Emma had struggled with the pressure of school learning. She initially had been pushed into a fee-paying primary school just outside of Ayr with high academic standards and even higher expectations laid on the pupils but from the start she performed abysmally and rejected with hostility the demands placed upon her by a system she was not old enough to understand.

She was classified and condemned as a failure by both her father and her form teacher from the age of just six years old. She would cry alone every afternoon in her room. Her despair only increased following her father's suicide, fuelling her rebellion against any hint of an academic goal and she bitterly opposed being forced to attend the local primary school in Dalmellington when she first arrived at Carsphairn Hall.

After two years at that same school, and with no sign of any improvement either in her attitude or her marks, a young and reportedly at one time brilliant university professor named Jackson Langley who had dropped out back in 1980 at the age of thirty-three and who spent most of his time working in the garden by day and most of his evenings chilling out with the support of some mind-altering mushroom or another, spent several unexpected afternoons just chatting with Emma and it became abundantly clear to him that, far from being an incompetent disrespectful slouch as she had been so often described by the teaching professionals, Emma was quite capable of learning, all she needed was some gentle coaxing out of her deep insecurity in the classroom.

Quite a breakthrough although hardly surprising given her circumstances and Jackson took this as evidence of the failure not of Emma but of the educational system itself. He was so convinced that he made a formal application to the local council, with the support of the Carsphairn Hall community, to take Emma out of school and to provide home-schooling under Jackson's own tutelage. This also fitted in remarkably well with the prevailing views in the community at Carsphairn Hall that stress-free education was best for the psychological development of a child, that the skills required for life were best acquired in a practical setting as and when the child demanded it, not the system.

The council caved in, fearing the onset of potentially damaging publicity if this whole issue were to end up in the courts, and Emma started classes with Jackson. This had the double benefit of helping Emma get a meaningful second chance to kick start her education and to provide Jackson with the motivation and self-esteem he needed to back off definitively from substance abuse as he dedicated himself to the educational requirements of a child.

To say this arrangement was transformational is an understatement. Emma's education had never even got out of the blocks but under Jackson's careful guidance and methods, Emma amazed herself, realising she could not only handle studying but that she was actually quite good at it, and she flew ahead. Her enthusiasm mushroomed spanning all the subjects Jackson presented to her but she was particularly gifted with an astonishing analytical ability in Jackson's own subject of physics which thrilled and spurred on both of them equally.

As a consequence of Emma's lasting and deep distrust of the school system, she took a special interest in Lucie's education particularly around the time when Lucie was coming up to primary school age. She begged the community to keep Lucie out of the system which had hurt her so much and with Jackson more than happy to double the size of his class, the local authorities approved the right for both to be educated at home in Carsphairn Hall.

As Jackson slowly but surely came to the realisation of the full potential of Emma's privileged mind he started to push her to consider applying to go to university to challenge herself further. But she would not even think about it. She would never abandon Lucie who was just nine at the time.

"Maybe when Lucie is older, and can come with me…then, maybe."

So, Emma dedicated herself to looking after and supporting Lucie while she herself followed the advice of Jackson on how to develop her own studies in physics without actually attending university. In the end, Jackson's physics study regime was without doubt even more challenging and more robust than any undergraduate course would have been and she quickly advanced beyond the not insubstantial capabilities of Jackson himself, much to his admiration and pride, even if it was wholesomely belittling and humbling to find himself in need of extra hours of study to keep up with his student.

But in amongst all this physics mania, Lucie's needs were never overlooked and the education she received certainly could hardly be considered subpar, far from it, although it differed from Emma's absolutely. The teaching Emma and Jackson together gave Lucie was well rounded and detailed but physics and mathematics or indeed any other academic discipline couldn't have been further from Lucie's mindset and increasingly, she focused all her energy onto art, in all its forms. And this received just as much support from Emma and Jackson; academia was only one of the possible ways to focus an education.

Lucie even started, from the age of about seven, to sketch the visitors to the kitchen garden and she was so good at capturing some internal spark in them that she turned it into a quite successful little business. Mind you, whenever possible, she would keep her earnings back from the community coffers, saving and hiding the proceeds in her room. Emma was in on it all and agreed that this was down to Lucie's skill, and insight, her vision. This should be Lucie's, and Lucie's alone.

The result was that Lucie ended up with a highly flexible, problem-solving mind. Unworried by testing and exam structures, she followed her instinct guided by both Emma and Jackson who were excited to see her explore the world in her own unique way, at her own pace.

Back in Lisbon, Lucie is now approaching the Santa Justa lift. Having identified that someone, a specific real guy, is following her, Lucie finds profoundly disturbing. What is she getting dragged into? What has Emma got herself involved in? Lucie pays her fare at the kiosk and goes into the imposing polished wooden chamber. On the outside it is crisscrossed with metal struts reminiscent of the Eiffel Tower in Paris which was indeed—Lucie learnt much later—its inspiration when it opened over a century ago. She is one of the first in and moves straight to the far end. She turns and stands facing the other passengers entering the lift. The lift capacity is just twenty people and it only half fills up but her tail is not intimidated by such proximity to her and does not hold back.

Knowing he is there, occupying the same space as her, makes her want to scream. She can see him so close up. It brings back to her mind events she has long kept hidden away deep inside. Being observed without her knowledge reignites such traumatic memories for Lucie. But she knows she needs to stay focused on the present, not to allow those fears to surge through her. Now is not the moment to be delving into all that. She focuses on her breathing, inhaling and exhaling slowly through her nose, calming her heart rate.

He is a young man, certainly still in his twenties. He has dark intense eyes, hair fashionably long and clean-shaven. He ignores her and avoids eye contact. He is wearing a leather bracelet with a double buckle and a metal ring, maybe platinum or silver, on a knotted leather thong around his neck outside of a tight-fitting white tee-shirt.

He works his body, no doubt on that front, and has a vain streak witnessed in a tattoo on his left upper arm of what seems to be a star with unequal arrows of light bursting from its centre half covered by his tee-shirt sleeve. All in all, it is a look which Lucie would usually find quite appealing and while he does not look in the least bit threatening, undoubtedly he is following her and that is enough to make her skin crawl. He turns to the side and stares impassively out at the view across Lisbon as the lift climbs noisily.

Finally, the lift clanks uncomfortably into its resting place and Lucie's tail is obliged to exit before her. He then he dawdles nonchalantly outside a shop window until she has gone past and resumes his pursuit.

There is nothing she would like more than to challenge him but she concludes that while the time for that may well come somewhere down the line, now is not that time. Actually, right now, it would be so much better just to be rid of him altogether. So, when a yellow and white tram eases into view around a corner, Lucie at the last moment sprints and jumps on at the last moment, squeezing through the door just as it is closing. The conductor is none too impressed with Lucie's absurd risk-taking. She moves quickly to the rear platform looking back down the street to her tail who after some metres seems to have given up on any hope of catching the tram on foot and he eases back to walking pace staring directly at Lucie, giving her an inordinate amount of deeply childish pleasure.

After only a short ride through the historic white stoned buildings of Bairro Alto, Lucie steps down off the tram at the last stop before it struggles up the hill towards the Basilica da Estrela. She then crosses the street which is fairly narrow at this point and stops in front of a doorway below a heavily corroded but still just legible sign reading Residencia Santa Rosita. Bizarre that Emma, such a staunched atheist, would have even considered staying at any place with such a clearly religious name and where some of her payment could end up supporting said religion. She presses the bell and after just a couple of seconds, almost too quickly for anyone to have reacted, the latch buzzes open on the iron gate at street level.

The entrance to the residence is up a dingy flight of stairs. Lucie hits the light switch just past the gate and a single bulb flashes on at the top of the stairs barely sufficient to light the way up, accompanied by a loud hum from a timer counting down the adequate amount of time for visitors to climb to the front door above. She goes up the stairs gingerly, taking them two at a time. The yellowish paint is peeling off the walls, damp patches a darker brown colour. A musty smell contrasts sharply with the suffocating heat in the street. There is no way that Emma chose to stay here for its style or comfort either.

The solid oak door at the top of the stairs has a large forged brass peep hole which makes not even a half-hearted attempt to hide the viewer and Lucie can see clearly that there is already someone keeping tabs on her, but the door steadfastly remains shut. No need to ring again, thinks Lucie. Let's get to it.

Lucie steps right up to the spy hole and raises her voice directing it with a touch of irritation at whoever is behind the door watching her, "I am looking for Emma, the English girl."

After some delay, the door finally opens revealing an elderly lady dressed entirely in black with a headscarf which suggests she must be from a religious order, a nun presumably given the name of the residence and its proximity to the Basilica.

"She gone," says the nun in broken English.

"Where gone?" Lucie replicates the nun's turn of phrase, mostly in an attempt to make herself more easily understood.

"She no pay. Fifty euro…You pay, I remember. OK?" Lucie is amazed, the old nun actually has the audacity to haggle with her but Lucie also has to admit that the nun is coming at this from a position of strength.

"And you can't afford a coat of paint for the stairs," Lucie says to herself taking a fifty euro note from her pocket. Lucie goes to hand over the cash but holds it back suddenly for a second, teasingly.

"…but you let me see her room too, OK?" The nun grabs the note with some disgust.

As the nun unlocks Emma's room, with a large old-fashioned key kept on a chain with a multitude of others, making her appear more akin to a gaoler than a nun, she explains, "Three guys. One week ago, on Tuesday…no, Wednesday. They come here…They arrest your Emma."

"Police?"

"Maybe, but no uniform. So maybe no."

Lucie gets nothing more of use from the nun but Emma's room does provide some food for thought, if no answers. It is quite a grand room for such a down at heel type of place. There is absolutely no trace of Emma at all. No belongings. There is no bathroom, just a chipped bowl and an elegant water jug on top of a chest of drawers in the corner.

Emma had to share the loo and shower with all the other residents which again is so un-Emma. The one thing that surprises Lucie is that there is an amazing balcony looking out onto the street, west-facing with the afternoon sun now streaming in. Lucie leans over the railing and can easily see the Basilica entrance. She could touch the overhead cables of the tram if she leant out just a fraction further.

Lucie also notices that the balcony offers an ideal spot to keep an unobtrusive eye on the comings and goings into and out of the yard and warehouse on the other side of the street of a company named Alves S.A. Lucie stares at the sign in disbelief. Alves? Really?

Alves was the name of the guy Emma got so excited about a couple of years ago. Emma doesn't have that many flings and one named Alves…Well, the name sort of sticks in the mind, doesn't it? There had been some lecture or something, Lucie couldn't remember the details. And then, they had gone off for the weekend together to the Wirral. Odd? Of course. But Emma never was one for Benidorm or Mallorca. Lucie had quizzed her endlessly when she got back but Emma never let on what happened.

"Listen, kid," Emma had always called Lucie kid, in the most affectionate and intimate way, when she pulled rank on her as now to explain something glaringly obvious that Lucie hadn't picked up on. It made Lucie feel warm inside whenever it happened. "He's old enough to be my father! It was work, Lucie. Nothing went on."

That was Emma's way of drawing a line under it. But Lucie knew something when she saw it. No doubt about it. Emma hadn't said anything about Alves being involved in her recruitment. Lucie had even mentioned Alves when the Lisbon position came up but Emma swore blind that Alves wasn't involved. So, what on earth was Emma doing with a room directly opposite Alves, S.A.? Too much of a coincidence.

Then Lucie feels a shiver go down her spine. Below her, on the street, tucked into a doorway opposite in the shade, Lucie's tail is back.

Lucie strides out into the baking heat on the street, she steps into the roadway and flags down the first cab to pass by and jumps in, asking to be taken to the nearest police station. Then she hunkers down in the back seat until she can see her tail in the passenger side wing mirror.

Annoyingly she notices that he too is already stepping into a cab. Of course, that must be what he did to follow her in the tram. Lucie feels a bit foolish that what she had thought was such a clever ruse had been so effortlessly side-stepped.

As she walks up to the single glass door with a rather tatty, sun-faded sign stuck behind it, confirming this represents the public access point for the 3a Esquadra—Bairro Alto police station, Lucie looks around carefully but she cannot see anyone following her now. Not surprising, she supposes, given where she is going, but she knows he is still there, somewhere in the shadows, watching her.

If the entrance of the police station was unassuming, the interior of the office into which she has just been deposited is downright joyless: a rusted metal table and two collapsible plastic-seated chairs, not even a 'Most Wanted' poster or two to liven up the blank, dreary walls. An antique-looking air conditioning unit blocks out almost the entire window, emitting an agonising whirring noise but next to no cool air, given the sweltering heat in the room. An old-fashioned bulky computer screen is the only evidence that would give away that this is in fact the twenty-first century and not the nineteenth. The uniformed officer who has been seated opposite her for the last ten minutes looks bored to death, like police work is way down on his to do wish-list.

Lucie tries to egg him on into some sort of action, "Aren't you going to at least go and talk to the owner of the residencia? She can confirm that Emma was taken away by three guys."

"Maybe she has a new boyfriend?" he shrugs and sniggers sardonically. "Or maybe a few." Probably the standard approach to investigating the disappearance of foreign girls, Lucie thinks.

The officer, passes his hand slowly through his thinning hair. In his late fifties, he seems to be somewhat in awe of the computer in front of him. He carefully puts his finger on the keyboard and presses enter.

"I can assure you that she was not arrested by the Lisbon Police Dept. Any arrests of foreign nationals would be in the system, no exceptions." The officer scans the computer screen without looking up. "There's nothing here. Not much we can do."

"Emma is not some tourist here to get laid," Lucie says with bitterness and exasperation. She then flat out demands to file an official missing person report. The officer grudgingly retrieves the relevant forms from a drawer under the table, takes down Emma's full name and asks in a mockingly apathetic tone for the address of the residencia.

"Hang on. I've got it here somewhere," Lucie hunts in her jeans pockets for the piece of paper where she had noted down Emma's address. "It's in the street that goes down from the Basilica. Just opposite the entrance to a company called Alves." She finds the piece of paper and hands it over to the officer.

"Alves?"

This for some reason has piqued some sort of genuine interest in the officer for the first time. He picks up a phone and moments later a plain clothes man comes into the room. He is young to be the senior officer but undoubtedly, he is the one in charge. His suit is good quality. Perhaps too good to be a work suit for a policeman or even a detective. And he has a Rolex watch which could easily be real although Lucie can never distinguish real from fake when it comes to watches. He sits down looking at the half-filled in form on the desk.

"What did Miss…Kelman have to do with Alves?" he asks, finding Emma's surname easily on the form.

"Nothing. I mean, nothing as far as I know."

"So why do you mention it?"

And so, just the merest mention of Alves had turned the reporting of a missing person into an interrogation of Lucie herself. Clearly Lucie has touched a raw nerve. Alves commands some respect around here or else is perhaps the subject himself of some ongoing police investigation. The younger officer in the end introduces himself as Detective Farinha. Then, his level of interest is elevated a notch higher when Lucie explains that Emma is working at the Bisset Institute.

"With Fernando Castro?" Farinha asks, his eyebrows raised as if in suspicion, doubting the veracity of Lucie's version of events.

"That *is* what I just said," Lucie is losing patience yet again. She must try to keep these tetchy impulsive remarks under control. No good comes from them, she knows only too well. But why does everyone treat her like she is lying through her teeth?

In any event, Farinha and his colleague seem to know nothing of Emma's whereabouts, in all likelihood about the exact same amount as Lucie herself. Farinha was more polite, though, as they brought the interview to an end and he even offered her his card and suggested her contacting him if she needed anything.

"Well," Lucie had said to the uniformed officer as she left, "at least Emma is now in *the system*." No reaction.

As Lucie walks back out of the police station she realises that her search for Emma has hit a dead end. So much for her being the next Hercule Poirot. He had been a Belgian like Lucie's mother but that is where the similarities ended. Perhaps it is time to take a different approach, more of a Bruce Willis sort of thing, not that he is Belgian, or at least Lucie doesn't think so.

Then, as she begins the long descent towards the main square of Restauradores, she glances over her shoulder and like magic, as she anticipated, there is her tail back on the case, standing out to her now like he had some post-produced arrow tracking his precise location through the urban scene. This has gone on quite long enough. She walks a couple more streets down the hill away from the police station and then she accelerates her pace, breaking into a run.

She races around a corner into a side street and immediately ducks out of sight into a doorway. A few moments later her tail rushes into the street and as he comes alongside Lucie's hiding spot, she lunges out grabbing him around the neck and entwining her legs around his, causing him to crash to the ground with Lucie on top of him.

"Bloody hell!" he groans. "I think you've broken my shoulder."

Lucie grabs his hair and jerks his head back until his face comes right up next to hers and says threateningly, "Who the hell are you? Why are you following me?"

"I saw you at the Science Institute," he says quickly, clearly in pain.

"So?" Lucie if anything tightens her grip.

"Look, I thought you must know something about Alves. Let me go, will you?"

"Who the hell is Alves?" Lucie shouts at him desperately. Alves again. Lucie can't believe it.

"OK, OK," he concedes defeat. "Just let me go."

It turns out Lucie's tail goes by the name of Zac. It makes little difference to Lucie what he calls himself. She is not going to be taking at face value anything uttered by someone who has been sneaking around, following her. Zac has certainly hurt his shoulder but broken it is not, just a bit bruised. That'll teach him for picking a fight with her in a cobble-stoned street. He is now sitting on the kerb, cradling and soothing his shoulder.

"Why did you have to do that?" Zac complains. "Why not just ask me politely to stop?"

"Just tell me why you were following me."

"Look, I'm just doing a background search," Zac says, stretching his arm out above his head, an agonised look on his face.

"What does that even mean?" Lucie responds harshly.

"You know, like what a private investigator does," he says, looking straight at Lucie, maybe almost proud of it.

"No way you are a private investigator. Come on."

"No, no. I'm not. I said *like*. Actually, I am in insurance. Honestly."

Lucie reserves judgement on whether to believe that too but oddly it sounds vaguely plausible or else Zac is a much better liar than her instincts suggest.

"So what do *I* have to do with insurance?" Lucie asks.

Apparently, a year or so ago, Alves had made a claim on the loss of some hi-tech gear which was on a ship that went down in the Straits of Hormuz en route to Lisbon. The claim ran to millions of euros and Zac's company which works habitually with Lloyds names on insurance fraud investigations had been hired to take a look at whether the claim was legit. Zac speaks Portuguese, well some; he has owned a time-share in the Algarve for a couple of years. So, he was given the job.

Lucie has to admit that Zac has been pretty upfront in answering her questions and he swears blind that he knows nothing about any Emma, missing or not. He is only interested in Alves.

Given the oppressive afternoon heat, they decide to call a truce and to adjourn to a table in the cool interior of an almost empty bar, the walls covered in huge antique-looking mirrors which make the place look massively bigger than it actually is. There cannot be more than half a dozen tables and a few barstools tight up against the counter.

The barman who is impeccably dressed in a white tuxedo and a black bowtie, doubles as waiter for the tables too and is placing two absurdly tall and narrow glasses of beer in front of them on top of two serviettes to capture the stream of condensation. Quite stylish, thinks Lucie.

"Now you tell me something. What were *you* doing opposite Alves, in that residencia?" Zac is the one asking the questions now, trying maybe to piece together who Lucie is and how she plays into his agenda.

"It has nothing to do with Alves. Emma was living there."

"Was?"

"Yes, she's gone, missing. Remember?"

Something tells Lucie she should, for the moment at least, stop short of levelling fully with Zac on what the nun told her, or for that matter on the disproportionate curiosity that the Lisbon police department, or at least Farinha, showed in Alves. And she certainly has no intention of revealing that Emma and Alves had known each other in the UK.

"How come Castro met you personally? You'd think, being the Director of the Science Institute that he would have more important things to do than seeing the friends of some summer intern."

Lucie had never thought about it. But Zac has a point.

"How do you know who I saw?" Lucie counters.

"I have a sort of a thing going with one of the receptionists," Zac winks. "Then I saw your courier stunt," he laughs. "That was when I decided to follow you."

"I didn't ask to see Castro. I just asked for Emma and he came to see me. But he couldn't tell me anything."

"Or wouldn't."

"What are you getting at?"

"First you go to the Science Institute and the Director himself sees you. Then you turn up outside Alves's offices. It seems your Emma and Alves are somehow connected. Look, the one thing I have discovered, pretty much the only thing to be honest, is that Fernando Castro is in cahoots with Alves. Alves has been pumping investment hand over fist into scientific research and Castro is managing the whole thing."

"What sort of research?" Lucie asks.

"It's something to do with quantum mechanics I think."

Lucie finds the very idea of opening up to any man she hardly knows challenging in the extreme. And to top it all this was a man who had been trailing her, observing her from darkened doorways. Even though many years have passed since Lucie left Carsphairn Hall, the events surrounding her flight from what was her home—the only world she and Emma knew—still cast a long and ominous shadow around her. But she has to accept that to have any realistic hope of finding Emma she really needs some support, so she decides a pooling of resources makes sense.

"Emma is a specialist in string theory which is linked to quantum mechanics too, I think," Lucie hesitantly contributes.

And so, while Lucie and Zac sit together and come up with a plan, she tries to keep her past from encroaching on her present—something vastly easier said than done.

At its best, Carsphairn Hall had been a beautiful shared experience. Hard work, for sure, none of life's so-called luxuries, and in return a stress-free and sustainable lifestyle in an awesome if somewhat austere natural setting. But it certainly wasn't at its best all of the time, that wasn't the whole picture; there was a much darker side which ultimately posed a very tangible threat for the two girls and in particular for Lucie.

Everything there transpired in cycles: people came and went, egos flourished and faded. But with Miles Sawcliff things went way beyond anything that can be described as a normal cycle. He joined Carsphairn Hall some six years before Lucie was born.

In his previous existence, he had been a lawyer or a judge, something legal or other, so he had a way with words and he eased his way pretty much unopposed into a position where he called the shots for the community as a whole. His long-time partner, Veronica, had always managed to keep a lid on his ruthlessness and his manipulative tendencies but once they split up, things at Carsphairn Hall changed irrevocably and, from then onwards, would head unstoppably downhill.

All the community ended up being dragged into Miles and Veronica's acrimonious breakup; the back-biting and the bitter rivalry, spread to everyone and drained their energy, arguments were left festering in the air, differences of opinion escalated into silent unbridgeable rifts. The day Veronica left marked a sad realisation at Carsphairn Hall that Miles had emerged victorious and his vindictive supremacy could no longer be tempered, on the contrary it would persist and intensify. From the over twenty people who were living there at the peak, their numbers dwindled in a matter of months to just nine.

For Lucie, this slide had taken on an altogether more sinister and menacing tone. As Miles distanced himself from Veronica, it felt like he was focusing more and more on her, as if he was closing in on her, like she was being forced into a corner, her way out shrinking daily. She talked about it to Emma but whenever Emma was around, Miles would ignore Lucie completely.

Miles was a tallish man and overly skinny, just bones and gristle Emma used to say, not in jest either. His face was marked with acne scars which his scant beard could not hide, a constant reminder to him, no doubt, of a difficult transition from adolescence. A tanned and heavily wrinkled neck betrayed his age at over sixty. Lucie found him quite repulsive physically, always had done. But after Veronica's disappearance as she turned fourteen and then fifteen years of age she increasingly seemed to find herself under scrutiny by his gaze which greatly disturbed her.

Then quite by chance, when Lucie was least expecting it, the situation tipped over into nightmare. She had been swimming with Emma down at the loch. Nakedness in a community environment is something wholly natural and Carsphairn Hall was no different in that respect. No-one gave it a second thought, men and women the same.

Some women even walked bare-breasted around the kitchen garden when it was open to visitors which raised multiple eyebrows amongst the lady customers and provoked undoubtedly some major dawdling in finalising their purchases amongst the men. Emma and Lucie were much more modest, always covered in public, aware of their bodies, particularly Lucie who was changing so quickly, but they still swam naked together if no-one else was present.

Emma had suddenly remembered it was her turn to help with the cooking and had picked up her stuff and run off back up the track towards the house the best part of a half mile away. Lucie didn't see any need to run and dressed in a wrap-around skirt and loose top with a towel across her shoulders against the now chill late afternoon breeze, she headed quietly after Emma.

He must have been there all along, watching them swimming from back behind the tree line. Maybe he had been there watching them other times that summer, the weather had been so good that swimming in the freezing cold water of Loch Doon could almost be called refreshing and not its usual description of torture.

Suddenly, he was there, blocking her way. The path was only wide enough at that point for single file traffic with the ferns and rhododendrons pinching into the route between the trees. As soon as she saw him, she could immediately see that he was aroused, his erection clearly noticeable in his trouser pants, making no attempt to hide it. She turned and tried to run again to the beach, maybe she could outrun him and go the long way home. But she was so stricken by fear that she only made it a few stumbled yards before he grabbed her and pushed her down onto the soft ferns along the edge of the path. She couldn't move beneath him.

"I'm not going to hurt you," he said absurdly.

"Get off me!" screamed Lucie. "Let me go!"

But no-one was going to hear. Emma was long gone and they were too far from the house for sure. He put his hand in any case over her mouth to silence her or perhaps it was just another layer of his perversion. She felt frozen like the trapped and silenced prey of some wild animal, helpless, terrified of what he could do to her. With his other hand, he was pulling at her skirt, groping her chest under her top and trying unsuccessfully to prise open her legs as all the time he rubbed himself against her.

Then almost as quickly as it had started, he uttered a deep guttural half-choked sigh and it was over. He must have ejaculated. Lucie was lucky if it's possible to call that luck. He ceased writhing against her and he withdrew his hand, his excitement and urgency waning. After a few moments still pinning her down, he put his mouth close to her ear and whispered menacingly.

"If you say anything, I'll slit your friend's fucking throat."

"If you touch her, I'll cut off your fucking balls."

He laughed. Really laughed. He then relaxed his grip on Lucie who got to her feet and ran off up the path. She could still hear him laughing for a good couple of minutes as she sped towards the house.

That incident marked the end of Lucie's childhood. She was certain that Miles would never carry out his threat against Emma but in some way she felt so deeply humiliated at what had happened that initially she said nothing of it. She knew that if she told Emma, she would go straight to Miles and the whole thing be known to everyone.

The protective wrapping around her existence had been torn down. No-one, not even Emma, had been able to prevent it. But it certainly wasn't Emma's fault, if anyone was to blame it was Lucie herself for allowing things to go that far in the first place. She should have acted sooner.

She could no longer be in the same room as Miles and it must have become abundantly clear to Emma that something had happened but it was Rachel who was first to decipher the signs.

Rachel was a relative newcomer to Carsphairn Hall one of the last before the slide. She arrived when Lucie was nine back in 2008. She had come to the community to "silence her demons" in her own words, although just what she meant by that was not clear. Rachel was a very private person and to lay out even that much in the public domain was telling but intended at the same time to draw a line under any possibility of delving further into the subject. She was a figure of seeming fortitude but behind that facade of solidity Lucie could always see traces of something far more fragile.

Rachel was an only child and had no close hand experience of kids, her own mother had been austere and distant and had died of a heart attack when Rachel was twenty-two, clearly a great blow deep down but she kept a lid on her grief externally. But there was something about Lucie which fascinated her, such an open, insightful yet playful mind, so honest even naively so and enthusiastic in everything even the dullest of tasks.

Lucie was special and Rachel quickly came to love her dearly, perhaps the child she never had although she would never admit to that. Emma was Lucie's guardian angel and Rachel had no desire to interfere, but Rachel nonetheless became a crucial more mature voice of reason in Lucie's life counterbalancing the more juvenile exuberance of Emma. At the same time, Lucie became a pillar in Rachel's own personal journey.

Rachel was well-spoken, with no traceable accent, neither posh nor otherwise, just neutral. But she had music which immediately brought her close to Lucie. Rachel had been a music producer for an experimental band way back called Virtual Noise before the term *virtual* had been hijacked by the Internet, in fact years before the Internet existed at all, when *virtual* meant almost or in essence but without factual reality, like an image in a mirror.

Rachel was an excellent guitarist. Really exceptional. Even if her preferred musical style was way off the beaten track. Lucie had never heard of any of the songs that Rachel played. Actually, Rachel and Lucie both preferred the instrumentals, focusing on unusual rhythms and progressions which seemed to come naturally to them both.

The other thing that endeared her to Lucie and to be fair to the rest of the community as well was that she had a clapped-out black Morris Oxford, which she had contributed to the community, more like a tank than a car, but with rather grand red leather seats which got incredibly hot when it was left out in the sun.

When Lucie thought about it later on, she realised that Rachel knew all along that Miles was a threat to Lucie, that he was a predator. She must have come into contact with others like Miles back in the music industry before *#metoo* put at least a minor spanner in the works for that type of character.

"Lucie," she said sternly, sitting them both down on the stools by the workbenches in the greenhouse which offered as good a guarantee of privacy as was to be found at Carsphairn Hall. "You must tell me what has happened. We need to deal with this now. It won't just disappear if we ignore it. It will happen again, you can be sure of that."

"I can't let anyone know…Especially Emma," Lucie burst at that point into floods of tears. She had been bottling it up for nearly a week. Lucie told Rachel everything. And then Rachel hugged her for several minutes, stroking her hair, gently comforting her. Then Rachel set about convincing Lucie that Emma had to be told. No-one else would have to know but Emma.

As Lucie had feared, Emma went ballistic but eventually the three of them concluded that any police involvement would end up with Lucie's word coming up against Miles's. And Lucie was some ill-educated nothing and Miles was Miles, a man. She would inevitably be portrayed as provoking him by swimming naked in the first place, tantamount to asking for it.

They also knew that Lucie and Emma could not stay on at Carsphairn Hall any longer. Rachel swore to make sure that Miles got his comeuppance in time, she would find a way to destroy him, and she delivered on her word claiming about a year later that Miles had tried to rape her. She had thought it all through and somehow even managed to conjure up a witness. Miles was sentenced to three years in prison. Nowhere near long enough according to Rachel but something is something.

For now, Lucie just wanted to be gone, she was thoroughly exhausted. Rachel gave Emma the address of an Irish lady down in London who rented out rooms without ripping you off completely. Lucie had been saving all the cash that she received from selling the sketches she did of the visitors and it turned out with the little money Emma had that they could pay for the bus tickets to London and they would be good for a few weeks' worth of food and rent anyway.

That night, once they had sneaked their meagre belongings unnoticed into the Morris Oxford before Rachel was to drive them to the bus station in Castle Douglas, she took Lucie to her room while Emma waited in the car. Rachel knelt beside the bed and reaching underneath she lifted out one short cutdown floorboard and pulled out from the cavity below a small wooden box no bigger than a cigarette packet.

"I have been keeping this for…just in case," she said removing the lid from the box to reveal a silver bracelet studded with shining jewels. "They are diamonds. Real ones." She held the box out to Lucie.

"No way, Rachel," Lucie refused shaking her head vehemently. "Just no way."

"You have to leave here and this will give you and Emma a fighting chance. You should get something like three or four thousand for it, if you are lucky. The receipt is in the box too so you won't have any difficulty proving it is yours."

"You must be joking. How could I possibly accept this? It is so beautiful and it is so yours. If Miles found out you had got this here, he would go crazy," Lucie laughed.

"It is just a relic from a past life which doesn't exist anymore. Actually, it never did exist either, now that I think about it. It will make me happy to think that it is gone finally and that it has helped someone so important to me."

Lucie tried to convince Rachel that she may herself need it more but Rachel was adamant this was the time as she pressed the box into the palm of Lucie's hand.

V
The Royal Society

London—1873

Precisely how and why he had plumped for the name of Oliver McNaught he never could say, it just felt right. That fictitious identity, cobbled together hastily in the days following his surfacing on the Moss to avoid being arrested as the murderer Duncan Chambers, had ultimately served him well. He had ingeniously hidden away every last trace of that tainted background and in London he had rebuilt his life with greater and greater success.

Although he would be the first to recognise that initially his escape from the law had lacked finesse, had—in all honesty—been downright messy: the Head Constable of Birkenhead dead, strangled ruthlessly, his young runner also dead with a meat hook lodged in his neck and there was no point in trying to allege he was not the killer in both cases. But the James incident was a different kettle of fish altogether. He was very much still a victim there. He remains convinced he had nothing to do with that.

Oliver McNaught's office is undoubtedly befitting of the illustrious status to which he has risen. A large uncluttered and meticulously polished mahogany desk lies at its heart, exotic Persian rugs cover the floor, a more informal snug area is nestled near a massive fireplace, and on all available wall space a floor to ceiling library is topped with the carved busts of celebrated scientists and explorers who survey proceedings with glum authority from on high.

Oliver leans back, pushing his plush burgundy-coloured leather chair out from under the desk, making no attempt to disguise his boredom. He has not the slightest regard for the sensibilities of his two clerks standing there before him. In all honesty, he is hardly more than vaguely aware of the buzzing of their voices and is certainly paying no attention to whatever they may be arguing about.

He gets to his feet slowly, ambles past them across the room—causing no interruption to their quarrel—and stands looking down out of the ornate window directly onto the Regents Park Canal where a horse drawn barge carrying coal is making its way serenely in the direction of Little Venice and the Grand Union Canal beyond.

His thoughts are elsewhere. Why does he keep reliving that same moment time and again? Why can he not just block out from his mind the memory of Jules glaring at him in disgust as he was tied to the cart outside the forge? That was the last time he had seen her. A full eight years have now passed since that ill-fated night. Yet there was still something in that look which chilled his soul—that was the precise moment she too had pronounced him guilty of James's brutal murder. Her expression of revulsion, suffused with despair, far from fading over time haunts him ever more often.

"Absurd! I want nothing to do with it," says one of the two men raising his voice just enough to rouse Oliver from his reverie momentarily.

"You press here," the other ploughs on also speaking a little louder, "and it forces that piston down which extends a rod onto that cylinder, down there. Then you rotate the cylinder shifting its position. It couldn't be simpler."

His clerks are engaged in what appears to be an impassioned argument, becoming more bitter by the second judging by the tone, although Oliver would wager, if he were aware of its subject matter, that it would be more akin to a childish squabble than anything resembling sophisticated discussion.

"Are you serious? All that for a single character?" offers the first again in a tone brimming with ridicule.

Sometimes, and increasingly so, it must be said, Oliver sees his two minions as no better than illiterate yes-men blindly seeking to propel themselves along the road towards huge fortunes by proximity to the real thing, as though just being in his presence would rub off on them and he would, as a matter of course, invite them onto the next rung up on some stellar career ladder. But that is totally missing the point. As a respected philanthropist and one of the leading fundraisers for ground-breaking scientific research, the spark of invention is precisely what he craves—originality, not some bland copy.

Oliver gradually becomes aware of a silence in the room behind him and he turns away from the window to find the eyes of the two men on him, awaiting eagerly his verdict on their respective deliberations. They are dressed almost comically in identical elegant, dark pinstriped suits.

Both are young, early twenties, around half his age. Their prattling on is stretching his patience. Aren't they here precisely to obviate the requirement for his being involved in every mundane decision, even though right now, what it is exactly he is being asked to adjudicate upon, eludes him?

Pritchard, who tends to believe himself to be the illuminati of the two, steps into the silence with some relish, perhaps even aware that Oliver has no idea what they have been discussing.

"That piece of junk quicker than a trained clerk? Impossible!"

Oliver follows Pritchard's gaze down towards the small table between the two clerks upon which is positioned some sort of mechanical device. It has a multitude of small pads on metal wires each with a different capital letter embossed on its surface forming a dome covered in the alphabet. Below this dome lies a cylinder with a piece of paper spread across its surface. Evidently some sort of new-fangled writing machine. As if he hasn't seen a dozen such designs over the past several years.

Saunders, the second in this double act who in the end can be guaranteed to take the side he thinks will most curry favour with Oliver himself, regardless of the merits of the argument, is not about to allow the subject to be restarted without also having his say, "The shape of the future, Pritchard. I'm afraid you are quite stuck in the past, my friend. All I am saying is that it could be worthy of further investigation."

"For the love of God, can't you two stop bickering for a moment and shut up?" Oliver finally intercedes before the discussion descends back into mindless buzz. "Investigation. That is after all why we are here, is it not? Saunders, set up a schedule for the writing machine's evaluation, could you? That will be all gentlemen."

As they scurry out the door, Pritchard looks disappointed it is Saunders who has been singled out for a task and not him.

"Oh, Pritchard," Oliver calls him back at the last moment. "Could you please draught a letter to Lord Wyndam to confirm that I will attend Sir Richard's dinner at the Royal Society next Saturday evening."

Pritchard closes the door behind him with a satisfied nod of assent.

The Royal Society dinners always attract a good gathering and the following Saturday proves to be no exception. The Great Room is overflowing mostly with gentlemen, all dressed to the nines in black frock coats, grey waistcoats, winged collars and bowties for the presentation of the medal for scientific achievement to Sir Richard Purleigh, whose research into thermodynamics Oliver has long been involved with, indeed he is his principal benefactor and some say not a minor source of the creative input into the science itself, although the reality, which Oliver prefers to keep back from public scrutiny, is that the entirety of the project has been based on his own ideas.

Oliver is standing stretching his neck upwards, more intent on surveying those present than on listening to the idle gossip another acolyte of his, Geoffrey Stourbridge, is peddling into his ear as though it were meaningful insight. But then something Stourbridge is saying riles Oliver and he interrupts him abruptly.

"Geoffrey, I told you six months ago to apply Bain's work on probability theory and logic to the development of neural networks. And what do you do?"

"I do not follow you, Oliver."

"Precisely, you ignore me completely."

"Oliver, you wouldn't believe the success I have…"

"I don't fund your research for any other reason than for you to follow my instructions. To the letter. Do you understand me?"

"But if you give me a chance to present my findings, I'm…"

"I do not wish to waste your time or mine. Listen carefully, if you do not turn things around in the next two months I will cancel your entire budget…"

Oliver stops in mid-flow. Something not quite discernible at the outer edges of his perception catches his eye and triggers a startling physical tremor throughout his being. It knocks him completely off balance. He strains to identify the source of this astonishing sensation but the crowd clutters his vision and all he can see is the chaos of normality. But then, in the distance by the doorway he glimpses Jules looking directly at him for the briefest instance, then she is gone again.

He draws in air sharply through his teeth. Was it really her? Jules…here? Deep inside he knows it was. He could never mistake that face even across a crowded room, the face that had witnessed his humiliation, the face he has never managed to keep out of his mind.

However, as his rational intellect retakes control over his spontaneous yearnings, his immediate response is to run. She must be here to ensnare him and is probably indicating his whereabouts to the police at this very moment in order to have him arrested once again. He would certainly not be in a position to be able to defend himself here with so many people around. He must leave as quickly and as surreptitiously as he can.

He cuts off Geoffrey Stourbridge's sycophantic defence of his funding requirements, curtly excuses himself and heads towards a door at the back of the Great Room, the most distant point from the spot of Jules's ghostly apparition. He scans the hall nervously but she is still nowhere to be seen and no sign of any police either, thankfully. And then just before he reaches the doorway leading to a service staircase down to street level and a back entrance to the Royal Society, Jules steps out boldly from behind a column and looks him straight in the eye.

"Mr McNaught, I believe." She holds his stare, unflinching. She seems to relish the shock her appearance has caused him. "I am so pleased to meet you. I do hope you do not have to run off. I have been longing for such an opportunity for so, so long."

He has no idea what sort of game she is playing. She knows who he is without a shadow of a doubt. Is she not afraid of him? Given the allegations against him, she most certainly should be.

"Miss…?" Oliver decides, however, to follow Jules's game plan, at least to see where it is heading.

"Mrs…" Jules corrects him. "Chambers…Jules Chambers."

"Delighted to make your acquaintance Mrs Chambers," Oliver laughs relaxing somewhat and faintly kisses her outstretched hand in greeting. It seems that Jules has no immediate intention of challenging his identity.

Jules is wearing a striking iridescent Portuguese-blue full-length evening gown which combines elegance with understated sensuality. No frivolity but a sassiness which suggests business mixed with more than a bit of pleasure. The effect is magnified by the contrast with the uniformity of all the men's attire and by so few other women being present.

The design of her dress is straight forward enough, even modest, but with a deeper more fashionable neckline which draws Oliver's attention to the rather too rapid rising and falling of her chest suggesting she too is more than a little excited at their encounter.

"And Mr Chambers?" Oliver says audaciously.

"Oh, he left home several years ago and has been…missing, if you like, ever since."

"That must have been most distressing."

"Actually, Mr McNaught, I have a strange feeling he may resurface at any moment," Jules says with a glint of humour in her eye.

A bell rings and the maitre d' announces the arrival of the guests of honour, Sir Richard Purleigh, accompanied by his third wife, Eleanor. A polite round of applause ensues, during which, Oliver leans in towards Jules and asks, "In what field is your association with the Royal Society, Mrs Chambers?"

Once the applause has subsided, Jules replies, "I fear I have given you the wrong idea as to my identity, Mr McNaught."

Definitely she is enjoying this. She is toying with him. She laughs out loud sending a shiver down Oliver's spine. She has aged a fraction but it renders her more captivating than ever.

She continues, "I merely report your grand achievements for a newspaper."

"A journalist?"

"Rather mundane, I'm afraid."

"Not at all, Mrs Chambers...Jules? May I call you Jules?"

She smiles invitingly.

"For which publication?"

"The Liverpool Mercury mostly and on occasion The Pall Mall Gazette and even the London Echo. Whichever pays most and first."

"I had no idea that women are now reporting on science. I thought it was just on matters...pertaining to their particular interests. I am impressed indeed."

"I fear my own contribution is negligible. It is the science itself and those driving it forward that are truly inspirational."

"Without your reporting," Oliver contradicts her, "those ideas would remain hidden in darkened laboratories without seeing the light of day. Reporting is a vital function in the process of discovery and enlightenment."

"Well said, Mr McNaught!" Again, she laughs.

"Oliver...please."

Jules smiles again but the way her lip curls this time makes Oliver less sure of her frame of mind. Perhaps using his false first name may grate excessively on her nerves but he can hardly allow any allusion to Duncan, can he?

"May I be straight forward with you?" Jules asks.

"Please."

"Some weeks ago, ever since I saw you in the background of a photograph taken here, in this very room I believe, which is on display in the ground floor lobby, I determined to meet you in the hope you would grant me an interview. I am extremely interested in how you have reached such a position of power in the scientific community." She has lost the playfulness of the early banter. Her tone is deadpan, cold even. "Our readers would be fascinated, I am sure, at your exploits."

"What I can tell you will without doubt fail to deliver on such high expectations."

"Let me be the judge of that. I will not be leaving for the Wirral for a few days. Could you fit me into your schedule at such short notice?"

"For you, a gap in my schedule could always be arranged." Oliver takes his business card from his waistcoat pocket and hands it to Jules. "How would tomorrow afternoon suit? Say at four in my offices?"

"Oliver! Oliver!" the towering figure of Sir Richard Purleigh with a long greying but immaculately manicured beard breaks the moment. "I need your advice on a matter of some urgency."

"Can't you see I am busy here, Richard." Oliver stops him in his tracks, clearly annoyed and showing remarkably little deference to the man receiving the accolades this evening.

When Oliver turns back to Jules to apologise for such a rude interruption, she has miraculously disappeared almost as mysteriously as had been her apparition. He almost starts to doubt whether the whole encounter has been no more than an elaborate figment of his own imagination.

The following day sees Oliver back in his office looking across his desk in a dispassionate manner as the unfortunate George Halford bemoans his sorry financial position. But once again, Oliver's mind is drifting elsewhere; he has slept very little, the image of Jules uppermost in his thoughts and now he can barely focus on anything other than the dizzying anticipation of seeing her again.

Clearly, he feels some trepidation, Jules represents a link back to a previous existence with all the threats that represents. But in those eight years Oliver has never felt anything that has moved him emotionally. His only objective has been money and his ultimate long-term scientific goals. But Jules is different. She fits so perfectly into his world, even though he recognises that his sentimental connection to her must break all the rules of the rationale behind his surfacing. But what harm can it do? The reality is that he still feels such a deep and inescapable passion for Jules. Maybe he really can dare to dream of some future for them together even after the shocking events on Bidston Moss.

"There must be something we can do, Oliver," Halford says, slumping ever deeper in the chair opposite Oliver.

"Come on, George. Get a grip. You knew the risks. The story is coming out in the Times tomorrow morning. The market has discounted the news. Java Shipping shares are already worthless. You are—I am afraid only one word can come close to describing it, George—finished."

Oliver smiles, understandingly. He cares nothing for the fate of Halford but there are still some loose ends that need tidying up. Halford's losses are way too serious for any real talk of saving his business, his wealth or his reputation, it's purely a matter of saving his skin and removing him from the game permanently in the most advantageous way possible for Oliver.

"Let me be frank with you, George. You have a stark but ultimately simple choice to make. Either you go down the bankruptcy route, which would end in you being tried for fraud, and your subsequent transportation to Australia with a real chance you don't end the journey alive. And even if you do, you'd be facing hard labour for the rest of your days, while your family rots in a London workhouse. Hardly an option at all in my book."

Halford has no response. He stares blankly into mid-air. Oliver lets this linger before continuing, the mood in the office turning ever more oppressive, at least for Halford.

"Or…alternatively…there is a ship sailing from Southampton tomorrow morning for New York…"

Oliver is interrupted by a knock at the door, followed by his second clerk, Saunders, poking his head around the door and announcing, "A Mrs Chambers is here to see you, Mr McNaught."

"Right, thanks Saunders. We are finished here, are we not, George?"

"But surely we can sell the house…"

"Gone, I'm afraid. Or will be once the story breaks. That's the first thing the vultures will swoop in for in any bankruptcy proceedings."

Oliver rises from his desk and accompanies Halford to the door, adding, in a more optimistic tone, as they cross the office, "But rest assured, the US immigration authorities will believe anything you tell them and you will get a fresh start out there. With nothing, of course, but we have both been there before, have we not? And that should not scare you. You would be alive, free and with your family still together."

Opening the door, Oliver barks his orders to his two clerks, "Saunders, could you see George out. And Pritchard, would you make sure all the necessary arrangements are taken care of for him and his family not to miss the New York steamer in Southampton tomorrow morning."

In the end, George Halford had no choice other than accepting Oliver's advice and he was unceremoniously and quite literally sent packing. What Oliver failed to disclose was just how much wealth he himself had made out of the calamitous fall from grace of his erstwhile friend and the demise of his Dutch registered company, Java Shipping, whose stock Oliver had shorted aggressively over recent days.

Most notably though, Oliver will secure the acquisition of Halford's stunning double-fronted property in the most desirable part of Blackheath looking out directly onto the heath itself and at the back of the house down to Greenwich, at a fraction of its true value by enacting the bankruptcy repossession clause he himself wrote into the deeds some months ago. Will he actually use the house? Oliver is unsure, perhaps he will sail down to Greenwich on the Thames and ride up to inspect his latest acquisition in person.

Suddenly, Oliver becomes aware of Jules standing in the outer office as the hapless Halford is ushered out.

"My apologies, Mrs Chambers. Please come through, won't you?" Oliver gestures for her to enter his office. "Pritchard, could you rustle up some tea, perhaps?"

Jules walks straight past Pritchard into Oliver's office. She luckily doesn't see the complicit snigger on Pritchard's face, aimed towards Saunders who is following Halford out of the front door of the office.

On a table in the corner, Jules spies the writing machine which was the subject of discussion a few days back between the two clerks and immediately goes over to it enthusiastically.

"I see you have a Hansen Writing Ball. This is marvellous. I saw a demonstration on one of these a couple of weeks ago at the Gazette. The speed of the operator and the machine were equally astonishing." She looks back, addressing Pritchard who is now standing in the doorway and adds, "You had better watch out or you may end up losing your livelihood to this kind of device in no time."

Pritchard ignores her as he closes the door but is visibly upset at the enthusiasm the machine has generated.

Oliver can now more fully appreciate her beauty. She is wearing functional attire, almost manly, in blacks and whites but that just heightens the deep impression that her grey-green eyes have on Oliver. Her hair is again tied up and discreetly draws attention to her elegant emerald earrings.

"Please sit down, Jules," Oliver suddenly says, remembering his manners. He indicates towards a comfortable armchair next to a small table near the fireplace. He himself takes the high-backed Queen Anne chair.

"You seem to have done pretty well for yourself," Jules looks around Oliver's office.

"I have been fortunate," Oliver is uncertain how to handle the situation. Is the pretence of the Royal Society to be maintained even when they are alone? Perhaps it would be more comfortable for them both that way. "Some of my largest financial gambles paid off handsomely."

"Only in finance?" Jules asks.

"I am not sure I follow you."

Jules takes a moment. "Do you think, for the clarity of my readers of course, you could go into greater detail as to your accomplishments in the period before you became so fortunate, as you put it?"

"Oh yes, of course. I had forgotten that this is an interview. I shall have to take great care not to incriminate myself if this is all liable to end up in the Mercury or the Gazette."

"You can rest assured that I will not print anything that I cannot fully substantiate."

Was that some sort of veiled threat? In any event, there is no point in rising to it. Better to stay calm and delve a bit deeper to ascertain precisely what Jules really wants.

"I was born in England but my parents emigrated to the Netherlands when I was just six years old. I moved around a lot; Japan, Singapore, Egypt." He makes a gesture to imply several more destinations too. "Then I came to London eight years ago, with next to nothing and fell in with some exceptional people and as I say I was blessed with no small measure of good fortune." All of this is actually the backstory of Oliver McNaught, so he will have no difficulty defending it, vigorously if need be.

"A fascinating story," Jules smiles knowingly. "And why the science? How did you get into all those weird projects you have supported?"

Jules has done her research into his scientific endeavours. Oliver feels flattered.

Pritchard knocks at the still half open door and pushing it open, he walks across the office, setting down a tray of tea things on the small table near the fire, before discreetly withdrawing again without uttering a word. He knows his place, if nothing else.

Oliver stands and walks to a sideboard where he pours himself a glass of whisky from a cut-glass decanter.

"Perhaps I can tempt you with a glass of sherry. I have an amontillado which I am told is particularly good."

"Later, perhaps."

"I have always been fascinated by science, and can think of no better way to make money than promoting some of the more exotic minds and projects, at the same time advancing the breadth of human achievement."

"But always in the background, like in the photograph?"

"I have no interest in fame…just the fortune part."

"I am sincerely hoping that fame is not all that you end up with." There is that threatening tone again from Jules. There is definitely something that Oliver is not quite getting.

Jules takes a deep breath, as though setting herself before asking her next question, lending it a certain more ponderous gravitas. "You seem to have a clear focus in the selection of projects. I would dearly like to glimpse, to share, if possible, the vision that is driving those choices. Where is all this leading?"

Oliver stares at Jules incredulously for several seconds before replying. "You are exceptionally perceptive, Jules. May I speak—off the record—for a moment?"

"Of course."

"You are right. There is indeed an overall direction of travel. It is no more than a far distant dream right now, but I believe that eventually it will be within the realm of science to bend the rules of physics to our own will, to see where the future may lead. At least to be better informed as to our options, to identify what we should be focusing on now, to achieve a better world. You will think I have lost my mind but in ages to come, this must happen. It will, I believe. It is my mission to lay the groundwork for that time. My projects may seem primitive but together, over time, they will grow into something vast and boundless, something essential to humanity."

There is a long, stunned silence. Then Oliver breaks the moment, "Or else that is just the whisky talking," he laughs.

"Perhaps I should have a drop too?" Jules laughs with Oliver.

"Absolutely, you must. I insist." Oliver fumbles nervously as he pours her whisky and then decides at the same time to refresh his own. Has he gone too far? Maybe he has made a fool of himself and has only succeeded in shocking Jules, in showing her just how much he has changed. But it is so easy to talk to her. He wants to trust her, to confide in someone.

"The future!" Jules proposes a toast. They chink glasses.

Jules changes the subject away from the seriousness of Oliver's science, at the same time shifting to a more light-hearted tone, although the question itself is complex, playful yet probing, "Are you married, Oliver?"

"No, absolutely not."

"Absolutely? A strange way of putting it…given the circumstances, I mean."

"What exactly is your point?" Oliver snaps at her. Perhaps it is he who still needs the veneer of his adopted identity more than Jules. He realises he is not yet ready to lower his guard to allow Duncan to set the agenda here.

"Well, you may yet," Jules backs off a little, "fall for someone new, you know."

"I have not done so in my eight years in London. So, I think any chance of that may well have passed me by." These are the words which come from his lips but they bear no resemblance to what he is thinking. He may no longer feel comfortable recognising Duncan but he has to accept he cannot keep this woman out of his thoughts, that his life before Bidston Moss is still brutally active and influencing him right now, that they have effortlessly fallen into an old, established pattern of conversation which is comfortable for both of them. Oliver is surprised by how much he enjoys Jules's company and it seems she too is more relaxed. When Pritchard alerts Oliver as to the time, they have talked for over an hour.

"My word," Jules jumps to her feet. "I had no idea it was so late. I must leave, I am afraid."

As she hurriedly gets her things together, Oliver observes, clinging at straws to come up with some reason to meet again, "I fear you haven't adequately fulfilled your primary objective this afternoon."

"That is undoubtedly true, Oliver," Jules says with a more serious tone of voice.

"If I may be so bold…On Thursday next week I intend visiting a new property I am in the process of acquiring in Blackheath, near Greenwich. Perhaps I could take you out for the day and I could give you some more material for your interview—on the record."

Jules smiles, "That would be most kind. I'd be delighted to join you."

This whole thing is becoming rather too complicated. But the temptation of extending his relationship with Jules is just too enticing to pass up. The risks are potentially devastating. He has no idea what her ultimate goal is but he feels certain that she does have one. Could she be laying a trap of some description for him? But somehow, he feels he must see her again one last time, to flush her out if you like, although he avoids admitting to himself that really, he is being driven by the overwhelming desire just to be in her company, to be close to her, once again.

The following Thursday, standing on the raised terrace balcony behind Halford's house in Blackheath, Oliver and Jules look down the long hill falling away from them to the wide loop of the river Thames winding around the Isle of Dogs on the far bank, opposite Greenwich. The new South West India dock on the far side of the river, opened just some months ago is clearly visible in the distance, a massive rectangle of inland waterway contrasting vividly with the irregular meandering of the river itself.

A chill Autumn breeze blows across the terrace. Jules shivers and pulls her cape tighter around her as she walks back through the double French windows into the large drawing room. It is completely empty, not even the carpets remain, just the bare and dusty floorboards. All the furniture, paintings, rugs, ornaments, every item has been sold off to pay down a small part of Halford's debts. A strange wariness pervades the house, an echoey hollow emptiness.

"Such a beautiful house," Jules looks around at the room admiringly.

"I first saw it a couple of years ago and made my mind up that this would one day be mine."

"You seem to always get your own way."

They had met at St Katherine's dock adjacent to the Tower of London. There they had boarded a spritsail barge with deep red-brown sails raised on large wooden masts. The journey to Greenwich took just under an hour and from there they had walked at a leisurely pace up the steep hill, past the Observatory and out onto Blackheath where Halford's elegant Georgian house is located.

"Duncan," she uses his real name for the first time, in a stern but nonetheless uncertain, hesitant tone, "I think the time has come for us to confront reality. It is absurd to maintain this charade any longer."

Oliver noticed almost as soon as they met that morning that something was troubling Jules and he is not surprised when she finally raises the issue of their past. It had to happen at some point and he had only avoided it because he didn't want their recently renewed intimacy ruined by bringing up the horrific events which had led them to this point.

It is strange and disturbing to be called Duncan again.

"It had its moments, though, wouldn't you say? You know, dropping the pretence will undoubtedly imply a heightening of some rather unappetising risks, at least for me."

"All that Oliver business has been doing my head in."

"How did you find me? How did you come across that photograph of me in the Royal Society?"

"A good friend of mine who is—shall we say—an expert in locating missing persons suggested you may have followed a science-based destiny, that maybe my being a reporter of scientific discoveries was a link, a sign which should not be ignored."

"And how could your friend come up with such an odd idea? I mean..." Duncan half laughs.

"There are many mysteries which science can still not explain," Jules says sternly, "but the day will come when psychological phenomena such as my friend's unquestionable abilities will be fully understood."

Duncan looks warily at Jules, "Listen Jules, what exactly do you want?"

"I want to know. All of it."

"All of it?"

"You know, on the Moss. With James?"

Duncan weighs his response carefully, acutely aware that the past eight years have essentially been condensed into a single defining moment.

"I believe I did not kill James although I cannot say for sure." This is the first and only time he has spoken about that incident to anyone. After a moment, he continues, "I can tell you for a fact, though, that when I came to, James's body was not anywhere around there. I would have seen it. Whoever killed him must have gone to the trouble of moving his corpse, of hiding it. When I said I had blacked out, it was true. And honestly, I was not in a state of mind to be capable of killing anyone. I was trying to get my head back together. I was alone, in shock."

"After all these years, you're still going to carry on with that amnesia stuff." At least, Jules's tone is no longer ridiculing his version of events out of hand.

"I have nothing to gain right now by lying to you, do I? I had no idea of who I was, no idea where I was or how I had got there. My memories were gone and they never came back. All I had from the past was an emotional tie to you. In fact, that is still all I have from before. Your face somehow inside my head. And a love for you which has never diminished. I think you know I am not lying. You too have witnessed it, have felt it, these last few days."

Duncan walks over to Jules and stands in front of her. Close, too close.

"You have changed, Duncan Chambers. But I can still see parts of you I recognise somewhere in the background."

"I feared I would never see you again," Duncan says.

It is as if he has stepped over a dividing line out from the troubles which have plagued his past into some unseeable future, a fragile dream which clings precariously to this current reality. They both accept each other, not as they are supposed to be, not as they used to be but as they are now. Jules says nothing but makes no attempt to pull away from him. He looks into her eyes. How can he even begin to tell her all the truth?

He reaches out his arm, touches her shoulder enclosing it gently in his palm. He feels everything cascading beyond his control. It is unstoppable, yet also unpredictable, like the wind swirling up the leaves outside on the terrace. He pulls her slowly towards him. He brushes his lips across her cheek nervously. He raises his hands lightly caressing her neck with his fingertips. The physical contact, the touch of her skin is electric: mortal and impetuous, fierce and undeniable. He hears her breathe and feels it on his neck.

Jules kisses him on the mouth with a delicate but searing passion. Duncan has thought about this moment for so long, never daring to imagine that it could happen. He is confused and frightened but also tinglingly alive, more so than in all the last eight years, beyond the scope of his entire memory. He has no idea what to do or how to react but Jules seems to understand that and she leads him. Maybe she always did.

Then when she feels safe, without uttering a word she steps back from him and unfastens all the ties down the front of her blouse allowing him to glimpse her breasts. She then loosens his shirt and raising it over his head, she kisses his naked chest. It is cold, his bare skin taut and responsive. She slips her hand inside his breeches, touching him, arousing him. This should not be happening but he has no desire or inclination to stop it. Delicately and tenderly he draws her blouse off her shoulders and, fearful of shattering the moment, lets it falls to the ground. He drops to his knees and kisses her breasts slowly in turn with rising intensity. They both remove each other's remaining garments and Jules leans back on the floor pulling him down towards her.

As gently as he can he eases himself forward, her hand guiding him inside her. She gasps. They are locked together as one. It is a throwback to Duncan's true self before surfacing, pure, visceral, instinctive, with Jules beyond the confines of time. Every movement however slight is transmitted in ecstasy across their joined souls. Her breathing harshens. She moves more agitatedly against him. He is engulfed within her soft, tense body. He writhes up, breathing in sharp painful gulps as he releases deep inside her. She holds him there, trembling involuntarily, letting out a series of hushed mournful whimpers.

They dress uncomfortably. Now they become aware of the intense cold in the unoccupied house; the passion which united them seems distant already. Duncan is sure that what has happened is a freak outcome. He had certainly never intended it to happen, and he is sure that Jules neither. It was just the past playing cruel games on them. Now far from a warm afterglow, he feels a chill nagging doubt that this could turn out to have been a mistake of far-reaching proportion. He fears the intimacy he so craves could end up destroying him.

Jules sits with her back against a wall. She too looks stunned.

"You never thought to contact me?" Jules asks breaking the uncomfortable silence.

"I knew any chance for us was gone. The look on your face when you turned and walked away as Kal tied me to the cart. You too had decided I was guilty. There seemed nothing left. No hope."

"I couldn't bear it. It wasn't that I didn't love you or that I thought you were guilty. Not then at least."

"Perhaps it was you who were guilty."

"What is that supposed to mean?"

"I discovered some time later the truth between you and James…"

"That is a lie!" Jules gets to her feet angrily. "You see? That was what he wanted all along. He wanted you to believe it. He tried to force himself on me once. I refused him. Absolutely! He spread the rumour to spite me and to poison what we had. But it is a lie, I swear."

"Right," Duncan says half-heartedly. He is not convinced. The rumour of Jules's infidelity had been widespread. Duncan had even tasked an assistant many years ago to find out whether there was any truth in it and he had reported back what local people believed and the story was consistent and damning of Jules, although the primary source had always been James himself, it has to be said.

"Why kill the Head Constable? You don't deny that too, do you?"

"He left me with no alternative."

"But the boy, his runner, he was only seventeen years old."

"That was collateral damage."

"You can't be serious."

"The Head Constable had every intention of lynching me. Of that, I am convinced. I would never have made it through that first night in the lock-up cells. You heard the veiled threats. If I had turned up dead the next morning, who would have questioned my hanging myself in despair and shame. He couldn't risk me revealing any of his arrangements on dock smuggling duties. I realised when he mentioned our strong relationship on contraband enforcement that he was testing me to see if I would keep quiet.

"But I could see that I wasn't saying the right things and I think he freaked. He wouldn't have done it himself I'm sure, but as you saw that evening, there were easily enough others only too happy to lend a hand. The boy was unfortunate. The Head Constable knew exactly the stakes. He was sloppy and the boy died as a result of that complacency."

"You have become a hard man, Duncan Chambers. Nothing like the man I once idolised." Jules too is being honest with him. Duncan realises with some trepidation that the gulf between them is growing ever wider as they go deeper into the past.

At that moment, there is a sudden loud and insistent pounding on the front door.

"Police! Open up."

Duncan looks at Jules. He is dumbfounded.

"Jules, how could you?" he whispers.

"Duncan Chambers! We know you are in there. You have no escape."

"It wasn't me," Jules begs but Duncan has shifted into survival mode and as he jumps to his feet, he has no doubt that Jules has betrayed him. The fact that they have just minutes ago shared an intimate act beyond his dreams is immediately banished from his mind.

They hear a loud banging, most likely some sort of battering ram to break down the door.

"Honestly Duncan, I had nothing to do with this."

"Quick," Duncan says as quietly and forcefully as he can. "*You* come with me!"

He grabs her by the elbow and half drags her out onto the terrace as they hear the front door caving in. Duncan is out of time. He pulls her over the terrace wall and they fall together onto the grass lawn eight feet beneath, winding them both. Duncan pulls himself together and drags Jules to her feet forcing her to take cover with him under the parapet of the terrace.

Duncan has snapped. He is so furious that Jules could have sold him out to the police, he is capable of anything. What has just happened between them just multiplies his rage towards her. He was a total fool. They can hear a couple of policemen are now in the room where they made love. One has walked out onto the terrace.

Duncan pushes Jules back against the wall supporting the terrace and covers Jules's mouth with his hand. He has to stop her from shouting out and giving away their hiding place. His right forearm is crushing into her neck and lifting her heels a fraction off the ground. She cannot breathe and Duncan is fully aware of that but his fury is now dictating his actions. She struggles against him but his strength easily overpowers her feeble resistance. She has been too much of a distraction.

Is he going to end her life, here, now? She has betrayed him. Clearly. His face is just an inch from hers. She is painfully beautiful. His mind flashes back to how he strangled the Head Constable in Bidston so unflinchingly. He can just as easily snuff out Jules's life right now. She has left him no option. He has no escape. His rage growing ever more severe. He loves her endlessly. He has to do it. Now.

"I must end this," Duncan whispers into her ear. "I trusted you."

Jules's lips are starting to turn the same colour as those of the Head Constable when Duncan ended his life. This is madness. Jules is close to death now. She has no more fight. Then suddenly, Duncan releases the pressure on her neck, letting her feet back onto the ground and allowing her to crumple at his feet coughing and spluttering as air finds its way back into her lungs. She rubs her windpipe trying to ease life back into it.

"You were going to kill me!" she chokes.

"They're over here!" yells the policeman on the terrace above them.

Jules continues, spitting her words at him, "You're finished. Your past has caught up with you now. You are nothing more than a cold-blooded murderer."

Duncan doesn't care. He will fight no longer, he will offer no resistance. All he knows is that he could not do it. In that last moment, he had recognised the depth of his love for Jules and his pre-surfacing, subconscious mind overwhelmed him and won out in the end. It had stopped him from killing her, even though he now knows that this will inevitably lead to his downfall. Duncan drops to his knees.

VI
On the Brink

Lisbon—Present Day

Bright and early the morning after their traumatic—and for Zac at least, physically painful—first encounter, Lucie sits alongside him in a hire car parked in an upmarket residential area of Lisbon, just down the street from what must be an impressive residence if the grandeur of the entrance is anything to go by. On each side of the wrought iron gates, a blue-painted tiled wall descends in an elegant swirl to just a couple of feet in height with a neatly trimmed box hedge above it running down the edge of the property. There are no overt signs of any security measures, no surveillance cameras, no barbed wire, no fencing or barricade walls, in fact there are some sizeable gaps in the hedge further down the street which you could quite comfortably step through.

Mind you, Zac remains adamant that Alves is pretty paranoid and for sure some Mission Impossible style hi-tech type solutions will have been set up to keep the place more than secure. They similarly have to rely on their imagination to conjure up what the house itself may be like as it presumably lies somewhere over the incline in the poplar-lined driveway which climbs gradually away from the gates through the freshly mown manicured lawns.

It is blisteringly hot already, even for eight forty-five in the morning; no breeze at all making it through the wide-open car windows. Their budget certainly doesn't stretch to leaving the engine ticking over just to keep the aircon going. So, Lucie is beginning to fear just how long they may be stuck here as the temperature rises degree by degree. It doesn't help when they hear the refreshing sound of the sprinkler system hiss into life to ensure that the grass is kept that unnatural astroturf colour.

Lucie spent much of the previous night in her hotel room trying to imagine what Emma would do if she were in Lucie's shoes right now. In the end, the only possible conclusion was that the ever-decisive Emma would tackle things head on. Lucie too is determined to seize the moment and do…what? Honestly, she has no idea. She had already exhausted all the more obvious courses of action: Castro had refused Lucie's attempts to contact him again; the police seem totally clueless and unwilling to offer any further support; and Alves, well, he remains phantom-like, ill-defined, always just out of reach. Actually, in a last-ditch attempt at diplomacy, Lucie had made a call to Alves while Zac was finalising the paperwork at the car rental firm but Alves's secretary had told her he was not available, nor would he be, for the rest of the week.

Hence, Lucie and Zac are now sitting here staking out Alves's private residence. By a stroke of luck—if anything to do with being stuck in this claustrophobic and stifling cheapo hire car can be described as luck—Zac, or at least so he says, had already, as part of his insurance search background checks, uncovered a late payment by Alves of a parking ticket from eighteen months ago which cited his home address.

And while all this has been going on, Lucie has been feeling more and more out of her depth and her concern for her friend's wellbeing has only steadily intensified. She has lost count of the times she has tried Emma's mobile but every time, as it again skips to voicemail, it just ratchets up her anxiety level, and increases her resolve to find her friend.

In the rear-view mirror Zac, who is in the driver's seat, sees the gates sliding open automatically.

"We're on," he says.

"Sorry?" Lucie is still miles away.

"The gate…" Zac nods at the mirror.

Lucie looks over her shoulder out through the rear window. A few seconds later an opulent looking red sports car exits the gate onto the street.

"Now that is a car!" Zac says with admiration laced with almost audible pangs of jealousy.

"Right," Lucie is focused on the driver as the car passes them.

"A Lexus LC, nice," Zac is still impressed mostly with the car.

"That's got to be him. Let's go."

Zac starts their silver Seat Ibiza.

"He's going to beat us for speed, I'd say."

But the Lexus doesn't just roar off into the distance, rather it plods along at a very sedate pace and they have no difficulty in following it through the Lisbon rush hour traffic.

Over the next couple of hours, they follow Alves at a prudent distance with nothing noteworthy to report. He heads to the main office opposite Emma's residencia, then to an open-air bar near the Bisset Science Institute where he has a coffee with none other than Fernando Castro. At that moment, it dawns on Lucie that their plan is flawed. All morning they had been hoping that Alves would drive them directly to the location of Emma's incarceration.

Woefully naive, she now thinks. She needs to do something far more confrontational than just limply tailing him hour after hour. What she really needs is to flush Alves out into the open, to force him to give her some answers. Then as he appears to be on his way back home, he pulls into a petrol station and fills the Lexus. He leaves the car and goes to pay. This is Lucie's chance. She jumps out of the car.

"What the hell do you think you are doing?" Zac shouts out of the car window.

"Change of plan...Upping the ante," Lucie yells back at Zac over her shoulder as she sprints across the forecourt to the pumps and stops next to the Lexus. She is finally going to meet the elusive Alves.

Just seconds later, Alves comes out of the petrol station shop, looks over at Lucie and smiles. He is in his late forties or maybe a well-preserved early fifties, with silver hair a fraction too long for it not to be a deliberate statement. His suit is immaculate, an 'Armani' or something of that ilk in a soft grey, a loose but perfect fit for his rather meagre frame. He walks completely unfazed back to the car, tossing his compact wallet up and down in the palm of his hand.

"Lucie," he says, as if to a child who is misbehaving albeit in an enchanting way. "Just what do you think you are playing at?"

"Where's Emma?" Lucie asks, raising her voice over the noise of a passing truck.

The car unlocks itself automatically as Alves approaches and with a wave of the hand he invites Lucie to get in on the passenger side. Lucie hesitates.

"Look, Lucie. You've been following me all morning. Do you want to know what's going on or not? Get in."

Lucie feels he's made his point and, if a little reluctantly, she gets into Alves's car hoping that Zac will be able to carry on tailing them as easily as he had earlier on in the day, although clearly their attempt to melt unobserved into the background traffic had been less effective than they thought.

"What have you done with Emma?" Lucie now demands as Alves starts the car.

He glances over at Lucie, genuinely surprised.

"Absolutely nothing," he says calmly, pulling out of the petrol station.

As Alves accelerates away far faster than at any other point in the day, Lucie becomes aware that her getting into the Lexus may have played straight into Alves's hands. She too may now have been plucked out of circulation, the same as Emma. Alves heads down the a motorway slip road and keeps accelerating as he joins the main carriageway, leaving Zac and the Seat Ibiza for dead. How stupid she has been.

"So, where is she?"

"She is in the lab, under a strict…lockdown protocol, if you like."

"Lockdown? She was abducted from her own room."

"Oh please. Don't exaggerate. She is fine…Better than fine," Alves says and after a small pause, out of the blue, he continues, "Let's eat. Are you hungry? I'm starving. I know a great place under the bridge. They do amazing fish."

"You just don't get it," Lucie says her frustration all too evident.

"Let's discuss it all over lunch, shall we?"

And in an instant Alves has moved on and there is no way back. He has no rewind button, almost as if he has morphed into an entirely different person. Either Alves had already planned well in advance on going to this particular restaurant or he is impelled by an astonishing spontaneity. Whichever it is Lucie has no time to decide as right on queue the Lexus turns the next corner and suddenly the massive red suspension bridge which spans the Tagus towers a couple of hundred feet above them.

Alves also has a strength of character, a natural aura which makes it hard to deny him. He brings the car to a halt at the edge of the river, beside a walkway down to a pontoon landing stage which houses the 'Lisboa Norte e Sul' restaurant.

He jumps out of the car and tossing his keys to the valet parking attendant, who clearly recognises him, says to Lucie, "This place really is very good."

Some minutes later they are seated at a table in the dappled shade offered by a pergola with vines trained above and bunches of not yet ripened grapes hanging down. The single span suspension bridge stretches away over two kilometres across the river to the southern bank where the iconic statue of Christ with arms outstretched immediately brings to mind Rio de Janeiro.

The location is stunning, the weather beautiful with a cooling breeze wafting up gently off the river and the food is as good as Alves had suggested; Lucie had seen nothing to be gained by rejecting Alves's lunch invitation. The longer she can be with him the more she may learn about Emma. She has to admit too that Alves is in no way threatening, in fact she finds him thoroughly charming and remarkably enthusiastic about being with her, which has caught her totally off guard.

"You really shouldn't have come all this way for nothing," Alves says as Lucie makes yet another attempt to bring the conversation back to the subject of Emma.

"So I'll just speak to her and then head home happy."

"Right now, that will not be possible, I am afraid."

Alves takes a long sip of the exquisite icy cold Vinho Verde.

"Let me explain," he says reassuringly. "Ever since Emma arrived here in Lisbon, what, just three or four weeks ago, I sensed we were on the verge of something momentous, like she was the final piece in the puzzle I have been trying to solve for such a long time. Emma is truly unique, as I am sure you, more than anyone, will fully appreciate and as I had imagined, once she saw the scale and scope of what we are trying to do here, she has thrown herself into the work unreservedly and as you also know, she can be quite single-minded.

"Now we are reaching the culmination of this crucial testing phase and Emma, along with all the technicians and the lead scientists will be in lockdown at our main laboratory until Thursday. Once all that is out of the way, of course you can see her. On Thursday. Just a couple of days from now."

"A call would do, just a quick call. That can't be too much to ask."

"Lockdown means precisely that. There is no communication permitted with the outside. I need to control all the data flow. I have had far too many issues with security in the past. Vital information leaks and data breaches, even via mobiles, would you believe? So, no. Not even a phone call…Coffee?"

And with that Alves puts an end to the whole subject of Emma's whereabouts. Of course, Lucie wasn't going to take any of what Alves has said at face value. Who the hell does Alves think he bloody well is anyway, to prohibit her from verifying the safety of her friend? And the lunch? It beggars belief that he could even think that lunch was appropriate when for all Lucie knew he could be holding Emma prisoner, kidnapped somewhere. It certainly didn't sound like she was taken from the residencia of her own free will.

Alves had driven her back into the centre of town and let her out in Bairro Alto, not far from the bar with all the mirrors, most likely believing that he had put out the fire behind Lucie's concerns but on the contrary as she now sits explaining how things had played out to Zac, she feels increasingly alarmed for the safety of her friend as though Emma might have been duped and inducted into some sinister cult. She could even see the extravagant charismatic Alves as a Charles Manson type, a manipulator, an obsessive control freak, a fanatic.

Alves had refused to tell Lucie anything about the project itself, scoffing that he hardly understood the basics himself and certainly wouldn't be able to explain it in a way that was even vaguely comprehensible. Well, maybe she is getting a bit carried away and to be fair, the lunch had been exceptional. Maybe they should just do as Alves had suggested and wait until Thursday, it is only two days after all.

Zac listened stony-faced to Lucie's story and then he explained that he had returned the hire car as it had proved completely useless in trailing a Lexus LC and had come back to the bar hoping—but by no means sure—that Lucie would meet him there after they had got split up. Lucie couldn't understand his doubting her.

The bar with the mirrors was the logical default back-up place to meet. Anyone with the tiniest bit of nouse would have realised that, although she kept to herself that, in fact, she too had become nervous approaching the bar as to whether she would find it empty and her heart had skipped a beat in relief when she saw Zac sitting there on his own waiting for her.

However, Zac seems to share none of Lucie's doubts about whether they should wait until Thursday. He is keen on carrying on with their plan B. He had even seemed a bit pushy in his questioning of Lucie about what had actually been said by Alves, as though she had missed out some vital bits from her account deliberately.

"He must have given you some hint as to where the lab might be."

"No, just that the whole trial process would be over on Thursday, the day after tomorrow."

"What did he say about me?" Zac asks, not for the first time. Zac had claimed that Alves was paranoid about security that morning but now Lucie thinks the one who is paranoid could be Zac himself. He seems manic, obsessed with everything Alves, taking it all far too personally, like there must be some deeper connection between the two.

"Zac, he didn't see you. I told you before, so how was he going to talk about you?"

"You can't believe a word he says. He has this hidden agenda, you wouldn't believe. I assure you he is quite capable of keeping Emma locked up while at the same time enjoying a nice lunch and a glass of wine with her best friend."

"She may just be complying with orders, willingly," Lucie can't believe she is now suggesting this but Alves was right when he said that Emma could be single-minded and would toe the line if she was convinced it was necessary.

"So, do we go ahead or not?" Zac puts Lucie on the spot.

"I have to know she is OK. Something *weird* was what she said. That was the word she used in her voicemail. And until she tells me herself she is good, we go on."

And with that the decision is taken. Lucie has the right to know the location of her friend and given Alves has declined to disclose that information, he is obviously obliging Lucie to take matters into her own hands and a minor, superficial bending of the law is fully justified in her mind to obtain that knowledge. Zac is absolutely up for it too, although Lucie is not quite so sure where his personal justification comes from.

Hardly what an insurance investigator looking into a claim on equipment lost at sea should be doing, Lucie thinks, but he seems to share her desire to get to the bottom of all this. Maybe he trusts her a little more now, or maybe she is starting to see something in Zac which she could eventually trust too.

A little after midnight that same night, Lucie can just make out the figure of Zac looking down from the balcony of Emma's room at the Residencia Santa Rosita. Ironically, she is standing in the same doorway Zac himself had used to tail her when she had been going through Emma's room with the nun.

Zac is keeping tabs on the security hut adjacent to the barrier which controls vehicles entering and leaving the Alves warehouse yard, as well as access to the main office building and the subterranean carpark. The last of the staff and any final shipments have finished for the day. All the executive level employees have departed the premises too. Even the red Lexus of Alves himself left a couple of hours earlier. Zac has explained to Lucie that overnight there is just a single security guy guarding the entrance to Alves's headquarters.

Lucie sees Zac look up and down the now quiet street a couple of times, then hears him whisper into her AirPods, "All clear. You're good to go." They have left a voice call open so they can communicate verbally but just to be sure, Zac gives Lucie a thumbs up from the balcony in any case.

"I get the picture," Lucie says sarcastically.

She pockets the AirPods and steps hesitantly from the cover of her doorway and as she comes into view from the security kiosk, she stumbles as if in a drunken stupor using the wall to steady herself. This is crazy, she thinks but then puts it out of her mind as she focuses on getting fully into character. She teeters precariously to one side and veers to avoid the barrier slipping inside the Alves entrance yard, grabbing at the second attempt the ledge going around the security cabin window. She plonks a two-thirds drained bottle of Johnnie Walker Black Label on the shelf in front of her, wobbles from side to side and doubles over as though she may be about to throw up.

That must have got the attention of the security guard as he jumps up clearly alarmed. Lucie turns and puts her back against the wall next to the window and slides down to a sitting position on the pavement under the ledge. She leans over again looking now perilously close to vomiting, she hopes.

"Não, não. Aqui não," the guard shouts, coming out of the cabin and urgently trying to get Lucie to move on.

"I don't feel good," Lucie slurs.

"Não vomite aqui!" he pleads, most likely hoping to get her to refrain from vomiting anywhere he would be obliged to clean it up. His attitude has no compassion, no suggestion of any concern whatsoever for Lucie's well-being, he just wants her off his patch.

Eventually he manages to get Lucie to her feet and he pushes her back around the barrier and then he stands shaking his head as Lucie staggers a zig-zag route up the pavement until she turns and disappears down the next side street.

"You are a truly convincing drunk, loads of practice, I suppose," Zac laughs into her AirPods as she slips them back into her ears.

Earlier that afternoon after a second and this time even more serious bout of haggling with the nun—which Lucie again lost dismally it has to be said—she had reached a deal on renting Emma's old room at the Residencia Santa Rosita for just one night.

"Some Dutch courage?" Zac had offered Lucie the bottle of Johnnie Walker with an ironic smile.

"Just get on with it, will you?" Lucie had chastised him.

Zac poured more than half of the whisky from the bottle into the water jug on the dressing table in the corner.

"That'll perk up morning prayers for some lucky nun," he had joked.

He had then emptied into the bottle a fine powder from a folded sheet of paper where he had just crushed up several pills.

"What is that?" asked Lucie.

"A type of Ketamine," Zac had replied without taking his mind off the job at hand.

"But won't that only get him high."

"Not with the sort of dose I'm giving him."

"How on earth did you get your hands on that, here in Lisbon?"

"What? You think they don't spike girls' drinks all the time here too? Come on, get real. You can buy this all over the place."

He had replaced the lid and given it a good shake. His confidence was reassuring but his familiarity with the whole spiking drinks scene and his ability to procure said drugs so easily here in Lisbon was more than a bit unnerving. However, she decided not to push the issue as after all this was the only plan B they had.

"That should do it," Zac had said, holding up the bottle to the light checking the powder had been fully dissolved.

Lucie re-enters Emma's room following her amateur dramatics session with the security guard and what a performance it had been. She has to admit that she had actually quite enjoyed herself. Obviously, she has had to push any moral questions to the back of her mind. But in the end, all she has done was to put temptation in the guard's way. She is not forcing him to drink her whisky, is she?

"He's been sitting there looking longingly at your bottle of whisky ever since you left him…I wouldn't give him more than a couple of minutes before he caves in and just has to try a wee dram," Zac's attempted Scottish accent is lamentable but it does seem to have done the trick as, lo and behold, at that very moment, the security guard grabs the bottle and takes a long slurp.

"I just hope you haven't put so much in that you end up killing him," Lucie says.

"I think that should be *we,* you are just as responsible as me in all this," Zac says, his tone a little too serious for Lucie's liking. Then he lightens up and continues, "Anyhow, don't worry. In half an hour, he will be dead to the world but not dead, dead."

They give it three quarters of an hour, just to be on the safe side, then Zac and Lucie head downstairs, cross the street and enter the yard which is still deserted. They approach the security kiosk and can see the guard with his head down on the desk, completely comatosed with his hand still clutching the now practically empty whisky bottle.

Lucie reaches through the window and gently slips the security guard's ID card from around his neck. Pressing the card onto the reader mounted on the wall next to the main door into the office building provokes a soft clunk as the lock is released and they are inside.

So far, so good. Just getting inside had appeared such a mammoth task that Lucie has hardly contemplated anything beyond that. Now, standing here in the dark and silent reception area of Alves's HQ, the enormity of what she is doing hits her. But apart from the unsurprising anxiety of what the consequences will be if she gets caught, she also feels an excitement, an undeniable thrill at really getting stuck in, at finally achieving something meaningful which may prove crucial in the search for Emma.

From the board behind the reception desk, they ascertain that the executive suite is located, as seems customary these days, on the top floor and they head up the four storeys of concrete steps in the emergency stairwell avoiding the lift, which Zac says may be protected by some fancy surveillance system or other.

Lucie is breathing heavily by the time she struggles up the last flight of stairs—Zac much less so, it must be said—but Lucie has not been in the gym in months so she couldn't really have expected anything else. The fire door is unlocked and as they emerge into Alves's office, she appreciates just how exceptionally plush everything is: a soft leather chair behind an antique hardwood desk; works of art on the walls; real carpets and rugs; and it is big, bigger than any office Lucie has ever seen before.

Alves's desk is pretty much empty save for a single page per day diary which Zac thumbs through using just the flashlight on his phone. Lucie rummages through the drawers but she finds nothing of interest there.

"Hey, Lucie," Zac whispers. "Alves's diary is full of meetings and schedules but then nothing after 21:00 Thursday. Then it is totally blank, like the world ends for Alves on Thursday."

"Zac, this drawer is locked," Lucie says pulling the handle aggressively. "This must be where he keeps the stuff he doesn't want anyone to see."

Lucie quickly scans the rest of the office for something she can use to force the lock on the drawer. She walks abruptly over to a sturdy-looking bronze art deco statuette with palms pressed together as if in some Buddhist prayer ritual above the figure's head. Lucie picks it up off its hefty looking black plinth and weighs it in her hand.

"Oh no, shit," Zac says under his breath. "That's all we need. I thought this was going a bit too well to be believed."

"What do you mean?"

"Look," Zac points to a tiny red dot on the ceiling directly above where the statuette was positioned. He shows Lucie a circular hole in the middle of the plinth and moving it to one side reveals the source of the red beam of light, built into the top of the display unit beneath. "That's infrared, some sort of burglar alarm."

"Too late to put it back, I suppose."

Zac smiles. It's all the confirmation Lucie needs.

"I reckon we have got five minutes before this place is crawling with police, tops," Zac says.

"Right. Let's get to it then," says Lucie, instead of running she is intent on maximising those five minutes. She looks at her watch, tilting it towards the meagre light which seeps in from the street and notes it is three minutes to one.

Lucie grabs the plinth from under the statuette too and brings both back to the desk. She slips the statuette's outstretched bronze hands into the gap above the drawer where the lock is fastened. She then swings the plinth into the base of the statuette. The noise seems deafening in the stillness of the night, but they have already revealed they are here, so who cares? She smashes the statuette a couple more times before the ancient lock can no longer withstand such an onslaught and breaks.

Inside they find a series of documents and charts, along with a map of Lisbon which Lucie unfurls across the desktop. It displays a series of concentric circles—well, more like isobars on a weather map—all the areas between them shaded in different colours radiating out from the centre in deep red to a faded light green further out.

"What is a Time Mesh Distortion?" Lucie asks.

"What did you say?"

"A Time Mesh Distortion. That's what it says here. See?"

"I'm not sure. I know Castro has been working on something time-related for several years. It seems Alves is behind that project too."

By the way Zac pores over the map, Lucie doubts he is letting on to his full understanding of what he is looking at. For Lucie the name 'Time Mesh Distortion' sounds offbeat, like some made up technology from a Dr Who episode, although it is somehow menacing as well. But none of the annotations she can see on the map or the other documents makes sense to her. It is all too technical, written in a scientific jargon beyond her comprehension.

"The epicentre of the circles, here," he taps a point on the map, "must be where the lab is. Look, there's an address too: Rua Lucio Vera, 302. That must be it."

Lucie glances at her watch; almost three minutes have passed since they tripped the alarm. She runs up the office to the secretary's desk closer to the lift doors.

"Come on, Lucie. We've got what we came for," Zac says. "Let's get out of here while we still can."

"Just a quick look, I promise," Lucie says flicking through the hanging files in the drawers in the desk. She finds a mass of receipts and papers related to a major removals contract. The whole office is being shut down and relocated. She makes a mental note of the name of the haulage company handling the onward move of items in the UK: TransWorldX from Croydon. But she finds no indication of any final shipping destination.

Then suddenly, the light above the lift doors flashes on and a hum tells them that someone is coming up.

"Oh Christ!" Lucie says under her breath.

"Run!" Zac half shouts, turning and rushing back out, leaving down the same stairs they had used on their way up, "Come on, Lucie. Move!"

Lucie bolts after him in shock. To reach the emergency exit she has to cross the whole office and as she follows Zac out into the stairwell she sees, over her shoulder through the slow-closing automatic fire door, the lift slides open and she immediately recognises the face of Fernando Castro. What is Castro doing here? How come he is answering an alarm callout at the HQ of Alves, S.A.? It seems the links between Alves and Castro run much deeper than either Lucie or Zac had suspected.

Lucie and Zac race down the emergency staircase and as they burst back into the main reception on the ground floor they are stopped in their tracks by none other than Detective Farinha, the young policeman she had seen when she reported Emma's disappearance, standing directly in front of the main door, their only hope of escape. More worryingly there is a gun in his hand. A real live gun. This is madness. Farinha smiles in victory.

Zac and Lucie are taken back up to Alves's office and then separated. Lucie has now been locked for at least twenty minutes in a meeting room in an annexe on the top floor. She cannot get her head around how Farinha and Castro even know each other let alone that they are working as a team. And then there is the small matter of Lucie having just been caught by a detective in the Lisbon police department breaking into the office building of the headquarters of a prestigious multinational science operation in a foreign country. She has really blown it, there will be hell to pay for the unholy mess she has made of things.

The door opens and Castro walks in. Lucie remains seated behind the only table on the only chair.

"Right, Lucie," he starts, letting out a sigh of annoyance as he paces up and down in front of her.

Lucie cannot quite pinpoint what it is she finds so disagreeable about Castro but since she first met him at the Bisset Institute she has always felt the same way. It's as though he believes he has some birth-given, natural superiority, like he sits on high with a trump card up his sleeve, while she scrabbles around, like some lab rat oblivious to his power over her, ignorant of how things are going to play out. He believes her to be no more than an annoying irrelevance—rightly or wrongly—but it is his taking all that for granted that so riles her.

"What are you doing here, Lucie?" he asks eventually in a measured tone.

"Me? What about you? This isn't exactly the Bisset Science Institute, if I'm not mistaken."

"Look, you're hardly in a position to be demanding answers. You have a simple choice to make here: either you answer my questions fully, in which case you get to walk away from here or if you don't, things get complicated. This little escapade of yours could see you end up in a Portuguese gaol for a heck of a long time. Do you understand?"

Lucie nods. However much she dislikes him she has to admit he now has her undivided attention.

"Good. So, what is your connection to Zac? That is what you call him, I believe."

"I don't have any connection to him. I only met him yesterday."

"You see. That is so disappointing. You have just broken in here and now you're trying to tell me that you only met your partner yesterday."

The grin which accompanies his snide observation suddenly thrusts Lucie back in time to when Miles abused her in Carsphairn Hall. Castro is taking the same sadistic pleasure in making Lucie uncomfortable as Miles had done. The realisation is spine-chilling. This guy too is a full-on narcissist, quite possibly psycho into the bargain.

Castro continues, "I don't think you understand frankly just how critical and dangerous this situation could be for you personally."

But the thing Castro is not cottoning on to at all is that while Lucie may be uneducated—by his own narrow standards—she is not intimidated by him and will not allow his egotism to dictate their rules of engagement. She has a quite unique emotional balance forged out of the harsh and brutal experience she endured in the past which allows her to see through his arrogance and threats, enabling her to identify an effective form of retaliation using the only weapon she knows may throw a spanner into Castro's playbook.

She counterattacks, "How about you listen to me for a second. My friend has been abducted and guess what? One of the people who took her was your man Farinha. Is that what you call him?" Lucie sneers, "You know, the cop who can afford a real Rolex."

Lucie somehow suspected from the outset that Farinha must have had something to do with Emma's disappearance. He was just too interested in Lucie being in the residencia in the first place. She also reckoned that the head-nun, the one who manages the place, was so in tune with the true value of things that she would have twigged that Farinha's Rolex wasn't fake and for an extra fifty euros, the nun confirmed as much when Lucie went back there to hire out Emma's room. Farinha had indeed been one of the men who had taken Emma away.

Castro blows air slowly out of his mouth in a soft and menacing hiss. He certainly hadn't expected that. Any trace of a smile has vanished from Castro's expression. He places his palms down firmly on the table either side of Lucie and towers over her.

"This is not some game. Don't you realise that? You and Emma, the two of you are in on this together, aren't you?"

His mocking tone is gone too, replaced by a deadly serious ruthlessness. She suddenly feels afraid of him, she senses he is so much more dangerous even than Miles.

"What do you mean? In on what?"

"She has been feeding you information," Castro is not asking anymore, he is stating a fact.

"That's ridiculous. I've come here to find Emma, not to steal anything."

"Yeah, right," Castro disregards her comment, he has reached his conclusion and is convinced she is lying. He shakes his head as if giving up on her and then roughly picks her up by the elbow. He doesn't ask anything else; her interrogation is over. He drags her out of the meeting room back into the main office where Zac is being looked after by Farinha, still with that gun in his hand.

"She knows nothing," Zac says. "Let her go."

"Oh, but she does. She knows far too much. The only thing she doesn't seem to have picked up on is just how toxic you are. You've really messed up this time. What were you thinking, bringing her in here with you?"

Castro turns away from Lucie and Zac and addresses Farinha directly, "She has even figured out that *you* were involved in taking the girl. Now that puts both of us in a spot of bother."

"I knew that suit was too good for a detective's pay." Lucie stares at Farinha defiantly.

"Cheeky bitch!" Farinha spits through his teeth.

"So suave, so stylish." Lucie doesn't appear intimidated at all, although she is not sure where she is getting all this unexpected courage from.

"Sort out this mess, Farinha," Castro says, staring unflinchingly at Lucie. He makes it sound so simple and routine, like taking out the recycling bin.

"Just let me talk to Emma and I guarantee you will never see me again," Lucie says, her desperation showing all too clearly.

"That is exactly what I am banking on," Castro laughs, a bit too loudly.

"I'm just looking for my friend."

"You should have picked your friends with more care," Castro says coldly.

"Shall we?" Farinha says, flicking the barrel of his gun in the direction of the still open lift doors. They have no real choice. Lucie is getting increasingly worried that as things stand, any realistic chance of escape is looking less and less likely before they get to the sorting out of the mess part of Castro's instruction.

This whole thing has gone from starting out as a bit of a lark, involving a trip down to Lisbon to see her friend, to some maniac with a gun threatening to end her life or at least that seems the only logical interpretation of where this is heading. Lucie cannot understand how all of this could have happened. You just don't get killed for breaking into an office building, do you?

In the lift, Farinha keeps the muzzle of his gun stuck tight into the back of Zac's neck and Lucie is placed with her nose almost touching the closed lift door which slides open slowly onto the basement garage. Farinha ushers them out of the lift towards the two lines of almost empty parking bays. They approach an imposing black SUV. Farinha has dropped back a couple of paces. Lucie and Zac are out of time.

Farinha presses a remote and the car bleeps and flashes its orange indicators.

"Open the trunk." Farinha says.

"The trunk?" Lucie laughs nervously.

"Just do it!"

Lucie opens the boot which is huge inside, quite large enough to fit a couple of bodies. Oh my God, Lucie realises Farinha is going to kill them both right here. She spins round just in time to see Farinha raising his gun to point directly at her chest.

"No!" screams Zac, throwing himself in front of Lucie as the crack of the gun going off echoes around the garage. Zac drops to the ground clearly hit by the bullet intended for her. Lucie lashes out spinning off her right foot, catching Farinha flat-footed before he has time to fire again and landing a powerful kick with her other foot straight into Farinha's knee which buckles with a loud crack.

He fires the gun again only missing Lucie by a fraction. She follows up immediately by lunging at Farinha's gun hand with all her weight, knocking him off balance and sending them both tumbling to the ground and the gun sprays from his hand, skittling across the floor.

Zac, from his position on the ground, manages to grab hold of Farinha giving Lucie a split-second advantage and she crawls as fast as she can the three or four metres to where the gun has come to rest. Farinha in the meantime has regrouped and is now sitting on the floor, leaning against the SUV holding Zac's head and forcing it into an unnatural position which seems could break his neck at any moment.

"Leave the gun or I kill him," Farinha threatens.

Lucie grabs the gun, rolls onto her back so she is facing Farinha with Zac way too close to her firing line to be sure she can hit the one but not the other. Who is she trying to kid? She has never even fired a gun before, but she knows instantly it is now or never and she pulls the trigger, the gun fires and recoils and Farinha falls away from Zac. Lucie fires again and a third time and then silence envelops the garage all the deeper for it following the sound of the gunfire.

"Jesus Christ, Lucie! You could have killed me," Zac cries.

Farinha is dead. Lucie hit him in the neck with the first shot, the second ricocheted harmlessly off a nearby car into the wall but the third has blown off a big chunk of his head.

"It was either that or you really would have been dead," says Lucie, checking Zac's shot wound which seems to have gone clean through his shoulder. "We have to get out of here…quick," she goes on calmly, looking in Farinha's pockets for the keys to the SUV.

She helps Zac into the passenger seat with a lot of moaning and groaning and buckles his seatbelt. Then she gets into the driver's seat and also belts up as she launches the SUV up the ramp to the exit of the garage just as Castro bursts out of the lift and starts firing at the car smashing the rear window and her side mirror. From the top of the ramp, she can see the barrier blocking her way into the narrow street beyond.

She accelerates hard, smashing the barrier to smithereens and careering straight into a parked car on the far side of the street whose alarm goes off loudly. Lucie shrugs, she was never much good at parking, she thinks, smiling to herself. She hits reverse backing away from the wrecked vehicle, slams the structurally undamaged SUV into forward gear and with a loud screech of rubber speeds away down the street.

"So now what?" Lucie wonders out loud. Zac is unconscious.

Lucie has no real idea of where to go. She is more than anything in shock after having killed Farinha, a detective with the Lisbon police…a policeman. That will not go down well. That is going to provoke a massive response.

VII
The Bell

Newgate Gaol—1874

A six foot long chain secures Duncan's right wrist to the back wall of a cell for the exclusive use of condemned prisoners located directly under the keeper's house in Newgate gaol. Given the gravity and the callous viciousness of his crimes—he had after all killed not one but two police officers, including the merciless strangling of the Head Constable of Birkenhead—the conditions he could expect to endure here were always going to be harsh, deservedly so, grotesque. The damp has seeped through all Duncan's clothing making this early January chill even more penetrating, mould clings to the walls, the floor is awash with a putrid swill, it is almost permanently dark except for a feeble light which filters for a couple of hours a day through a tiny opening protected by large metal bars, high on the far wall, which looks out at floor level onto a dank and dismal courtyard.

The foul stench at first made his stomach heave. Rats meander nonchalantly right up to him, audacious and unafraid—he is the intruder here. For someone so obsessed with cleanliness, the filth of this sewer must be close to overwhelming although it has surprised Duncan that you can become accustomed to virtually anything, it appears.

The keeper once a day unlocks and opens the cell door and with the steel toecap of his boot slides a bowl of murky water and a few chunks of stale bread across the squalid floor to within Duncan's reach—no point in wasting anything even close to edible on him. Not that Duncan cares; he no longer has the remotest interest in his own wellbeing. But that selfishness he knows in the back of his mind cannot be allowed to carry on clouding his thoughts indefinitely.

Following the incident in Blackheath, Duncan had withdrawn into himself. He made no attempt to speak to Jules and she likewise made none to see him.

There was no point. Jules had been deeply traumatised by his almost throttling her. That much was evident to Duncan as she was rushed away from him at the house half-sobbing, half-choking, accompanied by a police constable who had thrown his cloak around her shoulders as if that would offer her some protection from him. Duncan offered no resistance and he was chained up and taken away.

He feels already dead to the world, calm in the acceptance of his guilt. Just how long he has been here and how long remains before his execution, he would rather not bring to mind—at least not yet. In the eight years since his surfacing, Duncan had always been aware of the existence of the emotional ties to Jules but he hadn't come close to grasping just how deep those feelings went. He had no memories of his previous life with Jules pre-surfacing. He could only imagine how it must have been but that lacked any true personal engagement, like he was inventing some fantasy without any grounding in reality. Now, however, he had an actual physical experience to draw on: they had made love.

He had always known that there would come a time when circumstances would dictate he should move on, but he had envisaged that this would still be several years away. Duncan was just forty-two and in good health. But his upcoming execution cast a very different light on things all of a sudden. He could have chosen a successor easily enough. It is not as though he hadn't come into contact with suitable candidates in the weeks since his incarceration.

But more than anything else what had stopped him from taking such a pivotal and irrevocable step was his conclusion that any new surfacing would in all likelihood trigger a full purging of his emotional connection to Jules, leaving him alone. So, he allowed his final days to ebb away doing nothing, content to suffer all that indignity just to experience the proximity and intimacy of his feelings for Jules and his vibrant recollections of the moment they had shared.

There had actually been a trial of sorts although it had lasted less than a day. Jules had looked sad and a little ashamed, but Duncan also saw in her such beauty even as she testified against him. He had been disappointed that Jules had not sat for the whole trial in the gallery; she had only come in when called on to give her testimony. In fact, she had only looked at him directly for a matter of seconds just to confirm his identity when requested to do so by the prosecuting barrister and subsequently as she accused him of trying to kill her too in Blackheath. But she had got that all wrong; in the end he had elected to allow her to live. He chose her life over his own. This was a fundamental shift in his priorities which should never have been possible. And yet there it was, undeniable.

And then he saw Jules walk to the door of the courtroom and leave without so much as a glance in his direction—that hurt him deeply—and with that she was gone.

He had offered no defence. Again, there was no point. The date for his execution was set and as the clock quickly ran down on what was left of his life, he cherished ever more closely his admittedly vain belief that he had in some way saved Jules and as a result his love for her only grew deeper the longer he stayed in that grim cell until now only a matter of hours remain for him to live.

He is sitting in his customary position on the floor with his arms clutched around his knees and his head down to the side as Father Casey enters the cell. The priest is in full garb: a black cassock tied with a rope cincture, dog-collar, a silk burgundy stole edged in braid with a gold cross emblazoned towards both ends.

In one hand, he carries a candle which flickers in the draught. In his other, pressed against his midriff, he is carrying a Bible bound in well-worn leather. He raises the Bible and makes the figure of the cross in the air between them. The grandeur of the priest's attire strikes Duncan as fitting for this final ceremony and he raises his eyebrow in a gesture of approval.

"You've dressed up for this, I see," Duncan says.

"Maybe I can be of some help," the priest states in a grave tone.

Duncan smiles to himself. He hears the footsteps of the keeper move away up the staircase to the residence above and then he notices a muffled exchange of laughter way off in the distance; the keeper is clearly not interested in his last confession.

Father Casey seems nervous, fidgety, repeatedly folding down the corner of his Bible.

"New at this?" Duncan asks casually with a polite tone.

The priest looks at Duncan and tries to follow what appears to be a well-rehearsed script, "I wish to offer you some solace, a chance to cleanse your spirit before—"

Duncan raises his hand, interrupting him. "I will most assuredly not benefit from any of your rituals, Father."

The priest kneels on the floor in front of Duncan and places the Bible down to one side and the candle to the other as if beyond the boundary of their conversation.

"So why agree to see me?"

"With just six hours to go before my neck ends up in the hangman's noose, I am clearly in some need of salvation. On that, I am sure we can both agree. Although not, I would hazard a guess, on the way to achieve it."

"I am not sure that I follow you," Father Casey says, his confusion evident.

Duncan raises himself enthusiastically into a kneeling position mirroring the stance of Father Casey. He then offers out both his hands to the priest who looks at him, unsure of Duncan's intentions.

"Humour me, Father," Duncan reassures him.

Father Casey shrugs and offers forward his own hands, at which point, Duncan grabs both the priest's forearms in a strong grip. The priest will have realised instantly and alarmingly that Duncan's palms are covered in a clammy, cold sweat.

"What on earth?" Father Casey says, astounded. He jerks back his arms trying to pull himself free but this only causes Duncan to tighten his grip.

It only takes a few seconds for the icy secretion on Duncan's hands to penetrate the priest's skin and mix into his bloodstream. Duncan can easily imagine the dread the priest must have suffered as the first exploratory incursions spread across his mind, delving and probing into the structure and workings of his brain. Duncan holds the priest's wide-eyed gaze staring deep into his horrified eyes but he feels no compassion. This is essential and inevitable.

A viable connection has now been established. Once their skins have melted into each other, fused at the point of physical contact, there is already no way back. The rush Duncan feels is both disconcerting and yet at the same time intoxicating but that must have been nothing compared to the shock and upheaval endured by the priest.

But then, almost as quickly as the priest's anxiety had manifested itself, Duncan notices that the powerful sedative laced within the cold sweat on his hands must now have worked its way into his nervous system as the priest looks much calmer, almost serene. The nano-cybernetics will now be able, unhindered, to set about their much more fundamental and complex task of opening a workable pathway through to the priest's memory.

"There is no other way. This is…ordained to happen, you might say," Duncan says with a hint of irony even at this crucial point.

Their heart rates synchronise at an impossibly slow pace. Their breathing settles into a shallow unified pattern. Two different planes of consciousness shift across one another, identifying and establishing critical points of contact. They each mould themselves to accommodate the other, merging into a single tangled, labyrinthine coexistence. Neither can hide, neither can block out the other. Self-awareness lies at the very core of identity, the ability to recognise our emotions, our dreams, values and patterns of behaviour, what resides within and outside of our control. But now both Father Casey and Duncan are aware not only of their own individual psyches but also that of the other within a unique shared consciousness.

And then, before Father Casey has had time to grasp the enormity of what is happening, he notices a subtle change in the way his mind is functioning, just a gentle shift at first, no more than a barely discernible reordering of priorities, as if his mind is being deflected away from its instinctive, usual routines and responses, is being cajoled into adopting some little-frequented, untried direction.

Father Casey tries to refocus back onto who he is, onto his own beliefs, but he finds less and less there to cling to. Instead, he starts to see and to experience a mass of unconnected images firing into his mind. He feels a sharp sense of familiarity with them all, a feeling of oneness, which is both comforting but at the same time is intermingled with a niggling anxious doubt; these are scenes he feels he must have witnessed but he can't quite place them, he can't quite figure out where or when they happened.

There is some initial confusion, of course there is. Just try to imagine your own mind in a semi-anaesthetised state, your individuality crumbling, everything that defines you being stripped away, as innumerable unrecognised memories burrow into your mind, confusion is understandably the overwhelming reaction. The term that comes to the priest's mind is *déjà vu* but that doesn't even start to do it justice.

Father Casey dearly wishes this will prove to be the mystical, divine intervention he has longed for since he was a boy but which had always eluded him, had left his mind in a perpetual and disturbing fog of uncertainty. He has for so long craved clarity, an unequivocal vision of God, eliminating any room for that all pervasive self-questioning which tortures him.

But as the minutes pass he realises it is no deity generating the wild sensual experiences now cramming into his mind, the flood of images being absorbed into his being; they are all emanating out of the man kneeling opposite him on the floor of a condemned man's prison cell.

"Who are you?" Father Casey utters.

Duncan says nothing in reply. He doesn't need to. Father Casey is already able to discover for himself exactly who Duncan is, he can now see deep into the innermost recesses of the mind of this figure hunched down across the floor in front of him. He is at one with Duncan. Father Casey can hear the sound of the rain splashing onto the ledge and even though he is facing away from the small window, he can quite clearly see each and every raindrop hitting the courtyard paving stones beyond the open railings directly behind him.

He knows these visions and sensations are being channelled into his mind through Duncan. They are sharing every sensation, every thought. It feels eternal and infinite but both Father Casey and Duncan are also acutely aware that this mystical, ecstatic, unified consciousness can only last for the briefest of moments. They both know they cannot remain here, they need to accept their futures must diverge and each must follow their own separate path.

Duncan edges back becoming less and less distinguishable from the shadows which enshroud him. At the same time, Father Casey comes to the stark realisation that as all these amazing new memories and feelings coming from Duncan are layered across his mind, his own are being displaced, their intensity beginning to fade, their focus blurring.

Like mist rising up from a cold lake in the early morning, Father Casey can still see his past, his memories dance before him, shimmering, beautiful and enticing but now without clear form. They are already untouchable and dissolving, vague and agonisingly just out of reach. They dissipate slowly as the sun climbs ever higher in the sky until they eventually evaporate into nothing.

The process is complete. The only light comes from the single candle still flickering in the corner of the cell casting gigantic distorted shadows across the wall behind both Duncan and the priest. The priest's eyes are open although on the surface he appears devoid of emotion, inert, barely taking in the scene at all. However, that could not be further from the truth, he is now fully aware of what has happened, of his destiny and he is in awe of it.

Duncan hasn't moved for several minutes either, kneeling opposite the priest still holding his forearms but lightly now, his head bowed onto his chest, his eyes closed, a peaceful expression on his face too. The priest feels a fleeting sympathy for this solitary and tragic figure before him, he has a deep respect for Duncan, with whom he has been through so much and whose essence has now gone. Everything that had happened in the years since his surfacing on Bidston Moss, all his memories, motivations and experiences now belong exclusively to Father

Casey. Duncan himself is now little more than an empty shell to be discarded without undue concern. Father Casey will take things forward from here.

As dawn breaks, the hubbub outside the cell grows. At a quarter past five, the keeper leads several sets of boots noisily down the steps and with a rattle of keys, the cell door opens and the execution squad led by the police superintendent enters.

They unlock Duncan's chain and replace them with handcuffs. The priest does what he can to calm the increasingly agitated Duncan down, aware that Duncan is unable to remember any of the events that have led to him being here and his distress, confusion and indignation are entirely justified. As they bustle him out of the cell, Duncan has no idea even of where he is being led.

They walk in silence except for the head keeper who proudly explains that the passageway they are following is known as Birdcage Walk due to the wire meshing over its narrow open-roofed corridor. When Duncan sees the gallows in the courtyard, however, he falls to his knees in sudden fear, wailing to himself as he realises what is scheduled to happen to him here.

It is now six years since public executions have been banned due to the disruption they caused—literally thousands would pitch up and throw a massive impromptu party with untold mayhem inevitably ensuing—but that hasn't dampened the public's enthusiasm for an execution and the executioner confirms to Duncan that there is a good crowd in the street to celebrate his passing in any case. Duncan shouts at the top of his voice that he has done nothing wrong. He pleads his innocence to the priest, begs him to intervene to stop this madness in a heartfelt manner. Father Casey is touched. It is clearly unfortunate that Duncan has to die but honestly, what could he do to avoid it?

At the foot of the steps up to the gallows, all the participants in the execution are ushered into some semblance of a straight line by the official photographer. All stare blankly out while the photographer busies himself under a black cape draped over his head behind the camera mounted on a tripod. The photographer then shouts for them all to keep still as he removes the lens cap for several seconds. All part of some new documentation procedures, the police superintendent comments in an aside to the priest as the photographer gathers up his equipment and leaves.

The execution party then splits with Duncan, pretty much dragged up the gallows stairs to the platform by two constables with some considerable effort. Next, the priest is urged up alongside the executioner himself. As the police superintendent reads out Duncan's sentence in a commanding voice from the courtyard below, Duncan once again loses his grip on himself and crumples to his knees, his desperation now verging on the pathetic. The executioner places a black cloth bag over Duncan's head which thankfully muffles his whimpering for mercy.

The executioner places the noose around Duncan's neck and tightens its knot carefully lodging it into position. Duncan straightens visibly perhaps now conscious that his life is over. The only sound is Duncan's quick panicked gulps of air, sucking in and blowing out the cloth covering his mouth.

The executioner then turns and looks at Father Casey who realises with no little alarm that he is expected to utter some sort of final ritual or other. The priest has no idea what to say. He fumbles with his Bible nervously much as Father Casey had done when he had entered Duncan's cell the evening before. But then he notices his thumb snagging against a piece of paper stuck inside the cover of his Bible.

On it is scribbled a prayer from the book of Psalms, which the priest had probably placed there to be sure he would not fluff his lines at such an important juncture. Father Casey gladly reads the words with what he considers to be suitable gravitas. He feels relieved his duties seem to be over and nobody any the wiser.

The hangman pulls a lever releasing the trapdoor. It opens and Duncan is hanged, his body dropping with a sickening ugly snapping sound and then twitching for several minutes until it finally hangs still. A doctor pronounces him dead and the head keeper walks solemnly to a table behind the gallows and retrieves the execution bell. He rings it twelve times.

Only fifteen minutes later, Father Casey is walking out of the prison gates and he can fully appreciate the huge crowds in the street. Duncan certainly had his following. The priest pulls off the dog-collar and tosses it along with the Bible onto a pile of filth and rubbish on the corner of a squalid terraced slum as he walks by with a smile broadening ever wider across his face.

VIII
21:00:00

Lisbon—Present Day

Shock is starting to get a hold of Lucie, starting frankly to overwhelm her. Her knuckles grip the steering-wheel way too tightly. She is trembling, incapable of focus. How long has it been since she smashed her way out of Alves's offices? It can't be more than say five minutes but in that time, she has replayed in her mind a million times the moment the gun went off, the moment *she*—not anyone else—had shot Farinha in the head from pretty much point-blank range. But it is only now, as she realises she has escaped dying herself—or at least for the time being—that the enormity of that experience hits her.

She feels over and over the recoil of the gun snapping her hand back like a jolt of electricity slamming up her arm. She is struggling to cope with the moment—scorched indelibly into her mind—when the bullet impacted and blew away most of the right-hand side of Farinha's head, splattering the car door behind him and the way he crumpled to the ground with no resistance, the life instantly drained from his being.

Out of the corner of her eye Lucie half-recognises the forecourt of a petrol station. Could it actually be the very same one where she had jumped Alves that morning? She has been heading in roughly that direction. Or maybe that is just wishful thinking, an instinctive reaction, a way subconsciously to turn the clock back to before any of this madness happened as if that could give her another crack at things, this time writing out from the script such a horrific endgame. But she knows only too well there is no going back, no way ever to recover that carefree innocent excitement from earlier in the day.

She looks across at Zac. He's not doing so good either. He must still be conscious—at least on some level—because he moans under his breath pretty much all the time even though he keeps his eyes closed. Lucie tries to make out what he is saying but his murmurings are unintelligible. Seeing him in such a sorry state, his T-shirt soaked through in a mixture of his own blood and a good amount of Farinha's too, brings home to Lucie that this is all very much for real. She needs to think. First off, she needs to check out Zac's wound more carefully, stop the bleeding.

Going anywhere near a hospital with her having killed a police officer would be crazy. She rules that out; unless Zac is at risk of dying, that is. Ultimately, she may have to make that call at some point. Her priority right now though must be to get some distance between herself and the dead Farinha, that has to be her smartest move. But let's not go mad, no rushing, no stupidity.

Then Lucie certainly does recognise precisely where she is; this is the slip road of the A2. There is no doubt they came this way that morning. But after that initial stretch where Alves had shown off just how powerful his Lexus was, Lucie promptly misses the turning Alves must have taken as he had whisked her away to their lunch under the bridge. Instead, without any warning, Lucie emerges onto the bridge itself.

The first span from the Lisbon side is pretty much flat, you'd never suspect that you were on a huge suspension bridge at all. But the land drops away dramatically all of a sudden and you can see all the lights of Lisbon extending out below you and then you fully appreciate the massive drop to the black water of the river way down there with just the lights from what look like toy ships managing their way in or out of the Tagus. Lucie feels like she is in an aeroplane.

Even at this late hour there are still a good number of vehicles crossing the bridge but none with screaming sirens, no flashing police emergency beacons and no road block up ahead either, so maybe Castro has not been able to figure out which route she has taken since leaving Alves's headquarters. Just maybe she has got away from him.

But her sense of optimism lasts only the most fleeting of moments; in the rear-view mirror on the northern approach she sees a toll plaza and immediately knows she will have to pull up to pay a toll here on the south side too, and soon.

"Great," she says with irony to herself, "So, what are you going to do now?"

She has no cash, no credit cards and no mobile; all surrendered to Castro. She leans over scrambling around in the glove compartment in front of Zac and in the central console between them in the vain hope of finding some loose change. In Emma's car, there are always a few quid knocking around somewhere but not surprisingly, here in Farinha's fancy SUV there is nothing.

What is even more of a problem is that Zac, sprawled out, bleeding all over the passenger seat, hardly even half conscious, is in full view of anyone manning the toll booths which must be fast approaching. And if that doesn't get them stopped then there is the car itself, which is broadcasting tell-tale signs of having been caught up in some Bonnie and Clyde-like drive-by shooting. Any attendant—no matter how bored or unmotivated he or she may be—is not going to fail to notice that.

She can't do a U-turn; there is a barrier down the middle of the roadway separating them from the oncoming traffic. In any case that wouldn't avoid the whole issue of the toll. Lucie swaps lane a couple of times, edging ever closer to the extreme right of the carriageway. She knows she most likely will have no alternative other than to crash her way through the barrier, the same drastic tactic she used to get out of Alves's carpark, as there is no way she can talk herself out of this mess.

At least she knows it works. Then depending on how close the police back up is, she may well end up in some ridiculous car chase she is never going to win, and which could end horribly too, or more likely she will just have to give herself up meekly, and accept her life imprisonment for the murder of Detective Farinha. She shivers again.

But even well after the end of the bridge she sees no sign of any toll plaza looming into view. Amazing, but could it just be there is no toll for going southwards, only for going north into the city of Lisbon? Well that would be a first; Lucie getting lucky.

But if she thinks that will be the last of her problems, she immediately realises that she is going to be sorely disappointed. As Lucie accelerates away from the bridge, she sees in the mirror a young lad, from his hi-vis jacket clearly an employee of some description, or maybe even police, checking out the smashed rear window of her car, already speaking into the phone in his hand. Has he had time to call the police already or could he just be talking to his girlfriend, telling her about his odd day? Lucie cannot take the risk; she has to get off this road as soon as she can.

Once the bridge is out of sight behind her, Lucie takes the first turning off the motorway which is to a place called Costa da Caparica. She knows Costa means coast—at least it does in Spanish—so that means it should be close by.

Actually, Costa da Caparica turns out to be quite a big tourist town, a bit like Cascais and Estoril on the northern bank of the Tagus but without the money, no casinos here, nothing super-rich about it at all, to be honest. The place is shabby, faded, down at heel, laid out around a network of perpendicular streets which head ever closer to the sea, lined with closed-up shops full of tacky tourist gismos. There are a few restaurants that remarkably at well past two in the morning are still open but all the late-night stragglers are inside, it is too cool here by the sea for anyone to be sitting outside at this time.

There are no cars moving just a few parked up outside the restaurants. As Lucie gets further down the street she can see sand blowing across the tarmac, whipped up into small eddies by the wind. At the end, there is a huge almost empty car park. This place must be mostly frequented by day-trippers from Lisbon, Lucie thinks. Beyond, there is a massive beach which in the moonlight stretches away as far as the eye can see to the south.

The only way on from the car park is down a small unlit track which runs away parallel to the beach. She can't very well go back, that would be asking for trouble. So, she puts the headlights on beam and continues. As she leaves the town behind, the further down the track she goes the more remote things get. She meets no cars going the other way.

"Well," Zac coughs, quietly clearing his throat. "We made it out of there pretty much unscathed, wouldn't you say?"

Lucie is astounded. Just to hear his voice is bliss, such a relief. She thought Zac was out of it and here he is with an assessment of their performance, even if he does seem to be neglecting one rather crucial element.

"You have been shot, remember?"

"You are a constant surprise to me, you know."

"What do you mean?"

"Well we could both be dead in the boot. I mean, that's an amazing result. Look on the bright side for once."

Lucie is not sure if Zac is serious. He is losing blood. How much blood can you lose before you become delirious, before it becomes life-threatening?

"We have to stop the bleeding. You need proper medical attention."

"No hospital, Lucie. Don't even think about it."

"Gunshot wounds go a bit beyond my first-aid skillset."

"If you drop me at a hospital, there will be complications. I won't make it out of there alive. Castro would make sure of that."

"But why?"

"He can't let his involvement in any of this come out."

Lucie cannot fathom Zac. He suddenly seems to know a lot more about Castro than he had let on to her before.

"We have no idea what damage may have been done internally."

"I'll take my chances with you, if you don't mind."

Visible intermittently between huge sand dunes to the right which come up to and in some parts almost entirely engulf the track, is the Atlantic Ocean, a silvery sheen picked up from the light of the almost full moon. On Lucie's left is a wooded hillside of cork trees with just the odd house dotted about. After a few more kilometres, in a particularly dark stretch, she pulls the car off the road, well back in a hollow, hidden amongst the trees and switches off the engine.

She gets out and as she walks backwards away from the car, she realises just how secluded this spot is. The car cannot be seen at all from the track, that is for sure. She goes around to the passenger door to take a closer look at Zac's wound. Under the dense foliage of the trees it is so dark here, she has no alternative other than to risk switching on the interior light in the car. She needs to see how serious things are.

The bullet went in at the edge of his chest, close to his right armpit. She can see that much from the blood stains and the clear hole in his T-shirt. She rips the fabric from the hole outwards a few centimetres. The skin around the place the bullet entered Zac's body has a brownish tinge, like it is burnt somehow. The hole itself is very small and the bleeding seems minimal. She puts her hand around the back of his shoulder and feels dampness there too. She pulls Zac forward a fraction to get a better view.

"Jesus, that hurts," Zac complains.

There appears to be a second wound on the back of his lower shoulder which is bleeding more profusely. Lucie puts her hand down the neck of Zac's T-shirt. She can feel the ragged edge of the wound where the bullet exited. This is more concerning. Lucie steps back and takes off her own top.

"Now we are making progress," Zac smiles.

Lucie rips her T-shirt violently along the seam.

"In your dreams," Lucie dismisses Zac's banter.

She then straps her rather dubious-looking attempt at a bandage around Zac's shoulder as tight as she can. To be fair Zac doesn't complain too much but the look of exhaustion on his face when she finally lets him relax back into the passenger seat is telling enough.

"I'm going to take a look around," she says to Zac. "You stay here and rest up a bit. OK?"

"You are a real fusser, aren't you? It's just a scratch," Zac says closing his eyes and drifting off again. He seems to be doing OK given the circumstances. The bullet miraculously had gone clean through just under his shoulder without hitting anything vital, no major blood vessel punctured, didn't even hit his shoulder blade.

Lucie walks inland up an ill-defined, little used path which leads up a couple of hundred yards to a substantial house which sits dramatically above her set on stilts at the front with the back built into the steep incline behind. The access road must be somewhere on the other side of the property. The house itself is in darkness but it can't be much after three in the morning so it could easily be that the occupants are just sound asleep.

She notes that most of the rooms have the blinds pulled down fully. As stealthily as she can, Lucie climbs up the set of steps onto the terraced decking and goes around the side of the house to the front door. She checks the bins which are both empty. There is no car out front either and she sees no clear evidence of anyone currently living at the property. Her logic tells her that you would definitely have to use a car to get this far out of town, so most likely she concludes, the house could actually be empty.

She rings the bell and holds her breath listening for any sounds from within. What she would have said if anyone had answered she has no idea her dressed in only her sports bra. Luckily, she doesn't have to face that eventuality; as she had gambled, no-one is home. Eventually she plucks up the courage to put a hefty rock from the garden through a small pane of glass in the backdoor and is pleasantly surprised to find no alarm goes off.

As she looks around the interior she realises that this is most likely a holiday home, maybe even owned by a tourist from the UK. She wakes Zac, gathers him up from the car and installs him in the main bedroom. She pulls up the blind to reveal a stunning view of the beach in the distance and the sea beyond.

Zac is asleep in no time but even though Lucie herself is absolutely exhausted, she cannot sleep. She lies down next to Zac on the bed, her mind struggling to make any sense of what has happened. Surely there could have been something she could have done differently which would have avoided such a nightmarish outcome.

The more she thinks about it, the more it seemed like Castro could well have been intent on having her and Zac killed by Farinha from the moment he had caught them in the Alves HQ building. But how could that be? Why? In the end however, it was Farinha who paid the ultimate price, not Castro, even though Farinha had merely followed orders, not given them. But he can have no complaints either as he was playing by those same rules.

He was, after all, the one who introduced the gun into the equation and he was about to kill her; there can be no doubt about that and, in fact, he did shoot Zac. It is not guilt that Lucie feels—she was right to pull the trigger—it's a deep inconsolable sadness. However much she rationalises it, she has to face the reality that she extinguished a life, and she knows that will always torment her. She clings onto Zac tightly as she watches the first light of the dawn slowly colour the sky.

Later that morning, Lucie finds a first-aid kit in one of the kitchen cabinets and she wakes Zac briefly to dress his wound a bit more professionally. Mind you, professionally is somewhat of an exaggeration, she is of course making it all up as she goes along, but she is pretty good at that, even if she does say so herself. And certainly her nursing seems to be working pretty well; remarkably there is no more bleeding either the entry or the exit wound and no excessive swelling. He was so lucky. Undoubtedly, he could do with some serious painkillers as the first thing he does every time she wakes him is to groan in agony but there are only a few paracetamol tablets in the first-aid kit, and they don't seem to be helping that much at all.

Lucie also finds some old washing in a laundry basket in the utility room with a top she can happily wear and a tee-shirt to replace the blood covered one Zac still has on. She then hunts amongst the hoard of tins of food in the walk-in larder at the back of the kitchen and picks out a couple containing something called Feijão which looks from the label like some sort of a white bean stew type of thing.

She also finds a jar of instant coffee, so most likely the house is indeed owned by Brits; Emma had told Lucie enthusiastically just after she had arrived in Lisbon that no self-respecting Portuguese would be caught dead with evidence that they use instant coffee. She relaxes when she finds the fridge is empty except for a couple of bottles of a cheap looking Portuguese white wine—a clear sign that the owners are indeed away and the risk of them showing up is fairly remote, especially it being the middle of the week.

She checks on the car a few times too but it is also fine. Then she lets Zac sleep. That has to be best for him. And he really does, for most of the day.

As she warms up the feijão on the stove later in the afternoon, Lucie turns on the TV, more for company than anything else and to somehow fill that confused void caused by the whole Farinha thing. In the back of her mind, she also has a hunch that something about what had happened might be on and if that is the case it can only help to be aware of what is in the public domain even if she is obviously not going to understand the Portuguese commentary.

Then later on, as she is gazing out the full-length kitchen window to the beach where the strong off-shore breeze that has strengthened noticeably since the dawn is now throwing up imposing white crested waves, she hears the name Farinha and spins around to look at the TV where she sees a reporter standing on the steps of the Basilica da Estrela, just down the street from the Alves building. Next to the reporter a couple of paramedics are moving a body bag onto a stretcher. The next image makes her blood freeze. On the screen is her own face.

She immediately recognises the image. It is the ID photo taken at the Bisset Science Institute. There is no mention—at least not that she picks up on—of Castro, no mention either of Alves. The most likely interpretation of the news report is that Farinha's body had been dumped on the Basilica steps and she is clearly the prime suspect in his murder. Now as she stares at the screen in a daze, she is not so sure that she really wanted to know all this.

"You're famous," Zac startles Lucie. He must have heard the TV and thought he should investigate. He certainly appears noticeably better. Or perhaps what has lured him from his slumber is the smell of cooking wafting into his room. Zac walks over to the remote and with his left hand he flicks off the TV.

They eat their rather dull meal in silence or at least they avoid talk of their plight and the events of the previous evening, as though not mentioning any of it at all nullifies its existence. They even break out the white wine—what harm can it do? It is deliciously cold and through the lounge window they watch the sun sinking slowly directly into the ocean in the west. It's like they are out here in Portugal just staying at some Airbnb on holiday. It feels comforting, if wholly unreal and yet, eventually, Lucie's confusion and distress, maybe exacerbated by the wine, finally gets the better of her.

"What really went down last night, Zac? Castro actually wanted us dead. I just can't get my head around that. It makes no sense."

"We've got caught up in something big here. Off the scale, it seems. Castro is quite prepared to go to whatever lengths he may need to protect his project."

"But to kill us? Come on," Lucie laughs nervously.

"Listen, all we know for sure is that Castro thinks Emma is stealing critical and what presumably is highly valuable information. So, he kidnaps her…or worse."

"What is that supposed to mean? You think Emma could already be dead?"

"No," Zac backtracks sensing Lucie's distress. "I don't think so. I mean, they must need her for something. So maybe they thought they could stop the flow of intelligence by just eliminating the conduit for those leaks."

"Get rid of me instead, you mean?"

Zac says nothing, he merely raises his eyebrows suggesting it is more than obvious. It sort of fits, though. Completely insane, but isn't all of this anyway?

"Actually though," Zac continues his train of thought, "maybe they would have let us go if you hadn't gone and told Castro that you recognised that thug with the Rolex."

"Farinha," Lucie snaps, losing her patience now. How could he dare to insinuate that any of this mess is her fault?

"Right, Farinha. That was when things turned ugly."

"Hang on. Castro recognised you, not me. Toxic he called you."

"And you believe him rather than me. That's nice. Look, he must have seen some footage of me from the CCTVs around the Bisset Institute. That's all. He was just trying to confuse you. Angling for anything he could get to trip you up and turn you against me. Seems like he succeeded," Zac sounds peeved and disappointed in Lucie.

Lucie is none too convinced by Zac's spirited denial. But there is something else which has been troubling her in all this.

"Why did you do it?" Lucie asks.

"Do what?"

"You know. Step in front of me?"

"Oh that," Zac smiles. "Well, it certainly wasn't my smartest move, I'll give you that. It was instinctive, I suppose. I just reacted. That guy was going to hurt you."

Whatever doubts Lucie has concerning Zac—and there are an increasing number—in his defence, there is no denying that Zac wilfully stepped into the firing line of that bullet. That saved her life. She would have been dead, otherwise. That is a sobering thought all right. That colours your view of somebody, helps you choose who you should trust, whose side you should be on. Lucie feels that with Zac she is going to be a lot safer than without him.

"So, what do we do now?" Lucie finally asks.

"We need to get back home to the UK as quickly and as quietly as we can. Slip completely out of sight, off the radar—that is what they call it, isn't it?"

"Listen, after witnessing first hand just how insane Castro is, it's clear that Emma is in far more danger than we thought. I can't abandon her, not now."

"You killed a cop. Remember?"

"I haven't forgotten that, I assure you. Look, we now know two things. First, the possible location of the lab, Rua Lucio Vera 302. And second, that Alves's diary ends tomorrow. We know that his last entry just says Lab 21:00."

"You're completely crazy," is Zac's verdict on Lucie's suggestion of going back into the centre of Lisbon. "The whole of Lisbon will be on the look-out for you. You'll never get anywhere near the lab. It's not like you exactly blend into the background here, is it?"

"I don't care. Emma would never quit on me and walk away. And for sure this is my best, my only shot at finding her."

"You nearly got us killed last night and now you want to go one better, or what?"

"I have to be there tomorrow night; it is as simple as that."

"Oh great. I suppose you mean *we*," Zac says and then half-jokingly he adds, "Did I really just agree to go along with your insane idea."

That evening could have turned into something truly romantic, when Zac took her hand and kissed it gently, she so easily could have just gone with the flow, but it didn't seem quite right. At least not yet anyway. In any case, wasn't Zac mortally wounded? It didn't seem possible that he could have recovered so quickly but he certainly seemed up for anything all of a sudden. That said, and even though they had shared an earth-shattering near-death experience together, Lucie still finds intimacy something that cannot be rushed. She needs more time. But maybe not that much more.

The next day, out of a couple of pillow cases, Lucie pulls together a pretty decent-looking sling. Zac may have had his mind set on some sort of amorous endeavour the previous evening but Lucie couldn't really see how that was ever going to play out, except in his own imagination of course, as any proximity to his wounded shoulder is met with howls of pain. The sling helps keep his shoulder immobilised which should allow the exit wound to heal and maybe that can cure Zac's moaning into the bargain, if Lucie is lucky.

Next, she spends a couple of hours on the SUV's satnav writing down all manner of routes and directions they may need to get to the lab unaided by Google Maps. She is aware that once they leave the car behind, they will be out there on their own. The very idea of being off-grid is alarming enough in your own country but here they will not be able to go up to a helpful policeman to ask the way.

Then she takes a hammer she has come across under the sink and knocks out all the remaining glass from the rear window and the wing mirror of the SUV. That way the car is not going to stand out quite as much. But whatever she does, they are still going to need a huge amount of luck to get back into Lisbon unobserved. The police must be actively searching for this particular vehicle. Lucie hopes that taking an alternative and more unusual route may offer them some protection; they only need the car for maybe twenty minutes. That can't be too much to hope for, can it?

Finally, after much soul searching, Lucie grabs the old Dimple whisky bottle from the shelf above the mantlepiece in the living-room which is nearly full of the loose change collected presumably by the owners of the house and she empties out around thirty euros worth, but only enough to cover the fares they will need to get to the lab. After this final transgression, she is going to play things by the book from here on. After all, just look where breaking the law— ironically also with a whisky bottle—has landed her.

They would have preferred to head off under cover of darkness but sunset is too late at this time of year to be of any use to them. Going back up the main street of Costa da Caparica this time is genuinely unnerving, much more than on their arrival as to describe it as crowded would be a total understatement. People and cars are stacked all the way up to the turning to the A2 and the bridge. But everyone is in good spirits after a day at the beach and they see no police presence at all and remarkably there are lots of cars in far worse shape than theirs.

Now, instead of heading onto the bridge approach road, they go straight across the motorway and down towards the town of Cacilhas. In the outskirts, they ditch the car finally. It has served them well but they are mightily relieved to be shut of it. Just being in the car has brought back all too disturbing and gruesome memories to mind.

They look up at the Cristo Rei statue which is only a mile or so away. From this close, they can appreciate the scale of the structure, its night-time illumination already on, even though it is still nowhere near dark, adding to the aura of dominion over the whole area. But Lucie and Zac are not here to sightsee and they focus on melting into the background as they edge their way down the steep streets which lead towards the banks of the Tagus. At the bottom of the slope, they stop in an empty doorway from where they can see down to a square and on the far side the ferry terminal.

To enter the terminal building, Lucie and Zac split up and mingle with a group of rather boisterous American students clearly a few beers the worse for wear, who are stumbling off a bus maybe even coming from the same beach as them. Lucie and Zac fit in easily and the Americans are enthusiastic about adding another two to their number. They all buy tickets for the short trip to Lisbon and head towards the landing stage where they are corralled into a queue by an authoritarian-sounding member of staff. Lucie feels exposed.

After a wait of ten minutes or so swapping stories with their new friends, an orange ferry comes into view clearly heading towards them. It approaches the landing platform and the crew throw and loop ropes around the cast iron bollards fixing the ferry up against the wharf.

Lucie then feels the hairs on her neck spike up as she sees two uniformed policemen come out of the office on the landing stage and head straight towards her. She immediately turns away from the policemen and engages with another girl in the group, all the time expecting to feel a hand land on her shoulder, but the policemen walk straight past Lucie, and on up to where the crew are sliding back the metal doorway and putting in place the ramp to allow the passengers off.

The policemen half-heartedly check all the passengers alighting from the ferry and as the last one passes them, they shrug and head back into the office without so much as a glance at the passengers waiting to board. Were the policemen looking for them? Who knows. Certainly, if that were the case then they were only interested in people leaving Lisbon and not anyone trying to get into the city. Maybe the police think they are still in Lisbon. Who in their right mind when accused of murdering a police officer would voluntarily try to get back into the place they had just successfully escaped from? Lucie ponders that question as they make the crossing of the spectacular Tagus river and as the last light fades into night they approach the Lisbon ferry terminal at Cais do Sodré, where once again no checks on arrivals are enforced thankfully.

At around eight that evening, Zac and Lucie climb the steps emerging out of the protected cool of Moscavide metro station. It is like walking into a dark oven, a stifling heat pressing down from above, dusty parched air blowing up off the footpath baked throughout the day. Gone is any trace of the cool breeze on the coast. There is next to no vegetation here either. Only a couple of scragged trees which look to be suffering from the heat more than Zac and Lucie. It is still suffocating even though the sun has already gone down.

Lucie gets her bearings and they follow her planned route across a small square and walk a couple of blocks through lower class residential buildings. The streets are all but deserted. A few kids are out kicking a ball against a wall under the light of a feeble streetlamp. A mother pushes a buggy with a screaming toddler arching his back against the straps holding him in place. The woman seems more perturbed by Zac and Lucie than by her kid's screams but that might be surprise at seeing tourists out here, so off the beaten track at this time in the evening, rather than her having recognised them. They do stand out something awful here though, Zac was right.

They cross a complicated interchange through an underpass and emerge into a rundown industrial park made up of seven or eight large purpose-built units. Most look unoccupied given the amount of dirt and rubbish piled in the doorways.

"This can't be it. I must have made a mistake somewhere," Lucie says, disappointed. They are standing in the darkness, out of the pools of light from the inadequately spaced street lamps, opposite a building which looks like it has been abandoned for months or even years. The door and all the windows are boarded up. The place looks an absolute state.

"This is definitely the right address," Zac says nodding towards the rusted number 302 fixed above the boarded doorway. "Not very inviting, though, is it?" says Zac, mirroring Lucie's thoughts precisely.

"Hardly the hi-tech facility I was expecting, you're right," she says.

The lack of anyone around, encourages them to cross the street and to examine the building a little more closely. They find no sign of any bell or intercom system. Zac starts pulling at the boarding, nailed across the door, testing with his still serviceable left hand how secure it is.

"What do you think you are doing?" Lucie asks, nervously looking around to see if anyone is watching, but no-one is in sight at all.

Zac gives up on the door and moves on to a window next to it.

"This is encouraging," he says, peering through the gap between the boards, "the window is open behind here, I think." He manages to get a solid grip on one of the boards with his uninjured arm and pulls hard. It comes away noisily but pretty easily.

"Oh my God, that hurts so bad," Zac moans. "Come on, aren't you going to help at all?"

The window actually has no glass in the frame at all. It opens onto a small and mostly empty room apart from a set of metal shelves plonked in the middle, covered in a thick layer of dust and some discarded junk. There is just a single door which they can see is only pulled to, not locked although whatever may be beyond is obscured from view.

Between the two of them, they quickly detach some other boards, enough to be able to squeeze through the window. Zac helps Lucie up trying not to use the arm in the sling which makes his help close to useless but she manages to scramble through the opening headfirst, dropping to the floor inside on her hands.

She then helps to pull Zac through to join her amid bouts of altogether excessive whingeing and wincing. Breaking in has made such a din, that undoubtedly anyone inside could hardly have failed to notice their clumsy efforts to gain access to the building, so they now open the door slowly with more than a little trepidation.

The door opens onto a single square-shaped space and from its central point radiates a massive glass dome almost reaching the middle of each of the four enclosing walls. The whole place is empty, no-one anywhere.

It strikes Lucie as wholly impractical to have such an expanse of glass given how hot it must get in summer but then she notices a mass of solar panels covering the majority of the external surface of the dome, way in excess of anything a building such as this could possibly demand in terms of energy requirement.

And then she makes out an intricate pattern of metallic strips attached to and criss-crossing the underside surface of the glass all arranged into a circle that runs around the widest point at the base of the dome almost interlinking with but not overlapping the solar array at any point.

"What do you make of that?" Lucie asks, "Weird or what?" She then trembles in fear as she realises that she has used the exact same word that Emma left on her voicemail. The word that had triggered this whole escapade.

"That is some serious kit, that is for sure."

Zac walks towards a railing which runs five paces or so inside the circumference of the domed roof. Lucie follows him and from there, they look down at a second level way below them, maybe ten metres down, with a set of metal stairs descending to it from the opposite side of the dome. Again, there is no-one around.

Disappointingly, the lower floor offers no more information either on the purpose of the building or any hint as to where the people using the solar energy and that circular track may be. There are a few empty boxes strewn around and some more metal shelving stacked back against the perimeter walls, but that is it, apart from a mass of dust covering everything.

They circle around to the other side of the dome where through a door in the back wall they find the entrance to the small emergency staircase which links the two levels, encaged within an iron grille built into a low concrete wall, open on both sides and as they go down, on the outside of the building they can see down to a ramp which drops below the level of the building presumably to an underground car park.

"Well I never…Look who's here," Lucie points to a red Lexus parked almost at the bottom of the ramp.

"That must be the usual way in," Zac states the obvious.

"I wonder how many levels we are talking about under here," Lucie says as she starts to descend. At the first of three landings in the descent, Lucie hears a clunk and looks over the wall down to the interior floor. She then hears a swish as a mechanical door slides open and she hunkers down trying to hide as best she can. She is terrified that her and Zac's entry to the building has triggered a response and that whoever is coming out of that door will not take kindly to her appearance here and most likely will be intent on making her pay personally for Farinha's death. She turns to see where Zac is, but he is gone. She looks back up the steps. He has disappeared.

Lucie has no idea what to do. Without Zac she feels suddenly so much less sure of herself. From her hiding place, Lucie looks over the stair wall and sees that a hidden entrance door has opened in the floor itself. Down the steps inside, the scene she witnesses is one of absolute chaos with a whole load of people all shouting instructions at each other with all eyes glued to a huge screen on the far wall which seems to Lucie to be filled with a myriad of flashing and shifting colours and lights.

Then Lucie sees a figure striding purposefully up out of that chaos towards the quiet of the lower dome floor. Lucie recognises her immediately. It is Emma. Her Emma. Emma is safe, she is here. Lucie's ordeal, this whole nightmare is over.

Lucie stands up and shouts, "Emma, thank God you are safe."

"What the hell do you think you are doing here?" Emma says sharply.

"I was just checking up on you. You know me...I worry," Lucie laughs in relief.

"Worry? About me?"

"Yes, about you."

Lucie is shocked. This is not the reception she had anticipated at all. She carries on down the last two mini-flights to reach the same level as Emma saying as she runs down, "You disappeared almost a week ago. You left me a voicemail. Weird, remember?"

"Don't come down any further. It's not safe."

"What are you talking about?" Lucie ignores Emma and continues down the stairs.

"You're wanted by the police, Lucie."

Lucie stops and looks down at Emma.

"He was going to kill me. I had no choice. Zac got shot, for Christ's sake..."

But Emma interrupts, "Listen Lucie, you can't be here. This whole building is about to go up. You must leave now."

"Haven't you heard a word I am saying?" Lucie is desperate.

"I have to try to stop this. Get out, Lucie. While you still can." Emma turns and runs off down the staircase and before Lucie can get there the door has slid back into place.

"Emma! Emma!" Lucie screams banging her fists against the door but it remains closed and there is no visible way to open it from this side.

After a few minutes, it is clear that Emma is not going to reappear. Lucie suddenly feels very alone and scared. Where the hell has Zac got to? He was right behind her and then he vanished into thin air. She decides that she should head back to the upper level to look for him but when she is less than half way to the start of the staircase, the whole building vibrates stopping her in her tracks.

She then sees a ripple of the same fractured light she had seen on the computer screen rise out of the far wall, as if light were being fired through a prism, split into millions of dazzling coloured fragments. It is like the properties of reality itself are being broken down in a massive wave which Lucie now notices is not static but is moving, expanding out across the space. Lucie sees that her escape route to the stairwell she came down has already been cut off. If she goes back that way, she will have no option other than to cross directly through the wave.

She steps back, terrified. She has never seen or heard of anything to come close to explaining what she can see before her. The wave is still moving towards her and she cannot evade its path. She is going to be consumed by it. She backs away steadily further and further to the wall of the dome now opposite the stairwell. This is as far as she can go to escape it and yet it continues to expand, inexorably approaching her.

"Zac!" she shouts but hears no response.

In the end, when the wave is perhaps ten centimetres from her, she feels that it would be better, or at least preferable, to do this on her own terms. She tentatively puts forward the fingers of her left hand towards the front edge of the wave. She feels a slight tingling sensation as her fingers breach its surface.

There is no resistance, no pain. Then she sees that her fingers reconstitute themselves a few centimetres away on the other side. First her fingers and then her whole hand reappear after having been frazzled in the distortion but she can still flex her fingers and she feels nothing other than the tingling around her wrist where the wave slices through her body.

Slowly, the wave rises through Lucie's body. She stands on tiptoes trying to avoid it passing through her head but she knows now that is going to be impossible. Her heart rate is through the roof. What could this do to her brain? The tingling rises up through her neck and inevitably traverses her head.

Lucie blacks out momentarily. But in that same instant she breathes in through her mouth a gulp of freezing cold air and she sees the waters of Loch Doon stretching out before her. She is fully aware that she is not physically there on the pebbled shoreline, that all this has something to do with the shifting colours distorting her own personal reality and creating this alternative one. She hears the wind howling, curling down off the hills, cold on her face.

Squalls of rain are racing across the windswept moorland on the far side of the loch. It is a bleak and severe place but one that Lucie knows only too well—it is after all this harsh land that has moulded her, that made her into who she is.

The few desolate trees that survive here are deformed, bent over into wild shapes sculpted by the whims of the prevailing winds. But survive they do, as she must. They stand strong in spite of the extremes of such a hostile environment. And Lucie draws strength from that isolation and resilience, from the fact her roots are grounded in such a place.

Then she has a sudden feeling that she is not alone here. She shivers, looking around in terror. Along the stony shoreline she makes out a young man perhaps eighteen or not much more than that staring at her intensely, the waves of the loch lapping around his bare feet. She doesn't recognise the boy or how he can be here sharing this space with her. He has dark hair, cut randomly short in places and long in others. His complexion is pale as though he avoids contact with pure sunlight. He is wearing just some loose calf-length shorts and an oversized shirt, with only one button fastened, flapping and billowing around him in the wind, wholly unsuited to this place and this bitter weather, but he seems not to feel the cold.

Then she notices that where his bare feet disappear beneath the surface of the loch, there is no clear visible extension of his form below the waterline. It's like his hold on this reality is so fragile that it breaks down at the edges and merges into the background, as if fading in and out of existence itself. But his stare holds its focus tenaciously on Lucie. He walks slowly towards her and stops just a couple of paces away; a ghostly apparition flickering half in and half out of this immaterial world.

"You know her, don't you?" he says in a gentle but emphatic manner.

"Know who?"

"Emma, of course."

"Who are you? What on earth is going on here?" Lucie shouts out above the howl of the wind.

"Somehow we have to stop her."

Lucie gasps. And suddenly she is conscious again. She cannot come near to saying what had happened when the wave passed through her head. She feels exhausted. She sits down still trying to come to terms with what has happened, still mesmerised. It was the closest she has come to a mystical experience, something magical and special, but at the same time quite terrifying. Who was that lad? How come he knows Emma? And stop her from doing what?

She gazes upwards for several minutes watching the wave rise through the upper floor level and reach the lower part of the dome where it starts to cross the metallic strips. Sparks fly, there are multiple tiny explosions all across the leading edge of the wave where it overlays and comes into direct contact with the metal runway. The trailing edge seems to be failing to break through this point while the leading edge is now accelerating away upwards and outwards, stretching the distortion to reality over an ever-greater expanse.

The whole dome is becoming unstable. The violence of the reaction between the metallic strips and the wave intensify casting mini lightning bolts which fizzle across the floor. She has no way out. She pulls herself into the shelter of the staircase. She is trapped. Then, terrified, Lucie screams as she sees a sudden ultra-bright flash followed immediately by a massive explosion. Everything goes black.

When Lucie comes to, just how long she has been lying there in the debris after the blast she has no idea. The darkness is intense, thick like oil. A numbed calm grips the air. All her senses have been paralysed in an unnatural peace. Slowly, like the answer to some obscure puzzle, she alights on the idea that she must still be alive. But it is so difficult to resist the desire to drift back into unconsciousness and perhaps with it her own death. That doesn't scare her any longer. She would be comfortable with that and could even embrace it. But then, while she is right on the verge of succumbing, she notices some light flickering behind her closed eyelids. She focusses all her effort into opening her eyes and in the distance, she makes out some electrical sparks flashing from cables still swaying back and forth silently through dark heavy fumes. She feels small pieces of ash and soot, still falling to the ground, landing on her face. She can't have been unconscious for more than a few moments.

Lucie hears a terrible anonymous scream filled with pain, muffled in the smoke laden atmosphere. No echo, just a penetrating despairing shocking cry that cuts deep into Lucie's heart. The flashes become less and less frequent as the cables settle and darkness reigns.

Lucie can feel that she is lying on her side under a metal girder, twisted and awkwardly jammed up against the concrete wall. She can just move her arm but is unable to lift herself to a sitting position, her legs are trapped. She looks over her shoulder and from where she is lying she can make out in the intermittent flashes that pierce the darkness the tangled unrecognisable wreckage which she knows must have been only seconds earlier the doorway where she had seen Emma.

As her head clears she hears a gurgling, rasping breath close to her. No words, just a half-choking guttural cough, a frightened shocked whimper. It isn't a call for help but rather a more personal utterance not intended for the ears of anyone else, just a pure expression of unrestrained emotion. Lucie stretches out her arm and feels the stony ground around her. Amongst the shards of glass and twisted metal, her fingers touch an arm. The moan stops in mid-breath, interrupted by her touch. Lucie manoeuvres her hand down to allow her to touch the fingers of this unknown and unseen person, caught in the same nightmare. Could this even be Emma?

"Emma, is that you? We are going to get through this, OK?" Lucie says. "Are you OK?"

There is no reply, but what is there to be said anyway? It is clear they are not OK at all. There is no way that Lucie can do anything to help as she is pinned down by a mass of debris. She can't feel her legs at all, can't see how badly she may have been injured. But Lucie feels the stranger's fingers squeeze her own faintly.

There is an immense comfort in making that slightest of human contact in such an infernal horrific setting. She is aware of the force of life, the inner strength of the soul, she can feel it in that touch. Lucie closes her eyes and rests without letting go of that hand in the dark.

As the minutes pass with no sign of any help, fear and shock slowly intensify and replace the calm acceptance she had felt initially. She has no intention of dying here, not now.

She keeps drifting in and out of consciousness. There are no sounds apart from the screams continuing in the darkness. The heat and the fumes are suffocating adding to the claustrophobia. When she comes to again, she realises the screams have stopped. The silence is now absolute and as deep and frightening as the darkness that entombs her.

IX
Gryphon

London—1874

As Father Casey steps away from Newgate Prison after Duncan's execution, he feels a wave of relief wash over him. Not at having escaped the noose—he never had considered that even a remote possibility—the one thing that had worried him above all else in those final moments before transferring his persona into that of Father Casey had been that the process itself could eliminate his feelings for Jules.

Not the physical, fact-based recollections—those would still be there—but his passion, his subconscious engagement with those memories, that could have gone. He knew only too well that he never should have had any of those feelings for her in the first place and that there had been a real chance that an uninterrupted surfacing would mend that glitch and could purge his emotional connection with Jules definitively. So, as he walks towards Duncan's home in the eminently fashionable Eaton Square, he delights in the depth of that still strikingly present passion and in those memories of his brief but overwhelmingly intense amorous encounter with Jules in Blackheath.

To be fair, across the board, all the complex neural realignments had proved so much easier than had been the case with Duncan more than eight years earlier, none of the embarrassing post-surfacing blackouts, or the ugly and disturbing speech impediments. Also, clearly he wasn't faced by the sudden chasm of bewilderment—the logical consequence of that first surfacing—where in Bidston Moss, Duncan had been thrown headlong into a total absence of context with absolutely no memories to fall back on, either long or short-term.

Father Casey, on the other hand, had lost only his own memories, which let's face it were of no relevance anyway, while all of those pertaining to Duncan remained intact and mercifully those—he now knew—included every precious nuance of his time with Jules.

Father Casey prowls around the park in the centre of the square opposite Duncan's rented three-storey townhouse for several minutes making absolutely sure that no-one is keeping the house under surveillance before approaching. Obviously, he has not been able to return to the house since his arrest. From his cell, he had instructed his rather rattled clerks, Pritchard and Suanders, that his residence be closed up, the servants let go and even they too should seek alternative employment. He did, however, have them pay the rent through to the end of January, assuring that no other tenants could gain access to the property in the crucial handover period.

According to his clerks' reports, the police had cast a cursory and inept glance over the place, found nothing untoward, and that was as far as their criminal investigation went, it would appear. They had their man—case closed.

Instead of going up to the front door, Father Casey drops below ground level to the tradesmen's basement entrance. Hidden from the street by the overhang of the steps leading up to the main entrance above, Father Casey takes out the folding jack-knife he had traded only a half an hour earlier outside Victoria Station with a kid who couldn't believe his luck when Father Casey offered in exchange a real working pocket watch. This had been the only item of any value he had found on the priest's person in a small cloth purse tied crudely to his cassock cincture.

Using the knife, he sets about picking away the mortar surrounding a particular brick in the wall opposite the door. The mortar is soft and crumbles away easily. Father Casey then pulls out the brick and from behind it he extracts a folded leather pouch containing a set of a dozen keys at least. He selects one and uses it to unlock the door.

Once in the house he rushes upstairs to the second-floor landing and then climbs the steep and narrow set of bare wooden steps up into the attic. There he wrestles a large oak cabinet out from the corner some three feet to one side. He pulls up a couple of floorboards revealing in the space below a large metal box. Then he selects another from his set of keys to open the padlock which secures the latch. The box is crammed full of documents and an abundance of cash. Only then does Father Casey breathe a sigh of relief; everything is still here, everything has played out according to plan.

From an early stage Duncan always had an uncanny insight into which businesses would flourish. Not altogether surprising, given that more often than not those he invested in owed their success to ideas that he himself was feeding to the entrepreneurs and their scientists. Not to say that he was actually in possession of any privileged specific information or knowledge but rather that he was gifted with seeing where potential lay and in encouraging those that had the skillset to deliver his unique vision of the future. So, in a few short years he amassed an enviable fortune.

His problem resided far more in how to pass those funds on to his successor when he had no certainty over who that may be. Father Casey this time, but it could just as easily have been someone else. Inheritance, or rather the notoriously complicated litigations which some frustrated relative may pursue in an attempt to strip him of his hard-earned wealth, risked pushing his plans back to square one. He couldn't allow that to happen.

However, if there was one thing Duncan was exceptionally good at, it was contingency planning. So, he had avoided leaving any paper trail which could lead back to his own name and had moved large sums into cash and high denomination bearer bonds which his successor would then be able to use to rebuild his wealth under a new name without prying or greedy eyes scouring the legality of any contested last will and testament. Father Casey gathers up all the documents from Duncan's stash and then heads back downstairs.

As he enters his dressing room on the first floor, he is confronted head on by his own reflection in the full-length mirror, its ghostlike apparition stopping him dead in his tracks. He walks right up to the mirror and looks deep into those strange anonymous eyes. There is something unnerving in the confused gaze which stares back at him. He touches and pulls at the skin on his face, curious, even distrustful, failing to reconcile this external reality with his inner being.

But there is something more fundamental going on here. It isn't just the physical outer shell that is unfamiliar, there is also an unanticipated and startling shift in his psyche. Then gradually it dawns on him that, as had been the case with Duncan's surfacing, the subconscious pathways of Father Casey have not been fully purged, either. There are without doubt some remnants, some subliminal vestiges of Father Casey's mind which, while they will cause no real impediment to his routine mental performance, they will certainly find a way to influence his emotional state.

It is as if his emotional wavelength has been stretched. In Duncan's case—with the exception of his passion for Jules—the focus had always been absolute and unswerving but now he notices greater latitude for other conflicting responses. At one extreme he notes a distinct stoical, almost masochistic ethos of self-denial which actually is a pretty comfortable fit with the more clinical scientific mindset and thought processes of Duncan.

But where Father Casey differs wholeheartedly from Duncan is in his deep spirituality and while the religious emphasis for that is gone, his psyche is nonetheless still suffused with a mystical, otherworldly nature, tinged with a melancholic sense of loss. A vastly different mental condition to the unfailing optimism and sharp ruthless guile of Duncan.

He finally manages to drag himself away from the mirror. This is something he will have to learn to live with. But given the likelihood that this same subconscious seepage will most likely recur in any future transfers—a consequence of that corrupted initial surfacing—he now knows he will have to be careful not to just flit from host to host as that sort of build-up of emotional baggage could very easily become too much to handle. His mood swings could become far more turbulent and at the same time prove far less manageable.

He opens his wardrobe and picks out a shirt and necktie combination which will fit this new face with its rather more angular features. He then takes one of his favourite and most expensive suits with which to replace the priest's dreary and it must be said stinking attire.

Lastly, he pulls open a drawer and selects a gold pocket watch and attaches its chain to his waistcoat; much more befitting of his status. The priest and Duncan are of a similar build so when Father Casey stands back looking at his total transformation from a grubby pauper of a priest into this young and eligible businessman, he finds the result pretty convincing. He can live with this, no problem.

The next thing to go would have to be the name Father Casey. To all intents and purposes, that person no longer exists, at least in a practical sense, his mind now flush with the recollections, experiences and mental processes of Duncan. After much deliberation, he chooses to go by the name of Joseph Gryphon. He considers the mythical creature suitably represents the merging of two very different beings—Father Casey and Duncan—into one: the soaring, wild awareness of the eagle combined with the raw vitality of the lion.

A fraction overindulgent, he has to accept but the Duncan side of his character enjoys the tongue in cheek humour behind it while the Father Casey side considers in all honesty that this is not far from the reality of his new self.

Less than a fortnight later, a horse-drawn hansom cab enters the courtyard of a grand looking manor house just outside Bidston Village on the Wirral peninsula. The cabman reins in the horse and brings his cab to a halt just behind an open-backed cart which is loaded up with several sturdy-looking trunks and boxes. The cabman jumps down and opens the door for his passenger, helping him to alight from the carriage. Joseph Gryphon climbs down from the cab and stretches, breathing in the chill late January air, allowing his senses to soak up all that stands before him.

The house is Bidston Manor, Duncan's former home: a double-fronted two storey property with an entrance hall in the centre spanning both floors and an intricate stained-glass window in the form of a coat-of-arms which, he imagines, must cast a bold array of colours across the staircase inside. He walks up to the landing half way up the steps leading to the front door and then has to step briskly to one side to avoid someone almost entirely hidden under a hefty box perched on his shoulders which is leaning ever more precariously to one side, on the brink of toppling to the ground.

"I've got you," Gryphon shouts out, hopping down a couple of steps and propping up the corner of the box. Between the two of them they manage to bring the box safely down the final steps and load it onto the cart. As they set it down, Gryphon flinches. That forged hitch ring on the deck of the cart was where he was tethered when he had been hauled off towards the police lock-up accused of murder, eight years earlier.

Not just a similar one—no doubt about it—this is the very same cart. He shivers half in fear at the jolt back to such a distressing experience and half in anger at the gross injustice of all that followed that night. Then he glimpses the man carrying the box. It is Kal, the blacksmith who had mocked and goaded Duncan so cruelly when he was at his most vulnerable. Now Gryphon tries to keep his shock from showing as Kal, oblivious to who he really is, thanks him for his help and they go through the awkward formality—at least for Gryphon—of introducing themselves.

Kal then climbs up onto the cart, cracks the reins urging the horse to walk on. Gryphon watches until Kal has disappeared out of the courtyard, down the lane towards Bidston Village. He frowns as he turns and steps up towards the front door, which stands ajar, propped open despite the chill in the air with a heavy-looking doorstop presumably to allow access for Kal to load the cart outside.

From the threshold, Gryphon can see a woman kneeling with her back to the door, crouching down in front of a large display dresser at the rear of the entrance hall. He observes her for a second or two longer than decorum would suggest as appropriate before she must have sensed his presence lingering there and she shouts out without glancing in Gryphon's direction, "Make sure you don't forget to drop the spare keys off at Mrs Cawston's."

"I fear you mistake me for someone else," Gryphon says smiling.

Jules looks up at him in confused surprise.

"I'm so sorry. I thought you were…" she raises her hand squinting against the glare of the sunlight behind him, "…one of the packers."

She sounds irritated at her blunder as she struggles to her feet, wiping down her clothing, placing the large serving dish she has retrieved from the dresser in the box on a table next to her.

"I am looking for Mrs Chambers," Gryphon manages to say.

She is even more beautiful than he remembers. She is wearing a housecoat to protect her ankle-length blue dress from the dust and grime picked up in the cleaning and packing. Her eyes sparkle, an eerie reminder for Gryphon of their shared intimacy in Blackheath. Delicately she smoothes her unruly strawberry hair behind her ear. Her skin shines.

"And who might be doing the looking?" Jules is purely matter of fact, her tone cautious but without displaying overt suspicion.

It is uncomfortable and almost impossible for Gryphon to accept that Jules has never laid eyes on him before this moment, but that he knows is the reality for her.

"My name is Gryphon, Joseph Gryphon."

"Unusual name. For these parts anyway."

"I knew your husband…in London," he says, deciding to dispense with further pleasantries.

"Did you now?" Jules mulls this over. "You are a long way from home, Mr Gryphon. Won't you come inside?"

In the drawing room, Gryphon stands at the window looking back down across the walled courtyard, out through the wrought iron gates. The view over the rooftops of Bidston Village to the vast wetland of the Moss beyond, eventually merging into the northern shoreline of the Wirral and the Irish Sea, is quite simply magnificent. Gryphon is thrilled to be back within touching distance of where all this began.

Jules invites him to sit in a large armchair near the fireplace.

"Not many of Duncan's acquaintances even admit to having known him," says Jules throwing another log onto the fire sending a flare of sparks spitting up the chimney.

"I was no ordinary friend of Duncan. Close would hardly do it justice."

"Is your visit purely sociable…or do you have some ulterior motive?" Jules challenges Gryphon with her customary bluntness.

"He spoke of you often. I promised him I would make sure you were coping after…you know."

"Well, now you will be able to go back to London with a clear conscience, won't you?" Jules's tone has a bitter edge to it as if she has no intention of being drawn into any discussion which forces her to recall her pain at Duncan's death. Gryphon though, finds her utterly enchanting.

"I certainly am not here to clear my conscience, I can assure you of that," Gryphon throws back her brusqueness in kind.

Jules softens, "I didn't mean to doubt your sincerity. I am not used to much kindness of late."

They stare at each other for several seconds in silence. Then Gryphon clears his throat and continues, changing the subject, "I see you are doing a bit of a clear-out."

"More than a clear-out. I am moving out altogether."

Gryphon feels a wrenching emptiness in the pit of his stomach. If he is honest, he has, over the past few days, as he organised his visit, increasingly fantasised that somehow he would end up winning the heart of Jules all over again. It's not that far-fetched. Admittedly, he is now several years her junior. But what is age these days? And he retains Duncan's personality, at least in large part anyway and the addition of Father Casey's devotion and intensity can only make him more attractive, not less. But if she moves away it could wreck or, at the very least, complicate his plans no end.

"Oh, really?" is all he manages to say.

"The upkeep of the house has become too onerous financially. It has been for many years, to be frank. So, now that Duncan is never coming back, there is nothing that ties me to this place any more. I am sailing on Wednesday next week for New South Wales."

"No…" Gryphon blurts out involuntarily.

"Excuse me?"

"I mean…Australia? The journey is so perilous. So many passengers succumb to disease. And even if you get there, it's merely a penal colony, full of convicts. Hardly the place for someone of your standing. Are you sure?" Gryphon is having great difficulty processing the devastating news. The idea of Jules moving to Australia is just too cruel a blow.

"Oh yes, Mr Gryphon. Quite sure. My husband left me nothing."

It would be easy to conclude, understandably so, that his coming to the Wirral was all down to this Jules business, to his infatuation with her. His first stop had been Bidston Manor after all, well, apart from taking this pokey room at the Bidston Village Inn, that is.

But jumping to such a conclusion would be to ignore the scientific backing for his trip, which increasingly he tries to convince himself is every bit as important as the romantic justification.

Looking out of the tiny window, set deep into the thick walls in his room, he can see the forge opposite, not even twenty paces up the lane. He has long suspected that Kal knows a whole lot more about what happened that night eight years ago than he ever let on. He keeps remembering the look on Kal's face as he had furtively checked up and down the lane outside the forge to make sure that no-one had noticed Duncan's arrival.

Obviously as Duncan, he was never able to risk coming up here. He would have been recognised immediately and re-arrested with all the predictable consequences which he has only barely survived. But as Gryphon, he could use his anonymity to indulge that nagging curiosity over the origins of the surfacing interruption. And beyond that, he could for the first time undertake a meaningful reconnoitre of the Moss itself, perhaps even identify the precise physical location of the distortion which must play such a key role in any future reopening.

Since day one, this has been and remains his sole and overriding priority. As Gryphon, he could in a relatively short time have an impact far more dramatic and far reaching than Duncan's long years achieved. His plans now embrace the pursuit of this scientific investigation at the very least in parallel with his determination to prevent Jules going anywhere near that steamship bound for Australia a week from now.

He picks up his overcoat and throws it over his shoulders. He trudges downstairs, crosses the busy smoke-filled bar and heads out into the gathering gloom and the wintery cold outside. It is not even four in the afternoon but it is already almost dark; night closes in so much earlier here than in London.

Gryphon walks up to the forge and stands there in the darkness, observing Kal as he works. Such a lot has happened since he stood here, disoriented and on the verge of collapse. This was precisely where things slipped from his grasp, in this exact same spot eight years ago, and since then, he now recognises he has never fully regained control. It is like time itself hasn't moved on, stuck in some freak unending loop, delivering him back to the same place with nothing changed.

"Hey, Gryphon, wasn't it?" Kal sees him. "Come in, come in. It's far too cold to be standing out there."

Gryphon approaches the fire and warms his hands.

"I hear you knew Duncan Chambers," Kal states with no hint of emotion. He holds up the piece of metal he is working on, some sort of scythe blade perhaps, to the light of the fire, examining it carefully.

He then places it back down on the anvil and resumes his hammering, adding between blows, "Shocking business."

"I understand that you were involved," Gryphon says in an equally non-committal tone.

"Involved?" Kal stops his hammering and looks Gryphon up and down. "No more than everyone else around here, I'd say. What is it to you anyway, Mr Gryphon?"

Kal's smug, know-it-all hostility, betrays some deeper complicity surrounding those events back then. Gryphon is convinced of it.

"Duncan told me you were there," Gryphon pushes.

"What do you mean?" Kal seems rattled by where this is going.

"You know, when James was murdered." Gryphon hopes his clear provocation, a blatant attempt to flush Kal out into the open, will trigger a response and he certainly gets one.

Kal drops the scythe blade back into the fire and walks over to Gryphon. He pushes his face to within an inch of Gryphon's, indignation written across his scowl. Gryphon wants nothing more than to step back but he knows he has to stand his ground.

"Duncan said many things," Kal half spits out through his clenched teeth. "Almost all of them were lies. You should bare that in mind before you dare come around here spouting that kind of wild accusation."

"Are you threatening me?" Gryphon tries to sound unperturbed but his anger is seething just below that calm exterior.

"Why would I do that?" Kal laughs, stepping back. "Duncan was guilty."

"He paid a heavy price, that goes without saying."

"Had it coming, if you ask me," Kal says.

"He never confessed. Not even at the end when he faced the gallows."

"Actually, he did. He admitted it to me when he first came into the forge."

"He did?" Gryphon is appalled at Kal's shameless lie.

"Oh yes, he told me he stabbed him in the neck alright, in revenge for him touching Jules."

"That's not what he said to the police."

"Jules must have persuaded him to change his story."

"Why would she do that?"

"Because if Duncan confessed then the rumours of Jules carrying on with James would have been confirmed. He was protecting her reputation."

"And was she? Carrying on with James, I mean."

"Come on. Everyone knows. Why do you think she is going to Australia now, with that Moira Cawston? She can't hold her head up around here."

Gryphon is taken aback. Jules hadn't mentioned anyone accompanying her.

"She's not going alone?"

"The whole Australia thing is Moira Cawston's doing."

"Who is this Moira Cawston?"

"She's a complete freak. Ask anyone. And always hanging around Jules. Filling her head with all sorts of nonsense. It's not right, not natural, if you know what I mean. And now they are going off to Australia together. What more can I say?"

Gryphon is unsure he follows Kal's insinuations but this radically changes things.

"Where can I find her?"

"She works up at the Observatory. Does some sort of investigating."

The following morning Gryphon engages the innkeeper's wife in light-hearted conversation over breakfast and in exchange for some frankly undeserved compliments on her—what could only be described as—mediocre cooking, she is only too willing to share all the most recent gossip surrounding Moira Cawston, of which there is not an insubstantial amount. Such is Gryphon's level of agitation at what he hears that he decides there and then to head up through the woods towards the Observatory to find out just who the hell this Moira Cawston woman thinks she is.

Above the village, the double-domed building that houses the Observatory is perched on the northern edge of the huge outcrop of sandstone known as Bidston Hill, one of the highest points on the entire Wirral peninsula. The lighthouse next to it rises well above the tree line, so it is easily visible from all approaches and marching straight towards it, Gryphon has no difficulty in finding his way there.

He had asked the Observatory gatekeeper to inform Mrs Cawston that he wished to see her but he had no idea if she would agree to his request without any formal invitation or introduction. But only a few minutes later Moira Cawston herself appears and shows him up a sweeping wrought iron staircase and along a joyless and clinically plain corridor to her office on the first floor.

He hazards a guess that she must be close to fifty, but her fashion sense is far more modern and with her slender physique dressed in an elegant flowing black skirt and a close-fitting Spencer waistcoat also in black, over a pristine white chemise, she is certainly professional-looking. In contrast to her attire, her blonde hair is tied up casually with a hair pin giving an air of being comfortable within formality, not dissimilar to Jules. Her complexion though is totally different, covered in a mass of light freckles, which make her look much younger than her years. She exudes style and refinement.

"The lighthouse was opened just over a century ago in 1771," she says on the way, as if to avoid any nervous or uncomfortable silence. Her stock patter, providing him with a textbook background of the buildings, sounds like it has been used on multiple occasions to fill the same awkward void and seems calculated to last precisely the length of their journey to her office.

"At well over two miles from the coast, it is the most remote from the sea of any lighthouse ever built. The Observatory is a relatively new addition, occupying the same walled grounds and was built from the same granite stone but was only opened eight years ago, to house the relocation from Liverpool's Waterloo Dock of all the port's tidal research."

Moira Cawston stops right on cue before a door and takes a large key out of her pocket. Privacy must be of the utmost importance to her as, although she cannot have been away from her office for more than a couple of minutes, it appears she was not comfortable leaving the door unlocked for even that long. Either that or she is totally paranoid about her colleagues accessing her tightly guarded secrets. The key rattles in the lock as she opens the door and ushers Gryphon inside ahead of her.

Every available space is covered with large scale drawings and maps, even the floor. Mrs Cawston pushes the door back into place, forcing its stiff hinges to creak until the handle clicks into place and she then sits behind her desk, hardly a square inch of which is visible under the mess of documents littering its surface.

She indicates with her open palm for Gryphon to take the only other chair. It appears out of place, most likely brought in just for the occasion—the papers usually occupying its space pushed into a cluttered pile on one side. As he takes his seat, he looks around at the chaotic collage of charts and maps, with a mass of scribbled notes pinned across them. He is astonished at what he sees there.

"These charts have nothing to do with tides, if I am not mistaken," Gryphon declares, showing he is no newcomer to science but his genuine attempt to engage Moira Cawston in any meaningful discussion over what he has identified in those maps backfires. She takes exception to his comment. She must consider he is prying or maybe her being paranoid is not going to be that wide of the mark.

She ignores his observation and says coldly, "How can I be of assistance to you, Mr Gryphon?"

"I'm so sorry. Let me explain. Kalvin, the blacksmith, you know…"

"I know who Kalvin is," she cuts him off abruptly. This is going to be more difficult than he had anticipated.

"Yes, of course. Let me be blunt with you, Mrs Cawston. I hear you are providing a rather unique service in the local community, something quite exceptional."

Moira Cawston glowers at him. Her piercing stare is made all the more striking by her eyes appearing from behind a pair of oval-rimmed spectacles she had put on as she sat down and which previously had hung around her neck attached to a delicate silver chain.

"Something quite exceptional?" she queries with a derisive smirk. She manages to trivialise and undermine everything Gryphon says.

"You have quite a following, it seems."

"Some people seek my advice, that's all."

"But on matters beyond the grave? Really?"

According to the innkeeper's wife, Moira Cawston has seen spirits and what is more remarkable is that she claims she can communicate with them, and they in turn can relay back to her information on how our dearly departed of this life are faring in the next.

"You know Jules, don't you?" Again Moira Cawston changes tack. Gryphon feels as though he is permanently one step behind this woman.

"I knew her husband."

"Of course, Duncan. That fits."

"What do you mean?"

"So you come around here to see if you can pick up any leftovers. Is that it?" Moira Cawston has an abrasive personality which is starting to thoroughly annoy Gryphon, but he forces himself not to rise to her rudeness.

"Jules has just been through a horrific experience. The last thing she needs is for you to claim you can speak to Duncan. I am concerned for her. That's all."

"It just offers a bit of comfort. There is no harm in that."

"It has nothing to do with the other side," he says with conviction. "It is fraudulent."

"Are you trying to scare me, Mr Gryphon?" she scoffs.

"All I am saying is that you shouldn't prey on other people's weaknesses. Listen, you can't seriously be saying that the whole Australia thing is in Jules's best interests. You've got to stop that insanity. Anyone honestly thinking of Jules would never coerce her into risking her life on such an absurd and pointless journey."

"What Jules needs is a clean break from the likes of you. From your ego, from your lies and control."

As far as Moira Cawston is concerned, Gryphon only met Jules yesterday afternoon. Her comments suggest a deeper and more disturbing understanding of who he is. Obviously, even from this short exchange, he can sense that Moira Cawston has a highly developed psychological sensitivity, not unlike Father Casey's, he realises, although he is surprised that the priest has come to his mind at that particular moment. He decides to shift the focus back onto more comfortable ground.

He indicates to all the maps on the wall.

"That is Bidston Moss, isn't it?"

"Now you are an expert in local geography, Mr Gryphon, as well as oceanography," she sounds suspicious.

"Did something happen to you out there?"

"What do you mean?"

"Did you come across something which could have triggered your ability?"

"Why are you so interested in all this anyway? Do you want to ridicule me too? Like all the rest?"

"No, not at all. I know that when Duncan was out on the Moss that night, when James was murdered, he had a sort of a breakdown, if you like, a hallucination. I wonder if you might have had a similar experience out there at some point, a vision which touched you?"

"Listen, Mr Gryphon," Moira Cawston challenges him head on, "You are the one who is deceiving people. I can sense you skulking around in the shadows. But I know you are in there somewhere. Who are you? Why don't you level with me, right now?"

Gryphon is stunned into silence.

Moira Cawston continues, "There is something about you I don't like. Are you a priest, by any chance?"

"Not any longer." Gryphon is caught off guard. How can she have come to that deduction? By lucky association? He doesn't think so. It's as though she has somehow picked up on his thoughts of just a few seconds ago about Father Casey. What's more, he also has no idea why he confirmed her suggestion. Why didn't he just lie?

"I thought being a priest was for life," Moira Cawston now has a bold, disrespectful arrogance sewn into her words. There is something weird going on here and Gryphon knows that Moira Cawston is dialled into that same wavelength, too.

"I am no longer drawn to divine or indeed to any other spectral apparitions. I am only interested in science," Gryphon says, but what he can't explain is why he is allowing himself to be dragged ever deeper into something that he may not be able to handle.

"For a man of religion, you have remarkably little faith."

Before meeting Moira Cawston, Gryphon's mind had been wavering between taking matters into his own hands or just allowing things to play out, such was his confidence that he would be able to win Jules over, even with that glaring age difference. He now realises that he had been treating it all like a big game.

Meeting Moira Cawston though has changed all that and he now feels a sense of urgency. He has to protect Jules. And fast.

He had managed to get out of the Observatory without giving away anything crucial in spite of Moira Cawston's mental attrition or at least that is what he hopes. But coming into close contact with her left him feeling as though he had only just escaped from her clutches and at no point could he say he had been in control of that encounter. Having to bend to someone else's whim and fancy is something he has never experienced; he finds it all quite disturbing.

Moira Cawston had seen far too easily into his mind, somehow she had even been able to recognise Father Casey in the background. Could she be seeing even more than she has intimated? The uncertainty eats away at Gryphon. At all costs, he determines to stop Jules from leaving for Australia with this woman.

So, the next morning finds him bright and early in the well-to-do offices of law firm, Hand and Sons in Hamilton Square in the centre of Birkenhead.

George Hand, the son, who now runs the business following the passing of his father, says with an air of boredom at being forced to repeat himself, "I am sorry but as I said before, Mrs Chambers has already reached an agreement to rent Bidston Manor to the O'Shaunessy family. They are indeed, as we speak, in temporary lodgings in Liverpool waiting for the property to be vacated."

"Listen to me, Mr Hand. You are obliged to act in the best interest of your client, I presume."

"Of course. But you are too late, I'm afraid, Mr Gryphon."

"Let us not jump to conclusions, Mr Hand. I wish not to rent Bidston Manor but to purchase it outright and I am proposing to pay well in excess of its market value, closer to double, I'd wager. That would change things a little, would you not agree?"

"But why would you do that? I mean that is crazy."

"I want that house, Mr Hand. I really want that particular house. Let's say for sentimental reasons."

"But it will take too long to get the documentation prepared. Mrs Chambers is leaving in just over a week from now."

"In exactly eight days, Mr Hand," Gryphon says taking a fat looking leather document case from under his coat and removing a series of documents.

"Here is the entire sum I have mentioned, in cash, bearer bonds actually, along with a legally binding deed of sale which I had drawn up this very morning. Also, I would like two conditions attached to the deal: firstly, that if she so wishes, Mrs Chambers will stay on as a non-rent paying tenant at the property for as long as she desires; and secondly that my identity is kept secret at all times from Mrs Chambers. I would not wish her to know of my involvement.

"Please, Mr Hand, verify all the bonds and the title deeds at your leisure. Present my offer to Mrs Chambers and inform me of her decision, which I trust will be favourable, at the Bidston Village Inn before the end of Friday. Bring the deeds signed by Mrs Chambers and we will be able to conclude a very advantageous deal for all concerned. Amongst whom we should undoubtedly include yourself, Mr Hand, as I have included the payment of a commission fee of eight percent of the consideration, payable on completion, to compensate your estimable services in this transaction."

Over the next few days as Gryphon waits to hear whether his gamble has paid off, he hardly gets any sleep at all. He feels a way out of this mess and a more manageable future is so close he can almost touch it and yet it is dangling by such a thin thread, it could just as easily snap and fall to the ground, breaking into a million pieces. He spends hour after hour, walking aimlessly out on the Moss unable to remember precisely where his surfacing had taken place and he at no point felt any proximity to the surface deformity as Moira Cawston clearly had. But his strange encounter with her was never far from his thoughts either. And, at the same time, he could almost feel her thinking about him too. How could anyone weigh so ominously on his mind? It must be the lack of sleep.

In the end, Hand kept his side of the bargain. He was first and foremost a typical legal professional so a large enough fee cured all concerns as to impropriety, and the agreement with the O'Shaunessy's was unceremoniously relegated to the annals of history.

Gryphon, however, is none too thrilled at the details of the outcome Hand delivered in person to him early that Friday evening. Clearly, he is contented that Jules has accepted his offer to buy Bidston Manor but is left more than disheartened to hear she has rejected the possibility of her staying on at the property indefinitely.

To make matters worse, that meddlesome woman Moira Cawston somehow has managed to sway Jules into persisting in the crazy Australia venture. So, he will have to upgrade his charm offensive dramatically if he is to convince her otherwise before the two of them set sail, now in just five days' time. With that uppermost in his mind, he decides there can be no further time lost and he should go up to Bidston Manor right away to confront Jules directly. It is not quite dark yet and as seems almost inevitable here, it is once again raining as he walks out of the Inn and heads up the lane.

At the moment he enters the courtyard, he looks up at the house and glimpses for a second none other than Moira Cawston herself peering out through the drawing-room window. She has evidently seen Gryphon too, if her jumping back from the window is anything to go by. A chill runs down Gryphon's spine. He is infuriated by Moira Cawston's suffocating presence around Jules.

She has her hooks firmly embedded in her victim, like a leech sucking the blood out of its host. His reaction is way over the top, he knows; but she produces such an unnatural, visceral repulsion in him. He has great difficulty accepting that it is in fact jealousy he is feeling here. But what else could it be? He cannot allow that woman to take Jules away from him. It is unthinkable.

Taking a more rational approach to things, as he slowly walks across the courtyard, he recognises that this is the perfect opportunity for him to lay out the benefits to Jules of her taking up the second part of his offer and to tackle at source any pressure Moira Cawston may try to apply.

He climbs the steps and pulls the bell cord which he hears ring in the hallway. He is just about to ring again, such a long time has elapsed without any response, when the housekeeper opens the front door with a worried expression on her face.

"Mrs Chambers is not available to entertain visitors unannounced at this time," she says obviously following instructions albeit rather nervously.

"In that case," Gryphon walks straight past the housekeeper into the hallway and speaking in a voice loud enough to be heard by the two ladies who undoubtedly will be listening intently at the drawing-room door, says, "I will wait until she becomes available."

He takes a seat in the hallway opposite the entrance to the drawing-room. Gryphon is not going to buy this property and then let Jules or worse, Moira Cawston, trample all over him, even if they do not know specifically that he is the one behind the deal offered to Jules.

They appear to have reached an impasse. The housekeeper stands by the still open front door, unsure what her next move in such an awkward situation should be, and Gryphon is quite clearly not going anywhere.

After a couple of uncomfortable minutes, the handle of the drawing-room door edges downwards and the door slowly half opens to reveal Jules, a look of thunder written on her face.

"What exactly do you want?" she says slowly with ice-cold ferocity.

"What is *she* doing here?" Gryphon says staring beyond Jules straight at Moira Cawston. He stands up, pushes the door wide open and strides defiantly past Jules into the drawing room, uninvited.

"How dare you come barging in here, Mr Gryphon," Jules says, leaving the door to the hallway ajar, the housekeeper open-mouthed behind her. She walks briskly over to her friend who is standing with her back to the window, staring straight back at Gryphon.

The atmosphere in the room is heavy, laden with sickly sweet-scented incense fumes billowing out of a rose burner set on a table where the two women have evidently been sitting. It is also oppressively hot, Gryphon notes, a large fire blazing in the open fireplace.

"Well, well, well," Moira Cawston says with an ironic smile, "Look who's here."

Then Gryphon notices a miniature bottle with a cork stopper next to the incense burner.

"Is that…" he picks up the bottle and reads the label, "…laudanum? Really? Is that your science?"

"It just helps the spirits of the dead to manifest themselves," Jules explains in justification of her friend's actions.

"Helps her opium-induced rantings more like," Gryphon shifts his attention from Moira Cawston to Jules. "Tell me you are not actually encouraging her in this madness."

"She has done such a lot of scientific research into this stuff."

"She's not just a fraud, she is downright dangerous. She's messing around with *stuff*, as you call it, she doesn't even remotely comprehend."

"You see, Jules. It worked," Moira Cawston stares intently at Gryphon. "Now it all makes sense."

"What do you mean?" Jules asks, getting ever more confused, her patience wearing thin.

"I can feel his presence, Jules. I knew it was him."

"This is Mr Gryphon, Moira," Jules sounds baffled and concerned that her friend is losing touch with reality.

Gryphon though is shocked. He even questions for a few seconds whether Moira Cawston could even have had some influence over his own decision, of just a few minutes earlier, to come here at this particular moment. Moira Cawston has a crazed, wild look in her eye.

"Well? What do you have to say for yourself?" she says challenging Gryphon.

"I have no issue with you. I only wish to ensure Jules is safe."

"You frighten me, you know? I have never come across a spirit like yours," Moira Cawston says, edging towards the fireplace. "I know you are in there…somewhere."

"Jules, you can't go to Australia with *her*," Gryphon throws an exasperated glance in the direction of Moira Cawston. "I urge you to reconsider."

"You urge, do you?" Moira Cawston laughs.

"And why would I pay heed to your opinions on such a matter, I wonder," Jules is clearly still livid with Gryphon at his intrusion.

"This is absurd. You have to see that," Gryphon takes a step towards Moira Cawston, as if he has decided to take matters into his own hands, as if he is intent on placing himself as a physical barrier between her and Jules.

"Keep away from me," Moira Cawston shouts bitter and angry. Is she seeing right through him to Duncan in the background, somewhere inside Gryphon's psyche? She looks panicky, dazed and confused. "Keep your distance from him, Jules. He may try to take you, too."

Moira Cawston then steps quickly up to the fireplace and with both hands grabs a large burning stick out of the blazing fire. Flames dance along most of its length as she brandishes it out in front of her swinging it back and forth towards Gryphon menacingly. One of her hands seems to be grasping directly onto the charred smouldering wood but she is showing no sign of any pain.

"What do you think of that? Hey, priest? You know he was a priest, Jules. Was!"

"Just put the stick down. Please, you're going to set the whole house on fire," Gryphon warns. This is getting way out of hand. He is starting to question, remarkably, who wields the real control over the outcome here.

"Adjure te, spiritus nequissime, per Deum omnipotentem," Moira Cawston chants.

"What on earth? What are you saying?" Jules asks in an authoritative tone, trying to get Moira Cawston's attention, but failing.

"You have got to be kidding. Come on," Gryphon laughs nervously, and then in a much sterner tone he continues, "I am no demon. I am bound by neither God nor the devil."

"What is going on here?" Jules shouts, her desperation rising.

"She thinks I am possessed…by some evil spirit. It's Latin, part of a ritual of exorcism."

"I brought you here and now I command you to leave. Get out, now!" shouts Moira Cawston.

Gryphon decides that it might be wiser to go along with this direction and to take up the whole Australia madness with Jules when Moira Cawston is not present. He backs towards the front door while Moira Cawston aggressively thrusts her burning stick towards him.

"OK, OK," he tries to calm Moira Cawston down, "I'm going."

It then flashes through his mind that maybe he is again simply going along with Moira Cawston's subconscious instructions. He knows that is ridiculous; it is obviously just the laudanum pushing her over the limit. He is retreating on his own terms, no-one else's.

Once they are outside the rain hisses against the burning wood, the flames throwing eerie shadows across the courtyard. Moira Cawston looks drained, as if the rain or the cold has forced her to realise what she has just done and what Jules must be thinking of her. She suddenly looks down and seems to notice that her hands are being severely burnt and she drops the piece of wood onto the stone staircase. It cascades down to the courtyard end over end, spraying clouds of sparks as it drops down hitting each step.

"My God, Jules. Forgive me," Moira Cawston screams. "What have I become?" She runs down the steps, crosses the courtyard sobbing, and disappears out of the gates.

"Let her go," Jules says.

Some minutes later, back in the drawing-room, Jules pours Gryphon a whisky which he had readily accepted. She then, as if as an afterthought, pours herself a small glass.

"She will be fine. She just needs to be alone a while. She's been having a really tough time of late. Do not judge her too harshly, I beg you. I cannot apologise enough for that horrendous incident. I think her losing her job has really knocked her confidence."

"She lost her job? But I saw her up at the Observatory just a couple of days ago."

"When she spoke of what happened out on the Moss to her colleagues, she was treated as though she were losing her mind."

"So she did have some kind of experience out there?"

"Without a doubt. I think she must have blacked out and hit her head as she fell somehow."

"Why do you say that?"

"She told me she had been engulfed by something like a magnetic aura, that was how she called it, with all the colours of the rainbow changing and mixing around her. What else could it have been other than a blow to the head?"

"And that was when she made contact with the other side?"

"She is quite convinced her visions are a unique scientific opportunity to understand death and the human soul. It makes sense. Just look at the staggering advances in science just recently: the miracles of the telephone or the electric lightbulb. Moira believes, and I wholeheartedly concur that it is only a matter of time before death itself will have nowhere to hide and will give itself up to the progress of science. She sees her own experience with the world of spirits as evidence of our own immortality, if you like, that some part of our soul does indeed survive through death."

"But her colleagues were not so convinced, I imagine."

"To put it mildly. Their response to her insistence on carrying on with her studies into her visions shifted from sympathy to rejection, and then descended into outright contempt and ridicule. She had a massive fight with the chief science officer a couple of weeks ago which led to her being suspended, pending an investigation into her mental competency for her position. That's how the whole Australia thing came up in the first place. Suddenly there was nothing left here for either of us. They allowed her to keep attending the Observatory until she sails for Australia out of a show of respect for the many years she has worked there."

But none of Jules's explanation went any way to relieving Gryphon of his shock at finding that Moira Cawston had sensed Duncan's spirit. She seemed aware Duncan was inhabiting Gryphon's own body.

"You really should consider cancelling your voyage to Australia, at least for a time. Until Mrs Cawston can recover."

"Maybe I shall. Actually, I have just received an offer which would allow me to stay on here at Bidston Manor."

"How interesting."

Gryphon smiles to himself as he walks back down to the Inn. One thing he has inherited from Duncan is his ability to play around with different strategies until he comes up with an outcome which fits across all his requirements. And now he is starting to see an opportunity here to achieve a win-win endgame.

On the one hand, surely with Moira Cawston off the rails, psychologically-speaking, he should at least be in a position to delay any precipitous actions on Jules's behalf with regard to any emigration plans. And Jules and Gryphon had clicked in terms of personality, like he were still just the same old Duncan, their emotional engagement felt so comfortable and rewarding. It really could work.

And on the other hand, he is beginning to discern a way to restart Duncan's science development programme from here on the Wirral. Obviously, he cannot neglect indefinitely his primary objective, just so he can indulge some selfish pre-surfacing emotional gratification. But to pursue both through a single strategy would be ingenious, something Duncan himself would have approved of and indeed would have been proud of.

Ever since his visit to Moira Cawston at the Bidston Observatory, Gryphon has been mulling over some potentially revolutionary ideas which could lead to a whole new era of research there, away from its traditional shipping news focus altogether. Playing out that scenario in his head, he is sure funding strings could be pulled which would allow him to intervene on Moira Cawston's behalf with the head scientist at the Observatory, and he would be able to get her job back, for sure.

Indeed, he may be able to groom Moira Cawston as his prime conduit for feeding radical new proposals into the mainstream which could accelerate his plans. Of course, for this to come to fruition, he and Moira Cawston would have to patch up their unholy misunderstanding. If he can convince her that he can get her reinstated, it should be possible for her to accept that the whole Duncan manifestation was down to the laudanum and her extreme psychological stress. She would over time become accustomed to Duncan's presence and would no longer feel threatened by it.

Notwithstanding, it is with a real sense of dread that the following morning he approaches Moira Cawston's house. He had asked the innkeeper where Moira Cawston lived and he has followed the directions he received to a humble-looking cottage right down on the fringes of the Moss itself. Surely in the light of day, her mind will once again be calm enough to see him as he is. Or, well, he smiles to himself, as he isn't. But he is fully aware that his smile is merely a facade, hiding his trepidation.

He finds the door open, not just unlocked but actually swinging on its hinges and banging loudly in the fresh breeze. He stands there looking out over the Moss for a few minutes but cannot see Moira Cawston anywhere. He turns back to the cottage and enters.

Her front room is cold, no fire has been lit or even set. Now Gryphon feels a sense of foreboding as he shouts up the stairs to her with no response. He climbs the stairs and knocks on her bedroom door, which is also not fully closed. He carefully knocks again, trying not to open the door too far inadvertently in case she is still sleeping.

"Mrs Cawston?" he whispers but then on not hearing any reply he gently pushes the door open.

Moira Cawston had climbed onto the bottom end of the bed with a coiled leather bridle strap taken from the stables in her hand. She had thrown it over the middle oak beam which traverses the room, fixing it solidly in a clove hitch and had wrapped and tightened the strap around her neck making it fast and had quietly dropped into the void at the foot of the bed.

Gryphon instinctively rushes forward but as he touches her icy cold skin he becomes aware she has been hanging here for several hours. His disturbance of her body reignites the creaking of the taught leather strap as her lifeless form sways back and forth again seeking equilibrium. Gryphon is appalled. He is desperate first and foremost to stop that terrible creaking noise which he knows will have been the last sound Moira Cawston heard as she struggled towards death.

He grabs her around the thighs with one arm to stop the swaying and with his other hand takes his pocket knife and severs the bridle strap allowing her to fall into his arms. He lays her down on the bed and as he becomes aware that she can no longer register his touch, he collapses to his knees, aghast, embracing her tragic lifeless body. He smooths her hair back from her forehead and ever so gently closes her eyes. How could he have allowed this to happen?

At Moira Cawston's sad little funeral—attended ironically by all those colleagues who had fed her despair—Gryphon suffered a huge sense of guilt, laying the blame squarely at his own door for her wretched and heart-wrenching death. It had after all been he who had brought Moira Cawston into contact, albeit indirectly, with the surfacing deformity which had been the source of her visions and ultimately her madness but he had never thought in any way that her torment could have been such that she would take her own life. He had been incapable of understanding even his own mind—he had to admit—let alone that of a deeply troubled soul.

Jules had always stood by her friend but Gryphon's arrival had in some way proved a tipping point for Moira Cawston. They must have discussed the offer for the house and that had sown a seed of doubt in Moira Cawston's mind as to whether Jules would now go to Australia with her at all, and maybe more crucially, whether she could lose Jules to Gryphon altogether.

And then compounding that, she was also undoubtedly shocked at finding the energetic presence of Duncan within Gryphon. He imagined that she must have been terrified that she was indeed going mad and with the laudanum it had all become too overwhelming to handle.

Walking away from the Flaybrick Cemetery where Moira Cawston was buried, he accompanies Jules back up to Bidston Manor, protecting her from the drizzle with his umbrella.

"I presume you will now take up the offer to stay at Bidston Manor indefinitely." Gryphon has been thinking long and hard about how to broach this subject and now that he has done it, he suddenly thinks it sounds too pushy, but he couldn't contain his excitement any longer at the prospect of having Jules back permanently.

"No, no. I am still going. On Wednesday."

"But why? Surely you cannot even think of undertaking such a journey alone."

"The death of Moira has made it clear to me that there is now nothing here for me. Duncan is gone and Moira too. They were the only people I cared about in this world. I cannot face life here without them."

And that was that. She had confirmed her berth with the shipping line. It was all set. In less than forty-eight hours, she would be gone. Jules refused to discuss it further and even skipped away from him rather abruptly when they reached the gates of Bidston Manor, not allowing him to offer his umbrella to take her up to the front door. He stands there for several minutes, his world disintegrating around him. Duncan had no smart or fancy way around this problem and Father Casey was just devastated, defeated.

As Gryphon approached the ship tied up at the quayside in Liverpool that Wednesday at just after noon, he sees Kal, the blacksmith, rushing down the gangplank clearly distraught. As he races straight past Gryphon, without even recognising him, Gryphon can see tears are streaming down his face. He has no idea what Kal is doing here; it appears that Gryphon is indeed not Jules's only admirer.

A few minutes later, Gryphon is standing with Jules on the deck of the Australia Star in Liverpool watching as the final passengers and cargo are being loaded. They are scheduled to set sail on the high tide, in less than forty minutes. Jules had been massively affected by Moira Cawston's suicide and had refused point blank to see him in the two days before her departure but now she had relented and had invited Gryphon aboard to wish him farewell. He had misread both Moira Cawston's mental instability and how Jules would react to her death. He had failed on all counts, abysmally so.

Jules now would go to New South Wales if not a rich woman then at least with funds enough to start a comfortable new life there and she had been able to upgrade from steerage—where she would have been sharing a lower deck with all the other emigrants—to a first-class cabin, minimising the health risks on such a long journey, thankfully.

"I can't understand how anyone suddenly pays out that sort of money for Bidston Manor." They amble across the deck and look out over the river Mersey towards the Birkenhead side.

"It is a charming house," Gryphon defends his purchase.

"Not *that* charming!" Jules says and then continues, frank as ever, taking Gryphon totally by surprise, "Look, I know it was you who set all this up."

"How do you figure that?"

"You must have been a good friend of Duncan indeed. I am sure he would want to thank you for your safe-guarding my future."

"So you must also know how I feel about you in that case."

"You have known me for only just over a week. You have no idea yourself of how you feel about me. How can you?"

"You don't have to go. It's not too late…"

"Please…" Jules cuts him off, "We have been through all that before. I would ask you not to revisit those same arguments."

"But I love you, Jules. I always have. Since I first laid eyes on you. You have to believe me. Stay with me here in Bidston Manor. It could work. You'll see."

Jules is dumbfounded. Then she frowns and says, "I am afraid the only thing I can see is that you have lost your mind, Mr Gryphon."

And with that, she steps back from him and bids him farewell.

"No, please wait," he pleads but just as in Duncan's trial she leaves him without so much as a glance over her shoulder and retreats to the safety of her cabin.

Gryphon goes weak at the knees and has to lean against the railing for support. His position is hopeless, he knows, and he can do nothing else other than descend the gangplank back onto the quayside in shock and grief. He feels unable to face watching the ship set sail and he walks off towards the ferry back to the Birkenhead side of the Mersey moored at Pier Head, knowing full well that for both he and Kal too for that matter, Jules is gone.

X
Burnt Ash Lodge

Shropshire—Present Day

As Lucie is slowly regaining consciousness, as she pulls back from coming face to face with her own mortality, she grapples with disturbing and vivid flashbacks to the aftermath of the blast. But she cannot piece together any sort of clear picture, no sequence of events that she can follow coherently. Just vague unconnected and harrowing recollections: dazzling lights slicing through the darkness and thick smoke, like lightning in a cloud, the white beam from a torch maybe; the intermittent blue of what could have been a police emergency beacon way off in the distance; chilling tormented screams mixed with the whimpered moans of a more personal and intimate suffering; the silence of terrified solitude. And throughout her struggle, she refuses to give up searching with her fingertips through all the debris in her mind for the touch of that unidentified hand she held so briefly in the impenetrable darkness.

But it is gone. And the closer she comes to emerging back into full consciousness without re-establishing that spiritual bond, that shared destiny, the more intense becomes her panic and urgency. She tries to call out to that nameless soul and then slowly she fades back into deeper sleep as she is administered a further round of painkillers and tranquillisers to ease her agitation.

Outside, beyond her closed eyelids, Lucie senses someone else in the room with her, fussing around the bed, at her elbow, adjusting a tube which she can feel is connected to her arm somewhere above the wrist—a nurse most likely. And she is certainly keeping Lucie well supplied with drugs. In waves, Lucie goes from just a light drowsiness to feeling totally knocked about, like she has just gone ten rounds with Mike Tyson. But actually, she is not in that much pain. Mostly she is floating. Drifting.

Lucie instinctively knows she should feel safe here. Surely, there could hardly be a more appropriate place for her than a hospital after the shocking events in Lisbon. But even as Lucie's mind re-establishes some sense of order, pushing those still all to raw images of such a dreadful ordeal into the deepest recesses of her memory, just lying here peacefully with her eyes closed, there is something she finds inherently menacing about the place. What strikes her first and foremost is its eerie quietness. Apart from the shuffling of the nurse's sneakers across the linoleum as she hovers incessantly around her and of what must be the bleeping on a machine somewhere close to the bed of her own vital signs, there have been no other sounds at all since she has woken up.

But the longer she lies here, the more Lucie becomes aware that while she may judge her current surroundings to be a little unnerving—no way would anyone seriously try to assert this was anything close to your average run-of-the-mill over-stretched NHS hospital—this alone cannot justify her feeling this distressed. There is something self-deceiving and cosmetic in that, like wearing dark glasses when you're crying—it might stop other people noticing your tears, but not you, it won't stop you from hurting.

What has truly sent her reeling, what has rocked her to the core in fact, was seeing Emma. Lucie's immediate overwhelming sense of relief at finding her friend had vanished almost as quickly as it had arisen and had been replaced by a gut-wrenching confusion. Emma's ruthless, even cruel attitude had been so hurtful to Lucie that now in her hospital bed, with time to think things through, that confusion has multiplied many times over.

Emma must have been under such extreme pressure that she had blocked out all her natural emotions. Perhaps she had been blackmailed in some way, was being coerced into acting against her will. That could go a long way to explaining her bizarre nervous anxiety towards Lucie. But no amount of justification could get around the fact that Emma had known that the explosion was going to happen.

How could that be? She had warned Lucie to get out of the building. Like always, that was Emma looking out for Lucie. It had to be that. But more crucially how—knowing that—could she have left Lucie to face all of that pain and chaos alone?

And what of the explosion itself? Lucie had never considered she could be prone to hallucinations and yet how else could she explain away her witnessing that kaleidoscopic, distorted wave expand through the building just before the blast? Not triggered by the explosion but before it.

She clearly remembered it growing slowly, unstoppably during the four or five minutes leading up to the explosion. A multi-coloured shimmering fissure in reality advancing until it had passed through her own body. That was way out there, something Lucie couldn't even start to process or understand. It had even caused her to lose consciousness for a few seconds as it cut a pathway straight through her brain.

Then involuntarily, Lucie shivers as she had then too, just before the explosion, and she again drifts off into that same other worldly existence for a few moments. But it is still so real. So frightening. In fact, that same nightmarish vision has been kicking around inside her head ever since that wave passed through her. Basically, it is the same each time but there are undoubtedly subtle, yet clear, contextual differences: in the strength of the wind, the way the lad looks at her, how close he comes to her.

Could the hallucination itself still be active, still be defining itself? It reminds Lucie of the quick sketches she would do of the visitors to the walled garden in Carsphairn Hall before a full composition for a drawing would settle in her head. Is she going mad? Is this just a consequence of the trauma she has been exposed to?

But she knows, after this weird visitation or presence—whatever you want to call it—with this unknown lad asking if she knew Emma, actually mentioning Emma by name just seconds before the blast and then stating that Emma must be stopped, lying here in this hospital bed, Lucie knows that her search for Emma has not ended but has merely entered a new phase.

Lucie struggles against the glare and opens her eyes, finding that the devastating black void in Lisbon has been transformed into a clinical off-white colour and that faded green so typical of Victorian institutions, while the wreckage of Alves's laboratory under which she had been trapped has been replaced by this hospital bed she is now lying so comfortably in.

"How long have I been here?" Lucie asks, the words coming out as a spluttered cough, like gas bubbling through molten lava.

"Hey, you're back with us, are you?" The nurse turns towards Lucie, leans over and whispers gently in her ear, so close that Lucie can feel the warmth of her breath on her cheek as she says, "You're going to be back on your feet in no time. Don't worry."

By any stretch of the imagination, the nurse was being wildly overoptimistic. It would eventually take her several more weeks before she would be—in the nurse's own words—on her feet again, even with the help of crutches. But as over the coming days she slowly pieces together what had actually happened in the blank between the explosion and now she realises just how incredibly lucky she had been.

It turned out she had not been too close to the epicentre of the explosion but nevertheless suffered a massive blow to the head. Given the internal swelling and the risk of traumatic brain injury, she was put into an induced coma for almost a week. She could have died. She could have suffered permanent brain damage, could have ended up a vegetable. But she has responded well and the most recent scans show the swelling has subsided and her neural functions appear completely normal, thank God.

Beyond that, her right leg was broken in a couple of places and she had fractured multiple ribs; that is why she is having such intense pain when she coughs or tries to pull herself up into a sitting position. She also had a long and deep laceration on her lower back which miraculously hadn't severed any major nerve or artery although she had lost a lot of blood, nearly bleeding out before the paramedics got to her. But all in all, she had been remarkably fortunate; no vital organ damage, no life-changing brain injury.

"Can you tell me your name?" the nurse asks.

She is younger than her voice suggests, maybe not even thirty. A mix of racial ethnicity gives her an enviable skin tone which contrasts garishly—but not in a bad way—with her peroxide-dyed blond hair cropped almost into a crew-cut. She is wearing navy blue scrubs with white edging on the sleeves and a V-neck. A military-looking red badge with a gold crest is patched neatly onto her breast pocket, again certainly not NHS issue, not by a long chalk. She is definitely English though, a clear hint of Lancashire in her accent. "Is Emma OK?" Lucie asks desperate for news of her friend.

"Was Emma there with you when the bomb went off? Do you remember that?"

This is most certainly not the unequivocal straight answer Lucie had been expecting and hoping for. Her mind is already totally scrambled as it is and this type of evasive tactic, her question being foisted off with another, is only adding to her unease. She had only asked if Emma…Suddenly, a shocking thought dawns on Lucie.

"Is she dead?" Lucie says and then adds very quietly, "There was someone else…close to me. I don't know if she made it out of there."

"Who? Was that Emma?" the nurse insists.

"Did Emma get out alive? Just tell me that."

"I can't," the nurse says.

"Can't or won't?" Lucie blurts out, her desperation as ever getting the better of her.

Then she notices the metal bars on the windows.

"What sort of a hospital is this anyway?"

The nurse again ignores her, busying herself with some adjustment to the settings on the equipment presumably monitoring Lucie.

"Look," Lucie tries a different tack, "can you just let me use your mobile for a sec. Mine got lost, you know. I really must let people know I'm OK."

"I'm afraid I can't do that either."

"Why the hell not?"

"You'll have to take that up with the doctor. He'll be here in a second. I have already beeped him to say you are awake."

In a way the nurse is right; there is no point in exerting any further effort on questions she is quite clearly unable or unwilling to answer. But as Lucie settles back into her pillows she makes a solemn commitment to herself that from now on she will keep those few cards she has much closer to her chest than before; this time she will trust no-one.

Lucie must have dozed off as when she next comes to she immediately sees a man sitting directly opposite her, who has slipped unnoticed into her room. What's more, he is staring straight at her. Given the whole Miles Sawcliffe business, to awake and find someone unknown to her has been observing her while she was asleep is deeply disturbing and this particular face at such close quarters is even more off-putting given the deep wrinkles etched indelibly across it, made all the more prominent by his constant scrunched up expression as he tries to focus through a pair of tiny round spectacles perched crook-eyed on his nose.

Obviously, she thinks, this must be the doctor she has been promised. He is of Asian origin, as are so many of the NHS doctors these days, but by the way he is dressed it strikes Lucie initially—even though he must be in his late fifties, if not older—that he looks more like a porter or maybe the nurse's assistant rather than her boss; he is wearing a simple white lab coat with no distinguishable markings, no military crest like the nurse's, and under that just a plain T-shirt and jeans. But if his physical appearance is underwhelming, when he speaks, his directness and aggression more than make up for it, restoring instantly his natural authority over proceedings.

"Where exactly is Emma?" is the first question he asks, without releasing Lucie from his stare.

Lucie takes her time trying to clear her mind before answering in a tone as firm as she can muster, "That's what I have been asking your nurse here for God knows how long and she has been frankly unhelpful on that front."

The man looks over at the nurse, who shrugs.

"Lucie, we need you to tell us where she is."

Lucie is encouraged. If they don't know where Emma is, then surely that implies she can't have died in the explosion. This prompts Lucie to stand her ground, not that she actually has any idea of where Emma might be anyway but she is certainly not going to reveal that.

Instead, she demands, "The place to start would be you telling me just where I am and who the hell *you* are."

The man closes the journal he must have been writing in. Places his pencil down next to it and stands. A pencil? Really? He appears to be close to losing his cool at Lucie's disrespectful comment but he makes a visible effort to contain himself.

"My name is Doctor Jagdev Kahtri. I am the lead clinician responsible for your care. Your nurse here is Chloe and this…" he sweeps his hand around inclusively, "is Burnt Ash Lodge."

Lucie would find out over the coming days that Burnt Ash Lodge is a huge red brick Victorian mansion with three distinct wings radiating out from a central common hallway. It sits on a low hill nestled within woodland through which a winding single gravel track provides the only access at the rear of the property. A neglected lawn and several straggling ornamental flower beds slope away in front of the house offering glimpses through mature trees to some more imposing hills in the distance.

The wealth required even to contemplate building such a distinguished residence must have been eye-wateringly large back in the late nineteenth century. The good fortune of the owners, however, was short-lived; the building fell on hard times and was eventually abandoned.

It was requisitioned as a military hospital early in the First World War according to the locals and several old photographs in the main entrance provide documentary evidence in support of that story. Since then it has been maintained in public ownership through the National Trust but continues to be operated by the armed forces as a trauma centre for military personnel affected by extreme combat situations.

"Do you remember the explosion?" Doctor Kahtri asks.

"Bits," Lucie offers noncommittally.

"Did you see Alves?"

"I don't know any Alves."

"Was he at the lab when the bomb went off?"

"I tell you, I don't know anybody called Alves."

"Don't be ridiculous. Of course you know Alves."

"Listen all I want is to find Emma. Don't you understand? And Zac," Lucie says forcefully. "What happened to Zac?"

"We don't know any Zac, do we Chloe?" He looks back over at the nurse, who again just shrugs.

This is quite typical of their early sessions over those first weeks when Lucie is confined to her bed. Kahtri is her only visitor, apart from Chloe of course. And the more Lucie holds back, the more Kahtri's agitation increases, his nerves becoming visibly more frayed; he seems almost desperate, everything intense and territorial. Such a lot must ride on his getting to know the whereabouts of Emma. Quite astonishing and quite frightening, thinks Lucie.

"Don't you feel even an ounce of remorse?" Kahtri asks in a threatening tone late on in a session which has already dragged on past the hour mark.

"What are you suggesting? That I was involved in the attack? God, I really must be getting delusional? Come on, I was there. Sure I was. That's obvious, wouldn't you say?" Lucie puts on her own ironic smile before adding, "But at no point did I influence events; there were no consequences to any of my actions."

"Listen Lucie, I don't think you realise just how much trouble you are in."

"Oh yeah, well in that case, don't you *have to* let me make a phone call. All defendants at least get to call a lawyer, don't they?" Lucie demands getting her caustic tone spot on this time.

"Have to? Please, give me a break."

Kahtri chuckles to himself, although Lucie is uncertain what it is that has sparked his amusement, then he continues, "If I were you, I wouldn't even be thinking about making that call. It might end up very badly. For your own good, no-one can know you are here."

"Why the hell not?"

"Because you are a suspected terrorist."

"What? What do you mean?"

"You are wanted for killing a police officer and then you were seen on CCTV going into that building near the Moscavide metro station seventeen minutes exactly before a bomb goes off, killing thirteen people and you don't show up amongst the dead bodies. Hardly surprising that you end up being the prime suspect of the Portuguese terrorist squad. So you will understand our need for absolute secrecy over our extracting you from Portugal and over your actually being here in the UK, under the protection of the British Armed Forces."

"But you have to tell them. I had nothing to do with that explosion."

"At some point, we will be able to put that out there, obviously. But right now, trust me, it is better that your whereabouts remain unknown."

"Oh, for God's sake," Lucie says hoisting herself up on her elbows as though she intends to try to get up out of bed, although just that small effort makes it evident to her that she doesn't have the strength to do that.

"You must calm down. Chloe, can you give her something, please?"

The nurse is immediately there, readying a syringe to sink into her arm.

"I don't need any more drugs, I need to find Emma," Lucie shouts but is unable to avoid the needle and honestly the idea of sleep doesn't sound too bad, her head spinning, she is confused and thoroughly exhausted.

"There will be lots of time to talk," Kahtri says. Absurd and actually quite intimidating, thinks Lucie as her mind becomes befuddled and her world again fades to black.

Lucie can't keep the annoying intermittent creaking sound out of her mind, it grates like someone repeatedly scratching down an old blackboard with their fingernails. Neon lights on the ceiling blink on and off illuminating their progress down this long corridor. At the end in the reflection cast by a pair of lavish double mirrored doors, Lucie sees herself slumped in a wheelchair. That is where the creaking comes from; its rusty wheels struggling to turn as the nurse pushes her along from behind. The mirrors on each door are stunning, original art deco with multiple kite shapes one behind the other all edged in gold; simple geometric extravagance. But the multiple reflections cast in them breaking up Lucie's form into several broken images are a sorry echo of her own battered and fractured body. But at least she is out of that bed and out of that room.

Her leg is in a full cast stuck out in front of her on a mechanical support a bit like an ancient battering ram. But, even in this less than ideal and unglamorous posture, at least some new horizons seem to be opening up to her although she has already come to appreciate that this hospital—or perhaps she should call it a holding facility or, why not, just a prison—uses locks and keycards on almost every door; keycards which Lucie, it goes without saying, does not possess.

Two weeks have now passed since Lucie regained consciousness, more than three since the explosion. Chloe is with her almost all the time, at least when she has been awake which to be fair has not been that much. If Kahtri is the bad cop—and from Lucie's multiple debriefings, as he insists on calling them, he certainly is—then by extension Chloe must be the good cop. And generally speaking she does fit that bill. With Chloe, the talk is more comfortable and Lucie feels less threatened, allowing her to rebuild a sense of calm and order. But Chloe's attitude is starkly different whenever Kahtri is in the room.

The two of them clearly do not see eye to eye. In fact, Lucie has noticed that Chloe actually displays signs of a distinct physical aversion to Kahtri, recoiling from his very presence when he enters the room. But in the military, you can't just walk away, you have to button it up and carry on and Chloe seems well-accustomed to that sort of thing.

"I don't know how you can stand him," Lucie keeps probing Chloe for any chink in her military armour as Chloe pulls open one of the double doors and hooks the other on her ankle drawing it back with consummate ease at the same time as sliding Lucie's chair through the gap.

"He just takes his job a bit too seriously, that's all." Chloe has given no discernible signs of any chinks to date, though.

"Still, he gives me the creeps," is Lucie's considered verdict on Kahtri.

Lucie cannot quite believe the space she is propelled into; a huge ballroom stretches out before her. She had loved Strictly on telly and while this particular one has undoubtedly seen better days, it has certainly not lost all of its prior charm and grandeur. The original paintwork has been crudely covered over in a dull white magnolia colour from top to bottom, no gold leaf remains on the cornice frieze which itself is badly chipped with some chunks missing altogether, no glitzy chandelier hanging down from the ceiling rose, just neon strip lights and the parquet flooring is heavily scuffed up in places and completely worn out in others.

"Wow, I wasn't expecting this," Lucie congratulates Chloe.

An elegant—if a little over-elaborate—pair of French windows lead out onto a large terrace with a low parapet wall at the far end from where a flowing set of wide stone steps drop down to the lawns and gardens several feet below.

"Kahtri thinks it's time you met the others," Chloe sounds nervous. Quite a revelation to Lucie, who looks around the ballroom to see who the others might be.

There are three or four tables with mostly servicemen seated around them. Any activity they may have been engaged in had stopped suddenly as Lucie had broken into their world for the first time.

"Hey Chloe!" shouts this guy in half uniform with sleeves rolled up hobbling across towards them on crutches from a table near the French windows. Lucie sees he is missing the lower half of his right leg from just above the knee.

"Watch out, this one thinks he's God's gift to womenkind," Chloe says under her breath.

"Well, he does seem ultra-keen on seeing you," says Lucie with a whispered ironic smile, only for Chloe.

"You don't say," Chloe smothers her comment just before the crutches get within earshot.

"I heard we had a new inmate," the man's voice now less of a shout as he gets closer to them but still breathy from the exertion of crossing the ballroom so quickly.

"Lucie, this is Captain Phipps," Chloe introduces them with a casualness bordering on outright apathy.

"Jack, please. Delighted to make your acquaintance," he says confidently offering his hand. Lucie shakes it hoping her cringe at his over-formality isn't too obvious.

"Likewise, I'm sure," Lucie says. Chloe grins, happy perhaps that Phipps's attention may be retrained onto another target.

"That is Senior Aircraftsman Don Pearl," Chloe says more loudly. Lucie notices Don has lost both legs at the hip. It seems cruel to her that these men should be obliged to gather in a ballroom, dancing could not be further from their minds. Suddenly her own injuries seem so minor, irrelevant in comparison.

"And that, over there is Lieutenant Richard Sykes," Chloe points to a man sitting on his own next to the open French windows who has no obvious or at least visible conditions but who rocks back and forth, his arms wrapped together tightly around his chest, greeting Lucie with a nod only when he is sure that Chloe is not looking. "The rest I'm sure you will meet in due course."

And with that Chloe—perhaps because the simple idea of being anywhere in the proximity of Captain Phipps for anything more than a matter of seconds is too abhorrent to bear—makes her excuses and exits the ballroom leaving Lucie to fend for herself. The atmosphere then perks up no end.

"You see Jack, I was right, a woman," says Don, winking at Lucie in a friendly complicit manner.

"I must apologise for Don," Jack steps in. "He has lost his manners as well as his legs."

The summer weather has been gorgeous for days. This morning a dense mist sits down in the valley beyond the edge of the gardens and from the terrace outside the ballroom, it is like being on an aeroplane looking down onto a sea of clouds with islands of hills jutting up through them. There is virtually no wind, just a gentle rustling of the leaves in the tallest trees.

It is early, only just after six but it gets light at four thirty and Lucie has always loved the early morning, especially in the open air. The stillness and the freshness of the dawn somehow wipe the slate clean of all the previous day's frenzied and often confusing goings-on, a sanctuary in which to find yourself, before doing it all over again.

Lucie is now out of her wheelchair; the cast removed a couple of days ago. She still needs crutches to avoid putting her full weight on her leg but she is stronger with every passing day. She is in her favourite spot on the terrace, sitting on the low wall, where the sun slants through the trees casting long shadows that tremble in the light breeze.

Next to her is Captain Jack Phipps. He has become a steadfast companion on her early morning resets. She knows Chloe can't stand him but she also knows, from sharing time with him, that his interest in Chloe is genuine. But while he could be a bit of a mollusc—Chloe's word not Lucie's, clinging and wet—Lucie finds him, if not exactly charming, at least good company and a valuable source of information. However, just why Kahtri had decided to permit Lucie contact with the other patients and in particular with Captain Phipps always troubled her.

Was this some deliberate ploy on the part of Kahtri who was increasingly realising that his outbursts and threats directed at Lucie were not getting anything useful out of her. Could Captain Phipps be a plant? He might have been ordered to stay as close as possible to Lucie and to extract if possible the whereabouts of Emma which still seemed Kahtri's number one concern.

Maybe giving her access to Phipps constituted an attempt to get inside her protective outer layer, to soften her up using stealth rather than brute force. Lucie would have to be even more vigilant on what she let slip with Jack given he was so amenable.

Of course, Lucie has no hard evidence that can either confirm or deny her suppositions but regardless, she feels she has been played all along, ever since she was incarcerated here. And let's not hide the reality, she certainly is being incarcerated. Captain Phipps has outlined the security measures around Burnt Ash Lodge which are extreme to say the least.

In addition to the locks and controls on movement within the building which Lucie is well aware of, outside there is an electrified double perimeter fence and armed guards at all the checkpoints who are only too willing to use their weapons, Phipps has asserted. Chloe though is still an enigma to Lucie; seemingly on her side but at the same time she remains her gaoler.

The prosthetic limb guys fitted Captain Phipps artificial lower leg the same day Lucie ditched her cast. It irritates his stump so much that, like Lucie, he depends more often than not on crutches, both pairs of which, like props in a play, are placed against the wall on either side of them waiting to be called on again.

"How did you end up here, Jack?" Lucie breaks one of their habitual long but comfortable silences. She has been plucking up the courage to ask this for some days.

"Actually, we don't usually talk about how any of us got our injuries."

Lucie tries to apologise but Jack waves away her concern and continues, "I was in Pakistan a couple of months back with the UN Peace Keeping Force up on the Afghan border and I stepped on a landmine out on patrol. Bad move."

What can Lucie possibly say to that? She is so embarrassed; she should never have asked. Aware of Lucie's discomfort, Jack continues in a more philosophical tone, "Comes with the territory, you could say. But I've been lucky, like you; it could have been so much worse."

The wisest course of action for Lucie would probably be to move swiftly on but there is something yet more pressing on her mind.

"Why are they holding me prisoner here?"

Captain Jack Phipps looks over at Lucie, a frown appearing on his brow. She is starting to think their long silences are vastly preferable to this awkwardness. Unsure of where she is going to take this, she blunders on, "Well, I mean, there is something about this place that is not right. I can feel it, all around us, somehow."

"I've never understood why you were here," Phipps says in a conciliatory and rather sombre tone. "This isn't the sort of place for a broken leg, I'll give you that; broken souls more like."

Lucie is relieved and encouraged. She had been convinced that Jack would toe the military line but he seems willing at least to discuss her concerns. She presses on, "They could have de-bunked that whole terrorist accusation straight off, but they didn't."

"They want to keep you scared that if you ever get out of here, you'll be arrested and sent back to Lisbon to face the rest of your life in a Portuguese prison."

"Well, they're succeeding on that front."

"They think you know stuff, that you're holding something back from them. They're trying to wear you down. Pretty much standard procedure. Otherwise you would be out of here already."

"What is this place? I mean, who are these people? Jesus, Kahtri can't be for real. I know ostensibly I am a trauma victim but…"

"Oh, he's for real, alright," Jack interrupts. "But they're not regular military, that's for sure. I've served in all sorts of outfits but nothing comes close to this. Kahtri's team is outside the normal command structure. A big part of what happens around here is classified, no two ways about it."

The only other human contact Lucie has is with the oldish lady who, at least until her cast is replaced by the crutches making it possible for her to get down to the ballroom to eat, would bring her meals to her room three times a day and a guy who can't be much over thirty who seems to do maintenance and cleaning in Lucie's wing. Just how they both fit into the military hierarchy is unclear.

They do not wear uniforms so maybe they are outsourced but they have been well drilled not to engage in conversation with Lucie and certainly not to reveal any operational or organisational details of Burnt Ash Lodge. So, Lucie is flummoxed as to who could have been responsible for the envelope which slid under Lucie's door one afternoon. Captain Phipps would have been her first guess but why wouldn't he have just given it to her personally.

In any event, by the time she got to the door, grabbing her crutches, lifting herself off her chair, crossing the room, opening the door and looking out up and down the corridor outside, not surprisingly whoever it was had deposited the envelope there was long gone. Inside was no message, just what appeared to be a keycard. Who else could it have been? Chloe perhaps?

Lucie waits until nightfall. Then she picks up her crutches and tries the keycard against the reader in her room. It clunks open. So it works. Or at least it works on her door which is always going to be handy even if it doesn't work elsewhere. She glances up and down the corridor. No-one. She sidles out and hops towards the main access door at the end. The only sound is made by her crutches scuffing along across the tiled floor, interspaced with the light tapping of her single footfalls.

Her plan had been just to check if the keycard worked and reconnoitre the lie of the land outside before going back to her room and working out a more detailed escape plan. She has seen from the countryside on the ballroom side that the place is pretty remote. But the main access is on the other side and while Phipps has detailed the security measures in place, she needs to see everything first hand before going for any harebrained lunge for freedom which could see her back under lock and key immediately.

However, as has been the case so often ever since she headed out to Lisbon in the first place, things just don't want to work out as planned when Lucie gets involved. She only gets two thirds of the way down the corridor before she sees the beam from a torch, presumably of a guard on a standard routine check-up, just beyond the right-angled corner where the steps lead up from the kitchens.

It's already too late to get back to her room unnoticed and her only chance to avoid being seen is to jump up the adjoining flight of stairs and to head upwards rather than her chosen route down to the outside. Annoyingly the guard follows her up and she only just keeps out of sight. She is at her wits' end knowing that if he continues on upwards he will catch her on the third floor where she stops and tries to hide as best she can behind a buttress by the windows. Luckily the guard only goes up to the second floor before giving up and returning back down to the ground floor. Given the layer of dust over everything Lucie realises the third floor is not in use at all, thank goodness.

Then something gets Lucie's attention out through the grimy window next to her. Lucie pulls her shirt sleeve down over her hand and uses it to wipe away the dirt from the glass. From there, she can see down onto a small courtyard below which must be between her wing and the East Wing where on the far side, entirely covering the entrance, a large white tent has been erected, illuminated by powerful electric lamps.

Lucie is wondering what on earth could have prompted a tent to be set up in such an odd location when a guard emerges from under the flap carrying an automatic weapon of some description. Then two more figures follow him out of the tent. The first is dressed from top to bottom in what Lucie can only describe as biohazard gear: a full face mask with visor, gloves and a protective white gown. The second, who seems to be sharing a joke with him is none other than her own Chloe dressed in her usual uniform.

"What the hell?" Lucie wonders out loud.

Chloe is always on the move. That must be how she burns up so much energy, keeping her so slim. Not that she's anorexic-looking, far from it, but she is thin. Her spindly legs pop out of her oversized sneakers reminding Lucie of Olive Oil in the cartoon Popeye. But she is no sloucher on the fitness front. She is strong for someone with such a slight build, her upper body particularly is well-muscled.

Lucie has pleaded with Chloe to accompany her on a walk outside in the gardens, claiming she needs some fresh air and some space. But in fact, she wants to put some distance, both physically and psychologically, between themselves and the house before attempting to entice Chloe to open up to her about what might be going on in the East Wing.

After seeing the tent, she had retreated back into her room without incident. If she is going to escape that way, she will need to find out of any biological risk that could pose before taking that particular plunge and, given her joking around with the guy in the biohazard gear, this time Chloe is not going to be able to deny that she is in that loop.

They are near the trees and bushes forming the bottom end of the organised garden maybe a hundred yards from the terrace at their backs and the house behind dominating the whole scene.

"I box," Chloe explains her physique, "With the guys sometimes but mostly with a bag."

Lucie has never done any sport seriously. Actually, she did become quite proficient at throwing a frisbee back in her early teens at Carsphairn Hall but that would hardly count as a sport so she decides it doesn't warrant a mention.

"And you win, I bet."

"With the bag, always. With the guys, less so, though they are gentle with me, most of the time. But every once in a while, I land one…" She demonstrates her right hook, "and they go down hurting. That is so cool."

"What makes you need a punch bag anyway?"

"It's good to have something to take all this out on," she gestures to include everything around the house. Then she pauses before continuing, as if making a final assessment of whether to allow Lucie inside her guard for the first time, "You're getting to know Kahtri now, right?"

"I don't have much choice on that front."

"Well, the longer you know him, the tougher he gets. He can be…a real pain in the ass, to put it politely." She smiles more to herself than to Lucie.

Lucie senses that Chloe is not as strong as she had imagined and that Chloe could actually have no-one else to confide in. But at the same moment, she also finds it hard to read the timing of Chloe's sudden confession of the strained relationship she endures with her superior officer.

"You have to think of yourself first," Lucie encourages Chloe, who continues more freely now.

"I know what I *should* do, what the right thing is, but I keep putting off doing it. Do you understand? I feel like I am trapped, stagnating. The right thing is there, staring me in the face, but I just let things drift."

"You don't have to take shit from him, you know."

"The military would beg to differ with you on that, Lucie."

Chloe strikes Lucie as an odd character, out of synch with her surroundings. She has little of the natural caring spirit most nurses seem to have been born with, at least those that Lucie has come into contact with. But Chloe exudes honesty and Lucie's heart goes out to her for that. Kahtri is winding Chloe up like a spring and now only a minor increase in that pressure could break her resolve to avoid conflict.

Then Lucie hears a noise which vies for her attention, a clanging of metal or more like a rattle. She looks over at Chloe but Chloe remarkably seems to be unaware of it. Lucie can see her mouth is still forming words but she can no longer hear them. The rattling is blocking out every other sound.

Lucie feels a desperate urgency, a craving to find out where that noise assaulting her hearing is coming from, and what or who is causing it. She steps off the lawn and edges forward on her crutches, managing to squeeze through a gap between two rhododendrons scratching her arm as she pushes through the gnarly bushes.

Her heart is thumping and fear prickles the hairs on her neck. The noise is getting closer. Under the canopy of tall fir trees, it is remarkably clear, the ground covered in a soft layer of pine needles, very little undergrowth to impede her progress. Then she sees the double perimeter fence some twenty paces ahead of her.

Just behind the first fence, in no-man's land, stranded between the two, she sees the same figure from her Lisbon nightmare, the same boy. He is desperately shaking the mesh of the fence making the noise which has drawn her here, even though Lucie notices that where his fingers grab the railings they seem to melt into the mesh itself. Again he is bare-footed. When he sees her, he stops and stares unflinchingly at her, examining her.

"It's starting again. Can't you feel it?" The lad holds his head in his hands and sways back and forth as if possessed. "But so much bigger this time."

"What do you want with me?" Lucie stutters.

He grabs the fence desperately and presses his face right up against it. "You have to find her."

"Find who?"

"Emma, of course. Emma! Emma!" he screams.

And suddenly, Lucie is gasping for air on her back lying flat out on the lawn with Chloe kneeling beside her trying to ease her back down out of her frantic vision. Chloe's hand strokes Lucie's hair tenderly back out of her eyes. Shocked, Lucie then realises that she is the one who has been screaming for Emma.

Although Chloe at times might appear to be tough as nails, her gentleness now reveals an empathy Lucie had not anticipated. Maybe Chloe at some time experienced severe pain and loss herself, although Lucie can well imagine Chloe would have buried any details deep down and would never let slip their merest existence.

Once Lucie has regained her composure, she knows she has some explaining to do. You can hardly go losing it completely, uttering gibberish and then shouting out your friend's name like a madman without giving some sort of justification, however weak.

So, she tries to cover it all up telling Chloe that she has been suffering from vivid nightmares since waking up in Burnt Ash Lodge and some materialise as vicious daydreams, although she lies brazenly, preferring to keep the content of her visions to herself for the time being.

"It is hardly surprising," Chloe says, amazing but she doesn't seem too perturbed by Lucie's little turn. "Trauma victims often take years to readjust fully and nightmares are a way the brain has of processing all that stuff."

To give Lucie some more time to recover before attempting to get back on her crutches for the return journey to the house, Chloe too lies down on the grass next to Lucie in the warm morning sunshine.

"Chloe, what is going on in the East Wing?"

But if Lucie thought she had broken through to Chloe and that she would now gush out the truth about the East Wing, Lucie was going to be sorely disappointed. Chloe has the knack of being able to play along with Lucie but at the same time reveal little.

The East Wing was where they were testing some biological agents, that much Chloe could confirm, so it was all bio-secure, sure, but that was it. Nothing more sinister. Lucie though, would not be taken in by Chloe's bland explanation. But, of course, she had no grounds for questioning Chloe's version, so she backed off.

Every breakfast, lunch and dinnertime, the ballroom is set up as a make-shift dining room. A couple of long tables are brought in from the store room next door and are laid out end to end, reminding Lucie of some boarding school taken straight from a historical novel or a Harry Potter film, except that here only some of the place settings have chairs and others not, allowing access to those who are in wheelchairs.

Lucie and Captain Phipps are sitting alone at the table discreetly trying to shed some light on what the bio-secure unit could mean. Don has just had some medical intervention and is up in his room recovering. Lieutenant Sykes is on his own as usual up by the fireplace. He eats according to his own timetable, mostly not at all if his meagre and frail frame are anything to go by.

"Did you see anything like that in Lisbon?" Jack asks as he lifts a fork-full of some sort of stew towards his mouth and then hesitates as though something he has just seen, which he is about to put into his mouth, has prompted him to rethink his question, "Anything biology-based? Anything in the lab that could have been bio-secure?"

"Are you suggesting that there could be a connection between my being held here and whatever it is that's going on in the East Wing?"

"Your injuries are too run of the mill to warrant a stay here. The link must be Lisbon."

"Emma was involved in nuclear physics, you know, quantum mechanics and the like. She was never interested in anything biological. Just numbers. In any case, I never saw the inside of the lab proper. Just the solar array around the dome."

Jack tries the stew and shrugs his eyebrows. He really doesn't seem interested in any of the details Lucie is putting out there. If he is a mole, he is either a very accomplished one who blends into his environment perfectly or he is totally inept. Lucie thinks it could well be the latter.

Lucie carefully separates the grisly-looking meat to one side of her plate and picks at just the odd piece of over-cooked potato and carrot.

"Surely I wouldn't be sitting around here with you guys if I had been in contact with some dodgy biological agents in the explosion," Lucie says in a thoroughly disheartened tone.

She gives up on her dinner and puts her fork down neatly next to the knife on her plate.

"It's not real."

Lucie and Jack look up suddenly to see who has intruded on their conversation. The rest of the diners are still engaged in their usual banter. That leaves only Lieutenant Sykes sitting quite close to them, quietly in the corner near the fireplace. But he is so far out of it, they had been talking openly without concern over his overhearing them.

"I'm sorry, Dickie. Did you say something?" Jack asks.

"What did you say?" Lucie asks at almost the same time, both are clearly taken aback.

Then after some seconds, Sykes whispers, without looking up at them, "It's fake. The whole thing. There is nothing bio-secure about that tent, I can guarantee that. It's just to scare people like you away."

Lucie is standing by the window in Kahtri's office, waiting for the doctor to show up. Chloe had barged into the dining-room and had informed her that Kahtri wanted to see her immediately. She wouldn't say what about but it was clear that Chloe was upset. Then Chloe had delivered Lucie into Kahtri's office and had left her there alone.

It's the first time Lucie has been in Kahtri's office on the second floor of Lucie's wing and she has to say it is a joyless, dispiriting room very much in keeping with her opinion of him in general. Lucie spotted the lettering of his name printed on the door as Chloe opened the door to let her in, so she knows this space belongs to him.

Somehow the window fails to capture the light from outside and most of the illumination comes from a single standard lamp in the corner, woefully out of fashion, probably dating back to the 1970s. The gloomy half-light is in stark contrast to all other areas in the facility which are glaringly bright. It is almost as if this room was an oversight, the decorators found it locked the day they came down this corridor and never remembered to come back.

The fake wood-panelled walls add to the old-fashioned moroseness Lucie feels here. They are adorned with framed accolades and a solitary shelf holds several large tomes with suitably psychiatric titles, all there to convince patients of the scientific backing that their sessions hold, a bit like a dentists' waiting room, Lucie supposes, comforting yet there is no escaping the fact that you could be in store for something that is going to hurt. Odd, she notices that amongst the official-looking certificates backing up Kahtri's illustrious education and career, one cites a degree in virology which to Lucie seems strangely out of place in a trauma centre.

Out of the window Lucie can see down onto the car park, which contains a mix of civilian and military vehicles. For the first time in several weeks, it is raining; more a grey drizzle than rain proper. The summer seems to have broken quite suddenly. The drabness seems to infiltrate the building itself, dampening the red brick sheen to a wet mud colour.

Lucie is still trying to get her head around Sykes's assertion that the bio-security on the East Wing is all a sham. Phipps had confirmed that when it came to bio-security, Sykes was your man. He had worked for several years in a chemical weapons facility and if he said the way unprotected personnel are accessing the tent, as Lucie had actually seen herself with Chloe, constituted absolute proof the whole thing was a sham, that was good enough for him and should also be for Lucie.

The question now was why. If it wasn't bio-secure why were a covert military unit pretending it was? And what could they actually be hiding in there with such an elaborate hoax.

"You've been having nightmares," Kahtri says entering the room briskly without so much as a greeting. Lucie understands that Chloe has an obligation to report that sort of thing to her superior officer but it still hurts that the trust they seem to have built clearly only goes so far.

"More like I haven't stopped having nightmares," Lucie replies moving around to her chair and sitting down, placing her crutches against the desk under the disapproving gaze of the doctor. "Actually, my entire existence here is pretty much a living nightmare."

Kahtri asks her to go over her most recent event in detail. Lucie gives a traditional, if somewhat cliched, version of her nightmare: Lucie searching desperately for Emma; Lucie in amongst piles of rubble in the blast in Lisbon; lots of Lucie lost and wandering; she even goes as far as to say she was screaming Emma's name over and over. Kahtri is unimpressed and he writes nothing in his notepad.

"You take me for a fool," he says sharply. This is a more aggressive line of attack than usual, thinks Lucie.

"Oh, give me a break!" Lucie can play tough, too. "What is this place? There's a three-metre-high double perimeter fence and armed guards all over the shop. All very reassuring but not a run-of-the-mill medical centre, is it? What is going on in the East Wing?"

"Listen to me, Lucie." Kahtri snaps into a different persona at her mention of the East Wing. "You were lucky to get out of Lisbon with your life. Luckier than you think. Here we are keeping you safe and you should be grateful. You are still very much at risk. They may come after you. Maybe even here…"

"Come after me? Who? Why would anyone come after me? I did nothing."

"…and you will stay as long as we deem necessary and under whatever conditions we see fit. Get it?"

"*We*? Who the hell are *we*?"

Kahtri is again scratching with his pencil in his notebook. Her mentioning the East Wing seems to have sparked a flurry of activity on the note-taking front but he makes no attempt to answer her question.

"So that's it, is it?" Lucie says with a sneer.

Kahtri looks up and snarls at her, "The quicker you start to cooperate, the quicker we will be able to let you go."

"There's that *we* again."

Kahtri rises from his desk and leans right forward his face only inches from Lucie's. "Your cheap flippancy is starting to really annoy me, and I warn you. Get on side, Lucie, or things could…no, will get much more complicated for you. This is your final chance." He walks out of the office slamming the door. Chloe comes in immediately, obviously she has been right outside all the time.

"He's a bit tetchy this afternoon," Lucie jokes.

Chloe stands silhouetted in the window so Lucie has difficulty discerning her facial expressions.

"What happened?"

"I asked him about the East Wing."

"Oh, Jesus Christ!" This is the first time Lucie has heard Chloe swear. "I told you not to mention that…That's really blown it."

"Listen Chloe, I know that all that bio-secure stuff is fake, a facade."

Chloe slumps down in Kahtri's chair. Something seems to have cracked inside her. She takes her head in her hands.

"I'm sorry, Chloe. Really I am. But I need to know why I am being held here."

"This has all got out of control," Chloe says to herself.

"It's all connected, isn't it? The East Wing, my being brought here."

Chloe looks up at Lucie, "You have to be careful, Lucie. Kahtri is far more dangerous than you can imagine."

"So, level with me. Give me a chance at least."

Chloe stares out of the window, indecision twisting her face into an agonised frown. Lucie knows she needs Chloe's support if she is going to make sense of her own involvement in this tangle of intrigue.

Lucie plays a hunch, "It's not a biological agent you want to stop getting out of there, is it? You've got someone else in there."

Chloe says nothing.

"You have, haven't you?"

Chloe takes a look around Kahtri's office, as if weighing up in her mind if it really is worth it.

"For the last eighteen months…" Chloe has reached her tipping point. Lucie holds her breath, willing Chloe to go on. "There was a car accident. Mason O'Keefe—that is his name—he was badly hurt."

Suddenly, Chloe hunts around in the files behind Kahtri's desk, flicking through them until she finds what she was looking for.

"Here…" she throws an MRI scan on the desk, swivelling it around for Lucie to see. It is a meaningless mass of colours within the rough shape of what could be a head. Chloe points to a maze of cobwebbed lines linking the two larger areas of colours.

"The local doctors saw this and it spiralled up to us here pretty quickly. No-one had ever come across anything like this before. Our right and left hemispheres of the brain are separate entities while clearly still part of a single structure, but this entanglement between the two halves is unique. So much so, Kahtri considers it is not human. Do you understand? Not human in origin."

"So, you've got him here?"

"They decided to keep Mason isolated until his condition could be analysed, to see if it was safe for him to come into contract with the wider population."

"So, what do I have to do with any of this? Do you think my brain is the same?"

"No, no. Your MRI was completely normal." Chloe takes a breather. "But we have real time implants in his head and Mason's brain activity shot up, off the scale, at the exact time of the Lisbon bombing."

"I have to see Mason. Now!"

This time, Lucie couldn't complain about Chloe not laying it all out there. She must have broken all the military disclosure rules, jeopardising potentially her entire career. And then to agree to Lucie's request for her to see this Mason was massive. However, when Lucie thought back on it later, she never could say for sure if Chloe had been playing her all the time she was at Burnt Ash Lodge.

Chloe's sudden disclosure of Mason's existence had seemed just that bit too gratuitous, too easy. Chloe is clever, without doubt. She keeps out of the limelight. She doesn't need to voice her opinions. In fact, it ends up being impossible to know what her own voice actually sounds like. She seems to glide effortlessly above the day to day routines as though she is on some other plane.

But to say she is not aware of precisely what is going on around her would be a gross misjudgement; and Lucie had to recognise that it could just as easily be that Chloe had skilfully manipulated Lucie into thinking she was the one taking all the key decisions when Chloe herself could in fact be steering a vastly different, hidden agenda.

Once all the day shift civilian staff have departed from Burnt Ash Lodge and the patients all retired for the night, Chloe opens Lucie's door, checks up and down the corridor, as always and then silently beckons Lucie to follow her. They head down through the kitchens and at the end of a short underground tunnel, Chloe presents her pass card to a wall-mounted security reader and the lock on an unmarked door opens with a soft thunk. They carry on down a similar length tunnel on the other side into the East Wing, then climb an old wide wooden staircase up to the first floor.

Once through yet another security door, Lucie crosses the threshold and enters a huge room with a tall vaulted ceiling. It must be easily thirty paces long, almost the entire first floor of the wing. Near the door, to one side, piles of cardboard boxes almost completely hide a computer workstation. The room has in the distant past undoubtedly been the library, with an upstairs gallery running along both sides with alcoves filled with empty shelves where books once lay. There is remarkably little furniture, all located down the far end, the basic minimum of a table with a couple of dining chairs and a single armchair near the unused massive open Victorian fireplace.

There is a door at the end, next to the fireplace which leads off possibly to another room from which the exact same boy from Lucie's nightmares now emerges. Lucie is unsure for a second if this is perhaps another vision but Chloe is here with her and she evidently can also see the boy. He is bare-foot as in her earlier visions and he is wearing the same clothes which hang loosely from his skeletal frame. His shirt is unbuttoned and allows Lucie to see his hairless pale chest, making him look even younger than in her visions.

They stand observing each other incredulously, hardly daring to breathe. Lucie cannot comprehend how she could have seen this boy in her mind and now he is here, larger than life. It is totally impossible.

"Lucie, this is Mason." Chloe introduces them.

"Technically speaking, we have met already," Lucie says, aware of how absurd that sounds.

"You are Emma's friend," Mason pronounces each word slowly and deliberately.

"How do you know Emma? This is madness, Chloe. How does he know Emma?"

Lucie approaches Mason and stands just a couple of paces away from him, examining him. His eyes are a sparkling bluish-grey and his stare cuts right into her mind. He constantly fidgets with a gold chain around his wrist from which hangs a tiny gold amulet.

Lucie takes a deep breath, remembering just what a torment this young man has faced over the past year and a half. She asks calmly, "Who are you, Mason? What is going on here?"

Lucie senses the same energy bubbling up within her as when she had previously encountered Mason in her visions, the same urgency and anticipation. It is as though Mason has slipped inside her head, as if he were physically participating in the process of generating her thoughts.

Counterintuitively, it does not feel threatening at all, on the contrary, it is a liberating experience, there is a vibrancy to her mental agility which enthrals her, while at the same time terrifies her.

"You were there, weren't you…?" Mason says, "I felt you there."

"He means in Lisbon," Chloe clarifies. "The explosion."

"That was when it started…" Mason seems to be shivering, affected by some external force, "when I first saw you."

Then Lucie remembers suddenly the distortion, the twisted fractured colours expanding and passing directly through her body in the few seconds before the explosion. She swears she can feel the breeze rolling in off Loch Doon and she knows that Mason, standing right next to her is also experiencing it, through her.

"This is crazy," Lucie says.

Suddenly, Mason breaks away and turns to Chloe. "Is Kahtri going to lock her up here too? He could do a job on her as well. Kill her off, have a funeral. Emma could be there crying her eyes out. So touching."

Lucie can feel a bitter resentment surging inside Mason, verging on the insane.

"You know that's what he did with me. They can't let me go…ever…because out there, I'm dead!"

"Is that true, Chloe?" But Lucie knows it must be. Chloe frowns but makes no attempt to deny it.

"Eighteen months and twenty-six days, to be precise. In that sort of time, you can really do some thinking. You get less for murder, you know. And what did I do to deserve this? Nothing, Human rights? Shit. Means nothing here. Justice? They couldn't give a fuck about justice."

"I've seen the MRI," Lucie says firmly. "How do you explain that?"

"I don't really have much of an idea…Kahtri and his crew of stooges have been doing tests non-stop for ages. Ask them. But they don't really know anything either, or am I wrong, Chloe?"

"Well," Chloe starts but can't finish because Mason ignores her response.

"The question is what can I do that other people can't, I reckon. So far as the scientists go, not much. I have always known that I had something, though. An ability to read people, maybe. To understand their motivations. Like you, Lucie, I have moments when I can see the world in a different way to everyone else."

Lucie feels that he has included her with a specific reason in mind, but she just cannot understand what that reason is. Whatever it is, it makes Lucie feel warm inside and she is very happy to go along with it; somehow everything he says is perfectly in tune with her own thoughts.

Mason continues, "You should get away from here, Lucie. This place is dangerous. It is run by a bunch of fanatics."

"It's military, isn't it?" Lucie looks to Chloe for confirmation.

"That's what they say…Look," Mason runs almost the length of the room to the desk with the computer, and he starts looking amongst the papers there.

"Thanks to Chloe, I got access to a computer. I can't communicate with the outside world but I can at least see what is going on…Shit, I wasn't expecting all of this to be going down today! Where the hell is it?"

Mason seems to have accepted Lucie right off the bat, and Chloe too, for that matter. It's like he has the gift of knowing who he can trust without having to go through the whole process of building a friendship first. It is like instant admission. Like he has tapped into her psyche and at the same time has left some imprint behind as Lucie immediately feels she too can trust this young, wild kid.

"What are you looking for?" asks Chloe.

Lucie can see piles of website printouts, maps, typed sheets, hard copy emails with random handwritten scribbled notes on post-its dotted all around. Not an inch of the surface of the desk is visible. It's no surprise to her that he can't find anything. But this unintelligible collage shows Lucie that Mason has not been idle in his lockdown. Who knows what he may have uncovered.

"Here!" Mason grabs a computer printout.

"This is an email from Kahtri to his bosses about Alves. You know Alves, I believe, Lucie."

"How the hell did you get hold of that?" Chloe is shocked. But Mason now has eyes only for Lucie.

"This shower have been targeting Alves for months, trying to figure out what he is up to. This email proves it. But they are blind. You saw the lab. You saw the wave. A terrorist attack? Come on! Here, take a look at these."

Mason grabs a couple of photos from under a half empty coffee mug.

Lucie is stunned to find she is looking at two photos of herself, one outside Emma's Santa Rosita residence in Lisbon and the other in the park near the Bisset Science Institute.

"Where did you get all this, Mason?" Chloe's concern is evident but Mason again ignores her.

"Intriguing that the *military* as you put it, has been keeping tabs on you since before the explosion, don't you think?"

"Who took those photos?" Lucie demands.

"Who cares? The fact is that they had you under surveillance."

"What are you trying to say?" Lucie tries to calm the overexcited Mason down and herself at the same time.

Mason has an energy which is contagious. He is totally hyped, trying to pass on all the information he has been gathering over so many months. Lucie can understand this.

After she ran from Carsphairn Hall, she had struggled to find anyone she could trust, apart from Emma, of course. And when finally she did, she bled out her whole life story to him in one long burst, poor guy.

"There is some other organisation running this show, I swear. This is not official. It's way off limits. Covert. Serious power."

"OK, Mason," Dr Kahtri has entered the room and is accompanied by the armed guard Lucie had seen outside the tent, this time with a pistol in his hand. "That is quite enough."

"Oh amazing, that is all we need," Mason says striding towards Kahtri. "The bloody organ grinder himself, his fucking Lordship."

"That is close enough!" Kahtri's words cause the guard to raise his gun, pointing it straight at Mason, who clearly understands the situation well enough and stops abruptly four or five paces from Kahtri.

Lucie knows Mason feels no anger towards Chloe but she can feel a violent aggression towards Kahtri growing steadily, intensifying but so far still hidden behind his calm and even serene looking exterior. She can also sense a profound inner confusion at what is happening to him, an internal struggle which is tearing down any moral code he may have once had.

"Chloe!" Kahtri is almost shouting, clearly extremely agitated. "Go back to your quarters. I'll deal with your insubordination in due course. You are finished here."

"Dr Kahtri..." Chloe stages a half-hearted defence but is cut down by Kahtri's barked command.

"You are dismissed!"

"Don't take it out on Chloe, this is all my doing," Lucie says. "I insisted on seeing Mason."

But Chloe is already marching head held high out of the door at the far end of the hall and down the staircase, her future in tatters.

Kahtri slowly walks up to the table and says, "All *your* doing? Well, Lucie, you've really overstepped the line. What *do* you think you are playing at?"

"You could have told me the truth! You lied about Emma."

It is then that Lucie realises that Mason is on the verge of being consumed by his rage. He is about to do something extraordinarily risky and dangerous like a bow being drawn tighter and tighter, ever closer to its inevitable violent release. She has no idea what it is that he is going to do but she knows too that she also has some role to play in it.

Could Mason have been influencing her actions? If he was, it was with no external communication, he hadn't so much as looked in her direction. She never could say if she acted of her own volition, but certainly at the time, she was a hundred percent eager to help Mason out in absolutely whatever he had in mind.

Lucie breaks away from Kahtri and takes a few steps on her crutches towards the door, looking after Chloe, but also bringing her to within a couple of paces of the guard.

It is as if they had worked it all out beforehand; some choreographed routine as though they had rehearsed it thousands of times. Mason quickly advances on Kahtri. Suddenly, out of nowhere, he has some sort of weapon in his hand.

The guard raises his gun at the same time as Lucie lunges forward and swings one crutch up at his gun-hand. A loud crack sounds around the room as the gun fires and the bullet hits the ceiling causing a cloud of splinters to fall slowly to the floor from the beam it struck. By the time the guard has reacted to Lucie's surprise intervention, the dynamics of the situation have changed dramatically.

Mason has grabbed Kahtri around the forehead with one arm and in the other hand he pushes into Kahtri's exposed neck a homemade knife: a long sliver of glass from a broken mirror which is wound with string and cloth at one end forming a rudimentary handle of sorts. It has cut Kahtri's skin, a small surface wound raising a line of beads of blood but Mason holds back from inflicting any greater harm on Kahtri.

The guard now has his gun levelled again at Mason but Kahtri is clearly being held deliberately in his line of fire.

"Tell your man to lose the gun or I slam this home," shouts Mason for all to hear.

"Oh Jesus, you've cut me, my throat!" Kahtri whimpers.

"On the verge of it, I'd say, if you don't get Brains here, to get rid of the gun…"

"Do as he says," Kahtri mutters in terrified defeat.

"I wouldn't recommend that," says the guard, taking a distinctly hostile step forward. "He is not going to do it, or he's dead."

"I am *already* dead!" screams Mason.

"I am ordering you to put the gun down. It is not a frigging request!" shouts Kahtri.

Slowly the guard lowers the gun with a disappointed look on his face and stoops to place it on the floor in front of him. Lucie hobbles forward and picks it up off the floor. Then as gingerly as she can she approaches the guard and rips the security passkey from around his neck and moves to Kahtri and does the same and finally steps back and stands calmly next to the fireplace.

"Both of you, in the back room, quickly." Mason now clearly has the upper hand. The guard and then Mason with Kahtri still in a headlock and the knife pressing into his neck shuffle through the doorway into the room by the fireplace. Mason then releases Kahtri pushing him deeper into the room and steps back slamming the door shut, as Lucie presses Kahtri's passkey to the card reader locking it with a clunk.

It must have been at the precise moment Mason released Kahtri and she locked the door that Mason had slipped the tiny folded piece of paper unnoticed into her pocket. That was the only time they came even close to any physical contact. Amazing to think that at such an intense moment, Mason was capable of such a skillful sleight of hand. He was fully in control while she had no inkling of what he was up to. She would not find his note for a further five hours.

They both knew they had only seconds before a whole platoon of military personnel would arrive after hearing a gunshot. Lucie gave Mason Kahtri's keycard as they had rushed as quickly as Lucie could manage down the staircase outside Mason's room and had split up without so much as a farewell. Lucie handed the gun towards Mason but he raised a palm refusing it. She was more than happy to keep it although what good it would do her having it was less clear.

Mason disappeared into the night and Lucie made her way back to the trauma wing through the tunnel that she and Chloe had used earlier. Lucie still had her keycard which thankfully worked on all the intervening doors. As she distanced herself from Mason, her sense of a plan also seemed to fade, however. While she had been with him, everything seemed so clear cut but now as she enters the darkened ballroom, she is growing less sure of what her next move should be.

Lucie hears the frightening crackle of automatic gunfire somewhere outside the building. A deep shadow passes over her heart; Mason may be in trouble. She should have insisted he take the gun. What on earth is she doing wandering around with a gun in her hand? It is beyond surreal. Her certainty and clarity of thought have dissipated completely and have been replaced with doubt and anxiety. She carefully feels her way across to the double glass doors that lead out onto the terrace. More gunfire.

Then suddenly a hand grabs her from behind her in the darkness, slipping the gun effortlessly from her grasp, while covering her mouth and stifling any chance of her calling out for help. She immediately recalls Kahtri in his office just hours ago stressing that she may not be safe at Burnt Ash Lodge and that those behind the explosion may come after her, even here. The person now holding her could have followed her from Lisbon and be about to finish the job.

"Don't make a noise," whispers her assailant. Not that she could have done in any case but then she realises that two guards are about to pass the entrance to the ballroom across the terrace and she is immediately more complicit with her capturer's wishes. The guards are however in a hurry and rush past the point where Lucie is being held and disappear quickly in the direction of the East Wing.

Lucie can feel the wool of the balaclava the intruder is wearing. He could have shot her dead by now had he wanted to. But she is still alive.

"Hey, Lucie. It's me," he says in a hushed tone, releasing his hand from over her mouth.

"Zac?" Lucie is amazed, recognising his voice. She asks in as quiet a voice as she can. "Is that really you? I thought you were dead."

"You're disappointed!"

"Sure am!"

"Look, we have to get out of here sharpish."

"You got a plan? One better than in Lisbon preferably," Lucie asks hopefully.

"Well, it is still a work in progress but right now we don't have much choice but to run with it," Zac says while he puts Lucie's gun into an inside pocket in his flak jacket. He has no intention of returning it to her. Probably for the best, she thinks.

As they emerge into the open through the ballroom doors, it seems all the guards have headed out to cover the situation in the East Wing, leaving the way clear for Zac and Lucie. They are much more likely in the circumstances to put all their effort into recapturing Mason rather than Lucie who is still on crutches and is much less of a threat given her lack of knowledge of what has been going on here. They edge carefully around the terrace keeping their backs to the walls of the house.

Lucie decides she is going to have a much better shot at this without the complications of the crutches, so she dumps them behind some bushes as they cross the gravel driveway and plunge into the woods on the opposite side of the house to the East Wing. It is more difficult here for Lucie. Zac sees she is limping badly, throws his arm around her and provides as much support as he can. Then they turn down and away from the road near the edge of the lawn a few yards back into the trees.

Quickly they descend beyond the lower reaches of the garden and they are swallowed up by the banks of early morning mist. This allows them to relax their pace a little.

"How did you find me, Zac?" Lucie has been dying to ask, trying to square her image of Zac with the balaclava and the military scale operation he seems to have engineered to break her out of Burnt Ash Lodge. She has also been wondering just who the photographer could have been that had taken those pictures of her in Lisbon which Mason had shown her.

"You have been really well hidden away here. It has taken me weeks, but I knew you couldn't be dead because the newspapers were painting you as a prime terrorist suspect. As you know, I can be remarkably tenacious…and here I am."

"You seem to have learnt a heck of a lot about detective work since I saw you in Lisbon," Lucie smiles to herself but she feels somehow unsure of what is going on, of how much her trust in Zac has been undermined since he abandoned her in the lab.

They reach the fence and follow it round further down the hill.

"I crashed a part of their electric fence. They won't even be aware they have lost power down here yet. You can touch it anywhere you like on this lower section."

"I'll take your word on that if you don't mind," says Lucie. It all seems a bit too good to be true.

A bit further on they come to the place Zac has cut through the fence, hidden behind some tall bushes and ferns, ironically very close to where she had experienced her vision of Mason just that morning. They crawl through the gap, rush over the no-man's land and dip under the fence on the far side. Lucie is free.

XI
The Rise of Alves

Lisbon—2006

Alves resists the temptation to close his eyes. Somehow, he knows he shouldn't shy away from witnessing any of this however distressing it may be. He looks across at Bisset slumped up against the wall directly in front of him, his shirt collar loosened, his head back, his face racked in pain, his mouth gasping unsuccessfully for air, his left hand gripping white-knuckled onto Alves's own forearm.

Alves never once even considers withdrawing from Bisset's desperate cold sweat-laced grip. He would not abandon his mentor of so many years—more than that—his friend, as he embarked on this final journey. At that same moment though he becomes aware that something truly exceptional is happening to him. It is as though he is glimpsing for the first time some previously hidden world, his mind coming alive, veering off in radical, fresh and exciting directions.

And then he experiences something totally beyond the realm of his comprehension: he sees rain falling through the iron bars of a prison cell window; he hears a seagull squawk; the distraught face of a woman he has no recollection of glares at him in utter disgust; an excruciating emptiness at her loss freezes his heart. Instinct tells him he must be losing his mind but he knows that is not the case.

That confused rush of images lasts only a matter of seconds though before a new set of thought patterns establishes a foothold and instils an understanding and an acceptance that there is nothing to be concerned about here, that these are all just the natural real-life experiences and emotions from Bisset's past now being channelled into his own memory banks. Alves is breathless, he feels a strange out-of-body elatedness, a giddy sense of anticipation, brimming with unimaginable potential. And from then on, the deluge of data and information gathers pace steadily.

For a time, he is aware of the thoughts of both his old and his new self, co-existing alongside one another. Then as he slowly recovers perspective and control, with any last vestiges of confusion now fading, pitilessly Alves retrains his focus, settling ever more comfortably within this new identity while progressively peeling away and cutting back the links to Bisset's now redundant body lying strewn before him.

Once it is over Alves feels so vibrant and alive, so young. Irvine Bisset had been in his mid-seventies and to surface into a man less than half that age is indescribably exhilarating, like having another chance at life itself, like turning back the hands of time.

He reaches instinctively towards the desk behind him for his glasses at the very moment he realises his eyesight is no longer impaired by age. His heart, though, in spite of its relative youthfulness, will still require several minutes longer to calm down after sharing momentarily the agonised panic suffered by Bisset, his eyes now wide open in a deathly unfocused stare.

Alves only found out three months afterwards that Castro had witnessed the whole scene on the guardroom CCTV screens. Alves had seen Castro leave the Science Institute laboratory just a couple of minutes earlier but it turned out he had forgotten his pass card. So Castro had dropped into the security office to pick up a temporary one before leaving the building.

The room was only manned continuously outside of normal working hours but everyone knew that a couple of spare passes hung on the coat hook behind the door. The wall of screens fed by all the CCTV cameras on the site would have been on, as always. Castro must have seen Bisset grab his chest in pain and crumple to the lab floor. He would then have seen Alves kneel beside him, urgently loosening his tie and unbuttoning his shirt collar and a single flick of a switch would have opened the audio feed from the lab mic.

"What's wrong, Irvine? Just stay put for a second while I call the paramedics, OK?"

"No…No…" Irvine manages to say, grabbing Alves's arm tightly above the wrist.

Surely anyone with an ounce of humanity at that point would have rushed back into the lab or at the very least would have picked up the fixed line phone right there on the desk and called for the emergency services himself; but that's Castro for you.

Perhaps he was in shock, or he could initially have underestimated the gravity of what he was seeing—hard to believe, Castro is far too tough and calculating for that. Or maybe he thought he could learn something, overhear some snippet of conversation not intended for his ears which might prove valuable somewhere down the line—much more likely. Whatever the motivation, he did nothing.

Castro wouldn't have known that Irvine's hands were by this time already covered in the powerful almost hallucinogenic secretion not dissimilar to an ultrafast-acting scopolamine needed to smooth acceptance of the transfer surfacing. It entered Alves's bloodstream through the pores and hair follicles on his forearm causing an almost instant sense of acceptance of whatever Irvine wished to propose.

Bisset struggles to speak. He swallows shallow gulps of air.

"You have to see this through now."

"See what through?"

But Bisset does not elucidate further.

"I am afraid," are Bisset's last words as he recognises the cascading loss of his last memories feeding across the connection to Alves like the sand slipping unstoppably through an hour glass revealing in its stead the void of his now rapidly approaching and inevitable death. And still Castro does nothing.

Alves though feels the precise opposite to Bisset; his mind is shifting up a gear. Bisset had been fortunate enough to possess a truly privileged intellect but now, the myriads of electronic data pulses firing across the entire structure of his brain are being processed more clinically, more efficiently than ever.

Alves knows there is something more going down here, some unexpected natural process of selection which has filtered and kept back some of the superior routines from his own neural architecture, encouraging them to gel with those passed down from his previous selves all the way back to Duncan giving him a ferocious clarity he has never experienced before. This is unique, this is special.

Alves gathers himself, takes several deep breaths and gets to his feet. He steps backwards hesitantly until he bumps into the edge of his workstation not taking his eyes off Irvine Bisset for even a second. Alves picks up the fixed line and dials.

"Alves here. Get the paramedics down to the lab as quickly as possible. Professor Bisset has had a heart attack."

His enhanced mental procedures while undoubtedly more dispassionate and more accurate, could in no way prepare him for the avalanche of conflicting emotional responses flooding into his mind; over one hundred and forty years of often violently irreconcilable desires, impressions, beliefs, instincts. Duncan's undying passion for Jules, Gryphon's muddled and even quixotic but nonetheless heartfelt grief at her leaving for Australia, Bisset's stoical solitude, Alves with his glibness and his banter seemed hollow and insincere by comparison but that would be the only way he could deal with all that inconsistency.

Each personality added its own unique subconscious identity into the mix. Initially Alves struggled to cope with all the contradictions, and he even started to think that a tipping point must have been reached, but eventually he began to reallocate the different emotional strands throughout his psyche and he found or more accurately refound the core of his own personality, which in the end seemed capable of somehow keeping all that chaos at bay.

Alves sits calmly on the edge of his desk. Broadly speaking, at least in terms of how it affects his conscious thought matrices, the realignment is now complete although a host of minor adjustments are still going on in the background. The entire process of surfacing into Alves has taken a little under fifteen minutes.

Once the paramedics arrive, amid the confusion and the shouts of 'Clear' followed by the defibrillator smacking into Irvine Bisset's lifeless body, Alves recognises the stunning legacy and contribution of his erstwhile master and guru.

Just before the First World War broke out in 1914, Gryphon had surfaced into a German by the name of Klauss Hoffman, a reasonably competent physicist from Leipzig who kept things ticking over—although little more than that, it must be said—in the early and mid-twentieth century. But it was Irvine Bisset who really drove the acceleration which Alves has now inherited. He was a quiet, unassuming Frenchman who sought no accolade or recognition.

Neither did he possess some magical gift which miraculously placed all that technological knowhow at his fingertips, rather he knew where the destination should be and successfully stimulated others to deliver the route map to get there. He was a genius at suggestion and propositioning and, like Duncan himself, Bisset offered a combination of business acumen and scientific entrepreneurialism.

He found Portugal the ideal base, under the radar but sufficiently well connected, and from the end of the Cold War through to his death in 2006, Bisset laid the groundwork for his most important developments: from string theory to electromagnetic propulsion, from ultra vision optics to quantum computing, all vital to the progress towards the time mesh project.

But Bisset's accomplishments didn't end there; he also had an uncanny knack of spotting young and budding artists, recognising and nurturing new talent just ahead of their breaking through to widespread critical acclaim. So, amazingly both endeavours, art as well as science, proved to be exceptionally lucrative and he amassed one of the country's largest fortunes of that era with which he founded the Bisset Science, Art and Technology Institute in Lisbon, a charitable foundation primarily focused on supporting innovative scientific research, but which at the same time, housed and generously permitted the public to view his formidable modern art collection.

Alves feels humbled and more than a little insecure in his own ability to match these astonishing achievements. To others he always appears the most self-confident of individuals and he is competitive and ambitious, sure, but where Duncan and Bisset believed totally in their own capabilities, Alves can only hope that he will grow into that same level of competence and success. In awe, he realises that such are the advancements his predecessors have made that the honour of completing the project could even fall to him.

And only then as a calm descends on the lab, when it is already clear that Bisset is not going to respond to the emergency resuscitation measures, does Castro choose to make his grand entrance into the lab. He begs the paramedics not to abandon their efforts. Alves is totally enthralled by Castro's riveting performance; his tormented anguish at the loss of his friend is really quite convincing, touching almost.

"I am calling his death at 13:12," declares the lead paramedic, looking at his watch.

"He's gone," Alves says, stepping in and grappling with Castro to stop him from trying to resuscitate Bisset himself.

"Get your hands off me, Alves," Castro snaps at Alves bitterly, breaking free from Alves's grasp. He backs away, with a grimace of anguished despair on his face, but at least now seeming to accept that nothing more can be done for Bisset.

The fact that Castro and Alves do not exactly see eye to eye is hardly new, nor do either of them try to keep it from the rest of the team. No-one coming into contact with them would doubt they are both brilliant in their own way but are quite literally poles apart in terms of how their minds work: Castro always focused on calculated, mathematical probabilities, trying to block out irrelevant digressions; Alves the risk-taker, flirting with the exact opposite, unpredictability, juggling multiple potential outcomes before determining which strategy to adopt.

Castro, is cagey, quick to temper, with the bite of a shark when crossed, while Alves appears at all times comfortable in his own skin, affable and relaxed with a sharp but inclusive sense of humour. Until this moment, the animosity between the two had not proven to be an excessive constraint in their working relationship as broadly speaking their areas of expertise did not overlap that much: science, the exclusive terrain of Castro; with business, finance, logistics and art left to Alves. Any conflicts which did erupt would be quickly mediated and ultimately decided by Bisset. But with Bisset gone, a whole new dynamic would have to be determined.

From Bisset's own minutely detailed memories, Alves quickly pieces together a fairly extensive understanding of Castro and of what drives him.

Fernando Castro came from the humblest of beginnings and as a result in his formative years he never could tolerate privilege or, more to the point, the abuse of it. Curious and ironic given where his morality would ultimately end up. His parents had eloped together in their early seventies when they realised that they had no prospect of work in their rural farming community in a small village outside Covilhã in the foothills of the Serra da Estrela mountain range in north-eastern Portugal.

Like so many others at that time, they headed for the city, to Lisbon. Even though optimism was high in the capital following the Carnation Revolution in the spring of 1974, the reality was that life was extremely hard. When their scant resources were exhausted, they were left with no option other than moving into a derelict shack in a shanty town built into the railway embankment just feet from the mainline track running out of the city, where Castro was born at the end of that year.

He had only vague recollections of his father who disappeared suddenly when he was just five years old; something the boy had never understood nor forgiven. His mother remarried a year later and Castro always suspected that it was out of desperation rather than any emotional connection. Castro never accepted his stepfather and grew to despise him but he had to admit that the marriage did allow them to step up into something close to stability and gave Castro access to education.

He was exceptionally gifted and he studied assiduously, aware that this represented his best chance at providing a better life for his mother. It, therefore, came as a huge shock to Castro, changed his whole outlook on life radically, when she died of cancer in the very year he won a full scholarship to Lisbon University.

He was noticed by Irvine Bisset when he was still a physics undergraduate only a year or so after the inauguration of the Science Institute. In fact, it would be fair to say that Irvine groomed him from the outset, aware that he would have a key role to play in the future. He provided him with traineeships and grants, eventually taking him on full time as an assistant the moment he graduated. Castro even studied for his doctorate under Bisset's personal tutelage.

His stellar rise through the ranks at the Science Institute only heightened the sense of injustice he felt at his mother's cruel sacrifice, and with the motivation for his endeavour gone, he became more and more egocentric. His belief in meritocracy faded and he became increasingly impressed by the power of the individual to influence his or her own environment and that of those around them. This led to his adopting a more practical, and ultimately a more corrupt ideology where achieving the desired result, come what may, far outweighed the talent and endeavour required to deliver it. He became obsessed by power, control and the greatest enabler of both—wealth.

Irvine Bisset's funeral was a typical Portuguese Catholic ceremony even though he had been neither Portuguese nor Catholic, his casket cemented into a modest niche in a wall of tombs in one of the humblest parts of the Prazeres cemetery with just his name carved into the end-stone to identify it. Once the formalities have concluded and the few mourners who attended have dispersed, Alves and Castro stroll back towards the car park down a path hugging the interior wall of the cemetery lined on both sides with much more extravagant mausoleums, directly behind a row of tall cypress pines casting the last remnants of any late morning shade.

The heat is asphyxiating, the sky indigo blue, birdsong surrounds them, the city excluded miraculously from this tranquil setting. They can see why Bisset insisted on being laid to rest here: the peace, the view down the Alcantara valley to the Tagus river flowing out towards the Atlantic and to be in the company of so many of Portugal's greatest poets, writers, artists and musicians would sit perfectly with Bisset.

"We need to move now or we risk losing control of the Institute."

Alves is keen to set his stamp of authority on proceedings, even at this early stage.

"Yeah, right." Castro seems unwilling to engage, distracted.

"If we play our cards right, nothing needs to change."

"Come on, Alves. You know how things work here. It'll be another stitch-up and we'll end up having to bow and scrape to some political appointee who knows nothing. I don't want to hang around for that. Do you? That is all I am saying."

"Seriously? Where else would you get the independence you enjoy now?" Alves sounds a bit too desperate, he fears. He also cannot rule out that Castro is playing with him. He decides to take the opportunity to stress his commitment to the project.

"Irvine was clear as to the direction things should go. We must carry on. That is what he would have wanted."

"What are you going on about? All of that ends here. We still have our agreement, right?"

This throws Alves completely off balance. The wiping of his own memories in order to allow the rehousing of Bisset's and all the amassed earlier experiences from his other prior selves in their place means Alves now has absolutely no recollection of this so-called *agreement,* something Castro and Alves had evidently come up with behind Bisset's back. Alves feels exposed and vulnerable. He looks evasively down at his feet and says nothing, uncertain how to proceed.

Then Castro raises the stakes, "What happened between you and Bisset before the paramedics arrived?"

Alves stops and stares at Castro. So much time had already passed since the incident, and up to now there hadn't been a single word spoken about it between the two, that the poignancy of this sudden question is elevated dramatically.

"He had a heart attack; I tried to help him."

"You took rather a long time to ring for assistance," Castro states bluntly, with an edge of sarcasm in his voice.

"Precisely what are you getting at?"

But Castro shrugs dismissively and walks off. Alves lets him go. Castro's attitude resonates so violently against Alves that it sets off a shudder of realisation which grows and grows in intensity and then like a mirror shattering reveals a totally unseen and unimagined world behind it; Bisset had all along preferred Castro. Alves even has to lean against one of the mausoleums for support as the implications of this sudden realisation sink in. Bisset had always considered that his natural successor should have been the science-based Castro with the streetwise Alves merely providing the support.

But what is, if possible, even more disturbing, is that it is as though Bisset's own subconscious psyche has been deliberately concealing this thought from him and only now that Alves has seen Castro in a specific light, has witnessed the disdain Castro has demonstrated towards him personally, has he finally managed to remove the veneer of fog that has been blinding him to the fact that it was only Bisset's unexpected heart attack which had pushed things dramatically down this unintended and unforeseen route, almost like there is some reluctance to admit to Alves that he was not, and was never going to be more than a backup candidate, part of some hastily concocted contingency plan.

Where does this leave Alves? He sits down on a bench in the shade and tries to regroup. Doubting whether you can fully trust your own mind to level with you is devastating for Alves. That really is a type of madness, like he is schizophrenic. Gryphon had always thought there would be potentially damaging consequences from the uncontrolled passing down of subconscious emotions and this is perhaps the starkest evidence of that yet.

He painstakingly reviews the minutiae of Bisset's recollections of all things related to Alves himself in an attempt to throw light on any other potential ugly revelations that may be lurking unnoticed in the inner recesses of his mind.

Alves's father was an American from the East Coast rust belt where he worked as a blast furnace engineer in a steel plant just outside of Pittsburgh. His mother was a Brazilian, considered exotic by all who knew her but at heart she was more than happy to play the role of a typical suburban housewife. One of the reasons Castro had never trusted Alves is that he considers Alves benefited from a privileged upbringing but while he had certainly not risen out of the extremes of poverty Castro had endured, the reality of Alves's background was far less affluent than Castro imagined. They were comfortably off but no more than that.

Alves never got on with his father, who had a fierce temper of which he made abundant use in punishing Alves with little or no justification. His aggression towards his son was unfathomable to Alves and as he grew older so the violence became more physical and Alves felt forced to strike back and to retake control of his life. At sixteen, he forged the signature of his father on a cheque, stealing enough money—but no more—to buy a one-way ticket to Los Angeles and he dropped out of sight to all except his mother to whom he never stopped writing although he was always careful to hide his current location, lest his father come after him.

He then adopted a new identity, using the maiden name of his mother, and from that moment on he was always known simply as Alves. He spent four years back-packing around the world with no safety-net to fall back on. But he had the knack of always being able to turn a crisis into an opportunity and he never wanted for anything, far from it.

Alves was in no way academically brilliant like Castro but he did spend two of those years in Singapore studying with a computer genius and a further year completely redesigning the operating and data processing systems for a Tokyo-based Internet start-up. So no-one could accuse him of being intellectually challenged. He just never assumed anything he did was in any way exceptional.

When he arrived in Lisbon, on theoretically the last leg of his travels before he planned to return to the United States to knuckle down and try to find gainful employment, he met Irvine Bisset purely by chance wandering around the Institute Art Collection and his plans changed totally. Once the two of them started talking there was some sort of a meeting of minds which led to Irvine just three days later offering Alves a permanent position as laboratory assistant which surprised both of them equally.

Castro had always felt slighted that Alves was given the same pay grade and the same job title as his own when he considered the scientific team was in some way naturally superior. But Bisset recognised the need for organisation. Alves focused only on funding requirements and logistics around which he spun a web of businesses and financial interests Bisset himself could barely keep track of. Bisset would always be the lead on everything science based or on occasion in direct association with Castro. Bisset kept things simple. They all knew where they stood. But that was when Bisset was alive.

Now the onus would be entirely on Alves to guide the overall direction and the flow of the research. This would undoubtedly bring him into ever greater direct conflict with Castro who is hardly going to take kindly to Alves dictating his agenda. But most crucially, he is acutely aware that he will not be able to advance his plans at all without Castro.

Much as it pains him that Bisset favoured Castro, and oddly it does, Alves realises he is going to have to keep Castro on side, somehow. He needs to make this work. The idea of having to reset the project back to zero without Castro is a non-starter; it would be disastrous, setting back the timing on the delivery of the project by perhaps even several decades. It is unthinkable. So, he must come up with a way to incentivise Castro to stay on and to remain committed to Bisset's original project.

"This is all a total fabrication," says Alfonso Salgado, the chairman of the board of trustees. He points to the papers strewn on the desk between himself and Alves. "Where did you get all this? I have never been more insulted…"

The trustees of the foundation had set in progress a rubber-stamping process to select Bisset's successor and while clearly both Castro and Alves were already of sufficient standing within the Institute to warrant being included on the list of candidates, Alves feared that this was out of respect for the wishes of Bisset and that they were not to be given serious consideration. That was until Alves invited Salgado to see him to discuss a matter of the utmost urgency.

They are in the luxurious boardroom on the top floor of the Science Institute which Bisset completed only six months earlier. Alves is sitting calmly at the long table the top of which is made from a single piece of polished teak, imported from Brazil. You never could accuse Bisset of a lack of elegance. Salgado is standing, pushing around with increasing anger and anxiety, a jumble of papers, receipts and bank statements mostly. Taken together, the array of documents provides damning evidence that Salgado has been embezzling funds from the foundation, syphoning off vast sums into a numbered Swiss bank account.

"Of course, you must stand up for your rights and fight any slur against your character, any allegations of illegality must be fully investigated," Alves says coolly looking out of the window at the Lisbon skyline with the sun sinking into the west beyond the huge red 24th April suspension bridge. "Although, the media may jump to conclusions if they see all this, don't you think?"

"You are, aren't you? You are bloody well threatening me."

Salgado may have a shot at becoming President of Portugal someday but not if all this gets splashed around the press. Alves looks past Salgado, through the glass interior walls behind him into the tall corridor outside lined with modern artworks on a grand scale which tower over the heads of the clerical staff who scurry back and forth. Alves is in no hurry to respond; he wants the gravity of all this for Salgado personally to sink in. Besides, he is thoroughly enjoying himself.

"What do you take me for? I can assure you that all this…" Alves says finally waving his arm nonchalantly towards the documents, "It will all stand up to the closest of scrutiny, I have absolute confidence in that. So, no threat…just advanced warning, if you like." Alves eases back in his chair, smiling.

Irvine Bisset may not have had any chance to prepare Alves for what was going to happen to him in a physical sense, but he certainly had done a thorough job making sure his successor—whoever that might be—would have sufficient leverage to impose precisely the future structure and operating environment at the Science Institute required to deliver his plan to fruition and the dossier of documents Irvine left locked in a secret drawer in his desk are clearly making Salgado much more amenable to the suggestion that Alves now is making, regardless of whether or not the so-called documentation is actually legit or fake.

"If the board could see fit to put on hold the permanent appointment of Bisset's successor, shall we say, for an indefinite period, given the complexity of the search etcetera, etcetera, and install Fernando Castro as interim head in the meantime, to guarantee the impetus of the invaluable programme of ongoing projects, it may well be that any compromising financial transactions would get lost in the sheer volume of administrative paperwork involved in Professor Castro's running such a major and prestigious foundation."

Needless to say, Salgado rolled over without any big scene, a pragmatist at the end of the day, like so many other political types, and Castro was appointed interim head of the Bisset Science Institute, on a permanent basis, of course. A major coup for Alves and even more so for Castro. The two assistants had effectively taken over absolute control of one of the leading research and development labs in the world.

And granting the top job to Castro, instead of taking it himself, did indeed have the desired effect of guaranteeing that Castro would stay at the Institute. Needless to say, Castro was under the impression he had stolen a march on Alves, had demonstrated his natural power and leadership, blissfully unaware—as he was—of Alves having toyed with the process of his appointment. From then on, Alves made sure he kept a tight hold on all the purse strings though. He would have the final say on which projects were funded and he had no intention of allowing Bisset's focus to be watered down.

Alves always suspected that Castro somehow had managed to steal Irvine Bisset's last will and testament. What he did with it, who knows. But Alves knew for a fact that Bisset had definitely drawn one up; he remembered vividly leaving it in a specific office filing cabinet where it would easily be found in the event of his death.

So, nothing could have come as more of a surprise to Alves when no will can be found in said filing cabinet or anywhere in Bisset's office for that matter. Alves then went through all the records held by his lawyers but found nothing. And finally, after the better part of a week of increasingly desperate searching amongst his personal belongings in the beautiful mansion Bisset was lucky enough to call home, Alves had to accept that Bisset's will was not going to resurface.

Is it possible that Bisset had forgotten that he had moved it? He was seventy-two years old after all, but given just how lucid Bisset had been right up to his death Alves thinks that highly unlikely. But Alves is also very aware that Bisset never could really face up to the possibility of his own mortality, so maybe he could even have destroyed the will himself and pushed the recollection of it aside, banished it completely from his mind in a similar way as he had hidden from Alves that Castro had been his preferred successor. But Castro having swiped it remains the most likely explanation given he was undoubtedly the one who benefited most from its disappearance.

"Frankly speaking, this makes things so much easier," Castro says with a hint of a smile behind his otherwise expressionless face as they are bringing to a close their fruitless rummaging through Bisset's endless stash of files at the house.

"How so?" Alves looks up from the storage box he is sealing with brown duct tape.

"Well, who else was he going to leave stuff too? Except the two of us, that is. I mean he had no family. We should just split everything fifty-fifty, you and me."

So, Castro is angling for a half share in everything now, in addition to him, thanks to Alves, getting the top science job at the Institute. In the actual will, all the businesses were to go to Alves, to keep him sweet and loyal to the project, while Castro had been supposed to be Bisset's natural successor so wouldn't need any financial incentive. But Bisset's heart attack had well and truly put paid to those plans.

Alves lays out the reality which he knows Castro would already have deduced in any case but it still needs to be said, "Quite simply, without the will, we may well end up with nothing! You must see that."

"I have every confidence that you can swing things our way," Castro smiles, drawing a line under proceedings, which infuriates Alves no end.

And that is exactly how things would play out. Alves would have to fight multiple legal battles to secure economic control over all the different business interests and even then, to achieve that final closure he would be obliged to make a painfully large tax payment as well as substantial and ugly palm-greasing to smooth the process through. It would end up costing a small fortune but Castro seemed wholly unconcerned; things were working out famously for him.

At least, Alves would get to keep Bisset's house. Mind you, even this would imply another big payout, this time to Castro himself after he initially argued that it should be sold and the cash split between them. But Alves was not prepared to let his beautiful home be lost.

Luckily, Bisset had indeed followed Duncan's now time-honoured tradition of keeping hefty sums of cash in secure locations known only to his successors. So, Alves would be able to meet the payments to the tax authorities and to Castro with enough in reserve to keep the research projects adequately funded, supplemented by a few carefully selected art disposals. In any case, Castro wouldn't need to know where the cash comes from; has no right to know, if truth be told.

Alves would then embark on a wholesale restructuring of the group bringing control of all the various businesses under a single umbrella holding company to streamline all reporting structures directly to himself. He would rename the company Alves, S.A. in honour of his mother, not himself, as he was quick to stress. Castro couldn't have cared less so long as it made them money and as Bisset had foreseen, Alves would prove himself to be a highly accomplished business leader and with Castro driving the scientific projects, the performance of the group companies would go from strength to strength making both of them increasingly wealthy.

Inevitably though, around three months after the funeral, the so-called 'agreement' made its reappearance. Both Castro and Alves had kept their heads down in the meantime: Castro enjoying the status and freedom that came with his role as head of the Science Institute; Alves trying to sort out all the financial mess of not having found Bisset's will.

But now they are sitting in Castro's office facing each other across a flimsy self-assembled desk which wobbles every time either of them touches it, putting Alves's nerves on edge. It is not as though the budget is not there for a proper desk that would make a statement in accordance with Castro's new position. But Castro couldn't care less, seems to have no dignity at all, no style, thinks Alves. Castro is interested in wealth as a facilitator of power, not as a means of impressing others with empty cosmetic—as he puts it—statements. The office on the other hand is wonderful: a huge corner space on the top floor of the Science Institute with ceiling to floor windows on two sides giving a panoramic view to die for, out across Lisbon.

Castro is leafing nonchalantly through an old-fashioned ring-bound file open on the desk in front of him, flicking from page to page without engaging with the content in more than a cursory manner, revealing on his face an almost amused indifference for what he is finding there.

"You should keep to trading your artworks," Castro's tone reveals his ever-decreasing level of respect for Alves.

"We are way behind schedule already. It is as though you actually want to undermine things."

"*Things*—as you call them—are advancing quite adequately. It's just the direction that has changed subtly."

"The funding is available only for a finite number of initiatives and beyond these…" Alves indicates with his eyebrows at the file in Castro's hands, "…there can be no more than a minor involvement."

Castro closes the file and throws it to Alves.

"Listen, Alves. I don't like where you want to take this. We had an agreement which you seem conveniently to have forgotten completely. The trial on its own is dangerous enough. I thought we had established that conclusively. The containment field could hold stable, just about, in a laboratory setting but to consider scaling it up poses wholly unacceptable risks. Lose control of the wave and the sudden polarity shift may rip apart the time mesh itself, generating a micro black hole which could prove to be unstable. If that happens, all hell could break loose. Who knows."

"Oh, give me a break, Castro. Don't exaggerate."

"How can I say this in terms you might understand? A micro black hole the size of say…" Castro smiles to himself, "a pingpong ball could end up with a compressed gravitational mass greater than the moon…"

"Come on. The laws of physics rule that out, point blank," Alves tries to interrupt. He knows a fair bit about the science too but Castro has other ideas.

"…*that* could trigger an extinction scale event, the entire earth's crust could be swallowed in a period of less than three hours taking all life with it."

"You know only too well that is nonsense." Alves pauses. He is aware that placating Castro is his most important goal. He continues in a more conciliatory tone, "We can at least agree that we should take things forward as far as the lab trial. OK, I accept we could shelve plans to go anywhere beyond that until we can analyse the results fully."

"But what's the point in that? You were pushing harder than me to shut the whole time mesh project down. There are so many more intriguing options out there, moving on tangential lines, building off the same starting blocks which can deliver practical, risk-free opportunities. Now you sound even more obsessed with all that wave theory bullshit than Bisset was himself."

Alves stands up and throws the file back down on Castro's desk, his frustration showing. "You knew damned well all along where Bisset was taking things and I am convinced if we stick to his plans, the outcome could be immense."

"Wow, you've changed your tune, haven't you? Even Bisset had no idea where this would end up. And who are you? With Bisset this was dangerous enough; with you at the helm it is plain madness."

Castro has a point, Alves would have to recognise that neither Bisset nor Alves himself had all the answers. Actually, it went much deeper than that, much further back. All the way to Duncan himself, in fact. A full understanding of the science has always remained annoyingly just out of reach.

It must be right there somewhere, so close, it taunts him, makes him feel he must be able to figure it out if he just applies himself a little more. But the final piece of the jigsaw is always missing. It continues to elude him, while never leaving him alone, always nagging, somewhere in the back of his mind.

But his objective to reopen the time mesh distortion and the urgency with which he pursues it could not be clearer. It has always been at the crux of Alves's being. From the moment Duncan surfaced on Bidston Moss, this had always remained the ultimate goal.

Something in the process of surfacing had gone wrong. Something had interrupted the procedures. Alves is convinced that a successful reopening of the time mesh distortion with sufficient scale will produce something quite extraordinary, something astounding. He speculates that it could represent a one-off evolutionary step-up for the human race. The science he has already pushed forward over the past century and a half is already delivering that in part, but he knows this is just the beginning.

And obviously there were risks, Castro is right about that too. But none of these were great enough to make Alves question his proceeding with the project and certainly no amount of scaremongering from Castro would deflect him from his goal. Nothing could dampen his enthusiasm either at the potential of reaching such a point. He was desperate to achieve the outcome he knows will be life-changing for him and to find out what all this means.

"I saw it all, you know," Castro says calmly, out of the blue.

"Saw what? What are you talking about?"

"Why don't you come clean, Alves? Just tell me."

"Tell you what?"

Alves is getting increasingly nervous and annoyed at the same time. He can't work out what Castro is up to but he is sure it is not leading anywhere he wants to go. And at the same time, he loathes the way Castro goads and taunts his victims when he holds some unseen card, like he is teasing his prey. It is a trademark of his that when he knows he is touching a raw nerve, he draws out the moment as much as he can, enjoying the spectacle of seeing you squirm.

Castro smiles and finally continues, "I saw the whole thing on CCTV. When Irvine had his heart attack."

"But there was nothing to see, the CCTV feed had some malfunction and recorded nothing." Alves had made sure of that. "You must know that."

"I mean live, not a recording."

So, there we have it. Castro was incapable of keeping his secret any longer. Not bad though, he had lasted almost three months. This explains the subtle changes in Castro which Alves had noticed since the death of Bisset. Alves had tried to convince himself that Castro must have been more affected by the loss of his mentor than Alves had imagined, even though Alves never could really reconcile that interpretation with Castro's personality. Now it all falls into place.

"Well you've kept quiet about that, haven't you?" Alves says.

"Just answer the question."

"There is nothing to tell. Really Castro, Irvine grabbed my arm and held onto me for comfort, I think, as he died. I couldn't bring myself to break that embrace. I knew he was dead but I was too shocked to pull back. I just gave him, and me, a few moments of peace before the storm of calling in the paramedics."

Would Castro believe Alves's story? Of course he wouldn't. But that is not the point. He could have told him anything, the truth even, and he wouldn't have believed it, the truth least of all. It was irrelevant what he said. So better to paper over the cracks and try to take things forward as best he could.

"You let him die," says Castro icily. "You didn't call the paramedics in for fifteen minutes."

"That is not true."

"You made no attempt to save him. You actively contributed to his death."

"You don't know what you are talking about." Castro is pushing Alves too far.

"Why?" Castro himself provides the answer, "With Bisset out of the way, you get to run Bisset's whole empire. To control everything…Well, not me. I saw it all remember. *You have to see it through from here…*" Castro laughs sardonically, mimicking Bisset's voice, "*…I am afraid.*"

As Alves hears Castro ridiculing Bisset's final words, something snaps inside him and he lunges at Castro, grabbing him by the neck and lifting him, pushing him back into the glass wall causing a loud thud to reverberate around the room. Castro's secretary screams outside the office as through the glass door she sees them coming together.

"How dare you say that when you were sitting there watching it all go down, like you're at the bloody movies."

Alves slams Castro back down into his chair as the office door opens and two guys from the clerical team push their way in to stop things going any further.

"It's OK. I'm just leaving," Alves shouts as he walks past them out of the office.

Castro just smiles, adjusting his shirt and tie.

XII
Lucie Alone

London—Present Day

The rain is slanting down through the headlight beams and the windscreen wipers are working double time as Zac and Lucie hammer up the M40 towards London. It is now well past three in the morning. Apparently, Zac has a one-bedroom flat in Battersea and they need to keep their heads down for a few days to let the dust settle. At least that is what he seems to have decided. There certainly hasn't been any meaningful discussion as to what other options might be available. It is as though Lucie has traded in one form of captivity for another.

Well, that is a bit of an exaggeration but sitting here next to Zac she is filled with doubts as to where all of this is heading and just how she can refocus things back onto her principal goal which remains to find Emma. Lucie had been sidelined at Burnt Ash Lodge for well over six weeks and Emma's trail must have gone icily cold by now, but at least she is now sure that Emma didn't die in the explosion in Lisbon. But how heading to Battersea with Zac helps lead to Emma she has no idea. She has accepted Zac's extraction plan thus far just to get away from Burnt Ash Lodge but how long she will tag along with him she will have to see.

She is also keenly aware—from comments made by Zac—that her photo has indeed been plastered all over the national newspapers as a terrorist suspect, so the police could well still be keeping a look out for her. Zac is probably right; a low profile seems advisable for the time being.

This is the first moment Lucie has really had time to think since Chloe helped her gain access to the East Wing at Burnt Ash Lodge where Mason was being held. Things have moved on so quickly, she has been unable to keep up, numbed with the unspeakably mindboggling events which have transpired since then.

Meeting that strange young lad, that mental closeness, sharing that exact same wavelength, at least when she was in the same room as him was completely unique. But now it all feels so different, so far removed from the real world. But Lucie knows deep down that the explosion, Mason, Burnt Ash Lodge and Zac himself are all somehow interconnected and to get to Emma she will have to unravel the whole unfathomable conundrum.

The motorway is still busy despite the rain and the advanced hour. She stares out of the windscreen at the stream of red taillights stretching away in front of them, each of them distorted momentarily by the splashes of rain, flaring out of focus and then wiped back to a recognisable reality with a mechanical swish. It is reassuring in its reliability, almost hypnotic.

Zac has hardly spoken since they started driving. Lucie doesn't know what to make of him. In Lisbon, he jumped in front of a bullet meant for her. She has to accept that in terms of commitment that is about as undeniable as it gets. And she does really like him, that too is undeniable. He is quirky and calming at the same time, if that makes sense. An unusual but appealing combination. Lucie decides though that the time has come to get a few answers.

"You turned up right at the last gasp. Impeccable timing," she says although she hadn't intended it to come out with quite such a cynical and inquisitorial tone but luckily Zac doesn't notice or at least seems not to take it as a criticism.

"Actually, I found you a couple of days ago. You never saw me but I was in the woods when you feinted with that nurse. What a performance." He pauses as he switches lane to avoid a cluster of slower-moving vehicles.

Then he continues, "It took me some time to come up with a plan to get you out of there. Then when I heard a gunshot, it was pretty obvious you were in need of more urgent assistance. And here we are. Not a bad rescue, even if I do say so myself."

"Rescue? I mean you went to a heck of an effort to get me out of a hospital."

"Lucie please. You saw the electric fences and the guards. They were all military but I can assure you they weren't there to protect you but to keep you from getting out."

"Level with me, Zac. Who the hell are you, really? There's no bloody way you have anything to do with insurance."

"And I thought I was so convincing. What gave me away?"

Why can't he just answer a straight question for once. Zac concentrates on his driving as they pass a lorry which is throwing up a massive amount of spray, making seeing anything at all out the front a challenge. He leans forward squinting and accelerates to pass it more quickly. Once they are past it though, Zac just settles back and offers nothing more.

"Is that it, then? Just dismiss it with a laugh?" Lucie shrugs in disgust.

"Honestly, there's not much more I can add."

"Or what? You would have to kill me?" Lucie scoffs, "Come on. You can't be serious."

"Let's just say I work for a part of the government and leave it at that."

"A spy?"

"Hardly. More like a glorified civil servant," Zac smiles to himself, "Look, I am totally on your side, I assure you. You'll just have to trust me. That's all."

Yeah, right. That's so comforting. And with that Zac clams up again. This is not going well. Maybe she can get more out of him if she tries a less confrontational approach.

"You know I really did think you were dead," Lucie says softly. "In the blast. How did you get out in one piece?"

"When you went down, I went up. That saved me. I wanted to take a closer look at the gear set up around the base of the dome. Then, when I saw that kaleidoscopic…" he searches for a suitable word to describe what he had seen, "aberration, rising up out of the floor, I decided it was time to make a hasty retreat. No way I wanted to get caught and have that thing frazzling its way through me."

"You saw it too?"

"What did Emma say to you?"

"Nothing. She just warned me to get out of the building."

"She knew it was going to explode?"

Zac's sudden interest makes Lucie realise she may have let slip more than she should have.

Zac continues, "Where do you think Emma might be?"

Lucie is starting to feel nervous. This version of Zac is not as reassuring and safe as the one in Lisbon had been.

"You're actually asking me?"

"You know her. Where would she go?"

"So now you want to find Emma too. That's choice."

"She may hold the key to all this."

"To all what?"

And again, Zac ignores Lucie. She is losing her patience again. Didn't he just say they were supposed to be on the same team? Lucie has her doubts now. She decides to go back on the offensive.

"Did you secretly take photos of me in Lisbon?"

"What? Of course not."

"So who did? They exist. I've seen them. Outside the Science Institute and by Emma's residencia."

"Your guess is as good as mine. I have absolutely no idea."

Every line of enquiry seems to lead back to the same spot. Lucie is expected to divulge what she knows or what she guesses or what she imagines and in return she gets…ziltch.

Well Zac, it isn't going to work like that.

Lucie sees they are about to pass a service station.

"I need a pit stop. Besides, I haven't had a real coffee in six weeks and I'm starving."

They pull into the Oxford service station. Lucie climbs out stretching and heads off to relieve herself while Zac goes into the Starbucks to order her requested coffee and a bacon and egg bap but looking back, Lucie can see Zac is making sure he can always keep one eye on the entrance to the ladies.

As Lucie is pulling up her jeans, she feels something in her front pocket, something she is immediately sure had not been there when she went into Mason's room at Burnt Ash Lodge. She fishes out an obsessively folded sheet of paper. Opening it to its full A4 size, she sees it is a hand-written note in thick blue marker pen with a message scrawled in large letters across the top couple of inches of the sheet: 'Newgate Prison 1000/0828'

Lucie is confused by the numbers at the end of the message. They look like a barcode number. The place seems self-explanatory enough but the numbers? Maybe they could be a map reference, but they have only six digits, don't they? Or could they be a prison inmate identification number?

She takes a deep breath still looking in the mirror waiting for the one other lady to leave. Seeing Mason's message brings back into focus that in some way their destinies are aligned and that for the time being at least she must break away from Zac. She knows she has to get to Newgate Prison—wherever that is—and not with Zac.

That is clear to her now even if the exact meaning of Mason's message itself is a mystery. Quickly she re-enters the toilet cubicle and locks the door behind her. She reaches up and opens the small window above the toilet and with one last listen at the door to check that no-one else is coming into the ladies, she climbs onto the loo seat, manages to slip pretty snugly through the narrow gap offered by the window and drops onto her good foot outside.

She limps as smartly as is comfortable but without any obvious sign of panic across the carpark and into the area reserved for trucks. She approaches an HGV whose bulky driver is tiredly pulling himself back up into the cab.

"Excuse me…I'm in need of some help. Big help," Lucie begins. Then she explains that she has had a fight with her boyfriend and he has hit her. She has to get away from here and could he give her a lift to anywhere at all.

"I dunno." The driver hesitates. "I don't really want to get involved in anything…You know how it is."

"Oh God. Please!" she begs. "I can't get back in that car with him, I can't."

The driver sizes her up for honesty maybe and then comes down on her side.

"Oh, go on. Jump in."

Lucie sits stone faced in the cab as the truck rejoins the main carriageway of the motorway. She has left Zac to his own devices and she wonders with some amusement just how long he will wait for her to get out of the loo. He will be furious. But she needs some space and time on her own.

"No-one will know you in here, that's for sure," Matt declares confidently. He is sitting opposite Lucie at a pub table—actually more akin to a workbench—and what look like church pews with roughly carved ends down either side. It is midday, give or take. The tall windows reveal just how dreadful the weather has become overnight. Strong gusts of wind are lashing the rain into the panes of glass which are trembling noisily in their old wooden casements.

Matt has a natural upbeat positivity in everything and he even sounds enthused as he explains how shocked he and Zoe were to see her face on the telly. He was born only a couple of streets away from the Station Hotel in Hither Green which is where they are both now having a pint of lager and he is proud of never having strayed beyond his patch. He is in his mid-thirties, wears his hair short or at least what remains of it. He is going to be bald completely by the time he reaches forty and he covers up this glaring and uncomfortable reality with a Yankees baseball cap most of the time.

And he loves trainers, focusing attention as far from his head as possible. He cares little about the clothes in between. But the trainers are something obsessive:

new, special editions, celebrity-owned, classics. He has more than two hundred pairs, a whole room full of boxed trainers and he knows exactly what is in each box and their value. He even actively trades them online.

"I know you and Emma get up to some weird shit…but," he leans across the table smiling and lowers his voice. "Terrorism. Jeez, Lucie. That's proper." Lucie shrugs and changes tack.

"I'm afraid I need to ask you for a favour…Well, two actually."

"I'll do whatever I can. You know that, Lucie," says Matt. This is not the first time Lucie has sought Matt's help.

It is now Lucie's turn to lower her voice and make sure no-one is within earshot. "Well, I don't know any easy way to say this, so here goes…I need a gun."

"Now that, I wasn't expecting," he says slowly but not out of hand refusing to consider her request. "Listen Lucie, guns are never the solution, they just make finding one even more complicated. You know that, right?"

"I've got into something and I need to be able to protect Emma. Properly, this time."

"Are you sure you're not just getting further and further out of your depth?"

"Hell, Matt, of course I am. But I can't very well go to the police, can I? I have no-one to turn to but you. And this is getting more and more dangerous. I've thought this through and I am sure this is the right way to go."

For a moment, Lucie recalls how she had felt with Mason. He had been such a calming, reassuring influence. He seemed to know how things would play out. She had even picked up the gun off the floor at Burnt Ash Lodge in the first place, and then, she had let it go.

Mason had entrusted the gun to her, resisted taking it off her himself when she had offered it to him. He will certainly not be expecting her to have given it up to Zac without so much as a challenge. Or maybe she is just trying to convince herself that this whole gun thing is a good idea when she is really not that sure at all.

Matt then continues unfazed. "A terrorist asking for a gun. Well, I imagine that is the easy ask. So now you've got me worried what the difficult one might be," he says smiling.

"I need to see Zoe too…at home."

Matt laughs. "Well that we *can* do."

Matt has certain—shall we say—connections in the local community which run very deep. A crook would be too harsh a term to describe him. Matt bends the rules rather than outright breaks them but Lucie has no doubt that he can deliver on her first request too.

When Lucie and Emma ran from Carsphairn Hall to escape the clutches of Miles, they had no idea just how tough it would be to build a new life from scratch.

Firstly, there was always the risk of being found out. Lucie was only fifteen years old and Emma was not her legal guardian, Miles was. Logically, they hid their past in a fictional narrative with no mention of Carsphairn Hall at all. London was the obvious place to melt into a crowd so big as to go unnoticed. So, as planned with Rachel, that's where they headed. Emma was constantly tormented by what she was doing: hiding a minor in a dingy bedsit in Sussex Gardens of all places.

Every night the prostitutes would ensconce themselves back out of the light of the street lamps but any car crawling at close to walking pace would bring them all out kerbside. Lucie spoke to some of them in their darkened doorways and over time became friendly with one girl in particular, Janine.

"They're just kids, like me," Lucie would say to Emma and in terms of age she was right; some, like Janine, she was sure were younger.

"The difference is they are all hookers, and they all have pimps keeping an eye on them. I can't have you getting dragged into anything. Do you understand me?" Emma tended to be a bit over-paranoid, over-protective in those first few months which could make her seem uncaring. But Lucie understood that Emma felt responsible…for everything, even the Miles incident.

But Lucie saw those girls as victims, innocent of any wrong-doing except being unlucky and you can't be guilty of being unlucky, can you? They were just runaways, like Lucie. And most of all, they were truly alone, no Emma to look out for them. So much for safety nets. The police turned a blind eye or often worse. The whole sorry mess was accepted.

For Lucie though, this was exactly what she needed. Anonymity and space to rebuild, to process and to purge from her soul the claustrophobic final days of her time at Carsphairn Hall. And Janine certainly helped her recovery. She, like Lucie, had no past. They spent many hours in the tiny cafe just opposite Paddington Station on Praed Street and talked endlessly, both fully aware that some subjects were off limits and would remain off limits. The past was not the point. The point was new: a new life, a new friend, new hope.

Even with the help of Rachel's kind gift of her diamond bracelet, which sadly was only worth a fraction of what Rachel had always believed, Emma and Lucie's resources were minimal and dwindled alarmingly. And with no personal history to back up their identities, the job pool they could target was limited to say the least. Emma as the eldest of the two determined that she would have the best chance of finding work but it just wasn't that simple.

On the last day before they were due another month's rent on their grubby bedsit, which incidentally they didn't actually have, Emma was finally offered a job as a night receptionist at a shabby old hotel just off Bayswater Road called gloriously the Pacific Hotel where accommodation was thrown in.

Emma knew this was far from ideal and fraught with risks but beggars can't be…etc. etc. The owner was a fiftyish-year-old woman and she had a number of similarly dilapidated hotels and guesthouses in the Paddington area. She ran the staffing on an industrial scale. All the lower-end workers were illegal, just managers and above were legit and everyone knew they had to toe the line or else. That way, it gave the owner much more scope for downright exploitation with zero comeback.

All employees were paid net of their accommodation; disgusting rooms in another building which would have been condemned and closed down immediately if any inspector had come within a mile of it. But that was never going to happen as the owner knew the right people in the right council positions. Emma shared her room with Lucie. No-one cared, most thought she was just another worker. No-one ever checked up on her and none of the rest of the staff would ever have dreamt of snitching on a co-worker.

But this type of job has a limited lifespan; there is only so much abusive behaviour you can take and after two months of lip-biting, Emma finally lost her cool and snapped back at her manager, a reckless and definitive move, it turned out. The following evening, Emma was accused of stealing fifty pounds out of the till by her manager, who quite brazenly had opened said till in front of her nose and had taken a fifty pound note out and slipped it smilingly into his jacket pocket.

Emma knew her time at the Pacific Hotel was up, her word held zero sway with the owner. She was fired there and then and the manager even had the nerve to call the police. Obviously, Emma and Lucie couldn't risk being investigated and so they bolted. They were on the run again.

This time they went south of the river, to New Cross. They had virtually no money and nowhere to live but that afternoon proved to be a crucial turning point as Lucie took matters into her own hands. They were walking down Lewisham Way when down a side street, Lucie noticed a particularly rundown building. All the ground floor windows to the front of the property were boarded up and the garden had not been looked after in years. There was even a gaping hole in the roof so clearly no-one was in residence. It looked ideal to Lucie. Who could care less if they stayed there for a few days?

They pushed away the weeds clogging the gate and walked down the alley at the side of the house. There was a single storey lean-to with a small window through which they could see an opening onto a downstairs loo with the door missing and a large filthy Belfast sink, clearly a utility room of sorts. Lucie calmly picked up a large stone from the garden at the back and to Emma's shocked amazement shoved it through the window with a huge crash.

"Well, let's see if that gets the neighbourhood watch out in force," Lucie says jokingly, as she puts her hand carefully through the broken pane and opens the window with the latch inside.

"You're mad, Lucie."

Lucie then scrambles in through the opening and stands up looking back out at Emma. "We need somewhere to sleep and this looks like our best option at the moment, I'd say. What are you waiting for?"

And that is how the New Cross squat started. It was an awesome three-storey detached building in an amazing location, just a stone's throw from Goldsmiths College. But the property was in really bad shape: the hole in the roof over the stairwell was serious, and the rain and pigeon shit from the well-frequented roost in the rafters around it had left the stairs rotten and unsafe, so Lucie and Emma were confined to the ground floor initially.

The electrics were from some pre-historic age and had been cut off in any case so they had to rely on candles to provide all their lighting; the gas had similarly been disconnected; the house was damp and cold. Luckily, when Lucie turned the stopcock, they didn't find any leaking pipes and the taps in the kitchen worked and miraculously, the loo, by the window Lucie had smashed, did flush, even though they would be visible from the alley when using it if anyone came down that way and the half-broken seat was damned cold.

But there was a fireplace in the dining room they used as a bedroom and the garden shed, which was on its last legs, was only suitable for chopping up as firewood to keep them warm. The last of their money they used haggling aggressively at the Catford indoor market to buy a used but acceptable-looking mattress, a couple of not too moth-eaten blankets and a few bits of cutlery, some plates, a couple of pans.

Then after being in residence for a couple of weeks, and just as they were facing up to the fact that they had run out of both money and food, their endless trudging around all the pubs, restaurants and cafes, finally paid off as Emma got a job as a barmaid in a pub in nearby Deptford. That night they breathed a sigh of relief; some sort of future seemed at least plausible again.

In the next two months, they were unchallenged in the squat. Lucie used her gift for impersonation as a bona fide tenant to get the electricity reconnected, she put a new pane of glass in the window she had broken, had the lock on the back door changed so they could get in and out safely without climbing through the window, she renovated the fireplace and decorated both the dining room and the sitting room in stylish, bold and cheap colours. It might not have been the most comfortable place on earth but it did already feel like home.

Then while they are cooking dinner one evening, they hear a key in the front door and freeze. They have been caught.

Matt's face as he finds them looks almost as shocked as Emma's and Lucie's.

"Jeez! Who are you? What are you doing here?"

"We are living here," Lucie says boldly.

"But this is my house! You can't live here."

"Well you certainly have been neglecting the upkeep of the place," Emma says critically. "It's is a total dump. A deathtrap."

"Look, I need you to get out, right now. I have someone coming over to see me here in five minutes and you just can't be here."

"But we have nowhere to go," Lucie says. "You can't just kick us out."

"Like hell I can't," Matt seems agitated.

At that moment, there is a knock at the door.

"Oh shit!" Matt says in a forced whisper. "Look, you two get into the back loo and shut the fuck up. If I hear anything out of you, you are going to be in serious shit. Do you get me?"

That seemed wholly reasonable and they quietly filed out into the loo and waited for what seemed like hours. Then finally, a much more relaxed Matt called them back into the sitting room.

"Amazing. I never thought I'd see this house being used again. How did you get in?"

It turned out that the owner of the house had been sent to prison for some gangland-related crime back in the early 1990s, well before the area got its art-school revival. When he had died inside Pentonville from natural causes a few years ago, allegedly of a heart attack, the property passed on to his son, Matt. While Matt most certainly benefited from the illicit gains of his father, he never fully followed in his father's footsteps, just tinkered around the edges, if you like.

Matt took pity on Emma and Lucie and let them stay on in the house temporarily but he also told them that he had neither the cash nor the inclination to renovate the house which the council were keen on condemning and selling off at auction to a housing association which was presumably going to benefit some already well-lined pockets. A couple of weeks later Matt turned up again to tell them that the sale was set to go ahead before the end of the month.

"How can you even consider a hundred and fifty thousand for this place?" Emma says impudently.

"The council is going to pull it down. It's past saving."

"Rubbish! You are so being ripped off," Emma sounds as though she knows something about property valuations, which Lucie is sure she doesn't.

"Somebody's going to make a killing here but it doesn't look like it's going to be you."

Matt hesitates. He seems to know that he's getting legged over big time and he doesn't seem too keen on the house being demolished at all, just to be replaced with a sterile block of flats. Lucie can see a glimmer of nostalgia in his eye. She suspects that this had in fact been his home when he was a kid before his father went into prison.

Lucie jumps at her chance, "This house deserves more. Just look at it...I promise I will work night and day to restore this place. Emma can help on the technical stuff like fixing the roof. She understands physics, you know. And I'll put in the labour, all of it. That'll double the price you can get for it overnight. And that other thing that you use the house for, whatever it may be, we won't see anything. Right Emma? You can rely on us for absolute discretion."

Lucie knew then that he would agree. There was already some unspoken understanding between them. And a deal was indeed struck that stymied the council and allowed Emma and Lucie to become legal tenants; they could stay at the house rent-free indefinitely so long as over time they could do up the house.

Matt was happy to provide the materials but all the hard graft was down to the girls. At the same time, Matt could come and go as he pleased, using one room exclusively for certain undisclosed activities, the subject of which they would never ascertain nor did they ever try to do so. No questions asked.

Matt never could complain that Lucie didn't keep her end of the bargain either; she worked non-stop and learnt all the basic building trades and every time Matt came round he could appreciate Lucie's dedication and undoubted skill. So good was she that Matt ended up buying another derelict property in the same area and getting Lucie to take on that renovation too. Lucie effectively became an employee which in Matt's world was tantamount to being an honorary member of the family.

Matt even ended up marrying Zoe, one of Lucie's friends who was studying art around the corner at Goldsmiths. Zoe was local too, from Camberwell and couldn't have cared less either about the nature of Matt's at times dodgy dealings and Lucie and Emma went to their amazingly happy and exceptionally well-attended wedding at the registry office on Peckham Road.

In the next five years, Lucie and what grew into her gang, made up mostly of friends and helpers, including for a time, Janine, renovated another three properties for Matt. Matt was scrupulously fair in his apportioning of the gains on the sales once the renovations were complete and the income Lucie generated began to so outweigh the contribution from Emma working in the pub that Lucie nagged and nagged until she finally convinced Emma to quit and to take up her studies again.

With the help of Jackson, Emma was offered a post-grad place at Imperial College supported financially by Lucie. Emma was eternally grateful but Lucie knew just what a sacrifice Emma had made for her over the years and never forgot it.

"So, what would madam like today," jokes Zoe.

"I think the whole works, don't you?"

"Aggressive cut and then my absolute fave knock-em-dead newest colour?"

Zoe smiles at Lucie in the large mirror they have plonked on the kitchen table, snipping the scissors open and closed a few times as if stretching the muscles in her fingers before going about Lucie's hair with vigour and confidence. She has had many years of practice, refusing point blank to give any of her Universal Credit to a barber to cut the measly amount of Matt's hair that remains and she makes a pretty good job of it, usually.

Today is easy, she says, shearing off vast swathes of Lucie's shoulder length blonde hair, leaving her a short almost masculine style. Then she turns to colour. And gives Lucie something Zoe calls deep black, a natural dye which Lucie thinks it best not to inquire too strongly as to its precise origin.

Standing in front of the full-length mirror in the hall, now wearing some old nondescript baggy top which Zoe is only too happy to get rid of, a pair of jeans and with her new black shiny cropped hair, Lucie can barely recognise herself.

But in her new guise, Lucie quickly feels at home, so much so that she starts to think that this look is more her than she has ever felt before. She just may have to start getting her hair done at Zoe's on a regular basis. So relaxed is she about not being recognised, that she has even been down to New Cross and has walked round to take a look at the old squat. She immediately gives it a wide berth, however, as she sees a car up the far end of the street with someone just sitting there bored-looking finishing a last drag on a smoke and chucking the fag end without thought out the window.

Now that really never happens, you get into your car to go somewhere or when you arrive you get out and go into a house or knock at a door. Even if you a just a smoker without a garden to indulge your habit you hardly just sit there after you have finished your smoke.

Conclusion: he most likely is staking out her place. Given her new look though, she is confident that even Emma would struggle to recognise her from more than a couple of paces away. Notwithstanding, she does a quick about face and goes back down the street towards Lewisham town centre and Hither Green beyond.

Lucie is now sitting in a second-floor office in Croydon opposite someone called George McCartney. At least, that is what it says on his name tag. Actually, he really does look like someone from a Beatles tribute act with sixties length wavy hair and a shiny, drainpipe-trousered, single-breasted suit which looks like it could have been bought at one of the second-hand stalls in Camden Loch market. His thick cockney accent sort of spoils the effect though, but he just wouldn't hack it in the Rolling Stones.

Lucie too has a name tag pinned to her blouse—Giorgina Piotti—an over-exuberant alias, she would have to admit but she is deep undercover here.

"Let me take you through the ropes, it is all pretty self-explanatory." George has a lewdish smile which Lucie finds quite off-putting.

Lucie had phoned TransWorldX and a helpful but ultimately pretty gormless receptionist had confirmed that they were always taking on temps but was unable to say which agency they used. There was definitely one, she knew, but couldn't remember which one. So, Lucie has spent the last two days traipsing around all the temporary employment agencies based in the Croydon area, of which there were a remarkable number.

A temp's life can be a miserable one, particularly for those that cover short term positions. You are and will never be part of the team and boy are you made to feel that, to own it. Lucie is sitting in an open plan space at a desk behind a computer screen. She is introduced to everyone not by her own name but by the name of the person she is replacing, "This is Joanna's temp."

And the response is equally distancing and dismissive, "Oh right, how long are you with us?"

Lucie is booked for the rest of the week but has no intention of staying more than today. She will phone in sick tomorrow and that will be the end of it. She has fabricated a truly creative CV she thinks, including stints with other haulage operators and so when she applied for the five-day slot at TransWorldX she got the job, no questions asked and thankfully no-one checked the make-believe references she had provided. But they never do, do they for this type of job?

The work is mindless. Enter this number here, the date of invoicing here and then that product code over there.

"And that's all there is to it. Do you think you can handle all of that?" George smiles sending another shiver down Lucie's spine.

"I'll give it my best shot." Lucie tries not to let her sarcasm show through too much.

But Lucie is ecstatic as George gives her her very own computer access codes and leaves her to get on with the work. She has to rummage about a bit inside the system to find the terminated contracts but a positive by-product is that she finds just how much access they have given to her and that TransWorldX has a local branch in Liverpool based out at Speke, just by the airport. Then in no time she has on-screen the Alves account. She had been hoping that customer confidentiality would not be exactly at the top of a haulage company's list of priorities and her hunch pays off.

It was certainly a big project. In all, there were thirty-two lorries each with capacity for forty-four tonnes. Alves was shipping some serious kit, that is clear. Now the contract was complete and all had been delivered over the past six months from multiple locations across Europe, not just Lisbon, and then Lucie notes down the delivery address; Bidston Moss Industrial Park on the Wirral peninsula. Amazing, far too much of a coincidence, she muses.

"This never happened. You understand that?" Matt is sitting in the driver's seat of his rather sumptuous white Audi Q7. He hands over a Primark plastic bag which Lucie who is in the passenger seat next to him weighs up in her hand. Cleary it contains something much heavier than clothing. "Love the packaging."

"Zoe'd kill me if she knew."

"Got it. Thanks Matt."

"It doesn't come with a user manual but from what I gather about your encounter with the Lisbon police, you already have that off pat." Lucie immediately knows that he is referring to her shooting of Farinha.

"Come on, Matt. I never wanted to do that. I'm still having horror flashbacks all the time."

"But you opt to double down," Matt says turning to look at Lucie eye to eye. "Just be careful Lucie."

"I'm not planning on using it. It's just for leverage."

"Well that type of plan has a habit of going tits up…Look, seriously, if you manage not to use it, just toss it. It's clean so even if someone finds it, it won't be traced back to me."

"Matt, you know more than most about prisons," Lucie supposes.

"Never set foot in one," Matt counters although Lucie cannot tell if he is serious or not.

"Right. But anyway, could 1000/0828 be an inmate number, maybe?" Lucie pulls out Mason's note and hands it to Matt who looks quizzically at it for some time.

"Well, I suppose so. It's possible. But…"

"But what?"

"It could just be the date. You know, backwards, like the Americans do. 9/11 was the eleventh of September. I know it's quite common these days even over here, with computer geeks especially."

"You mean it could be the 28th of August?"

"At 10:00 in the morning."

"Oh my God. That's two days from now! Matt, you're a crack."

XIII
The Auction

Lisbon—18 Months Ago

What was the worst that could have happened? The gravitational discharge was always going to be met by an equally powerful opposing force in the shape of an electromagnetic pulse. Had it lasted more than a second or two, it would have crashed IT systems across the entire globe, would have caused aircraft to fall out of the sky, would have fried permanently all computer operating systems, all cell phone networks, everything electronic would have been compromised. But it hadn't, had it? It had lasted less than one thousandth of a second, exactly as planned. To Alves it had been a resounding success.

As he and Castro analyse the results of that pulse, which actually will form the backbone of the live trials now no more than a couple of years away, Castro again disappointingly only has eyes for the negatives. Obviously, the wave had become unstable when measured against Castro's own criteria. True to form, Castro has remained surly and ill-tempered throughout the process.

It is as if he has never accepted that Alves could play such an important role in the scientific strategy as Castro himself, as if all along he harbours a deep-seated grudge. He even goes as far as to claim he is so shocked that he is reluctant to engage any further with the whole time mesh project, but Alves can see in his eye the amazement at what they have achieved. No way is Castro walking away from this now. It's all just for show. They are so close.

"We just need to improve the alignment and to narrow down the electron beam, that's all," Alves seeks to reassure him as they stroll through the gardens outside the Bisset Institute.

"All? You know, I've had a team in Iceland contact me and some research lab in Vladivostok. Both picked up the resonance fallout and from that they've been able to track it back to us here. So much for being undetectable. If they put two and two together, we will be locked up in no time."

"We're just a blip on their screens. Adding two and two in this case is way beyond them. Nobody has the faintest idea what we are doing."

"Precisely. And nor do we either."

"Oh, come on. If you could only commit to the procedure with a bit more energy, we will be able to hone the calibration and ramp up the power enough to allow us to keep the wave pattern within even your own overly cautious limits. We could even avoid any pulse at all. Before anyone can figure out what's going on, we will have done it. You'll soon change your mind once you see that it works."

Remarkably for Alves though, this has not been the only thing vying for his attention at such a momentous time, he has been fully occupied also with putting the finishing touches to his flash new headquarters near the Basilica da Estrela in the Bairro Alto area of Lisbon which he also feels has taken forever, it must be said. But now, with that too finally done and dusted, strange as it may seem, Alves immediately starts to miss that whole rather banal process: the endless choices of colour schemes, of materials, of textures and finishes.

Not that he would change anything either; he is more than satisfied with the end result. He is particularly pleased with the elegance of his own office occupying the entire top floor where he had allowed his imagination free rein to propel the design in unusual directions, bringing in several of his favourite artworks from the Bisset collection along with a few extravagant, plush Persian rugs and wall hangings in homage to Duncan's first office in London and the subtlest of lighting schemes which would have made Gryphon gasp in amazement, even if Bisset himself would have considered the whole thing far too self-indulgent.

The costs, needless to say, have also spiralled out of all control, stretching the budget ever wider with each step up in specification, with every additional luxury. So, to finance the last phase of the construction works and the lavish interiors on such a grand building, while at the same time having to accommodate the ramp up of funding to deck out the lab in Moscavide to allow the trials of the time mesh project to go ahead on schedule has taken far more in terms of investment than the cash-cow ventures in the group generate and Alves has had to resort to selling a selection of the paintings owned within the foundation collection to make up the shortfall. And this is how he first comes into contact with Patrick Doyle.

Alves remembers that day only too vividly. The auction room at Christie's in St James's of Mayfair is pretty much full as he first becomes aware of Doyle staring at him unwaveringly across the hall. Alves has such a strong mental presence that rarely does he come across anyone even close to that degree of vitality and Alves feels drawn irresistibly into the aura of this guy's audacious gaze.

Doyle is among several people standing at the back behind the last row of chairs, virtually all of them, with the exception of Doyle, with mobile phones pressed to their ears, representatives of some more guarded, privacy-minded bidders.

There is something uncanny about the way this perfect stranger stares unblinking at him, as though some invisible filament joins them, a thread of consciousness intersecting the space between them. It is as though some form of communication has already been established when Alves has never laid eyes on this man before, he is sure. The rest of the room seems to edge slightly out of focus, and even when Doyle raises his hand to bid once or twice, it is somehow blurred and set to one side. Alves is intrigued—more than that—he is mystified by the intensity of this outlandish psychic intimacy.

Alves is standing up at the front of the room, close to the auctioneer's podium, beneath a screen showing an image of the lot now under the hammer: a painting by a little-known Portuguese artist who Alves has been promoting for some time. This particular painting is a modern depiction, bordering on the surreal, of the Bisset Institute itself with shapes in bold brushstrokes of garish, almost neon colours and striking sharp palette knife-scraped lines rendering the building unrecognisable in all but the most emotional of contexts.

It is a painting that has hung on the walls of the Art Collection for the last three years but Alves has decided that now is the time to realise some profit and to take the artist's recognition to another level. If there is one domain where Alves has already surpassed Bisset, it is in his appreciation of art.

"Well, that was a fine result, I'd say. Quite reasonable given the rather—although I hate to say it—dubious quality of the artist," Doyle has somehow sidled up beside Alves unnoticed at the end of the auction.

They are standing in the crowded viewing gallery, everyone clutching onto a glass of champagne, amid a general buzz of banal arty conversation. Both are examining the actual painting Alves has just sold, which in reality is much smaller than the screenshot in the auction room had suggested.

"I'm sorry?" Alves makes no attempt to disguise his irritation at this uninvited and unannounced intrusion.

"I mean…The buyer would have gone a lot higher. I pushed him up a bit for you but he…"

"You pushed him up a bit?" Alves cannot believe the gall of this joker. But neither can he rid his mind of the feeling he experienced while in the auction room during the sale just minutes before.

"On a couple of occasions, to be precise."

"Do I know you?" Alves confronts him.

"Patrick Doyle," Doyle introduces himself, offering his hand.

Alves ignores Doyle's outstretched hand, snubbing him for an uncomfortable beat. Doyle though is far from flummoxed. He looks down at his hand but does not withdraw it. If anything, he extends it further, challenging Alves.

There is nothing Alves hates more than the sensation that the control over a situation is slipping away from him, particularly in opening encounters; Doyle is really pushing his luck here. First there was that stare, then the insult that the sale price was too low, and now to butt in, invading his personal space, thrusting out his hand. But Alves cannot deny that a part of him is still gripped by curiosity to find out just who Doyle is.

And in any case, Alves has no option other than to accede to Doyle's demand for Alves to shake his hand and introduce himself as a couple of other patrons on the lookout for gossip as they pretend admiration for the next painting along have turned their heads noting the bitterness of their encounter and are now waiting open-mouthed to see if it might deteriorate into something even more vulgar and entertaining.

"Alves," he says, shaking Doyle's hand distractedly and then continues in a biting cold tone, trying to regain the upper hand, "What are you selling, Mr Doyle?"

"Ouch!" Doyle laughs.

On the face of it, Doyle seems to fit in comfortably with this crowd but Alves feels something odd about him, something out of place. Doyle is in his mid-forties, and is well enough dressed: a suit, clearly made-to-measure, a gaudy tie, shoes shined to a mirror finish. He is tall, clean-shaven. Perhaps what Alves finds off-putting is that his heavily greying hair is surprisingly dishevelled.

Or maybe it's the obnoxious smell of some expensive, over-liberally applied aftershave. Actually though, Alves concludes that he really does look pretty much like a salesman, maybe from the fancy Bentley's dealership around the corner in Barclay Square or maybe an upstart city broker trawling for high net worth clients around London's top auction houses.

Doyle nods to refocus attention back towards the painting, "It's hardly worth the price you got for it, so I wouldn't complain."

"Just wait and see what it's worth a couple of years from now," Alves says dismissively. He has his own way of assessing the value of a painting: an intuitive appreciation of where art is trending, a natural ability to distinguish between lasting original creativity and crass superficiality. There can be no doubt it has worked exceptionally well for him up to now and he has no reason to suspect it will not continue to do so in future.

"Be that as it may…" Doyle is far from backing down, "I was never going to go as high as your buyer, so what's the point?"

Alves turns to face Doyle head on, who he finds is also no longer looking up at the painting but rather is staring straight back at him.

"How do you know that wasn't his final price?" Alves asks.

"Oh, call it a pure speculation, if you like," Doyle smiles. "I enjoy the odd flutter with fate."

And there it is again, that weird, uneasy feeling that Alves is not quite getting the whole picture. He has a strange sense that Doyle may really mean every word he says. There is something about this guy that Alves finds uncomfortable and yet at the same time seductive. Just who the hell does he think he is?

"I am just a negotiator. Not a full-on player, like you."

Doyle is answering directly Alves's unspoken question. This whole thing is beginning to freak Alves out. He is starting to feel threatened by the precocious insight of this clown.

"A negotiator? Yeah, I bet you are," Alves says sarcastically to himself as he walks away. But he also notes a touch of disappointment at breaking the spell.

Back in Lisbon, back in his comfort zone, Alves is discussing Patrick Doyle with Castro although he has chosen to omit the more surreal moments in Christie's. He could hardly disclose any of that without risking another bust-up with Castro. It's been hard enough to keep Castro on track over the years and now, when they are so close to the end, he certainly doesn't wish to give Castro any reason—and to be fair it would be a pretty substantial one—to question his sanity.

"Is that it?" Alves waves a thin cardboard folder in the air in front of Castro.

"Farinha has been through all the UK and EU records. There really isn't much more out there."

"Seriously, an art dealer with no provenance?"

"It seems he has covered his tracks with a great deal of care. Obviously, he doesn't want anyone digging around in his past. What difference does it make?"

"I found him sneaking around the Art Collection at the Foundation, yesterday. I can tell you, he's not here on holiday."

Alves had indeed met Doyle again in the Foundation. It was almost as if Doyle had planned the whole thing. He seemed to know where Alves was going to be and just when to saunter out from one of the collections into the lobby.

"Hey, Alves. I was hoping to see you again," Doyle had said with a smirk.

"Doyle, you really should have called. My schedule is massively overloaded today."

"Yeah, sure it is."

And with that snide remark the whole Christie's vibe seems to be picking up where it left off in London. And immediately Alves notices he again feels—how can he describe it?—enthralled is perhaps overstating the issue but certainly entertained would seem to sum it up adequately enough.

"What are you doing here?" asks Alves abruptly.

"You have an amazing collection," says Doyle without seeming to address Alves's question at all. "It is so inspiring."

There is something about him which is bizarre, unique. It's like Doyle is throwing out clues to some mental puzzle of his own creation but the answers for Alves are tantalisingly always on the tip of his tongue but stubbornly refuse to come to mind.

This time though Alves senses a similar degree of anxiety present in Doyle too. Like he has a hidden agenda which he is struggling to get into play.

"What do you want from me, Doyle?"

"I'm just getting to know you."

"What the hell is that supposed to mean?" Alves feels threatened. Doyle is scrutinising his every action. None of this makes any sense. But he also knows he can't just leave things as they are. He has to find out who Doyle is behind that smokescreen.

And then, at precisely the moment Alves becomes concerned that in some involuntary way he may already be relinquishing control, letting slip to Doyle far too much, he suddenly blurts out, the words forming themselves in his mouth without his brain seeming to have any intention of saying them, "Look, Doyle. I have a few paintings at the house you might be able to help me with. Why don't you come over for dinner tomorrow night. At eight, say?"

"I thought you'd never ask," Doyle says, stepping away.

The huge loft, built into the sloping eaves of Alves's mansion, is turned over entirely to art, his one enduring obsession, which had originated way back when Duncan's first transfer took place. Father Casey's deep love of religious icons and paintings was never wiped from his subconscious and from that moment on, it had lasted and deepened.

Gryphon became similarly infatuated but, without the religious influence, he was bowled over more by the hypnotic intermingling of colour and movement of the Impressionists, the sheer audacity of essence winning out over detail, the faithful representation of reality being pushed out of the limelight. And then, as with pretty much all things, Irvine Bisset had polished and given scale to this passionate endeavour, adding huge numbers of modern artworks to the Foundation Art Collection.

Into the roof Alves has added an array of angled skylights which fill the space with the last beams of late evening sunlight. There are paintings everywhere: stacked in piles, some overtly on show, propped against walls, some in elaborate frames, some just bare canvasses. In the centre is an easel with a sheet covering another work.

Alves clicks an app on his mobile phone as he ushers Doyle in and the artificial lights come on, filling in and mixing with the fading natural light.

"This is what I wanted you to see," Alves says, pulling the sheet off the easel. "What do you think?"

The painting in question is a dark, melancholic work. A heavy storm-laden sky weighs down upon a fragile woman, standing on an exposed heath, her red hair flares behind her in the wind, the only colour outside of the multiple shades of grey, intensifying to a near pure black.

"It's yours, isn't it? That's hardly fair."

"Just tell me how much you think I might expect to get for it. That is your speciality after all."

"That would depend on who the buyer is."

"What sort of an answer is that? Come on Doyle. Indulge me."

"Are you sure you are willing to part with it. It is really rather good. Who is the woman?" Doyle avoids committing to a specific figure.

"What does it matter who she is?"

"She clearly matters to you."

Doyle steps closer to the canvas and looks carefully at the figure.

"I knew her a long, long time ago," Alves replies, failing in his resolute decision not to confess to Doyle the motivation behind his painting. Actually, it is his interpretation of the last time Duncan saw Jules as she wandered away from him across Blackheath into the gathering storm after his arrest, after he had come close to throttling her. But Alves at least manages to quell a sudden desire to tell Doyle any more.

"She seems oddly familiar," Doyle peers quizzically at the painting. "You have captured her quite beautifully but there is such despair in her expression, she is so tormented. I find it deeply disturbing and quite exceptional. Name a figure, I will give you whatever you want for it."

Alves cannot understand now why he felt the need to show this painting to Doyle. He has never shown it to anyone else before. It is just too personal. But Doyle somehow strips back the layers of protection around his deepest feelings and lodges his own priorities in their place. Alves finds it unnerving. But the way both of them appreciate art and even just how they think is also distinctly familiar.

Alves's phone bleeps, announcing a text message. He looks at the screen and ignoring Doyle's offer, throws the sheet back over the painting saying, "Shall we go down to dinner?"

A couple of hours later, once the maid has left the dining-room, laden down with the last of the serving dishes, having completed her duties for the evening, Alves decides this polite charade with Doyle has gone on for long enough. He refreshes Doyle's glass of cognac and says, "Tell me, Doyle. Who are you? Really."

Doyle says nothing in reply initially. He looks at Alves as if trying to glimpse behind the mask to reveal the unseen intricacies in Alves's question. He exhales slowly and chooses his words with care.

"I do not wish to disappoint you, but there's nothing exotic, nothing out of the ordinary, I'm afraid."

"You have *no* past."

"You have checked me out. How vulgar!" Doyle laughs loudly and then in a more serious tone continues, "Having no past and deciding not to publicise it, are two very different things. I have chosen the latter. My background is not at issue here, and I certainly do not intend to relive any of it for your or anyone else's entertainment. Let's leave it at that."

"Don't keep dodging the issue."

"Alves, please. Let me propose something to you. Tell me about your work into the connectivity between time and space."

Alves stares across the table at his guest. He is stunned. This has turned things on their head. Alves may have researched Doyle's background but he has found out nothing. Doyle though seems to have had much more success and has a far deeper understanding of Alves than he has previously let on.

"None of that has anything to do with me," Alves says trying to hide his growing alarm at the sudden shift in the direction of their discussion. "That would fall under the remit of the Science Institute. I am only responsible for the Art Foundation. The two sides have zero overlap. You would have to talk to Professor Castro. He is the head man there."

Alves feels as though Doyle is somehow dredging through his thoughts, rekindling odd unintended memories in his mind. Alves tries to resist this pressure but the effort to block Doyle out is firing up such a severe headache that Alves is finding it difficult to focus on the here and now. Doyle at the same time, however, seems wholly comfortable behind this thin veil of normality.

"Now you are taking me for a fool," Doyle counters. "I saw you give a lecture at Imperial College less than a couple of months back. What was the title? Oh yes, 'Time and Other Boundaries Waiting to be Broken'."

Alves is dumbstruck. He clears his throat, in an attempt to regain his composure. There is no denying that Alves had indeed given that lecture but he has no recollection of Doyle being present. He had felt none of the psychic presence of Christie's or indeed of here right now. But Alves had been exceptionally focused on other things at that time so perhaps he had just failed to pick up on it.

"You were there?" Alves asks, "Why?"

"Didn't understand much of it, if I'm honest," Doyle smiles to himself and then continues in a deadpan seriousness which surprises Alves, "What are you trying to achieve here, Alves? What is your endgame?"

"There is nothing more I can say on that subject."

"You see. You are the one shrouded in secrecy, not me. I have discovered that you are responsible for that huge electromagnetic pulse last October. But why? That is the question."

"How can you know that?"

"It was triggered here in Lisbon. The epicentre was right here."

"Who's taking who for a fool now? Where the hell did you get that information?"

"It is disruptive and unstable."

"Nonsense."

"I felt it. And not only that, it blinded me for several minutes."

"That is impossible."

"I tell you, it is dangerous. Massively dangerous."

"This has gone quite far enough. I think you should leave," Alves says, losing his patience. It is so unlike Alves to let anyone get under his skin like this, but his head is spinning. Doyle's smile turns into an aggressive stare.

"You must stop."

"Is that a threat? You know nothing of our work here. Nothing! Do you hear me? How dare you come here making baseless and absurd accusations."

Doyle picks up a carving knife which the maid for some reason had forgotten to clear away. Alves had not noticed it up to now, either. Doyle grasps it like a dagger in his fist and holds it over Alves's hand which is stretched out on the dining table in front of him.

Alves is terrified to see that he leaves his hand out there directly under the point of the carving knife. He breathes in a few deep gulps of air. Can he pull his hand away or is he just determined to show Doyle he is not going to be intimidated?

Doyle then says darkly, "Listen to me, Alves. Stop meddling with that stuff; you're not as invincible as you think."

Doyle plunges the carving knife down at the exact moment Alves pulls his hand back and the knife slams into the table precisely where his hand had been. Both Alves and Doyle look in amazement at the carving knife which vibrates back and forth, its long, thin blade stuck in the tabletop.

"Jesus Christ! You're insane! Get out. Now."

Alves stands, clearly shaken, and walks unsteadily to the door. He holds it open. Doyle slowly gets to his feet glaring intensely at Alves all the time but it is as though he has realised that his time is up.

As Doyle gets into his car, he says in an ominous tone, "Watch your back, Alves."

"Right. Thanks for that," Alves says sarcastically as he walks quickly back up the steps and enters the house, slamming the front door behind him. As Doyle drives away down the long driveway, Alves feels his headache ease. At least, there is no way Doyle can get anything more out of him. Or maybe he had already by that time got what he came for.

Alves's only reason for giving the Imperial College lecture in the first place was that it had given him the chance to meet someone else. He had no idea that Doyle had been there. That other person would, like Doyle, have an important, if even more unorthodox impact on upcoming events.

Alves first became aware of her existence when he stumbled across a research paper by a young quantum physics postgrad named Emma Kelman in the UK. It was astonishing on two counts: first, the scientific analysis was beyond anything he had come across before, outside of Castro and Bisset, of course; but second, amazingly, it related to Bidston Moss.

Despite several trips to the Wirral over the years, from Gryphon's ill-fated long stay to his own short exploratory visits and even after the vast sums he had spent on developing the most hi-tech and sensitive of testing equipment, he had been unable to ascertain the exact location of the structural scarring of the time mesh inevitably left by his surfacing all those years ago in 1865. And he knew all too well that, if he was ever going to complete the project, he would need to identify its position.

Emma had termed it a cosmic radiation singularity, which in essence is true but she had failed to grasp the monumental consequences behind, or more precisely, within such an anomaly. But Emma's work was nonetheless breathtaking. So much so that Alves had taken up the offer from Imperial College to give its Invitation Lecture purely as an excuse to meet Emma face to face.

"Emma," Professor Melville, the head of the physics department, calls to her just after the lecture has ended, "Would you mind joining us down here for a moment?"

Emma stands up and looks down from her place in the fourth row, her mouth agape as though she can't quite believe it is actually her being called down to the stage to meet Alves.

"I am honoured to meet you," Alves says, shaking Emma's hand vigorously.

"Oh please! You must be mistaking me for someone else. How could you think…" Emma suddenly clams up, whatever she had been intending to say must have gone, her mind left blank. Her face turns pink and then contorts into an embarrassed cringe as she looks bashfully down at the floor.

"Bidston Moss?" Alves comes to Emma's rescue.

"You've read my paper?"

"I have never read anything quite like it before," Alves compliments her.

"Is that good or bad?" Alves can see that Emma is honestly unsure as to which way his verdict may lean.

As Alves discusses Emma's findings and what it was that had originally drawn her to Bidston Moss, he becomes increasingly charmed by Emma's unassuming candour, her beguiling naivety, her genuine enthusiasm for everything regardless of its apparent value or indeed its lack of it.

Only three weeks later, they hug awkwardly when they meet again, this time in the centre of Bidston Village, exchanging kisses on both cheeks. Alves has flown in direct from Lisbon into Liverpool John Lennon airport while Emma has travelled up by train from London.

They had agreed to meet outside St Oswald's and now with the church at their backs they are looking up towards Bidston Hill with Duncan's old home, Bidston Manor, only a hundred yards or so away, the roof actually visible above a row of mature sycamores that Joseph Gryphon himself had planted.

"This is the way," Emma strides off along a small track near the wall surrounding what Alves still considers his own estate. Actually, he really is still the owner of Bidston Manor although he has never used it as his home and it has now been empty for decades. He walks after her up through a wood of tall silver birch trees and they emerge onto the ridge upon which Bidston Observatory and its adjacent lighthouse are built.

The sandstone outcrop goes along as far as an old and disused windmill at its southern end. The Observatory and the surrounding buildings are all closed and locked and look deserted, their damp austere-looking granite walls belying the fact that such major tidal research had been undertaken here up until the 1970s.

"This is the best place to see the Moss in its entirety," Emma explains looking out from the highest point, oblivious to the fact that Alves knows this area much better than she does.

The view is stunning. They can see all the way across Bidston Moss itself and Wallasey beyond, down to the coast a couple of miles away. To the east is the estuary of the river Mersey with the city of Liverpool rising up out of the far bank and to the west of the peninsula lies the river Dee with the Welsh hills just about visible in the murky distance. Alves feels a deep affinity for this place, the ghostlike allure of some previous life.

As he looks down onto the Moss he is actually less interested in the geography than he is in Emma herself. In fact, he has come here in large part as an opportunity to spend some time with her, to assess her. He has to admit she is certainly very attractive: her dark hair cut to a no-nonsense shortness, her face while portraying no immediately notable, standout features, seems to flow and to draw you in towards her vibrant hazel coloured eyes which dart back and forth with enthusiasm and vitality.

Her dress sense is like her, unstuffy, practical. Her frame of mind—her presence if you like—is humble, even shy, yet clearly, she is capable of sharp, decisive action. Alves can imagine she could have a quick temper but also would move on, not be one to hold a grudge. The longer he is with her, the more struck he is by her captivating, positive aura.

"And where exactly did you find your anomaly?" Alves asks.

"Oddly enough, it's not far from that shopping centre they built down there. Can you see it?" Emma points down less than a mile or so beyond the rooftops of Bidston Village. So much has changed over the last one hundred and fifty odd years that to all intents and purposes the whole area is unrecognisable: the housing developments which have all but entirely swallowed the old village, the recycling drop-off, the docks mostly now unused, and the large, ugly shopping centre a hive of activity with its huge car park outside a strip of stores along one side and a busy road behind it leading to the M53 motorway which curls away down the middle of the Wirral peninsula.

Emma continues her explanation, "It's actually in between the back of that DIY store at the far end and the main set of docks, on that expanse of marshland which still exists today. But it is on private property. There is nothing there except a massive fence and signs everywhere warning trespassers will be prosecuted. I never could make contact with the owner."

And the owner here too, would be Alves. He knew perfectly well that Gryphon, Bisset or himself had already acquired all of the land that Emma is referring to.

"But could you pinpoint the exact location of your cosmic radiation singularity?"

"If I had the funding to build a kit sensitive enough, sure I could. The science is simple." Alves is thrilled. Now it really could happen. She has passed the audition.

Alves hasn't heard anything from Doyle thankfully since their calamitous dinner the week before. But he still can't get him out of his mind. The fact he seemed to be in possession of critical data relating to the time mesh project was deeply disturbing.

The gates to the Alves mansion open automatically and he drives his red Lexus towards the house which is set back from the road at the end of a long driveway lined with towering mature poplars. In the evening, they are illuminated by spotlights making their white bark gleam as though the trees themselves are the source of the light.

Alves drives around the extravagant fountain forming the centrepiece of the grand circular end to the driveway and parks at the foot of a wide flight of steps leading up to the front door.

Castro has been going on about leaks for ages but Alves always imagined it had been some sort of a ploy to slow down progress. Maybe there really is something in it. Could Doyle be involved?

As he opens the driver's side, the low growling throb of the engine cuts out and is replaced with the gentle sound of cascading water. He climbs the steps and taps his phone, unlocking the front door but then his excitement vanishes instantly as he crosses the threshold. The alarm system has failed to emit its customary facial recognition bleep that should announce his entry to the house and should at this time of night automatically switch on the hall lighting.

But the hall remains in darkness. The security system has been compromised; someone may have gained access to the house, and that someone may indeed still be in the house right now.

He steps back a pace and extends his hand, feeling for the manual light switch. It too has been deactivated. He switches on the torch on his phone. It casts a pale unfocused light which hardly penetrates more than a few feet into the darkness. He heads to the end of the hall and descends a staircase into the basement where what he calls his quiet room is located, where all the most private and most valuable data is kept.

Even Castro doesn't have the codes to get in here. At the same time, his mind darts back to the fleeting sensation of the multiple passcodes flashing through his mind just for an instant while escorting Doyle to his car.

He walks down the basement corridor and stops nervously outside the quiet room door. As he presents his passcard to the reader outside the door, he hears a feint noise immediately following on from the usually reassuring clunk of the lock releasing; a switch being flicked, a torch being turned off, if he had to guess. He pushes the door open slowly.

The room is in darkness, the absolute black of a subterranean space with no windows. Here, even the light from his phone seems stronger, flooding across the floor, its edges sharp, nothing discernible in the intense shadows. Alves stands hesitantly in the doorway.

"Who is in here?" he shouts out, stepping forward boldly and as he does, his peripheral vision registers some movement just behind the set of floor-to-ceiling metal shelves which form a divider of the space between the pure office and a more comfortable environment for relaxing. The shelves tip forward. Alves tries to push back against their weight but clearly whoever is pushing them over from the other side has unstoppable momentum and Alves is thrown to the floor with the shelves and all their books, tools and half mounted instruments come crashing down on top of him. A glass decanter shatters and loose papers flutter gently, as if in slow motion, to the floor.

Alves sees a silhouetted shape jump out of the door and hears footsteps run down the corridor and up the stairs. The figure he glimpses could have been Doyle or Castro, or indeed some other unknown intruder. He has no idea. Again though, he hadn't felt any psychic presence, at least nothing like the other times he had come into contact with Doyle but he hadn't felt anything at the Imperial Lecture either so he can't say for sure it wasn't Doyle.

By the time he pulls himself out from under all the debris, his assailant is long gone. Clearly whoever it was knew what they were looking for and where to find it. Alves retrieves his phone and eventually manages to reset the systems, restoring the lights. He finds the safe wide open. Some key documents have been stolen and one file in particular containing the most sensitive information of all is missing. This will come back to haunt him for sure.

XIV
Identity Matters

London—Present Day

Matt's help had revealed the meaning behind the numerical part of Mason's enigmatic note, but that was not the end of it. Mason cited Newgate Prison, presumably as the location for him and Lucie to meet, but that, in and of itself, presented Lucie with another significant problem: Newgate Prison had been demolished in 1904.

On that location now stands the Old Bailey, the central criminal courthouse in the whole United Kingdom. Why on earth Mason had picked anywhere a heightened police presence would be inevitable is beyond Lucie. They are both fugitives from the law and Lucie is accused of something which could hardly be deemed trivial: terrorism and prior to that killing a cop. That must put her right up at the top of the police most-wanted lists. She pulls forward the hoodie she had earlier purchased for precisely this reason, trying to shield her face from the pedestrians passing by, who for all she knows could be off-duty policemen.

Making matters even more complicated, Lucie hasn't been able to ascertain precisely where the entrance to the old prison would have been. She decides her safest vantage point is in a quiet doorway a few yards back from the pavement close to the corner of Newgate Street and Old Bailey. From here, without drawing attention to herself, Lucie should be able to spot Mason if he turns up anywhere around the steps leading up into the Old Bailey itself and she can at the same time see all the way down the adjacent street to where a Roman gate in eras past gave access to the city and incidentally its name, Newgate, to the prison which would centuries later lie upon that same spot.

While she waits, she ponders whether perhaps she should have gone off on her own, should have focused exclusively on finding Emma. She already had a pretty good idea that Castro and his cronies must be holding her somewhere close to Bidston Moss so she could have ignored Mason's proposal of a date and gone straight there. But she also knows that both Mason and herself had been kept prisoner at Burnt Ash Lodge and that could be no coincidence; it was all tied in with Alves and Castro's project. To have any realistic chance of finding Emma and then of actually getting her out of wherever she is being held, she is going to need to have a better understanding of what is going on, so meeting up with Mason has to be her smartest move.

It is however a measure of just how much this whole Mason thing is getting to Lucie that as she stands there she starts to wonder if she may actually be feeling his physical presence getting closer and closer. Get a grip, Lucie, for crying out loud. Is she really getting *that* excited at the prospect of seeing Mason again?

Lucie is of course expecting the self-same Mason to walk towards her as she had seen in Burnt Ash Lodge. So, when a lad with an aggressive crew-cut walks by wearing a knee length navy blue coat with straight-fit jeans and black trainers, she doesn't immediately recognise him. Lucie's new look must be confusing Mason too as he walks straight past her without so much as batting an eyelid. Just where the psychic link has gone all of a sudden, who knows. But then, he turns his head and the two look quizzically at each other for a few moments before bursting into laughter. Then they hug still laughing.

Stepping back, Mason takes in Lucie's full transformation and says, "Wow. You look *soo* amazing!"

Lucie can see in his eyes signs that he is being genuine even if it didn't come out quite right, like he hadn't really believed she could ever look that good. In fact, to many this might not appear a particularly flattering comment at all but for Lucie it certainly is. Right at the top of her all-time list of the best compliments ever. And it's been a long time since anything up towards the top end of that particular list has come her way at all.

Lucie immediately feels less concerned about the police, about everything in fact, as if just being with Mason again throws a protective shield around her. Nonsense, obviously. But his mere presence here is conducive to her comfortably going along with whatever plan he may have, if he actually has one that is. That sense of security, that warm glow she had felt in Burnt Ash Lodge when she first laid eyes on Mason in some small measure at least is back.

Talking of security, Lucie points out that meeting on the steps outside the Old Bailey is probably not the brightest of moves given that the whole place is swarming with police and surveillance cameras. So they agree to look for some more anonymous and private location where they can quietly discuss their next move. All the usual coffeeshop chains of Caffè Nero and Costas are teaming with tourists—hardly surprising given they are just down the street from St Paul's. But when they head into the backstreets behind Blackfriars the hubbub is instantly left behind. They come across a rather gloomy, locals-only looking pub, the Rising Star. At this hour of the morning, they are practically the only customers, ideal.

Mason orders coffees and then as he is paying, on the spur of the moment, he asks for a couple of whiskies, to calm the nerves, of course. Lucie has no complaints; it will do her no harm to take the edge off the morning. They take their drinks to an ornate cast iron table with a cracked marble top, set away into a small niche with multiple bullseye glass windows behind them that must render them completely unrecognisable from the outside while those passing are transformed into blurry deformed shadows.

"Just what is going on, Mason? I mean between us. All the hallucinations, the psychic mind games. Jesus, it's doing my head in. Are we really telepathic?" Lucie realises just how off the wall this sounds. She would never have believed she could have uttered such a question in earnest.

"Come on Lucie. Are you serious? Listen to yourself," Mason has a point. It's true that Lucie has no belief in any of that sort of telepathy mumbo jumbo, actually in nothing supernatural whatsoever, either religious or otherwise. But since finding Mason wandering around inside her head, all of that has been thrown into doubt. And Mason is very much for real, that much is irrefutable.

"OK then, so if we are not…" Lucie avoids repeating any of the more extravagant terms she had used to describe their relationship, "Just how is it possible that I saw you on the shore of Loch Doon when we had never laid eyes on each other before?"

"Was that where we were? Loch Doon?"

"So, you accept we were there?"

"Great name," Mason smiles.

Lucie ignores Mason's facile comment—her desperation spilling over—unwilling to allow this to be taken so lightly, "Not once either, twice. When you were locked up in the East Wing, you were at the exact same time screaming at me through the perimeter fence."

"Hey, it wasn't my doing, I'll have you know," Mason sounds annoyed, a defensiveness bordering on childlike peevishness at being called out which Lucie had not noticed until now. She suddenly sees him more as just a young lad, his immaturity showing through.

"I'm not accusing you. I'm just trying to figure this out," Lucie states in her no-nonsense voice.

"Right," Mason is less than convinced.

"So?" Lucie throws back at him bluntly and then waits in a huffed silence for Mason's take on things. No way is she going to let Mason duck her question.

"Well, there has to be an explanation. Something scientific. To me, the whole feel of it was a bit like virtual reality. Neither of us were actually there in a physical sense but we could see each other and speak to each other. For me, that's science…not telepathy."

His description is quite close to how it had felt for Lucie too. But of course, there had been no Internet, no avatars, no computers, no virtual reality headset. It all happened inside their heads. Her own reality of the lab in Lisbon had been blocked out and another superimposed upon it, while Mason had never left Burnt Ash Lodge.

"I was in that fake alternative reality for so much longer than the couple of seconds I actually blacked out. It felt more like half an hour at least, like in a dream, I suppose."

"You blacked out before the explosion?" Mason sounds interested for the first time.

"At exactly the moment, that crazy wave went right through my head. That was when I first saw you."

"You were *inside* the wave?"

He is fully engaged now.

"Then the whole place blew up."

"That wave is the key, it must be. That's what Alves has been trying to create for some reason. It must have brought us together somehow. My mind was in total overload due to the wave and I blacked out too, you know. We were together right there on the same wavelength, linked in both in space and time. It's quite astonishing. I too had that same sensation of time playing tricks on me as I walked along the shore of Loch Doon. It seemed like an age, when like you, I was unconscious for such a short time."

"But how?"

"I don't think…" Mason hesitates as if still formulating his idea, "I don't think this was part of the plan. No-one saw this coming. Amazing, but it may well be that no-one is aware of our connection as we speak. That could give us an edge at some point. Did you tell Kahtri about seeing me in your visions?"

"No way. I told him nothing. What does all this have to do with you anyway?"

"That's what we now have to find out. And with us both out of the clutches of those madmen in Burnt Ash Lodge at least we can have a more serious look into things ourselves."

Lucie takes a long slug of her whisky which she had left untouched to this point.

"How did you get out of there in the end?" Lucie asks. "I heard gunfire after we separated."

Mason then tells Lucie his own get-away story. He had been preparing to break out of Burnt Ash Lodge for ages and then Chloe had sided with him and she played a vital role in putting those plans into action although from the way Mason tells the story it isn't clear how much—if any—direct influence he had over her volunteering that support.

From Lucie's perspective, when she burst into Mason's room, provoking the showdown with Kahtri, events appeared to be spiralling out of control but it seemed that for Mason and Chloe this had just triggered some minor rearrangements to their existing plan.

When Mason had run down the stairs and out the front door, into the darkness outside, he somehow knew that Chloe would be there waiting for him. Without a word, she bundled him into the back of a military jeep and covered him with a tarpaulin. She then drove quickly to the edge of the compound and jumped out leaving the engine running. She led Mason through the undergrowth and bushes as confusion broke out around the main gate a hundred metres or so from where they now crouched down.

A flurry of activity saw most of the sentry guards rush off presumably to quell the uprising Mason himself had set in motion and Chloe took this as her cue to get him out. Some days previously she had dug out a channel under the concrete base which houses the foundations for the perimeter fencing. Then she handed over some keys to Mason.

"There is a Land Rover twenty metres beyond the second fence. It's full of petrol and should get you to London no problem," Chloe says bidding Mason goodbye.

"Thanks," is all he says. At least according to Mason's account, although Lucie has some doubts as to whether their parting may have had some more intimate details which he has chosen to leave out on her behalf.

Chloe had run back towards the jeep and roared away, wheels skidding in the gravel while Mason crawled under the fence and as quickly as he could he ran across the no-man's land between the two fences. A guard spotted him from a sentry post and shouted out to him, then an automatic rifle fired several rounds in his direction but they were all wide of their target thankfully.

This must have been the gunfire Lucie had heard. Mason scrambled under the second fence as a couple of shots thumped into the ground just in front of him, this time their aim was much more life-threatening. He rushed forward reaching the Land Rover in seconds. More firing hit the rear of the car as he pulled away but he disappeared into the night and was gone.

Briefly Lucie tells Mason her own story but surprises herself by leaving out any mention of Zac from her account. She had been lucky, had found a gap in the fence, had hitchhiked to London. But why she had hidden Zac's involvement is unclear to Lucie. With hindsight, she now recognises that in Lisbon she had been overhasty to throw in her lot with the first friendly face that came along, and she really doesn't feel like sharing any of that with Mason for the time being.

Or is this just self-delusion and ultimately she doesn't want to jinx Mason's interest in her by throwing some other guy into the mix. Now who is being defensive and immature? She panics a little and hopes to God Mason is not picking up on any of this.

She quickly shifts the topic of conversation onto safer ground to something less crazy, more factual which, to be fair, has also been nagging at her mind ever since she found Mason's note.

"Why here? Why Newgate? It doesn't even exist."

Mason holds up the chain around his wrist. She remembers having been surprised to see it around Mason's wrist in Burnt Ash Lodge.

"This. Somehow…this must be important." He unclips the chain from his wrist and holds it up to the light, the amulet dangling over the table.

"My father always said it was Welsh gold." He opens the delicately worked lid in the form of a Japanese acer, a symbol of eternal life, a tree which Lucie has always adored. Mason flicks out a heavily faded ochre coloured photo of a rather stern-looking man's face.

"It's just got 'Newgate Prison, January 1874' on the back," Mason says, showing Lucie the message written in minuscule well-penned letters on the reverse side to the image.

"There is some sort of engraving on it, too," Lucie notices, squinting as she tries to read the tiny inscription.

"It says 'For Jules, forever Duncan.'"

Mason knows it by heart.

"Where did you get it?"

"I stole it…from my father."

"Stole it?"

"I only wanted to have a closer look at it. He would never let anyone near it. Certainly not to open it and see the photograph inside. I was only nine. He had left it on the sideboard and I just slipped it into my pocket when he wasn't watching. Then, when he found it had gone missing, he went ballistic. He could be quite intense, volatile, if you get my drift and I was too frightened to say anything. I was going to put it back that evening but then he left."

Mason keeps fiddling nervously with the chain bracelet he has once again wrapped loosely around his wrist as he continues his story.

"My mother was freaking out, screaming at him. I was so scared I shut myself up in the attic and hid in the dark behind an old kitchen cabinet used for storage. I could hear everything, I could feel all the rage of my father, as well as the panic and anguish of my mother.

"Then I realised he was looking for me. He eventually pulled down the attic ladder, switched on the single electric lightbulb and climbed up. He came straight over and stood directly in front of the kitchen cabinet. Never did he try to look behind it. He knew I was there. He stood there stock still for what seemed an age. He didn't speak.

"I was holding my breath with his gold amulet pressed desperately in the palm of my hand. Then, suddenly, he was gone. I was devastated; he never came back. I have felt guilty ever since. I always thought that he had blamed my mother, and that was why he had left. But now I am sure that he knew. That was the last time I ever saw him."

After undertaking a swift bit of Google searching—virtually the first thing both had done with their newly won freedom had been to buy a new mobile phone—Lucie and Mason leave the Rising Star, determined to identify the mysterious man in the amulet photo and head across Smithfield Market towards Clerkenwell from where they cut through St James Church Garden before emerging onto Northampton Road opposite the London Metropolitan Archive, which also according to Google, houses a good portion of the Newgate criminal records.

As they walk, Lucie has been trying to digest what Mason has told her but uppermost in her mind is the uncomfortable truth that she has no idea just who or even what Mason is. It's not that she doesn't trust him; she does, instinctively. But Kahtri's description of Mason's brain rewiring as non-human has been flashing repeatedly through her mind, impossible to ignore. Obviously, that term was just a way of saying that it was unique, hadn't been seen before, not that Kahtri actually considered Mason to be an alien.

"So when did you first realise that you weren't like everyone else?" Lucie asks as they stop outside the rather drab modern exterior of the LMA.

"I only found out about the MRI scan after the accident. But I suppose I've known pretty much always that I was different, for sure."

"Different? In what way?"

"Well, I was always a bit paranoid, a bit manic. And then some smart-arse teacher joined all the dots and came up with idea that I must be attention deficient. You know, hyperactive. Once you get," Mason lets his fingers add some quotation marks in the air, "*diagnosed*, that's you done. Take the pills, shut the fuck up and stop bothering everyone. But as I got older, I slowly came to realise that it wasn't a deficiency I had, and certainly not of attention. Totally the opposite, as the MRI finally confirmed, I actually had a massive attention surplus. I was processing not only my own emotions but also those of anyone I was coming into contact with. It is hardly surprising I was a little manic."

"How old were you at that time?"

"I was only eleven. I was only just starting Junior High School in New Jersey."

"In the US?" Lucie asks in surprise.

"My father was English but I was born and went to school over there."

"Amazing. I would never have guessed. You don't have any accent," Lucie says, clearly puzzled.

"I always liked the way my dad spoke."

When it comes to Mason, there is always some unexpected extra surprise thrown in. Is he really suggesting he deliberately faked his English accent? Lucie cannot rule it out. As has so often been the case with Mason, Lucie gets the idea he is being genuine with her but just maybe he is the source of the trust she feels in him, maybe his own unpredictable and random thought processes could influence her to such an extent that she ends up getting lulled into a false sense of security, into believing his seemingly continual contradictions. It is so confusing…well, thinks Lucie, that at least is clear.

Mason continues, "That was when I first started to distinguish between external stuff I was picking up from other people and my own emotional state. Can you imagine? My mood was being affected by everyone around me. It's not like you are sitting there, looking in from the outside like you're at the cinema. It is a dynamic experience, you participate fully in those emotions. It didn't take me long to realise that this was unique to me."

"And you didn't tell anyone?"

"I learnt pretty sharpish that it was better to keep quiet about it. Kids can be cruel. As time went on, though, I got much better at handling all the conflicting emotional data and could even start to use it to my own advantage. It does have some amazing plus points: to know what people think of you really, particularly girls. Can you imagine? To really know."

Lucie can't really say any of this is a surprise to her. It is almost as if she had been prepared for this by her interactivity with Mason already. But what she certainly hadn't realised was just how routine this was for him, how much a normal part of his life it was. Can Mason see how she feels about him right now? Is he weighing up her emotional responses to him as he speaks? Is he even brazenly bragging that he knows just how interested she is in him? She has to put a stop to this, right now. Lucie walks up the steps and opens the door of the LMA courteously gesturing for Mason to enter first.

Inside, they pore over Newgate Prison committee reports, prisoner records and all sorts of administrative documents for more than an hour or so with no success; they are on the point of having to concede defeat. They have searched all the electronic databases and have sifted through all the relevant physical records and yet they still have no idea of the name of the man in the photo. They have found no reference to either a Jules or a Duncan at all. Their search of anything pertaining to January 1874 in Newgate is not helped by the fact there are virtually no photographic records available.

A student librarian who has taken an avid interest in their unusual investigation suggests that while mugshots were only just being adopted around that period those that remain are kept mostly at the National Archive in Kew. So, they head south on the tube and after a further hour looking through a mass of photographic data both online and actual physical prints, both are thoroughly disheartened.

There is something that is still nagging at Lucie. And maybe now could be the most likely moment to get a straight answer out of Mason. She just has to know.

"So..." she asks, "can you influence the emotions you pick up from other people, change how they feel? Can you affect their behaviour?"

"Lucie, listen. It's not like that," Mason is categorical. "I can read what some people may intend to do, their impulses and desires, what is pushing them along a particular line of action and to some extent being on that same wavelength, matching a neural pattern and experiencing a shared emotion can lead to them adapting their own decision-making process. It's not just one-way, there is a live connection, a real coupling but it's not me, as such. There is no lever I can pull."

Lucie is not sure she is any the wiser for the explanation, although she has to accept that Mason is again doing his best to be open and frank with her.

"I know how confusing all this can seem," Mason says a bit too knowingly for Lucie's peace of mind. How dare he claim to know how she may be feeling.

"Are you bloody kidding me? Are you messing around in my head right now?"

"No, Lucie. Honestly."

"Just answer me this then. At Burnt Ash Lodge, did you manipulate me in any way whatsoever? You know, when I knocked the gun out of the hand of that guard. Was that you?"

"No. That was you. We were perfectly matched, I admit. But it was you who took all the crucial decisions and you who put them into action. It wasn't me."

But Lucie's eye has been drawn to an expression she instantly recognised in a photo Mason has just discarded. She picks it up and stares at it in disbelief.

"Mason, this is it!" cries Lucie, raising a disapproving stir amongst the other researchers.

She continues in a hushed whisper, "It's the exact same photo. Wow! Look at this."

But this is not a mugshot, it is a fully posed scene. Presumably that is why Mason had discarded it. At the foot of some steps leading up to a gallows, there is a line-up of dignitaries and participants in an execution. From the text accompanying the photo they identify the Chief Constable, the head gaoler, the executioner and at the end of the line the condemned man side by side with a young fresh-faced priest. A sorry bunch, all stand expressionless and insecure. None more so than the man about to face his maker, who Lucie discovers is named Duncan Chambers.

"Chambers? Did you say Chambers?"

Lucie nods.

"My name is Mason Chambers."

"But Chloe told me your surname was O'Keefe."

"O'Keefe is my stepfather's name. My biological father was Harrison Chambers."

"My God, Mason. That means you must be directly related to a triple murderer."

Lucie can feel Mason's initial awe melting into something more akin to dread. He picks up the photograph and stares hard and long at it. He seems to recognise something deep inside himself. His hand slowly strokes his face.

"I have to find my father. He must know how all this fits together."

Later, Lucie will recognise that this was the moment Mason grew up fast. His understanding of his roots was something he had lacked throughout his life to that moment and now this photo and its context were to become the driving force behind him.

Gone was the childlike version of Mason and in its place, Lucie would now see a more mature, more committed individual with a clear goal etched in his mind. He was no longer bitter about his treatment, he no longer wanted revenge for the hardship he had been put through. He wanted to assume his natural position, to accept his fate—whatever that was to be. And the first part of that journey was to discover who he really was and how he had ended up this way.

But where Mason's biological father might actually be turns out to be not that simple either. Mason hasn't seen him or heard from him in over ten years and has no idea as to his whereabouts. They first try to access any NHS records but they are blocked by confidentiality rules.

Mason then tries calling Chloe and enlists her help but there appears to be nothing on anyone named Harrison Chambers after 2009 when he left Mason and his mother. He had literally disappeared off the face of the earth. The photo inside the amulet seemed to have revealed all its enigmas but provides no clue of where they should now try to find Mason's father. So as a last resort they turn their attention to the amulet itself.

Lucie knows that Matt's dabblings have at times had something to do with jewels of imprecise if not downright dodgy origins and she is confident when she calls him that he will be able to recommend someone who can offer an honest appraisal of the amulet and it turns out that Matt does indeed have such a friend who works buying and selling gems and precious metals. So, Lucie and Mason take the tube to the Elephant and Castle northern line station and emerge into a dingy and run-down shopping arcade built right on the top of it. There are a few barber's shops, some nail-bars, rows of unoccupied orange prefab seats, places to buy phone cards or for transferring cash overseas and a couple of shops claiming to buy all types of gold and silver.

As they enter the store that Matt had recommended, a doorbell is triggered in the back room. The inside of the shop is even dingier than the rest of the shopping arcade if that is possible. A counter spans the entire place with a secure looking rusty grille stretching right to the ceiling. There is no display of anything for sale.

Just a couple of soiled and worn sofas which Lucie would much rather avoid sitting in. There is just a single small opening in the grille through which to transact any business. The place looks more like a minicab hub in a dangerous part of town rather than anywhere you might consider buying jewellery. Quite depressing.

The jeweller who comes out from the back room recognises them immediately although a smile is not a part of his way of communicating.

"Matt sent you, in it?" His accent is southeast London mixed with some deep-seated tinge of Eastern Europe.

The whole feel of the place is of plastic, not gold. But Lucie has absolute confidence in Matt so she prods Mason to get him to hand over the amulet.

Matt's jeweller friend looks through his loupe magnifying glass lodged in front of his eye. Lucie is fascinated that it is held in place by just the jeweller's frowning eye which has been moulded through years of practice to a shape ideally suited to deliver that gravity-defying feat.

"How much do you want?" the jeweller asks.

"Oh no, we are not selling," Lucie explains. "We just want to find out about its origin."

"Well," the jeweller again looks at the amulet. "It certainly is unusual," he says mysteriously.

"In what way?" Mason asks.

"Well, it is a reasonable piece. Beautifully worked. But…"

"But what?" Lucie insists.

"But…the hallmark has been tampered with. A sort of vandalism which casts doubt on its true origin. This seriously reduces its value, I am afraid. Why someone would do that is beyond me. Makes no sense."

"How has it been changed?" Lucie demands.

"The original hallmark is from a well-known London maker, Jon Klein. Made in 1863. And then…" the jeweller pulls a thick catalogue along the counter and flicks through its pages without removing the loupe. And then tapping a specific page knowingly, he continues, "…someone added another mark belonging to a small relatively unknown maker in Dolgellau in North Wales founded in 2004."

"Welsh gold," Mason murmurs.

XV
Trial Run

Lisbon—Two Months Ago

Alves never truly came to terms with not being able to trust his own mind. Or—as he often chose to think about it—he never could quite get used to Bisset's side of his personality not giving him a chance; he even half-accepted now, after so long, that Castro would indeed have been much better than him. It wasn't like Alves hadn't tried to live up to Bisset's expectations. Oh, he certainly had.

Yet always he felt like he was having to peer cautiously around corners just in case he was about to be jumped by some sneaky unexpected revelation. Sad, maybe. Mad, most likely. Annoying, without a doubt. But he knew these same contradictions were an integral part of his psyche and even now, seventeen years after Bisset's death, were still contributing so much, albeit in a subversive, behind the scenes, sort of way.

The only thing which none of his personalities dared to go anywhere near was his love for Jules. That love had touched all his various incarnations and Alves was still shocked at how painful he found just thinking of her even after more than a century and a half had elapsed since as Gryphon he had last laid eyes on her and most likely she must have died a minimum of seven decades ago. But that deep anguish never stopped him going over and over all his most nostalgic memories of her. How is it love can last so long with such brightness?

A bleep brings Alves back to the here and now. He taps a key on his phone angrily activating the speaker and says in a disgruntled tone.

"Yes?"

"There is a Miss Kelman down here, Sr Alves. We can't see her in your schedule but she is extremely insistent that she must see you now."

"I bet she is," Alves says to himself. This was so inevitable. Why he hadn't pre-empted this when he had the chance, he has no idea.

When Emma first arrived in Lisbon, Alves had taken a backseat role. He had left things pretty much up to Castro and his team. It made sense, Emma had been offered the post by the Science Institute and the business side of things, which he ran, should not be seen as driving academic recruitments.

It had been a hard sell to get Castro to consider appointing another junior member to the team. But after a month or so of complicated bargaining and after seeing the quality of her thesis, he too could see she may be helpful and capitulated.

Now though he wonders how much it had actually been nerves at how Emma might react when she found out that Alves had been instrumental in her appointment. He feels apprehensive now that it becomes clear he has been rumbled. Absurd, he knows.

"What shall we do with her. She is refusing to leave the building."

"It's OK," Alves says finally. "Send her up."

Just a few deep breaths later, the lift opens and Alves can see Emma across the full length of his office. She looks so much younger than he had thought and more beautiful than he remembered from their trip to the Wirral.

"Alves!" Emma runs over to him and hugs him eagerly, kissing his cheek lightly and comfortably this time, as though they have been the best of friends forever. How things have moved on since he first saw her timidly descend towards the stage in the Imperial College lecture hall.

She then steps back and looks at him somewhere between inquisitively and accusingly.

"You have been trying to avoid me," she says.

"That is not exactly true," Alves manages to reply lamely, still unsure of how to approach Emma being here in his own space.

She looks around taking in for the first time the scale and luxury of Alves's office and her mouth opens in awe.

"Wow! Is all this yours?" Emma asks.

"Yeah, you're right. It is way over the top, I know. Look, let's get out of here," and Alves grabs Emma's hand and pulls her back towards the still open lift doors.

They are now sitting in the most sumptuous of soft white leather armchairs in the naturally cooled wine cellar just a few doors down from the Alves building.

The wine racks are illuminated with uplights making them stand out all the more in the quiet and subdued area around their low table in a secluded corner. On the table stands a bottle of dry white port wine the contents of which both Emma and Alves are sipping from exquisitely curved port glasses.

Just what Alves had been afraid of, why he hadn't been upfront with Emma from the outset, he now cannot comprehend. Emma seems to approach everything with such a straightforward, practical and uncomplicated mindset. She clearly didn't understand Alves's motives for keeping her in the dark over his role in bringing her to Lisbon but she had always imagined that he was there in the background anyway and she accepted whatever reason he had for his privacy but when she came across the Alves S.A. plaque outside his office purely by chance—or so she said—she couldn't resist forcing him out into the open. And then it was forgotten, as though it had never happened and they carried on as if there had been no interruption in their relationship since the Wirral trip.

Alves is truly in awe of this woman. Not in a physical attraction kind of way—he is more than twenty years her senior—but in a straight character sense. She is forthright, unprejudiced, free from all the baggage he himself drags around.

"What's wrong with Castro?" Emma asks.

"What do you mean?"

"Well, it's like he hates every suggestion I make. Takes it personally."

Alves finds it difficult to defend Castro when he recognises so keenly Emma's allegation. He shifts the focus to a more positive interpretation of Emma's complaint.

"To be fair I couldn't believe myself the results of your recalibration of the mesh exposures," he says. "I suppose Castro is just envious. You know his team has been working on that same problem for God knows how long and then you come in and slash the tolerances across the board. It's hardly surprising he's a bit put out."

"It's more than him being a bit put out. It's as though he cannot see the true potential here."

"Oh, he gets it alright, I assure you," Alves says with a smile.

"He just keeps going on about the risks more than anything else. I never dreamt this sort of project could ever see the light of day and yet, here it is. But Castro seems to be pushing against the flow."

Alves never could pin any blame directly on Castro for the frustrating delays which had beset the project, although he always assumed that Castro, where it was within his reach to do so without detection, would actively undermine progress as Emma is suggesting.

Needless to say, there had been endless arguments over deadlines not being met, over staffing levels and supply issues, over the need or not for time-consuming safety procedures. Castro was a master at conjuring up excuses out of nothing. But none of those disputes ended in wholesale paralysis, and headway of sorts, even if at an agonisingly sluggish pace, had consistently been achieved and now, basically since Emma has come onto the scene, things are moving at pace. Emma has the scientific backing which can expose any sham or pretence and Castro is only too aware of that.

Alves has gone from eternal frustration to being on the verge of fulfilling his dream. He knows he shouldn't be getting ahead of himself but talking to Emma gives him real hope that he could now be the one to realise the ambition of all those who had gone before him, all the way back to Duncan. In just a matter of months, he could be reunited with his destiny. His gamble of bringing in an outsider is paying off, handsomely.

When Alves returns to his office after leaving Emma at the door of the residencia where she is now staying, bizarrely right opposite Alves's own new headquarters, he finds Castro pacing up and down outside the lift, waiting for him. The bottle of port and Emma's innate enthusiasm has left him with a warm glow.

"I don't like it," Castro says in his customary scrappy, negative tone. Alves makes no attempt to hide the roll of his eyes as though he is already convinced Castro's comments will be a groundless waste of everyone's time. Castro, seeing the gesture, glares at Alves and continues, "It's like she's spying on us."

"Spying!" Alves is incensed. Castro cannot be serious. "She has just shaved five microns off the wave tolerance. You've been trying, and failing, I would remind you, for the last four months, to achieve less than half of that. Hardly the action of a spy."

"She's taken a room opposite here." Castro walks over to the window. "Look, you can bloody well see it from here! She could be observing us right now."

"She has just informed me about that herself, Castro. In any case, just what would she be hoping to see? Listen, that residence is a total dump. It must be so cheap. Maybe you should consider paying her a bit better."

"Well, in the last few weeks, more or less since she arrived, there have been a series of attempted breaches of the firewall and Farinha's team has spotted someone taking photos of all the people coming and going into the Institute. A bit of a coincidence, wouldn't you say?"

Alves had never told Castro of the break-in at his house. On the one hand, he actually thought the intruder may have been Castro himself, and if that were the case, what would he gain by accusing him without proof? And on the other, if it hadn't been Castro, then him finding out that key data had gone missing could potentially cause a major raucous and with the final trial only days away, now was not the time for honesty on that issue.

But Alves was certainly concerned that someone, maybe Doyle, who has disappeared off the face of the earth ever since the exact day of the break-in, or else some associates of his, may be mounting a concerted campaign to stop the project completely or to take all its potential value away from him.

"Well, tell Farinha to get a grip and to apprehend whoever is behind all that. But don't try to include Emma in your spy plot, please."

"We have to bring her in. You know that. We can't put it off any longer. We can't have any of the latest data getting out. It's critical." Is Castro being cynical? Does he know that key data has already been stolen? Alves cannot say, but it would be precisely the sort of game he would play.

"She will freak out…She could run…That would be disastrous," he says in an overdramatic tone.

But Alves knows that Castro is right. It is just how Emma might react to their wanting to take her freedom away even if it is only for a matter of days that worries him.

"Are you losing your bottle, Alves?" Castro sneers.

"What on earth do you mean?"

But Castro clams up and just smiles knowingly at Alves.

"Alright, alright," concedes Alves. "But I will have to be there. It is the only way Emma may go for it. We don't need to use force, just make sure that thug of yours, Farinha, knows that."

The next afternoon, a Wednesday, just over a week before the final trial is set to go ahead, Alves is standing in Emma's room, looking out of the open

French windows across the small balcony and over the narrow street into his own office two floors up in the modern building opposite.

"So what *is* going on here?" Emma asks. Alves turns around noticing that she has raised her voice deliberately, he assumes, so she can be sure the busybody landlady listening down the corridor will be able to overhear without any difficulty. "How dare you come barging in here."

"You should watch your lip," Castro says bitterly, "I am still your boss and I could have your stay here terminated immediately."

"Oh yeah? Really?" Emma is fuming. Alves was right about Emma being quick to anger but he still hopes his other initial view that she would be quick to move on and not hold a grudge is also true. But for the time being that is unclear, she is still incandescent with rage. She continues, "Sack me then. Go on!"

"Calm down everyone, please," Alves tries to ease their belligerent egos back down a notch. "As I have already said, we cannot afford to put the project at risk. From here on, I will control the information flow. It's only for a week and I would feel much happier if you were safe."

"Safe! Have you lost your mind?"

"Don't be so melodramatic, Emma. We're just going to offer you alternative living arrangements for a week, that's all. All paid for. Think of it like a business trip. It's really very luxurious. When you see it, you'll be thanking me for getting you out of this hovel for a few days."

Castro still hurting from Emma's sniping lack of respect, orders her to accompany them.

"Are you going to kidnap me? Is that the deal? Really?" Emma is incredulous. She addresses Alves, "You're serious, aren't you?"

"You are such an important part of all this."

"Why don't you just fuck off! All of you, get out of here. Now!"

Emma turns away from Alves and takes a step towards the door. Farinha crosses her path and touches the inside of his jacket clearly suggesting he is in possession of a concealed weapon.

"Oh, right. Brilliant. Just brilliant," Emma sarcastically accepts her position is useless.

"We will take great care of you," Alves states. "You'll see."

And Alves really did believe that. Obviously, he considered that removing Emma's freedom of movement and of communication would in no way undermine his commitment to taking great care of her. Emma had no alternative.

Alves was convinced that Emma was smart enough to realise it was either scream like hell and end up on a flight back to London or take it on the chin and stay part of the project. And Alves was quite sure which way Emma would lean and his gamble again paid off.

Later when he analyses her mobile records that evening, he notes that she had made a call to a friend called Lucie in the UK just minutes before they had *barged* into Emma's room, but the call duration was only seconds. So maybe she hadn't been able to talk at that time or perhaps she had just left a short voicemail. Regardless, he will deal with any fallout. Just having Emma here, on site, lifts his spirits no end.

The 'lab' as the whole complex is known to the team, is located outside the centre of Lisbon in Moscavide on an old industrial estate. From the outside, the building looks so run down that anyone passing would think it must be unoccupied, but nothing could be farther from the truth.

The only way in is through the subterranean carpark accessed from a ramp behind the block. No-one comes here without strict invite so no need for any reception area, branding logos or signs. All the windows and doors at street level are boarded up.

The large operations room is two floors down, below street level. Multiple live feeds and data processing units are linked to desktops and to large wall-mounted screens connecting through to the mesh containment chamber which is built some fifty feet below ground level, encased in eight-foot-thick reinforced concrete walls and a steel door more usually seen protecting gold bullion in central bank vaults than in a research lab.

To create the simulation of a mesh surface deformity in Lisbon they have had to develop a revolutionary new advanced particle accelerator just a fraction of the size previously designed for electrons to reach close to the speed of light. And so far, it was working, totally glitch-free. So much for Doyle's alarmist danger talk. And so much for his little threats. Even Castro himself had been impressed.

The pipe, as everyone calls the accelerator, runs around the circumference of the specially designed domed roof of the building with multiple hi-performance solar energy arrays built on the exterior roof of the dome to provide the power source, stored in batteries which avoids any direct connection to the electricity network.

This should give rise to a wave simulation triggered within the containment area allowing the team to test equipment calibration in preparation for the fully scaled-up run in Bidston Moss, even though the development of this last part of the project is still secret from everyone, and particularly from Castro.

Alves himself shows Emma around her *alternative living arrangements* and his description of luxurious is not far off the mark. Emma's living quarters are on the floor below the main control room. There are five huge bedrooms of which Emma is taking the last. The others are already occupied by three lab technicians and an IT specialist. There are another two floors with accommodation for the rest of the team and the deepest level is reserved for Alves and Castro's own rooms although they are not bound by any of the most stringent terms of lockdown imposed on all the rest. They are free to come and go at will.

There is a fully stocked kitchen on Emma's floor which miraculously is replenished daily. The lounge area is sumptuously decked out and has the most comfortable sofa and armchairs that Emma has ever sat in, with perhaps the exception of the wine cellar near Alves's office.

"I am sure that once you realise that this is the ideal working environment you will not think of trying to leave. You will feel no privation here. Anything you need, you only have to ask. Of course, with the one caveat that we remain in lockdown until after the end of the trial. So, no phones, no communications with the outside. But I hope you will agree that this is for the best and will dedicate yourself to the task in hand."

One of her colleagues who is in the lounge when they are looking around says rather blithely, "It is a bit like Big Brother, you know, the TV show. Lots of cameras and locked doors. But here you get to work on a project which may change the course of humanity rather than doing a challenge to win a few extra likes and a bottle of some cheap booze."

Alves had been right to trust that Emma would understand that a communications blackout was the safest way to assure secrecy. All the staff are also under the same intense lockdown rules and everyone is ultra-committed to the project; Emma fits in seamlessly with all the other members of the team.

Alves is also quietly confident that with Emma's latest recalibration the tolerance will be sufficient to allow them to take the accelerator up to full power firing up the controlled wave simulation they are looking for. Sixteen people in total are involved in the project at this time, and all spend those final days working at full tilt. Even Castro seems to have knuckled down and remarkably has put in more hours than the rest.

Alves is on his own in the containment area making the final checks to all the manual adjustments to the resonance synchronicity valves inside the accelerator target field to make sure they have all been implemented correctly. It is the one thing he refuses to trust to any form of automated procedures or indeed to anyone else on the team, it is personal, even though it requires lying on the floor of the containment area half-in and half-out of an uncomfortable hatchway with a ratchet in his hand stretching to reach each of the valves in turn. This is after all the culmination of such an agonisingly long process and now finally there are just under two hours until the trial runs for real.

Alves finds his mind drifting off onto the issue of Emma's friend Lucie. He thoroughly enjoyed their lunch just a couple of days before at the Norte e Sul. She is bright, scintillatingly alive, quite different to the scientific precision and prudish bashfulness of Emma, it has to be said. Lucie's mind has a refreshing uncluttered take on things. Maybe it has something to do with her being so much younger than Emma. In eight years you can live a lot, build a lot of protective barriers.

The two girls think in such different ways, communicate with vastly different styles, they are in many ways both unique, yet they remain committed to each other totally. Lucie has demonstrated over the last few days a deep loyalty to her friend and a fierce tenacity in her search which Alves can only admire. In fact, he would go as far as to say he feels envious of the intensity and profoundness of their friendship.

Clearly he is now aware of what had happened with Farinha and even that Lucie has been suggested as her killer which is blatantly ridiculous. Quite laughable. You only had to meet Lucie to know she could never do anything like that. Alves has no idea how her name ended up being leaked to the press. He wipes the sweat from his forehead. It's hot. Strange, he thinks. Or maybe it's just that he's not used to this much physical exertion. The air-cooling systems should keep the temperature pretty stable in the run-up to the initiation of the accelerator.

He stretches to reach the final valve turning awkwardly on his side. He struggles to attach the node scanner and then flicks at the switch on his phone on the floor beside him to take the initial reading. It really is so stuffy in here.

"Emma, are you there?" Alves asks. There is no response.

He pulls himself back out of the hatchway and gets to his feet. Emma should still be monitoring all this from operations. He taps the manual intercom mounted on the wall.

"Emma, what's going on? Are you seeing the temperature in here?"

Again nothing. Just an eerie sound of white noise.

Then he notices a tiny mirage-like flickering disturbance no bigger than the smallest of coins in the very centre of the containment chamber. He has never witnessed this phenomenon before but he instantly knows exactly what it is. As quickly as he can he moves to the door, leaving the hatchway open and all his tools and his phone strewn across the floor. He pulls sharply at the handle but it is locked. He taps his code into the keypad and waits for the automated clunk to open the lock. Nothing.

The disturbance is steadily growing and is now a clear sphere approximately the size of a tennis ball of flashing, sparkling lights. He rushes over to the back wall of the containment area and checks one of the array of instruments. He looks down aghast at the numbers on the screen rising quickly. He cannot explain how this could be happening.

The bar graph representation shows the readings are climbing beyond acceptable levels into the red zone on the display. It measures the level of ionising radiation inside the containment area and it is going off the scale. Somehow the accelerator has been started with himself still inside the target area.

"Emma!" he shouts, his desperation getting the better of him.

The shimmering fractured light at the centre of the room is the least of his worries, he knows that. It's the radiation being emitted here inside the containment area which is potentially lethal. That's why the walls are eight feet thick.

That's why no-one can be in the chamber when the accelerator around the dome is fired up. There are so many safeguards in place to make sure it could never happen. He calculates that at the current levels, he has maybe ten minutes before he will start to suffer from ARS—Acute Radiation Sickness—and if he is not out of here in thirty, he is dead.

He tries to keep calm. There is no way this could happen accidentally. Impossible, too many things would have to malfunction at the same time: the live mics, the manual intercom, the accelerator start-up, the door lock, his passcode failure. Which means that someone has to be behind this and he could hazard a guess at who that person might be. When he gets out of here, his retribution will know no bounds, he will show no mercy. More like if he gets out, he starts to think.

The radiation level continues to rise. He has maybe fifteen minutes before he has no way back, less before he gets the first symptoms.

The data screens all over operations should be screaming at the rest of the team. They must be seeing this…unless whoever orchestrated all this has also tampered with the feeds and up there they are all still seeing everything as it was an hour ago. No-one would hear the accelerator, it's way up under the dome. And no-one would hear his shouting either. With the accelerator operating, there is no way his phone will get any reception down here—that is why Emma couldn't hear him earlier. He needs some other way to raise the alarm.

Then it dawns on him that perhaps if he could divert a signal showing the current level of radiation through to Emma's desktop, bypassing the main feeds, a backdoor into only Emma's personal system, it just might work, that is if Emma happens to be at her desk and if she twigs that there is something wrong with the main feed. Not much better than a maybe but it is all he's got.

By the time he has completed his personal SOS message, he is already feeling quite nauseas. He sits down on the floor next to the door. He is mesmerised by the disturbance which has grown to the size of a bowling ball and as he looks at it he can now see that it is hollow at its centre, it already has the form of a wave, growing slowly and unstoppably. He suddenly wretches and vomits blood and mucus down the front of his shirt. The radiation sickness has progressed more quickly than he had anticipated, the dial has been slammed at past the maximum for the best part of thirty minutes.

He is losing focus. He regrets more than anything how things had turned out with Jules; he had only been with her for the briefest instant. But that one moment they were together was the defining moment in his entire life. He would have given up everything for the chance of a lifetime with Jules.

So absorbed is he in the shifting flickering colours and in reminiscences of his time with Jules that he hardly notices the clunk of the door unlocking. It opens and Emma is there. He coughs involuntarily as he sees her; more blood. His message worked but he already knows it is too late for him.

Emma struggles to drag him through the door as quickly as she can. Alves himself can barely offer her any assistance; he feels drained, totally spent. Once outside, Emma slams the steel door shut and helps Alves into a more comfortable position with his back up against the wall.

"You saw my message," Alves is having difficulty speaking. He was in there for over forty minutes.

"It must have been Castro," Emma says. "He checked all the feeds this morning."

"I figured that out," Alves chokes. "I have been exposed too long. I am going to die."

Although Emma clearly doesn't want to accept this, Alves can see that she too knows he's right. His time is up.

"What should I do?" Emma pleads. "The radiation spike will overload the wave structure. It could be impossible to maintain the containment field. This whole place could explode in less than an hour. It may already be too late to stop it."

"You will know what to do," Alves grabs Emma by the forearm tightly, his palms sweating profusely.

Emma freezes. Alves understands her instinct to pull away from his touch but he has no choice. Emma too has no choice.

Suddenly she sees Bidston Moss stretching out before her. She is kneeling in the freezing waterlogged mud. She feels her own consciousness mutating and fluid. This is something beyond her understanding, she has no response to it, no way to halt or even influence its progress, no alternative other than to engage with this new reality. She looks deep inside Alves's eyes. She feels his pain. But what shocks Emma is not what is actually happening to her but that during the entire process what Alves keeps uppermost in his mind is Jules, constant and unbudging. He refuses to let go of her.

Even as his memories of her flood in an unending barrage out of his own mind and into Emma's, as his own recollections inevitably fade, his love and passion for Jules persists throughout with an intensity and clarity which is astonishing. For Emma, it is perhaps made even more tangible and pure by her being a woman, by being able to fully appreciate just how much Duncan had hurt Jules, abominably so. It wells up from so deep within Emma that it makes her balk at its ferocity.

She recalls, can see vividly, the policeman throwing his cloak around her shoulders as he led her away from him, the sky dark, her hair burning against the blackness of the storm clouds. She sees Jules's despair at Moira Cawston's suicide, the rain pelting against her coffin lid as it was lowered into her grave. The look of disgust on Jules's face as she abandoned him shackled to the cart outside the forge. The desolation of Gryphon wandering listlessly around their home in Bidston, mourning her loss when she left for Australia.

And then in the end, she knows she has to break away; it is over. She leans back weeping for Alves, for his feeling of devastating failure in the end at not completing the project and more than anything for his anguished unfulfilled love of Jules. Emma resolves to be so different from Alves. But she vows never to renounce that love and to live up to his legacy. She also vows to be so much more ruthless. This is her time.

Emma is sitting at Alves's desk, less than an hour has passed since she gained access to the containment area and pulled Alves out. She is still in a state of confusion at what has happened. It is too much to assimilate. And at the same time as dealing with that shocking new reality, she has tried with two other members of the team to get the radiation spike under control and to shut down the accelerator but so far they have failed.

Containment is holding but only just. Following orders shouted by Emma, a couple of the more junior assistants have taken Alves down to the living quarters to be showered and decontaminated as much as is possible. Really just to make him comfortable. He isn't going to make it and now he doesn't even seem to have any meaningful grasp on who or where he is. Emma can see his image on the CCTV downstairs, he is just lying in bed with severe burns now disfiguring his skin. He shivers continuously. Emma knows his mind must be wandering, listless. His brain with no point of reference. Blank. Only registering physical pain.

Emma knows now that once the wave breaks out of the containment field, it will expand freely and unstoppably through the building and beyond, accelerating until it reaches critical extension, at which point it will snap back, collapsing in on itself at close to the speed of light, triggering a massive explosion which will destroy not only the entire building but also a good part of the surrounding area as well.

Then on another screen Emma sees Lucie standing inside the front door of the lab looking up in awe from the gallery, staring at the tech around the dome and the solar panel array.

She must have broken in through the front of the building somehow.

"Oh Christ, Lucie! What the hell are you doing here?" Emma shouts at the CCTV screen. She rushes over to the door and taps a security code into the keypad while shouting over her shoulder, "How the hell have we got someone wandering around up by the pipe? I thought we were supposed to be in bloody lockdown. This is the last thing I need to deal with right now."

Emma goes out through the automatic door and climbs the stairs up to the level directly below the dome and walks towards Lucie.

Lucie looks so lost. She has no idea of the danger she is in. She could die this evening. She deserves at least a warning. Emma is now aware of the lunch Lucie had with Alves just a couple of days before and of the remarkable tenacity she has demonstrated in her search for her friend. Emma looks at Lucie with a deep sense of regret that she can no longer fulfil that role although she now knows that thankfully she has not lost all her feelings towards her friend in the process of transfer. It is still there, in the background. It still drives her, no doubt about it. She has no feelings for the other members of the team, however. They will have to take their chances if they choose to stay put. But Lucie is special.

Emma shouts for Lucie to stop coming any further down to see her.

"Listen Lucie, you can't be here," she pleads. She then tells Lucie that the building is going to explode. "You must leave now!"

What more can she do? Emma goes back into the ops room and slams the door shut, hoping that her harsh words will have the desired effect and will convince Lucie to get out of there in time.

The team is rushing around in total chaos, shouting aggressive but meaningless orders at each other like in some out of control computer game running on auto-play. They still seem at least partially convinced that they can avoid a breach and no amount of screaming by Emma that they must evacuate now does any more than add to the bedlam but she knows it is already too late and she has to get out of the building.

As Emma is taking the lift to the car park, the surface deformity wave slowly crosses the space in the lift car, the containment field definitively breached, its multi-coloured chaos fracturing reality as it expands, passing directly through her body. This was not supposed to happen. Her eyesight blurs momentarily.

There is a presence here. She can feel it. As powerful as she is herself, maybe. And she feels Lucie here too, who clearly has still not evacuated the building but there is nothing more she can do for her friend. The wave fades through the wall of the lift car behind her and she is left with a sense of longing. She must hurry, critical extension is now so close and the wave could collapse triggering the devastating blast at any moment.

Emma jumps into Alves's red Lexus parked there. She drives up the ramp and races away from the building. Only a few seconds later there is a massive flash; a huge explosion rips through the area behind her and the lights across the entire city of Lisbon go out. She stops the car and gets out. She is engulfed in total, absolute darkness.

Then, suddenly, as she looks up, Emma can see billions of stars in the sky. Deep down in her psyche she knows she has only once before seen a night sky so vibrant and alive, standing next to Lucie on the shore of Loch Doon in the purest of Scottish nights; just a feeling, though, the embers of a memory but she has no doubt it actually happened. She thinks of her friend Lucie and hopes maybe that someday they get the chance to witness such beauty together once again.

XVI
Welsh Gold

Snowdonia—Present Day

Up here the gloom on this Welsh mountainside is such that Mason has had to turn the headlights back on although Lucie can see from the dashboard clock that it is still before noon. Even on full beam they are pretty much useless, incapable of penetrating more than a few yards, the light getting clogged up in a layer of dense cloud, like the car is feeling its way through soggy cotton wool which enshrouds everything.

The higher they go, the wilder the countryside becomes and the less defined the road. To be honest, the term road gives a bit of a false impression; it is little more than a track. Very few other vehicles could have made this particular ascent recently given how the gorse and the brambles are protruding into their path. Luckily the Land Rover which Chloe presented to Mason has made light work of the climb but the wet dreary late morning certainly does nothing to lift their spirits.

"I don't get it." Lucie says, looking over at Mason, "Why didn't you try to find your father sooner?"

"It wasn't that simple," Mason replies after a lengthy pause.

Lucie keeps quiet, allowing Mason time to consider how best to frame what could well prove a difficult and even painful explanation. Mason eventually turns to her taking his eyes off the road momentarily, a stern look in his eye.

"What can I say? Look, it's like we had some sort of an understanding," he says, peering back out through the windscreen into the swirling foggy drizzle, "…an unspoken arrangement, if you like. Don't ask me how, but I felt as though I knew what he wanted. For me to keep out of sight, not to expose myself, to stay safe. In his way, he was protecting me, I guess."

"Walking out on you is a funny way of going about it," Lucie says.

"I was struggling just to understand what was happening to me while at the same time I was trying to cope with my father not being there. What could I do? I was only nine years old when he left. Later on though, as I got older, I did look for him, of course I did. But I found out that the police had been investigating him. He worked for one of the big American banks, Morgan Stanley. He'd been setting up some takeover—that was his job—and he ended up in trouble when all he ever did was to use his admittedly *special* negotiating skills to help determine just how far deals could be pushed."

"Oh, right. Your father was a banker," Lucie gives a sneered edge to the term, jumping to the cliched conclusion, only later realising she was failing to pick up on the full implication of what Mason was saying: that his father shared his unique abilities.

"That is unfair, Lucie. He did nothing wrong. The police just couldn't get their heads around any of it. Hardly surprising, I suppose. Actually though, it was the police themselves who acted unethically. For a couple of years, I sensed their presence lurking in the background all the time, keeping an eye on me—that can't be right, can it?—hoping to ensnare my dad through me. It was terrifying. So I backed off from trying to find him. I didn't want to make things worse for him. In any case, he was long gone. I found out later he had skipped the country ages before that."

"Quite a guy, your dad," Lucie says, the rabbit hole she is falling into spiralling ever deeper by the minute.

"Once I reached eighteen though, I decided the time had come to find him and to get some answers. So I started looking for him seriously again. That was when I came over to the UK and then, almost straight after arriving here, I had my accident and as you know, from that point on, all hell broke loose."

After finding out from Matt's specialist jeweller in Elephant and Castle that the amulet had indeed offered up a viable clue as to the whereabouts of Mason's father, or at least a credible starting point for their search for him, Mason and Lucie had not wasted any time in heading out of London. They spent that night at a Premier Inn near Leicester in separate rooms—although Lucie cannot say what might have happened if Mason were to have intimated otherwise if she were completely honest.

An early start the following morning and a few more hours on the road, saw them entering Dolgellau in southern Snowdonia. They trudged up the rather drab and damp high street and rang the bell outside the goldsmith's workshop gallery.

They then presented the amulet to the owner who himself had opened the door. He had studied it for what seemed an excessive amount of time for such a tiny object before saying in a broad Welsh accent, "It's really exquisite but I am afraid I don't buy. I'm only a manufacturer."

"You recognise it though, don't you?" Mason states rather than asks.

The goldsmith eyes Mason warily for a second or two and then, holding the chain up to the light, admiring the amulet, he continues, "Well, it looks familiar, yes. All I can say, though, is that the gold may have been mined just up the valley from here in the mid-to-late nineteenth century, if I am not mistaken. How did you come by it?"

"Was it you who added the extra hallmark?" Lucie asks, abandoning the niceties.

"What are you talking about?"

"Come on. Don't deny it. It was you, wasn't it?" Lucie pushes.

"I did nothing illegal. Who are you? Police?"

"Police? No, not at all," Lucie clarifies, fearing she may have freaked the goldsmith a bit too much by her directness. Falsifying hallmarks must be illegal so she can see why he is nervous. Mason's father must have paid through the nose to leave his personalised clue as to his whereabouts.

"So answer my question then. How did it come into your possession?" The goldsmith challenges Mason and Lucie again, his tone still one of distinct mistrust.

It is clear that if Mason wants the goldsmith to reveal anything about where his father may be, he is going to have to give some account for his ownership of the amulet.

"It's been in my family for generations," he says. "Actually, it belongs to my father. His name is Harrison Chambers."

"That name means nothing to me. Where were you born?"

"What does that have to do with anything?"

"If you want to convince me of who you are, just tell me where you were born?"

Mason accedes to the goldsmith's demand, "In Saint Vincent's hospital, in New York City."

"So you really must be Mason."

"You know my name?"

"I never thought it would work, mind. It must be ten years at least since he came in here, only a couple after I set up shop here. I certainly wouldn't be doing that sort of stuff now."

"So where is he now?" Lucie asks.

"I suppose he must still be up at the ruins. He just said to explain to you how to get there."

"The ruins?"

"Rumour has it he bought vast swathes of land, way up around the mine. The gold seams dried up back in the 1950s. So why anyone would want to buy so high up in the hills, I have no idea. They said he must have been connected with the mafia somehow. Laundering dodgy money. Then, by all accounts, he built a massive wall around the whole place. Completely crazy, if you ask me. When he came in here, that was the only time I ever saw him. He is not exactly community-minded, if you get my drift."

The goldsmith mutters something under his breath in Welsh as he rummages around in a disorganised-looking chest of drawers, eventually coming up with a map of the area.

"It's a bit off the beaten track, though," he says. "You got a good car?"

The Land Rover rattles its way across a cattle grid. Visibility is much better now they have climbed out above that dismal layer of clinging mist and cloud. The terrain has levelled out somewhat and is more easy going too. They continue ever upwards. The last village was some miles back. Whoever had decided on building a home in this location must have been seeking total isolation; over the last couple of miles even the sheep are few and far between.

Then Mason and Lucie make out the wall in the distance and immediately recall the comments of the goldsmith. This is certainly not one of the typical dry-stone dykes separating fields but a proper solid affair, to stop intruders from getting in. For the last mile or so before they reach the entrance, the road is flanked on one side by the barren moorland rising steeply to a craggy peak above them, part of the steep rim of rugged mountains at the head of the valley, and on the other by the wall which close up they can see has rolled barbed wire and broken glass cemented into its top.

Lucie also notices that at strategic points along the wall a series of cameras are mounted looking outwards onto the road. All way over the top, thinks Lucie, or maybe a sign of total paranoia on the part of the owner. She cannot for the life of her imagine how such security measures could be necessary; there are no people up here after all, no houses, nothing.

They pull up in front of a pair of rusty-looking gates. Through them they can see down to the ruins of some ancient building or fortification perched on a small hilly outcrop below them, some two hundred yards away.

"Are you sure you want me to come in with you?" Lucie says. "I can stay in the car, if you like. It's not a problem."

"No, absolutely you should come with me. Right now, that is the only thing I *am* sure about."

Lucie gets out and tries the gates but they are locked. She looks around for a bell or an intercom, but finds nothing. She shrugs at Mason, who is still in the car, at the exact same moment she hears a loud clank as the lock on the gates is opened remotely. Somebody must be keeping an eye on those camera feeds. Lucie then struggles to open the gates enough to allow just herself to squeeze through, let alone the car, so jammed up are they with weeds and the hinges caked almost solid under thick layers of rust.

After trying to budge the gates himself for a while as Lucie rolled her eyes at his failed machismo, Mason finally parks the Land Rover and slips through the opening to join Lucie inside.

"From here, we go on foot," he says as though this had always been his plan.

"Right," Lucie lets it go.

Everything looks abandoned, left to the forces of nature. The driveway itself is lost beneath a knee-high mass of meadow grasses, its form only recognisable in the magnificent beech trees planted originally on each side in some earlier age.

The tall and thick tree-trunks are completely covered in bright, almost luminous, green lichen which draw the eye easily down the slope to where a small half-collapsed stone bridge crosses a loud gurgling brook which over time has eaten a deep scar into the terrain before the driveway rises up again on the other side around the base of the ruins.

Mason and Lucie walk down between the line of trees and carefully pick their way across the bridge. Of the ruins themselves little more than rubble remains, a few isolated walls, any roof long gone. It must date back hundreds of years. Lucie's light jacket has not been made with this climate in mind. She pulls it around herself a bit tighter but it does little to ease the cold.

"Look, Mason," Lucie shouts out. "Over there."

She is pointing beyond the ruins, way down close to where the brook disappears from sight, swallowed up by a large deciduous wood which seems to follow its path down the valley. From out of the darkness amongst the trees, they see a figure emerge walking across the field towards them.

As he gets nearer, Lucie can tell he is certainly old enough to be Mason's father but any further similarity with Lucie's expectations of a well-heeled, smarmy investment banker is decidedly lacking: his greying hair hasn't seen the inside of a barber in months; he has an unkempt half-grown beard which is in parts oddly darker than the hair on his head; he is dressed just in jeans and a black T-shirt, over which he is wearing a faded airforce trench coat with its collar pulled up against the cold; his well-used hiking boots are covered in mud. But there is some undeniable family likeness which stands out behind the obvious generational differences.

Lucie can only imagine just how much Mason must have craved to have any sort of opportunity to speak to his father, must have played out this very scene over and over in his mind, role-playing all of the possible outcomes. But here in some abandoned ruins, most of the way up this desolate mountainside in Wales was never going to be high on any list of probable scenarios and Lucie can see he is struggling to come up with anything appropriate to say at such a massive moment for him. Mason's father slows hesitantly to a nervous stop also. Could this be even more difficult for him? He too seems lost for words.

"Well, you certainly took your time, didn't you?" Mason's father finally breaks the awkward silence with a casual throwaway admonishment, hardly the opening Lucie was expecting.

"You're not the easiest person to find, you know," Mason replies slipping into the same comfortable banter which most likely was ever-present in their relationship when Mason was a kid. Dramatic childhood emotional outpourings were probably something Mason's father would have frowned upon back in the day. Far better to keep any evidence of their unique connection totally under wraps, to maintain at all times a facade of normality.

How, she cannot say, but Lucie senses a surging unstoppable undercurrent firing back and forth between them. She also notices that both are edging nervously forwards and then all of a sudden they pass some unmarked threshold and the whole thing tips over; they both rush forward, the power of all those years apart taking them by storm and they embrace tightly for what seems an age.

Mason finally breaks away, realising that Lucie is still standing there witnessing all this.

He looks embarrassed almost.

"This is Lucie. She is my friend," Mason says to his father.

"Is she now?" Mason's father says smiling knowingly and offering out his hand to Lucie.

"Lucie, this is my father."

Lucie steps forward and as they shake hands she notices his eyes are the same piercing bluish-grey as Mason's and she feels the same depth and intensity in his gaze, the same penetrating prying scrutiny. But then quite abruptly Mason's father turns his back on Lucie and walks briskly away, back across the open field down towards the woods.

"We have to talk. Come on," he shouts over his shoulder.

Under a canopy of tall trees they follow the brook downstream on a barely discernible footpath. No words are spoken. This is neither the time nor the place for the major exchange which Lucie can sense bubbling up only just under the surface.

After some minutes, they come out into a small clearing at the far end of which stands a stone cottage. Well, stands is hardly the right word to describe it. A large tree uprooted by storm years ago lies fallen across its roof and a mass of ivy and other undergrowth have almost completely integrated it into the structure. The cottage looks more like an organic part of the scene rather than something built by outsiders but this is undoubtedly where Mason's father is heading.

He pulls open the door of the cottage and draws aside a heavy red carpet-like material which must help keep the cold out. There is no sign of any electricity and no gas. A single tiny window set deep into the thick external walls has a wire mesh protective layer to stop the glass being damaged. That is the only natural light source in the cottage but a fire burning in the grate gives off a comforting cosy feel.

Lucie's mind backtracks to the hitech security measures and she concludes that paranoia indeed seems their most likely explanation; so far, she has seen nothing of any value whatsoever within the walls, apart from the CCTV cameras themselves that is. But where the monitors are located leads her to think there could yet be more to this place than meets the eye.

Mason's father indicates for them to pull up chairs from the back wall and to sit down at the large oak kitchen table.

"Why did you never even try to contact me?" Mason cuts to the chase. "Never call. Nothing."

Mason's father pours boiling water from a charred kettle on a Primus stove into three chipped mugs each already prepared containing a finger of milk and a single teabag. Everything seems to be following a set preordained plan. Mason's father even shows no surprise at his son's question; he must have known all along this would be the first thing his son would ask.

"God knows I wanted to. Believe me," he replies sitting down and sliding the mugs across the table one by one to Mason and Lucie. "But my getting involved would have led to all sorts of risks. It made sense to leave you be, to wait until you needed me."

"You could have let me know you were alive, at least."

"It was better this way. There is a right time for things to happen. And this, now, is how and when we were destined to meet again."

Lucie raises an eyebrow thinking that maybe Mason's father has spent too long out here alone in these woods. But she can feel Mason is getting more out of this than she is. The way the two exchange glances seems to hide a myriad of unseen levels from her.

Actually, she feels quite an outsider here, which in any event she undoubtedly is, she recognises that. Let's face it, she is not on anything like the same wavelength as these two. But her closeness to Mason is something she can hold on to, something to make her feel somehow still a part of all this, even if only a minor one.

Mason pulls the amulet from under the cuff of his shirt, unclasps it and holds it across his knuckles, offering it to his father.

"This belongs to you," Mason confesses. He breathes out a long deep sigh of relief. He had waited over ten years to have a second chance to give the amulet back to his father.

"No, no," his father replies immediately. "It was always going to be yours."

Mason just looks quizzically at the amulet still dangling from his hand and then asks, "How did you get it in the first place?"

"We have found out who Duncan was and what happened to him," adds Lucie. If she is to be here at all, she will not allow herself to be a mere spectator.

Mason's father looks across at Lucie and then says, "I'd wager you didn't find out Duncan was innocent though."

"What? Duncan was innocent?" Mason mutters in shock.

"Just imagine the guilt his adoring wife Jules must have suffered; she had after all—unwittingly or so she always swore—led the police to Blackheath where Duncan was arrested. Imagine then finding out he was innocent after he had been executed. No wonder she wanted to leave the Wirral altogether, to get as far away as was physically possible."

Mason's father takes a deep breath waiting a few seconds to allow his revelation to sink in. Lucie cannot figure out Mason's father at all. He seems beyond any frame of reference she has ever come across before. He is odd, but not amusing odd, nor bizarre odd. So what kind of odd is he? Eccentric odd, perhaps. He does seem blissfully unaware of his being outside of what the rest of us call normality, breaking the accepted rules without intending to, or even being conscious that he is. He is courteous enough, sure. Yet he is also suspicious of her she feels.

"The other thing you won't have found out," Mason's father continues again looking at Lucie, "is that by the time Jules sailed from Liverpool she would have known that she was carrying Duncan's child. That must have seemed doubly cruel. Jules and Duncan had been married for six years before the murder of James but they had never been able to have children.

"And then, years later they meet for the briefest of moments and by some sort of miracle she ends up giving birth to Duncan's son on the first days after making landfall in New South Wales. Jules never remarried so the boy kept the name Chambers and before she died she passed on the amulet to him, and so on down the generations, eventually on to you, Mason."

"So, I am directly related to Duncan. OK, I accept that. But how can you know categorically that Duncan wasn't guilty?" Mason asks.

"What I am going to tell you," Mason's father continues after a pause, "is Jules's own account of events, told to me by my mother—your grandmother—just before she died back in 1986. That was when she passed the amulet on to me. All of it is based on what Kal, the village blacksmith, told Jules on board the Australia Star just minutes before she set sail for Australia only six weeks after Duncan had been executed."

"Kal's story, however, relates the events surrounding James's murder almost nine years earlier in 1865, in a place called Bidston Moss, a large wild area of marshland on the Wirral peninsula, just below Bidston Village."

Lucie cannot believe her ears. The Bidston Moss Industrial Park is precisely where TransWorldX has been delivering all the truckloads of gear from Lisbon and from several other locations all over Europe. She decides to keep this to herself—for the moment at least—although she has doubts as to her ability to keep anything from Mason or indeed from his father for that matter.

"Duncan was a successful shipping line owner. Pretty well-off, I suppose we would say today. But everyone was only too aware of the bad blood between Duncan and his lawyer and accountant James, who had been recalled from his cushy position in Jamaica accused—although nothing was ever proved—of having had his hand in all the tills he could. But I believe what pushed things over the edge was more personal, when Duncan found out that James had been making a play for Jules. On that cold November afternoon, the two had a massive bust-up. Duncan stormed out of Bidston Manor where he lived with Jules and was followed by James only a couple of minutes later.

"Kal, the blacksmith, as I said, who was working in his forge just across from St Oswald's Church in the centre of the village, must have seen something in the look on James's face as he rushed by just after Duncan that caused him to suspect something serious could be going down, so he dropped everything and followed them out from the village and onto the Moss."

Lucie can feel herself slipping under the allure of Mason's father's story. The longer he speaks the more vivid her experience becomes. It is hypnotic, his voice totally absorbing.

"As Kal emerges from the trees, he sees Duncan way down, nowhere near any recognisable path, kneeling in the marshland of the Moss itself, up to his haunches in mud and stagnant freezing water. It is sleeting and bitterly cold. Duncan looked to Kal as though he were praying, his eyes closed, quite peaceful, in some trance-like state. Just why he had gone down there in the first place is anyone's guess.

"And somewhere between them Kal sees James too, stumbling and splashing his way across the marsh, screaming at Duncan although Kal is still too far away for the words to carry to him. Kal jumps down from the track and he too begins wading towards them.

"Then the story shifts dramatically. When James gets to say within twenty paces of Duncan, something utterly bizarre happens. The whole substance of James's body starts to shimmer like he was stepping in slow motion through a rainbow—those are the exact words used by Kal to describe it years later—and from that moment on, James seems to lose momentum, he starts slowing down, his progress towards Duncan getting more and more laboured with every step. Kal closes the gap on them.

"As Kal approaches the spot where he guesses the rainbow effect must have taken place, he wonders whether it might be wiser for him not to go any further but he can see James now only ten or fifteen paces ahead of him and he takes a deep breath as he decides to push on regardless. He sees the same multi-coloured turbulence surge through his own body and he trembles."

Lucie too trembles. She can feel the sleet striking her cheek. She sees the shimmer climb through Kal's body as he walks forward.

"This is just how it happened to me in Lisbon," Lucie says, "but it wasn't static, it was moving. I couldn't get away from it."

She then realises that Kal is not trembling from the cold. A rush of panic has engulfed him as he suddenly is aware of how things will play out here. Somehow, he knows the outcome of what lies before him. It has in effect already happened. Kal is confused. It is that same fear Lucie had experienced as she blacked out and found herself bizarrely on the shore of Loch Doon, the moment she saw Mason for the first time, sharing impossibly that space with her when she had never laid eyes on him before.

Time here too has gone haywire, is breaking every law known to physics, is shifting at a slower pace the closer Kal gets to where Duncan is kneeling. At the outer edge, nearest to the rainbow effect, Kal is less affected by the freak time disturbance and he can easily anticipate James's every move. He can see everything unfold, before it comes to pass. But what terrifies him all the more is that he also knows there is no way he can stop any of it.

Kal knows James is going to take a knife out of his pocket, he has already seen its blade glint in the dull afternoon light. He knows too that James has every intention of killing Duncan but at that same moment he realises he is about to intervene, to change the course of history, to disrupt the flow of time itself. The knife suddenly is no longer in James's hand but in his own, although he has no clear recollection of it getting there.

"Oh my God, Mason. Can't you stop this?" Lucie shouts out, becoming increasingly agitated as she too sees where this is leading.

"This all happened in 1865, Lucie," Mason says.

"How can you say that? Don't you see?"

Lucie feels the knife plunging once, twice into James's back. James has no time to react, he just turns and stares at Kal, a muddled and imploring look on his face. Lucie in shock then experiences how Kal grabs James around the head and she suffers first-hand the sensations of the knife this time slicing right across James's neck as though she had cut his throat herself.

James inevitably would then fall to his knees, blood spurting from his severed artery, splattering the impassive Duncan whose eyes are still peacefully closed, oblivious to the horrific events that are happening. For Kal—and for Lucie too—all the events appear to be out of sync, their order hideously jumbled, like a mirror has been smashed and each sliver of glass put back in the wrong place.

Mason's father finally falls silent. Lucie takes several deep breaths, trying to compose herself. Her total immersion into all the graphic and gruesome detail of his story has left her stunned. How could she have even seen—let alone to have actually felt—the physical sensations behind any of those actions? She looks across the kitchen table at Mason who like her seems dazed. It occurs to her that he could have had an even more intimate encounter with the appalling incident via his links to his father or indeed those going all the way back to Duncan himself.

"I have frankly no idea what prompted Kal to confess suddenly to Jules," Mason's father offers a few seconds later in way of conclusion, "and neither can I imagine how she managed to handle the fact that Duncan was innocent. But ultimately, she knew there was no point in staying in the UK to try to secure justice for Duncan; that would never bring him back. So she just left in sorrow, knowing that she was carrying Duncan's child."

"I feel we are further than ever from understanding all this. Everything is just spinning out of control," Mason says in a more downbeat tone than Lucie is used to from him. "What actually happened to Duncan out there? That's what we have to establish."

"Well, clearly there is no way that time disruption could have happened by chance," says Mason's father. "I mean, it is not some natural occurrence, is it?"

"What worries me," Mason takes up that same idea, "is that whatever is behind it, whatever, or whoever, caused it back in 1865, that very technology is precisely the one Alves has been trying to replicate for years. And now it seems that effort is being taken to a whole different level and is close to completion. That is what you got caught up in, Lucie. You know, in that wave, as you call it. And we have both experienced how life-changing any connectivity with it can be."

"Jules certainly did say that from that day in 1865," Mason's father explains, "Duncan was a changed man, he was never the same again. He claimed he had lost his memory and Jules believed he wasn't faking it."

"Could your MRI have something to do with it?" Lucie asks in something close to a whisper, worried that all this science goes so far over her head that with such a question she may be making a complete fool of herself.

"What MRI?" Mason's father demands.

"The scan they did after the accident. It identified a rerouting of the neural pathways in my brain. I always thought it must have been some freak of nature, a one-off but I'd say you just might be right, Lucie. Now I would bet my father has the exact same anomaly and that its origin could well be out there on Bidston Moss."

Lucie immediately thought Mason's father, who clearly wasn't aware of the MRI, would want to go much deeper into this but instead he chooses to shift his focus entirely onto her, once again drawing her under his penetrating stare. She feels his presence, stronger than before.

"You trust her fully?" he asks his son, still looking intently at Lucie.

"I do," confirms Mason.

"But you know just how close she is to the one who helped Alves."

"Emma! She has a name, for heaven's sake," Lucie makes a stand. She is not going to let such an obvious lack of respect to her friend go without at least making Mason aware of it.

Mason's father continues to address his son but he doesn't take his eyes off Lucie for an instant as he says slowly and ominously, "Both of them may be too dangerous for you, Mason."

"Lucie is with me! She is good here. Back off, won't you?"

At least, Mason is showing he's on the same page as Lucie. She feels a huge sense of relief and a warmth towards him.

"All right," Mason's father says, casting his eyes down to the floor in the corner.

Strangely, Lucie had only become aware of the full strength of that magnetism in his gaze and of her inability to evade it, once he had looked away, effectively releasing her.

"I have to show you…something important," Mason's father grunts, getting to his feet and moving to the back of the kitchen. He pulls back a rug and opens a trapdoor revealing a set of steps descending into the floor. As he disappears below ground level he orders, "Follow me."

Mason and Lucie look at each other and shrug in acceptance. They too descend the steps which lead into a twenty-yard-long passage with just a single weak bulb half way down but at least that means they are entering a world where electricity exists. At the far end a door opens automatically, triggered by a sensor as Mason's father reaches it. The steady but rapid move up through the ages to what is clearly a hi-tech environment is hugely comforting to Lucie.

Beyond the door they walk out onto a metal gantry some five metres above the floor of a cavernous space cut out of the rock hillside itself. As Mason's father descends, lights progressively flicker on, the whole place coming alive as if by magic. He is already almost at the bottom of a spiral staircase which leads down to the floor.

"My God! This is amazing," says Lucie in awe. At the far end of the cavern, mounted on the wall, is a series of five monitors all currently switched off—the feeds from the CCTV cameras no doubt. Lucie immediately knows that this must be where Mason's father followed their progress up the mountain and from where he must have unlocked the gates. There are also three more large oak tables, the same as the one in the kitchen upstairs covered with photocopies and printouts strewn randomly across their surfaces.

Lucie is struck by just how much the disorder reminds her of Mason's room at Burnt Ash Lodge. Even the scale of this space itself is reminiscent of the library where he had been incarcerated for so long. It's like unknowingly they had been sharing far more of their lives at a much deeper level than either could have imagined.

"What is this place?" asks Mason, his voice betraying the fact that he certainly wasn't expecting anything like this either and maybe he, like Lucie, has recognised the same surprising similarities with his previous abode.

"It is part of the old mine…the goldmine," Mason's father says over his shoulder. "The cottage upstairs is just for show. I live down here mostly. It's comfortable enough. I have spent much of the last decade down here, to be honest. I needed a bit of privacy."

"A bit of privacy?" Lucie jokes sarcastically.

"What do you mean?" Mason's father snaps at her. He clearly doesn't see the funny side of things, Lucie concludes. A bit too serious. Thank goodness Mason is not like him in that respect.

"Come on, I mean you are a bit paranoid about intruders, wouldn't you say?" Lucie refuses to back down as she skips more confidently down the last few steps to the floor.

"You have no idea what they are capable of," Mason's father says in a tone however, which sends a disturbing chill up Lucie's spine.

But with that Mason's father has already moved on—subject closed. He is rummaging around in some untidy desk drawer, pulling out some papers. He clears a space for them on the nearest available table and spreads them out for her and Mason to see.

"Look at this," he points to what appear to be two photographic prints with some sort of bar code charts on each except in colour going from blue at the top through to orange lower down with some red bars interspersed along the way.

Lucie and Mason study the images. Mason states the obvious, "They look identical."

"That's because they are. They are exactly the same, down to the tiniest detail. These are the DNA test results of two different people: Irvine Bisset who, as you may know, founded the Science Institute in Lisbon and Alves, who was responsible for and was killed in the Lisbon bomb blast. You heard about it, I suppose."

"Alves is dead?" Lucie asks. She had always hoped that Alves too would have escaped unscathed from the lab, even though she knew that he had been responsible for the project which had nearly killed her.

"How can Alves and Bisset have the same DNA?" Mason has no such concerns for Alves's safety, he is focused only on the science.

"I've no idea, but according to this, they are essentially the same person."

"That's impossible," Lucie says instinctively.

"Where did you get this?" asks Mason.

"Ever since I heard Kal's story, for years, I tracked any research projects looking into revolutionary theories in their approach to time and space, anything that could maybe eventually offer some sort of an explanation of what had happened to Duncan: the weird time perception shifts, that rainbow effect. And then a couple of years ago, the name Alves started to come up a bit too often to be pure coincidence.

"There seemed to be a pattern which always pointed back to Alves and to Bisset before him. I found out that Bisset had died of a heart attack in 2006 and from then Alves was the one running the show. There was very little overlap. Alves had been just a junior assistant who inexplicably was launched to prominence when Bisset died. I attended a lecture given by Alves at Imperial College getting on for two years ago when he met your friend Emma."

Mason's father glances over at Lucie with a hint of an ironic smile. Well, at least this time Mason's father has remembered she has a name.

"At the same time, I was desperately trying to find you. I knew you hadn't died in that accident. I was blinded too for a few minutes by the same pulse that caused your crash. I was absolutely certain they had faked the funeral. And that in some way you were involved too. So I tried to put two and two together and came up with five when I thought Alves had somehow whisked you out to Lisbon and that you could be playing a crucial and involuntary part in his experiment. So I orchestrated a meeting with Alves face to face."

"You met Alves?" Mason asks.

"You know, he had an amazing mind, Mason. Quite exceptional. His thought processes, the way he interacted with the external world was not unlike our own. Uncomfortably similar, in fact. So I broke into his home hoping to find you there but instead all I came up with was this, locked away in a safe."

"But this doesn't get us any closer to understanding what actually happened to Duncan, does it?" Lucie interjects.

"Somehow…" Mason says as though he is still figuring it out, "Duncan's DNA must have been changed."

"Right. In 1865. Out on some marsh. You can't be serious…" Lucie says but she is interrupted by a muffled high-pitched intermittent alarm which sounds somewhere strangely close by.

"That's all we need." Mason's father pulls out his phone and looks down at the screen with a worried frown. "You were followed, Mason."

Using his mobile, Mason's father activates the line of monitors along the back wall of the cavern. On one of the screens, Lucie can see a black Mercedes climbing the track up towards the gate outside the property. It advances out of camera and the shot flickers to another angle which again captures the car as it now slows up outside the main gates, stopping next to their own Land Rover. Lucie is impressed by the tech running Mason's father's surveillance system.

"The two of you need to get out of here, and fast," Mason's father blurts out, getting up. He rushes down to the far end of the bunker and unlocks and opens a door which Lucie had not until now noticed.

"This tunnel comes out on the far side of the wall where the old mine entrance used to be. It's all overgrown by the woods now so that should keep you hidden if you are careful. Follow the brook for a mile, then a track leads off to the right over the hills to the next valley. Hide there until it is completely dark. Then head down till you hit the main road."

"This is crazy. I've done nothing wrong." Lucie is adamant. She avoids mentioning that she has just recognised the guy who has got out of the Mercedes. It is none other than Zac. "Maybe I can create some kind of diversion to give you enough time to get away."

Mason looks at his father, and then at Lucie. Later, she would come to the conclusion that Mason and his father were both aware of her knowing Zac. That had to be the case. But initially at least Mason does seem reluctant to leave her behind.

Zac will listen to her, she says to herself. Won't he? He'll understand why she dumped him at the motorway service station. They'll patch things up and she'll convince him to let her leave in the Land Rover and then she'll pick up Mason under cover of darkness. It just seems so reasonable. What could possibly go wrong? What indeed, she worries.

"Go! I said." Lucie shouts at him rising to her feet. "I will pick you up outside that jeweller's place, OK?"

"She's right," Mason's father backs her up. "She may be more useful here. She is not a threat to them. You most certainly are. You have to get away from these guys."

Mason must have realised that no amount of argument was going to change Lucie's mind and with a smile he accepts it and with a shrug disappears into the darkness of the tunnel.

"Hey," Lucie shouts out remembering something important. "Car keys?"

"You see how in control I really am?" Mason jokes, re-emerging after a couple of seconds.

He hunts through his pockets and holds out the keys to Lucie.

Lucie walks over to Mason and takes the car keys. He pulls her towards him and kisses her full on, almost desperately. Lucie melts.

Mason stands back stunned at what he has done.

"That was quite something, eh? I mean…good something," he says smiling as he lunges out of the bunker and this time he stays gone.

It's just too much for Lucie to process in one go: Kal's story, the DNA, Mason's father's part in all of it. And then throw that kiss into the mix and it has pushed Lucie off the cliff edge. She wants to scream, partly out of confusion but also in no small measure out of pure elation.

She has always considered herself pretty level-headed and all this sort of stuff just doesn't happen to her, or at least never has before. Specially the kiss bit. But right now is not the time for any considered reflection along these lines; she will be able to do that later, when she picks Mason up in Dolgellau, she thinks glowing inside, already looking forward to that moment.

For now, all she can do is follow Mason's father up the spiral staircase and back into the cottage where he stops briefly by the window, reaching down behind a cabinet propped up in the corner. Lucie is totally gobsmacked when he pulls out an automatic rifle, like one of those Russian ones you see all the time in the movies.

"Jesus! Just what are you planning on doing with that?" she shouts out at him.

"I know this guy," he says calmly, checking the rifle is fully loaded and grabbing a backup magazine. "He may have been OK with you so far, but that is because it suited him. I assure you he is absolutely ruthless."

This is when Lucie realises just how much Mason's father has gleaned from her. She had definitely not told him that she knows Zac but not only is he aware of that, he seems to have some idea of how their relationship has panned out thus far. Then to make matters worse she realises she herself has left Matt's gun in the glove compartment of the Land Rover. A lot of use it will be to her there if things escalate out of control and with Mason's father armed to the teeth she most certainly can't rule that out.

"It's better to let them know how seriously I am taking things from the outset. That may give Mason a bit more time and he is the most important thing here. I have done my bit now."

"You know Zac?" asks Lucie but Mason's father either doesn't hear her as he has already pulled back the rug curtain and marched out of the door, or else he has deliberately ignored her. She should have left with Mason. What was she thinking about?

When they reach the tree line, hunkering down to keep themselves hidden, they can see Zac and a thuggish-looking companion of his just getting to the foot of the ruins, looking around with lost but wary expressions on their faces. Both are dressed in jeans with black jackets which look all the world like standard FBI issue but without the yellow lettering on the back. That easy approachable look Zac had in Lisbon is gone without trace. An insurance inspector. Please.

"You stay here, Lucie," Mason's father orders, his tone leaves no room for discussion. He walks straight out into the open and fires his rifle a few times into the air just to get Zac and his buddy's attention which it certainly does. Both of them immediately drop to the ground behind the outer wall of the ruins, pistols magically appearing in their hands, aiming down towards Mason's father, who seems unconcerned and continues to walk towards them.

Zac yells, "Doyle? Is that you?"

"You shouldn't have come here Zac," Mason's father yells back. He now has the assault rifle pulled hard against his shoulder, his aim trained directly on Zac. "This is only going to end badly for you."

"Calm down, Doyle. We had no idea you were here."

"You don't say."

"We need to talk a bit, that's all. Then we'll be gone." Zac jumps down from the ramparts to the path leading around the edge of the ruins, putting his gun away in his belt behind his back. He doesn't feel threatened in the least by Mason's father even if he is toting an assault rifle. Zac's sidekick likewise nonchalantly descends to the track but he keeps his gun very much on show, taking a back-up position from where he can easily cover Zac.

Mason's father stops some ten paces or so from them. Lucie can't believe that they actually know each other. And why is Zac calling him Doyle?

Zac and Mason's father are now just out of earshot and Lucie knows she has to hear what is being said, so she nimbly skirts around the border of the woods until she reaches the brook. She ducks down below the tall lip overhanging the bank and edges steadily further up, her back tight under the ledge keeping out of sight from the ruins. From here, she will be able to pick up most of the conversation going on above.

"…and here's me thinking all this time that you were dead," Zac is saying in a scornful tone.

"Listen Zac, get your mate over there to back off. To the bridge, say," Mason's father demands. "If he tries to sneak off a shot, I might even kill both of you with this thing before I'm done."

"Vaz, give our friend Doyle here a bit of space," Zac says firmly to his companion. Lucie can hear Vaz's boots crunch across the path just above her head as he backs off slowly. If he goes much further, Lucie will be in full view. Another brilliant plan, she thinks. Can't Mason's father pick up that she has moved here? The one time you need him to tune in, his psychic gifts go missing. Thankfully, the footsteps stop; what can only be inches now keep Lucie hidden.

"Tell me Doyle, where is Mason?"

"It's only me here," Mason's father says coldly.

"Come on, Doyle. Give me a break. We are going to find him."

"You swore you were going to put a stop to Alves," says Mason's father, "and that never happened, did it?"

"On the contrary. He's about as ceased functioning as you can get."

"We were talking about his playing God with science and that has far from stopped. Actually, it's starting up again, as we speak."

"All we want is the chance to give it a once over ourselves before shutting it down, that's all."

"Sure you do. You saw what happened in Lisbon. Wasn't that enough?"

"Where is it 'starting up again' as you say? Not up this godforsaken mountain, that's for sure. So, the question is where are Mason and Lucie heading to after here."

"You tried to have me killed in Lisbon. Remember?"

Lucie has to do a double take. Zac tried to kill Mason's father in Lisbon. That can't be right. She knows Zac. He would never do something like that. Well, she thinks she knows that. Her doubts about him now snowballing.

"We had a deal. You were going to give me whatever you found in Alves's place and then—what do you do?—you hand it over to Castro, of all people. That blew any trust I could've had in you. I should have gone ahead and killed you myself then."

Vaz takes a further step backwards onto the bridge itself and Lucie is suddenly in full view. She freezes but it is too late. Mason's father must have immediately understood the look on Vaz's face when he spotted Lucie on the bank.

"What the…" Vaz shouts out but he is interrupted by a shot hitting him full in the chest. A second shot echoes around the ruins, Vaz falls to his knees and topples forward over the low wall and tumbles head first down into the stream with a loud splash and thud as he hits the water and the rocks below.

"Why the hell did you have to do that?" Zac says, annoyed. Lucie then hears a gun clatter onto the track, followed by someone falling heavily to the ground immediately after it. She realises that the second shot she heard couldn't have been from Mason's father's rifle but actually came from Zac's pistol. She can hear someone gulping for air. Mason's father must have been hit.

Lucie scampers manically along the bank and rushes towards her only protection now, the bridge itself, so if Zac comes to check if Vaz is still alive he won't see her. Lucie could save him the trouble though; she has already witnessed his wide-open staring eyes looking out from under a foot of water in the brook as she clambered past his body and into the opening under the bridge.

"You're in way over your head, Zac," splutters Mason's father. Speaking so coherently must mean he cannot have been hurt that badly.

"Right," Zac ignores Mason's father's comment. "Listen Doyle, I can get a medical team up here in no time. That part's easy, you know me."

Lucie climbs out on the far side of the bridge and from there, risks looking over the lip of the bank. Zac has his back to her, his gun back in his hand. He is standing over Mason's father, who is lying face down in the grass verge in the middle of the track. Mason's father's face is lying towards Lucie and she sees a glint of recognition in his eye that he has seen her.

"You are losing your grip on this, you know," Mason's father manages to say in a half-choke, half-cough.

"Oh yeah? Really? Listen, you can stop the project dead in its tracks," Zac says, "stop it from being taken to the next level. That's what you always said you wanted, wasn't it? You know where Mason and Lucie are going. So, just tell me."

"Don't you get it?" Mason's father spits out angrily. "I am in control here."

"For God's sake," Zac sounds as if has become bored suddenly. "You're pathetic, Doyle. You really are."

Mason's father says nothing.

"Right. I can't mess around here with you any longer. Tell me where Lucie and Mason are going or I will finish right now what I should have done ages ago in Lisbon."

"I wouldn't tell you even if I knew, which I don't."

"I just can't be bothered with this anymore," Zac says leaning over and pushing his gun into the back of Mason's father's head.

"Last chance," he states almost as if he has no expectation of getting the result he needs. He waits a few seconds and then, as if in a gesture of annoyance, he fires twice from point blank range killing Mason's father instantly.

Lucie shivers, screaming inside. She has just witnessed the cold-blooded execution of Mason's father, there is no other way of describing it. Zac looks up breathing deeply. Lucie ducks down again as Zac turns and she hears his boots advance to the bridge and stop right above her position.

If he comes down to retrieve his partner's dead body, he will see her through the opening under the bridge, she will be discovered without doubt. But instead, Zac takes out his mobile and holding it to his ear gives details of his location. Lucie then hears him walk back up towards the ruins. She breathes a sigh of relief, Zac had seen Vaz is dead from where he was and has no intention of pulling him out of the brook himself.

From where Lucie is hiding at the far edge of the bridge, she can see the Land Rover parked just on the other side of the entrance gates but she has no way to get to it without revealing herself to Zac and after the scene she has just witnessed she fears that would lead nowhere good. Her confidence in being able to talk Zac around is shattered. She has no intention of testing the strength of their relationship right now, or ever again for that matter.

Getting back down to the cottage to follow Mason's escape route is similarly out of the question with Zac prowling around close to the bridge. She has to get to the car unobserved before the cleaner-uppers arrive. But how? The walls on both sides of the gate are impossible to climb with their barbed wire and broken glass inlaid topping.

First things first, she makes her way along the bank trying not to dislodge any stones the sound of which might give away her location. If she can make it upstream to where the woods beyond the ruins resume, then maybe she would be offered some cover from any new arrivals who as things stand would see her directly from the gates.

As she edges her way along the bank, an idea occurs to her which is, at the very least, worth investigating: the woods curve away following the brook upstream towards the wall and given water of necessity must flow downhill, at some point it must have crossed the wall and the track Mason and herself had driven up earlier, so maybe there is another bridge they had failed to see on the way up which she can use to get under the wall, not over it.

So far so good. She reaches the woods and, without the risk of being seen, can climb up out from the bank of the stream. She can see Zac walking nervously around on the bridge looking down at his dead colleague. Had she stayed put he would have caught her by now.

She follows the brook upstream a couple of hundred yards but her excitement at seeing the brook up ahead coming out of a culvert which undoubtedly crosses under the road lasts only seconds; her master plan falls in tatters around her. Mason's father it seemed had already considered this entry point to the property and had taken measures against its being used.

There is indeed a circular concrete pipe maybe seven or eight feet in diameter bringing the brook across the track and under the wall, but the end is covered with an iron grille blocking any access to it. Also, the stream being forced into such a tight space means it is gushing through the grille with force and the culvert is pretty much full of fast-moving water.

But then she notices that the grille seems like the gates on a castle drawbridge, going down only so far. It doesn't appear to be fixed into the ground under the water. She grabs a long stick and probes the lower part of the grille. There is indeed a gap under the surface which could be big enough to squeeze through at a push although it is more than five feet under the turbulent water.

If Lucie needed any proof that she is certifiably insane, this is it, she thinks as she lowers herself into the gushing current, holding onto the grille to stop herself being flushed downstream. She has convinced herself that she can hold her breath for thirty seconds no problem and at a push can probably get close to a minute, so easy enough time to drop under the surface and to pull herself through the gap in the grille.

But she hadn't realised just how cold the water would be. My God is it cold. And the force of the current was far more aggressive and destabilising than she had imagined when looking at it from the bank. But now she is here, up to her neck in water, taking deep breaths to expand the size of her lungs for her to eke out a few extra seconds underwater just in case, there is no going back.

One huge gulp of air and she pulls herself under allowing her feet to follow the rushing stream out behind her. The other thing she hadn't taken into consideration was how she would immediately become blind once under the surface. She can't see anything and has to feel her way down the grille. The gap is just about big enough but as she is half way through and starting to think her Houdini act is all but done, her belt snags on the bottom edge of the grille, halting her progress.

She is stuck. She needs both hands to pull herself through the gap so she has no way to detach the belt from the grille. She struggles, her fingers are going numb. Her lungs are already close to bursting. In a last ditch attempt she relaxes, allowing her torso to shift backwards a touch and then jerks herself downwards. The belt is free but now she is starting to doubt if she will have enough air to make it but somehow she keeps going and once her feet are through and make contact with the base of the culvert she can push her head up and out of the torrent of water, pinned to the grille by the current, spluttering into the tiny space in the uppermost bit of the pipe. But she can breathe.

To get to the other end of the culvert, she still has several yards to navigate with just her head above the level of the water, holding herself in place with her arms extended to the roof of the culvert and slowly shifting one limb at a time. A few minutes later, she emerges onto the other side of the track where thankfully no grille had been deemed necessary.

She clambers trembling uncontrollably up onto the track and half runs to the Land Rover, jumps in and first things first, she checks the glove compartment, takes out Matt's gun and stuffs it quickly into the bottom of her bag still where she had left it on the front passenger seat. She's not going to leave that behind again in a hurry. Then, taking one deep breath for courage and maybe for luck too, she starts the engine.

She does a nifty three-point turn—even if she does say so herself—and hits the accelerator powering the Land Rover away from the gates. In the rear-view mirror, her last recollection is of Zac now shouting into his phone and staring directly at the Land Rover as she speeds away. She knows she may only have a few precious minutes to get down the mountain before Zac's guys cut her off, so she pushes the Land Rover as hard as she can down the narrow track. It is tough driving.

The rain is falling quite hard now and judging distances is perilous; it is now almost dark. She emerges from the track onto a stretch of proper tarmac road and accelerates. She just might make it. Then as she rounds a sharp bend she is suddenly confronted by two black vehicles blocking the road completely with dazzling blue flashing lights on their roofs. She has no time. She brakes hard but the car spins out of control, smashes into the rear of one of the cars and piles into a ditch down the side of the road. Lucie is thrown forward violently as the airbag explodes and she loses consciousness.

This time, as Lucie comes to, her first thought is that she is back in Burnt Ash Lodge; it has all been some strikingly over-elaborate dream. All that stuff about non-human brains, the visions, the MRI, even Mason himself, all of it just a fabrication of her own super-vivid imagination. She can even hear Chloe's reassuring voice in the background. She is recovering consciousness after the Lisbon explosion, that must be it. But when she opens her eyes and sees the cramped interior of an emergency ambulance, that comforting version of reality breaks down. Suddenly she is aware that Mason is very much for real, as was his father's death, her escape from the ruins, the crash as she raced down the hillside, the whole lot. And yet she can still hear Chloe's voice.

"She's coming around," Chloe is saying.

"Chloe?" Lucie pulls herself up onto her elbows. "What the hell are you doing here?"

Then Lucie notices that the person Chloe is talking to, in the driving seat of the ambulance, is none other than Zac. She shivers in fear as she sees his face glaring straight at her through the rear-view mirror. This is the guy who a question of minutes ago had murdered Mason's father, more than that—if anything *can* be more than that—had executed him mercilessly.

"Oh my God! Don't tell me. You two together. How cute!" Lucie says but neither Chloe nor Zac provide any response to her outburst. Instead, Zac just starts the engine and pulls the ambulance out into the road, waving to a uniformed army officer outside, and heads off through the steady rain down the valley in the direction of Dolgellau.

Lucie decides to go on the offensive. She swings her legs off the gurney but finds that her right wrist is handcuffed to the bar along the side of the stretcher.

"Let me out of here, now!" she shouts out.

"Lucie, calm down," Zac snaps at her. "We need to talk."

"Talk, you say," Lucie quips, unable to believe her ears and then adds in a voice laced with sarcasm, "For starters, how the hell did you know to come to Wales. A bit of a coincidence, don't you think?"

"Lucie, we need to find Emma and the only way was to let you and Mason lead us to her. When Chloe told me that Mason was planning to escape from Burnt Ash Lodge, I provided the Land Rover and planted a tracking device in it."

Lucie stares at Chloe with disgust. "You sold out Mason to this lying bastard! I thought you could be trusted. Just goes to show, eh?"

"That was my doing, not Chloe's," Zac offers in Chloe's defence.

"You were working with Kahtri all along. The two of you in on all of it. You kept Mason locked up in Burnt Ash Lodge for eighteen months. Would have kept me there too for good, no doubt. How could you do that, Chloe?"

"It's not that simple, Lucie," Chloe says but her words only raise a further ironic smile on Lucie's lips.

"And you," Lucie says, looking forwards towards Zac, "when you gallantly broke me out of there, you were actually the one holding the bloody keys all along. And you wonder why I have issues of trust with you?"

"You are the only one who knows where Emma has gone to ground."

"Why do you think I know where she is? It's astonishing. All of a sudden everyone is desperate to find Emma when a few weeks back I couldn't get anyone to even accept that she had gone missing."

"We can't allow her to carry out the final stage of her plan," Zac says.

"Her plan? Emma never had any plan. Who the hell are you Zac? I am fed up with your bullshit. You want my help, you're going to have to be straight with me."

"Alright, Lucie," Zac takes a deep breath, "Chloe and I work with something called TAU—that stands for the Threat Assessment Unit—an outfit which functions in tandem with MI6."

"Secret then, I take it?" After so many lies, Lucie finds it difficult to take anything Zac says at face value anymore.

"Actually, you'd find it doesn't exist at all," Zac confirms.

"And what threat do you imagine Emma can pose to anyone?"

"The Emma you knew, no longer exists," Zac states bluntly.

"You see. There you go again," Lucie yanks against the handcuffs aggressively. It is blatantly obvious that she has no way out of here using brute force alone. She is going to have to come up with something more finessed than that.

"Lucie, can you please shut up for just a second?" Chloe shouts out in anger, shocking Lucie into silence.

"I was there in Lisbon. I was undercover as part of Emma's team. I can assure you that the Emma that arrived in Lisbon has gone. Please, listen to what we have to say. It is vital that you do."

"You were there?" Lucie asks, amazed. "So you're not a nurse? I always thought that didn't quite fit with you."

"I did train as a nurse originally but in Lisbon I managed to infiltrate Alves's IT support team. The Emma I met there was a highly talented physicist, but at the same time, as you know, she was never one to sing her own praises, she was down to earth, humble even. Not shy exactly, as she would certainly stand up for herself, but she never sought to be the protagonist. You met Alves, he was always the top dog, the leader.

"Alves and Emma worked together non-stop in those final few days before the trial and then that whole dynamic changed—unbelievably so—just a couple of hours before the explosion. Emma was quite literally transformed."

"Go on," Lucie says. Everything that Chloe has said rings true, even the shift in Emma's personality which Lucie herself had witnessed when they met in the lab.

"Alves had for years been funding all manner of research projects into the bizarre time distortions which occur close to the event horizon of micro black holes, all very targeted, all very discreet. As I understand it, these distortions are like tiny folds in the space-time mesh which holds the entire universe together. As the folds fluctuate in position due to the effects of gravity mostly, they at times can draw near to one another and Alves was convinced he could create a fissure—as he always called it—linking two different folds."

"You mean he was trying to join together two separate moments in time? That's crazy."

"Maybe, maybe not. Emma and all the physicists had certainly bought into the science," Chloe says, "but something went seriously wrong and the containment field was breached. They lost control of the entire process. And well, you know only too well how that turned out. But Alves wasn't killed by the explosion, he was exposed to a massive and lethal dose of radiation beforehand.

It all happened so quickly. He was totally out of it, couldn't speak a word. And then inexplicably, out of the blue, Emma stood up to the plate and took over.

"Everything. Do you understand? The change was incredible. Everyone was in shock at seeing Alves so sick. But Emma took charge of things. She left Alves slumped on a bed downstairs. She rejected the idea of calling in the paramedics; there wasn't time, she claimed, and to be fair Alves was never going to survive, whatever Emma did. And by that stage, we could all see from the data readouts that the situation was fast becoming critical. The whole team was scared. There was no real discussion about it. When Emma started dishing out commands right, left and centre, the rest of the team recognised that she represented their best option of getting things back under control. They trusted her, but without doubt Emma was only too aware just how dangerous the situation was, and yet she was virtually the only one to get out of there alive."

Lucie cannot believe her ears. "How dare you accuse Emma like that? There is no way Emma would do any of the things you are saying. No way."

"But that is the whole point," Zac states turning around sharply from the driver's seat.

"Exactly what are you trying to say?"

"Whatever happened to her with Alves," Chloe tries to explain, "altered her profoundly. Something to do with that project, maybe the potential she saw if she could complete it. That's the only thing I can think of. That must have shifted her whole outlook on life so radically that she was prepared to let innocent people die to keep the project going. It's like she became a different person altogether."

"So how did you get out?" Lucie asks, still angry at Chloe's insinuation.

"When I realised Emma was abandoning everyone, I followed her out. She knew the whole place was going up and she was prepared to let everyone die, even you. Is that how your friend Emma would have handled things? Listen Lucie, I don't need to tell you what risks a scaled-up version of that mesh distortion could represent. We really need your help to stop all this."

"And you are both committed to shutting down the whole operation?"

"Absolutely," Chloe says firmly.

"Or...maybe you just want to give it a *once over* first, to check Emma hasn't missed anything?" Lucie sneers.

Zac darts a vicious look at Lucie in the mirror. She knows immediately that Zac is now aware that she heard everything that was said between himself and Mason's father at the ruins, that Zac never had any intention to shut down the project, that he simply wished to take over control of it. She also knows disturbingly that Zac cannot leave her alive at the end of this either or she will be able to testify as to what she has seen, that she witnessed his execution of Mason's father.

"Why come to see Doyle?" Zac asks, maybe his curiosity and arrogance getting the better of him. "What did he have to do with this?"

"You have no idea who he was, do you?"

"What do you mean?" asks Zac.

"First, you tried to have him killed in Lisbon?" Lucie can see from the expression on Zac's face in the mirror that he is shocked at the depth of knowledge she has about what has happened. She is doing a good job of getting under his skin. She needs to trigger a reaction to make it clear to Chloe who her only potential ally here is and just how dangerous Zac has become.

"Oh, come on. That's absurd. Doyle was a double-crossing conman. He was playing some other game…and he lost."

"And then at the ruins, you finished off the job."

"Lucie, he killed Vaz," Zac laughs. "He gunned him down without provocation. He would have killed me too if I hadn't stepped in."

"That is rubbish. I saw what happened. You executed him. I was there. I saw it with my own eyes."

"Lucie, Lucie…" Zac tut tuts. "You really don't know your station in life, do you?"

Chloe looks at Zac, confused. She didn't know. Zac hadn't shared with her the details of what went down at the ruins. That could be crucial.

But before Zac can say anymore he slams on the brakes as, rounding a corner, the headlights pick out Mason, standing in the middle of the road with both hands held high above his head in a gesture of surrender. The ambulance comes to a halt maybe fifteen yards from Mason. He is soaking wet, oblivious to the rain. How he had known that Lucie was in this particular ambulance is impossible to say. Maybe it was Zac's presence here, not Lucie's, that had drawn him to this spot. This is the first time Lucie has seen him since his father's death. He looks wild, insane with rage.

"Well, look who we have here," says Zac.

Then at a leisurely pace he climbs out of the ambulance, tucking his gun into his belt behind his back.

"Chloe, we have to stop him. He's going to kill Mason!" Lucie whispers to Chloe.

"Don't be ridiculous," Chloe freezes.

Zac walks towards Mason and shouts, "I was half-expecting to run into you again. Great timing." He pulls the gun into view.

With no order from Zac, with no suggestion at all, Mason slowly turns his back on Zac and kneels down. He lowers his arms and tilts his head forward. Eyes downcast. To Lucie it looks as if Mason is offering Zac the back of his head to perform the exact same execution he had done on his father.

Lucie says coldly and calmly, "Let me go, Chloe. I can stop this. If you don't we are all dead. Zac killed Mason's father, Doyle, I mean."

"Mason's father?" Chloe is amazed.

"That means he must kill us all: Mason, me and you. He's mad, completely deranged. You can see that, can't you?"

Finally, Lucie has got through to Chloe. She grabs a black holdall and rummages energetically around inside it pulling out a stubby looking weapon of sorts, not like any normal gun, though. That is for sure.

"Chloe! Unlock me. For God's sake."

"I need you to stay in the ambulance," Chloe says climbing out of the back door, leaving Lucie handcuffed to the stretcher, "If Zac sees you outside he *will* freak, believe me. Then things really could get dangerous, you're right."

Through the front windscreen Lucie can see Chloe walking resolutely through the rain towards Zac who now has his gun pointed into the back of Mason's neck.

"Zac, is Lucie right?" Chloe demands.

"It's OK, Chloe. I've got this covered. Get back in the ambulance."

There is no way Zac could have missed seeing the weapon in her hand, even though it certainly was not raised in a threatening manner, just held loosely at her side. He must have imagined Chloe intended to back him up, covering him even though Mason is not offering any resistance whatsoever. Zac seems to have complete confidence in his superiority over Chloe.

Chloe ignores Zac and says calmly, walking right up to his side, "You can't do this, Zac. You have to let it go."

"What the hell is wrong with you? I gave you an order, Chloe."

Chloe quickly raises the weapon in her hand and presses it onto Zac's neck, Lucie hears a fizzed crackling sound. She realises it must be a taser even though she has never actually seen one before. Zac's body spasms uncontrollably and his gun falls from his hand onto the road as though he had dropped it accidentally. As the taser blast ends Zac drops immediately to his knees.

"I am putting an end to this right now," Chloe says as though the most logical, rational statement ever. Chloe fires the taser again for another few seconds this time. Zac falls to the ground.

Mason jumps forward and scoops up Zac's gun. He now has a cold ferociousness written across his face.

Zac fights against the pain and manages to place one hand on the ground to prop himself up while the other he holds up behind him in a pathetic attempt to shield himself from his own gun, now in Mason's hand. Mason walks right up to Zac and pushes the gun down into the back of Zac's neck. Chloe says nothing. Lucie holds her breath.

"You showed my father no mercy," Mason states without emotion, just a matter of fact, a setting straight of the record.

"Your father?" Zac looks up in confusion.

"Why should I spare your life?"

"Mason, is this really what you want? This is not the way," Chloe pleads with him. "Let him spend the rest of his life in a prison cell."

Mason looks towards Lucie in the ambulance and as their eyes make contact Lucie is sure that Mason is going to go through with it and execute Zac in precisely the same manner that Zac had done to his father. To Lucie, it feels right even, justice of a kind. But even so, she prays for Mason to show compassion and humanity towards Zac.

She doesn't want any more death here, not even for a man so unashamedly guilty. Several seconds pass. No one speaks. In the end, Mason steps back. Perhaps he had listened to Lucie's appeal for mercy, she never could say. Chloe takes that as a signal to fire the taser once more, this time for way longer than before, fully incapacitating Zac who, once it is over, lies unconscious on the tarmac.

Once Zac came to, he had made no attempt to justify his actions, he shut up shop completely, said nothing with just an angry blank stare on his face, all the way down the mountain. Chloe drove the ambulance. Zac was handcuffed with the same cuffs from which Lucie thankfully had been liberated. She sat up front with Chloe while Mason kept an eye—and his mind too, no doubt—focused on their prisoner.

They had pulled in at the Dolgellau police station and Chloe herself had jumped out of the driver's seat and gone inside. It must have caused quite a stir when Chloe announced to the young constable on duty that they were handing over a murderer. He had come outside with Chloe looking not a little confused to see for himself precisely what was going on. His training had certainly not included dealing with anything remotely like this. Between Mason and the constable, they bundled Zac out of the ambulance and locked him in their single holding cell.

"The whole TAU operation was thrown into chaos by the Alves issue," Chloe explains to Mason and Lucie in front of the ambulance. "And then, when you were brought to our attention, after your accident, that was so big, it transcended the whole command structure of the place. Kahtri was in shock. Zac was convinced Kahtri wasn't up for taking the right decisions and, after the explosion in Lisbon, Zac did indeed start to push in a different direction. I had been aware that this was going on for quite a while. He was my handler in Lisbon and I could see he was becoming less and less rational, more and more obsessed by what Alves was up to, I could tell he was close to…going rogue—if you like—but I still had no proof."

"Well you have enough of that now, I'd say," Lucie says.

"You two need to get out of here. I have always believed Mason is the only one who can decide the right way to handle all this Alves stuff. He has the right brain for it, wouldn't you agree Lucie? Take the ambulance. I won't report it missing until tomorrow morning which will give you time to get away."

"What will happen to you now?" Mason asks.

"I have no idea. I will most likely be court-marshalled for not following Kahtri's orders and for allowing you to escape from Burnt Ash Lodge and again now, I suppose. But I can't do this anymore."

"You could come with us," Lucie suggests.

"Somebody has to stay here to explain what Zac did to Mason's father," Chloe says.

Chloe gives Lucie a hug and then approaches Mason more nervously.

"Well, I suppose you know how I feel about you anyway, so what the hell," she says planting a long kiss firmly on his cheek and then she skips up the steps and goes through the door into the police station.

Lucie climbs into the driver's seat of the ambulance and fires up the engine with the keys that Chloe had left in the ignition. For some reason, she knows it is right for her to take the lead here and to drive.

"I don't think I can take much more of this, Mason," Lucie says in shock, staring out through the windscreen.

As she drives the ambulance across North Wales and through Conner's Quay onto the Wirral peninsula, Lucie cannot get out of her head that somehow Mason played a much bigger part in everything than he has admitted to.

As they are passing along the shore of a long and deep looking lake, Mason asks Lucie to stop for a moment. He gets out of the ambulance and walks up to the edge of the road. He then hurls the gun that had killed his father into the dark as though he can no longer tolerate its presence there with them. They hear the splash as it hits the water.

There is nothing else to say and they drive on in silence through the night.

XVII
Entangled

Bidston Village—24 Hours Ago

Emma walks up the overgrown track towards Bidston Manor. Nobody has been up this way for years, most likely. The brambles and giant nettles remind her of just how ensnarled and venomous her own Medusa-like head is becoming of late. Involuntarily, her mind keeps flitting back to so many irreconcilable and dissonant moments in Lisbon: the explosion itself of course, clashing with her vivid memory of all those beautiful stars in the darkness; the intimacy of her connection with Alves colliding into his agonising final moments. His unjust suffering has left her anxious for—she wonders how to describe it—closure would be the politically correct term, but revenge feels so much more satisfying and honest.

And more disturbing even than all that, Emma cannot get out of her head the look of horror and disappointment on Lucie's face when Emma had pushed her away so harshly. Of course, she had acted in Lucie's best interest, getting her out of there fast had been her sole objective and it must have worked because Lucie definitely was not amongst the dead.

So where is Lucie? Emma has been unable to find any trace of her. And she has tried. Hard. The void left by not knowing has been eating away incessantly at her insides over the past weeks. Couldn't she have been a little gentler? Lucie had come through such an ordeal just to get to the lab. Couldn't Emma have shown just how excited she had been to see her? It is ripping her to shreds: she can't sleep, for the first time ever she is plagued by troubling nightmares, so off the wall that they push themselves into her waking mind.

As Emma reaches the gates, she can appreciate how neglected and run down the property is now: grass growing between the cobblestones in the courtyard; several of the steps leading up to the front door, cracked and dislodged; the bell cord Gryphon had pulled all those years ago, dangling down almost to the ground from its broken wall mounting, swaying uselessly in the breeze.

She takes out the set of keys left for her by Alves, unlocks the gates and goes inside. Despite having had no inkling that circumstances could conspire to make it necessary, Alves had nonetheless taken all the same precautionary measures first devised and implemented by Duncan—which had served so well in the past—to pass on vital documentation and to maintain the integrity of his financial position. So Emma, straight after the explosion in Lisbon had driven the red Lexus into the car park under a luxury Lisbon apartment block.

She had made her way up to the penthouse whose ownership Alves had kept a tenaciously guarded secret and used the key codes located in the memory she had inherited from him to open the door and gain entry. She then broke away the false rear wall of the built-in bedroom wardrobe and tapped the combination into the large safe hidden behind it.

In addition to the usual cash and share certificates, there were a number of documents assigning the legal ownership of Bidston Manor and several other properties on the Wirral to the fake identity of Carlyle Flanagan. Alves had thought of absolutely everything, even that Emma may one day be his successor and so he had picked a name suitable for either male or female when he had written up the documents transferring ownership, just in case she would have to represent that person as the legitimate owner one day. There were also two valid birth certificates from County Cork in the same name one for a boy and one for a girl so she could apply for an Irish passport as back-up if she felt like it. Alves was nothing if not resourceful and detailed.

Alves had secretly set in motion a massive UK based operation focused on a wide expanse of marshland on Bidston Moss and a mosaic of old docks and warehouses towards the eastern end of the Great Float, connecting the Birkenhead docks into the Mersey between Seacombe and Woodside. He had hired a team of engineers and specialist builders to lay all the groundwork for the project.

Needless to say, it caused quite a stir amongst the locals—new investment in that area was all but non-existent and all manner of rumours abounded. The one that gained traction was that it all had to do with the development of some new power generation technology, something akin to cold fusion, although actually this had been circulated by Alves himself as pure smokescreen.

The entrails of the project were—as had been the case in Lisbon—underground but this time on a massive scale. It was so much easier if nothing was visible at ground level to the naked eye. Just a single entry point was located under an old and disused pump house, hidden ingeniously under a tangle of rusted nineteenth century machinery.

And now all of that is done. It had been mostly completed before the Lisbon trials started. The explosion and Emma's taking over control of operations had little impact on things. Lisbon, in spite of its calamitous conclusion had proven beyond doubt that the technology worked—Alves's personal recollections of the initial phase of the generation of the waveform was evidence enough of that—and so, after a few weeks of intense effort, all the final installations were complete. This time the whole thing was built so there would be no need for a team of scientists and technicians as had been the case in Lisbon. Emma would be able to finish this on her own. It just felt so right that way.

Emma draws open the curtains in the drawing-room throwing a cloud of dust into the air which is caught in the shafts of late afternoon sunlight streaming through the windows, like an old cinema projector cutting through a dark smoke-filled auditorium.

All the furniture is covered with dust sheets, even the mantelpiece is protected by a large faded sheet held in place by the same doorstop Gryphon had noticed on his first visit. The rugs are rolled up and pushed to one side out of the way.

When Jules had left for Australia, Gryphon had gone back to Bidston Manor. To this very house. It took many months before he recognised that he would never get over her loss. Sometimes it felt like he was trapped in a maze, as if he could leave one room and wander for days without finding the way back to that same room. He found it overwhelming but not for a single moment did he consider leaving. His memories did not include knowing this place as a home with Jules but just being here gave him some solace. He could feel her presence in every nook and cranny, on every wall, every surface. Here even now, Emma can breathe in her essence, like Jules's ghost is accompanying her in her desolation.

As she looks over towards the fireplace, she sees Moira Cawston swinging that burning stick the night of her suicide, a distant but still raw and painful recollection brought vividly to life by merely her presence here in this place.

Perhaps Moira Cawston had been right all along; Gryphon had indeed been possessed by some unholy spirit.

Then she notices something odd, something that doesn't fit. There are several unmistakable footprints in the dust on the floorboards by the dining table: recent, given the clarity of the impressions. She gets down on her hands and knees and examines them from close up. She carefully slides her middle finger into the imprint, slowly breaking its outer edge. Or is her mind playing tricks on her, another hallucination sent to torment her?

The pattern looks so familiar. These could very well be her own footprints from her own trainers left just seconds ago. Lifetimes of deception finally coming back to haunt her, laughing brazenly in her face. Is she now finally starting to lose her grip on the one thing that has defined her over the past one hundred and fifty-plus years: her mind? Is she now failing to keep all these disparate and conflicting emotions in check?

She sits back on her haunches and closes her eyes, in the exact same posture that Duncan had assumed on the Moss. She shivers as the chill air in the house gets under her skin.

"I'm sorry?" Emma mutters, as if to herself.

"Are you feeling OK?"

"Me? I'm fine," Emma says, looking around the plain office and trying to appear as though she is fully aware of where she is.

"It's just…you seem distracted. Like you slipped away, like you weren't here with us at all for a moment."

This is not the first time. She has had some similar equally disturbing moments, when she has momentarily lost touch, has drifted off into some other space, like falling uncontrollably into a dream.

"No, please go on. I'm here now."

"Well, the source of the problem was the sudden surge at the East Float repeater substation, right on your patch," says the second guy, who up to now has been sitting quietly in the background. Police? He hasn't been introduced, Emma is sure, so maybe.

Emma had been summoned here by the Wirral Council energy department and she felt, given the blackout the whole of Wallasey and most of Birkenhead suffered the previous night, that it would be asking for trouble if she ignored their request.

"And you are?" Emma confronts him.

"I am Detective Inspector Williamson."

There you go; Emma can spot them a mile off, she smiles, definitely one of Alves's better attributes.

"Has there been some crime committed?" she asks.

"No, no," says the council guy, whose name Emma has already forgotten. "It's just hard to see how such an overload could occur without a circuit breaker malfunction."

"Malfunction? I'd say so," Emma senses her chance to put the whole thing to bed once and for all.

"Huge issue, actually. But I can assure you it has all been taken care of. Definitely won't...*can't* happen again. Any damages, of course will be met in full."

Better for Emma not to mention that the East Float repeater substation was the target of some clear act of sabotage. Nor indeed that this is not the only tech outage she has had to face recently; they are becoming commonplace, a pattern starting to emerge. Actually, when she says 'taken care of' that is not entirely accurate either. She has identified the problem but the 'taking care of' bit, the remedial action, has certainly not yet been implemented.

Emma continues, "What might your interest in all this be, Detective Inspector? I would have thought this was a bit mundane for your elevated pay grade."

"Not when eighty thousand people are left without power. What exactly are you doing down there in the East Float?"

"We are just testing some new tech. Nothing at all to do with the power surge, actually. Everything council-approved stuff, it goes without saying." Emma sidesteps the issue.

Emma can see the Detective Inspector is not taken in by her explanation. He must have been tipped off. Probably by the same character who has launched the sabotage campaign against her. No way could he have figured out unassisted that something worth looking into was going on in an electricity substation.

Emma takes deliberate deep breaths in through her nose, trying to re-establish her inner calm. She is still kneeling in the drawing room at Bidston Manor. She knows that. Her eyes are still closed. She senses that things are drawing towards an inevitable conclusion. Critically, she has realised—without doubt—there can be no more transfers. The time for that is gone.

Gryphon had been right after all. He had been the one who had recognised from the outset that some fragments and relics from Father Casey's subconscious personality had persisted through the surfacing procedures and could influence and even exert at times some control over Duncan's natural behaviour. And then there had been the whole Jules thing. That, far from dying back over time, seemed to only increase in intensity. Gryphon had realised that this accumulation of emotional psyches would in the long run become overwhelming; each surfacing adding more background noise, each with its own meddling and clogging interference contributing to Emma's current inner turmoil.

She is not praying but she is certainly somewhere close to it, caught within a conscious trance. Strangely, and perhaps at the same time worryingly, she seems more reassured and peaceful in this glazed state where she doesn't have to interact with the tedious details, with the cold indisputable facts and logic of reality. She finds it soothing to leave all of that behind, to inhabit a world filled only with undefined impressions and moods which she cannot assign to any specific experience or memory, without any source she can pinpoint directly, all of them seeping seamlessly one into the other.

It is like she is walking through a room with multiple veils hanging down, hiding the spiritual essence they embody. Drawing aside one ghostly shadow only reveals another billowing in a chill breeze behind it, waiting to engulf her with its own concealed sensations of yearning, of loss, of passion, of hopeless despair. By their proximity, by the very fact they exist, even in some faint, intangible form she finds profoundly comforting. They belong to her only. And here, at least while she keeps her eyes closed and her mind empty, she can feel them all.

"Are you a gambling man, Jordan?"

"I've been known to have the odd flutter, Mrs Flanagan." To Jordan, Emma has always been Mrs Flanagan.

"Of course you have. I can tell, see? And why wouldn't you?"

Jordan seems nervous. He is not used to this kind of conversation with Emma. Actually, he is not used to any sort of interaction with her. He must have no idea why he has been called into her office in the deepest enclave of the Bidston Moss subterranean facility or where this may be heading and the longer it goes on, the more uncomfortable he appears, the more he fidgets, pushing his glasses further up his nose again and again.

"What were the odds on you getting found out? What did you think? Maybe fifty-fifty? Less likely than that, no? Say eighty-twenty against?"

"I don't know what you are talking about."

"Well said. Keep that going and you never know; she might just believe you in the end. Is that the line?"

Jordan shrugs. Emma hates that. This cretin oozes cocky, smug insolence.

Biting her lip, Emma carries on, "Well, here's the thing, Jordan. I know you tampered with the relays on the electromagnetic switches at the East Float substation. I know that for a fact."

Now Jordan is looking really worried.

"But, Jordan, what I don't know is this. What are the odds on you accepting a way out of this mess."

"I am afraid I truly do not understand what you are going on about," Jordan says. Disappointingly, he still looks capable of denying any involvement in the overload.

"OK, right. Chips down, so to speak. Here's what you do. Tell your handler, whoever he or she may be, to show up at Bidston Manor, alone, next Tuesday at eight and you disappear from my sight…forever." Jordan is part of the last group of workers still on site and his contract terminates at 17:30 that Friday in any case. So his being fired should not be an issue. Emma then takes things to a whole new level, "Or if not. I take your daughter away from you…also forever."

Emma smiles at Jordan, waiting for this to sink in. She has obviously done her homework on him. He does indeed have a daughter, who is just eight years old. Then she continues, "And yes, that is a threat. And yes, I am that mad. And three yeses, I will do it, you can be sure of that."

"Listen, you've got this all wrong," Jordan is squirming now.

"So far, Jordan, it's you who are getting this so wrong. Not me. Get out of here. I expect never to see you again. Just do as I ask. Do yourself a favour. Do your family a favour." And with that Emma presses a button on her desk which automatically opens the door to her office with a swish to one side into the wall, "Out! Now!"

Jordan would rush straight back to his boss and would tell every last detail of their brief discussion. Even though that showed just how sloppy he had been in his sabotage efforts. Jordan may well have thought Emma would never carry out her vile threats but regardless of whether he had absolute confidence in the protection his boss could afford him or not, why would he risk his daughter. He wouldn't, of course, particularly when he takes into account the pittance he must have been paid to do the odd disruption job on Emma's tech, and just how little Emma had asked him to do to placate her.

Emma opens her eyes. She gets to her feet and slowly walks across to the window. The Autumn evenings are closing in so quickly; it is close to dark and just ten past eight. The trees have grown tall since Gryphon's time here and now block any view of Bidston Moss but she can sense its presence there all the same.

She knows instinctively that Jordan's boss will show up. In the end, this is all personal. He is just playing it cool, turning up a bit late, politely late as it used to be termed. He would make no attempt to disguise himself. What would be the point? He would face her head on, that is a given. And so, she is not surprised in the least to see a figure she immediately recognises enter the courtyard a couple of minutes later.

Emma had opened the front door before he had even half-crossed the courtyard.

"Castro, I thought you blew yourself up in Lisbon," Emma says in greeting.

"Quite a place you have here," Castro says cautiously. He stops six feet short of the steps leading up the front door.

"It's been in my family for generations."

"Yeah right," Castro smiles sardonically. He is cagey and alert, his eyes alive, darting distrustfully back and forth as though he fears he may have been lured into a trap.

Emma continues, "It's OK, there's only me here. Won't you come inside?"

"Listen Emma or whoever you are, whatever you are. Let's get one thing straight, shall we?" Castro pulls a gun out from behind his back and levels it directly at Emma's chest. "You don't come anywhere near me. Do you understand?"

"Sure," Emma puts her hands out to either side, showing she has no intention of resisting such a show of strength.

Castro steps forward now; it is remarkable just how much of a boost to confidence a gun can provide. He indicates with it for her to retreat back into the house. She turns around abruptly, hopefully displaying little of the fear she feels and leads him into the drawing-room, Castro lagging a prudent distance behind.

Emma may have wholly underestimated how dangerous meeting Castro could be. She thought she had undertaken a deep enough risk assessment and had concluded that she could not allow another interruption in the surfacing procedures this time.

Duncan's surfacing had been compromised by external events and as a result Emma has had to wait a hundred and fifty-eight years to get a second chance. She is not going to squander that this time. Even if Castro is a vicious killer she cannot let him ruin all her work. She must take care of him first, make sure that this time everything goes off without a hitch.

Now though she has her doubts. She had thought she would be able to control the situation, keep the upper hand easily at all times, but maybe her insomnia and let's face it her fixation on making Castro pay for Alves's death have led her to misinterpret the delicate balance of power between the two of them.

Obviously, the gun is not a surprise; she had fully expected him to come armed. But she had not anticipated that he would show his hand so early or that he would threaten to use it as his opening gambit. Could she have misjudged him so badly?

"Sit over there," Castro points to the far end of the large dining table which like all the other furniture in the room is covered in dust sheets. "Keep your hands on the table."

Castro has thought out exactly how he wants this whole scene to play out. Emma desperately needs to regain the initiative. But for the time being she has to do as he asks.

"Now, tell me exactly what you are doing on the Wirral."

"Bidston Moss was the start of everything, of my very existence, if you like."

"What the hell does that mean? Your very existence?" Castro looks so angry, out of control almost.

"We have to finish this in the same location as it started and at precisely the same time."

"The same time? I'm warning you, don't push it."

"That was the reason for all that effort we put in. You and me. So we could get back here right now at this exact time."

"Oh Christ, I can't stand this anymore."

Castro points the gun at Emma and pulls the trigger. A loud crack resonates around the room. The bullet misses Emma by a wide enough margin but shocks her to her soul. She felt it crash into the wall behind her. The gun has left a bitter, acrid smell in the air.

"What the hell?" Emma gulps.

Smoke curls slowly up out of the barrel of the gun anchored steadfast in Castro's hand, retrained instantly on Emma.

"You don't seem to have got the idea, do you? I want you to explain what's going on. I don't want any more of your nonsensical riddles."

Emma has known Castro for such a long time, but she realises she can no longer predict what he will do. That used to come so naturally to Alves. Perhaps killing Alves has hardened Castro, changed him deep down more than Emma can imagine. Castro has shown he is comfortable taking a life, and now she can be under no illusions that he will be capable of taking another, hers.

"Let me show you a map. With the blueprints of all the installations, how it fits into the geography of the Moss itself." Emma starts nervously to get to her feet, "It's in the back cabinet, over there."

"Stay put! You do not move, at all," Castro smiles. He doesn't trust her. Hardly surprising. Rightly so.

"It's in there," Emma nods towards the dust sheet covered dresser along the side wall. "In the top drawer."

Castro walks over to the cabinet and pulls the dust sheet back without shifting the aim of his gun or even taking his eye off Emma for a second. He seems genuinely surprised not to discover some sort of a concealed weapon there; all he finds is indeed a large rolled map. He takes the map back over to his end of the table and puts his gun down next to him so he can unfurl the map fully, brushing away a layer of dust from its surface with his hand.

"You'll recognise the design," Emma says enthusiastically, "It's pure Alves." Castro studies the map intently, poring over the detail.

"Oh my God! More like *pure* madness. It's massive. You can't seriously be thinking of going through with this."

Castro is not here seeking reconciliation, Emma must not forget that. There is no way back to how things used to be. He killed Alves and now he is here to destroy her and then he will pick through her bones and scavenge whatever remains. He is hooked on greed, both intellectual and financial and he will forever feed that addiction. Once she has given him all he needs or once he tires of the process of trying to extract it, he will kill her pitilessly without so much as a thought.

So, she now has to make sure Castro can see she is still holding back some critical and valuable information. She needs to keep him intrigued, even tease him with the science to stop him from going back to the gun and pulling the trigger, to convince him that at least for a time, she is of more value to him alive. It only needs to be for a matter of seconds, a couple of minutes tops.

"You shouldn't be thinking about *what* is going on, but on *who* I am. That is where things get interesting."

So enthralled is Castro in the details of the blueprints and the science that this hardly seems to register with him and his response when it comes seems casual, almost throwaway, which is totally outlandish given the essence of their conversation.

"I know Alves wasn't human and you're the same, I'd hazard a bet."

"Oh, but I am. I really am every bit as human as you are. More so, actually. I have more humanity gathered together over several precious lifetimes than you could ever dream of."

"Your definition of human is…debatable, to say the least," Castro looks up from the blueprints. "You always had a naive arrogance, you know. I have seen proof that whatever infected Alves altered his DNA."

"You didn't do the break-in yourself, did you? It was Doyle, wasn't it? He passed the DNA results on to you." Castro makes no attempt to refute Emma's assumption.

For Emma, Doyle remains an enigma. There was something about him which felt overly familiar. She had half-recognised the way he had zoomed in his focus on Alves, entrapping his gaze from across the auction room at Christies. There was something in the way he thought, the way his mind tested and probed, like a butterfly flitting around a garden, seemingly in a random, haphazard progression but with an underlying pattern directing its movements even if not readily discernible to the casual spectator.

But Emma could hardly be considered casual, could she? It was so close to her own way of thinking but taken even further, to a new level, one she had not yet been able to achieve. Alves had taken Doyle on and had been overwhelmed by him. Audaciously, Doyle had even lifted Alves's personal security codes directly from his mind, had stolen the DNA results and now it turns out he had handed them over to Castro willingly, it would appear.

"Alves wasn't infected. There is no mindless virus. And this is not some random coming together. It all has meaning. It's all moving towards a single objective. That is what gets passed on from one *human* to the next," Emma emphasises that human connection. "That is what you witnessed on the CCTV between Bisset and Alves. Imagine each of my incarnations is like a separate transparent photographic slide with a watermark embedded on it. When they are all placed one on top of the other, the detailed structure of that plan, of that design, far from being lost, is actually reinforced. It becomes clearer. The rest of the image can be massively different and confused, that doesn't matter; the watermark is identical, it has remained consistent throughout."

"It doesn't sound very human to me."

"You're the one who is inhuman," Emma snaps back at Castro unable to contain her anger any longer. "You rigged the whole damn breach in Lisbon. Just to murder Alves."

Castro had given no thought to the suffering that Alves had endured. Emma tries to breathe calmly as she suffers multiple flashes of the utter terror she had experienced in Alves's death throes as he engaged with her mind and transferred to her his shocking awareness at his own destruction.

"I clearly didn't do a good enough job of it though, did I?" Castro picks up the gun again. Emma is out of time.

He continues, "And you know I can't let you go through with this, either. If you lose control of the containment field, the devastation will be unthinkable. Lisbon was nothing. This could destroy the entire Wirral, most of Liverpool. Hundreds of thousands will die. It's madness. But you knew that, didn't you? And yet you still invited me here."

"But just think about if it works. And it will." Emma is clutching at straws, she knows, appealing to Castro's ego. "The Lisbon trials showed conclusively that the tech is good. Just imagine, you could end up having your name on the first time mesh distortion in history."

"Time mesh distortion? Is that what you are calling it now? You're mad…talk…ing…rubb…ishhhh."

His final words slur into each other and then he is silent. Confusion mutates into shock. Castro tries to raise the gun to point it at Emma but it drops from his hand onto the table with a resounding clunk. He looks at it in amazement. Then his head droops ever so slowly forward and his cheek comes to rest gently on the table just a couple of inches from the gun. His eyes stare unblinking at it.

"Are you not feeling yourself? Too bad, too bad."

Emma now jumps to her feet and moves confidently around the table. She pulls back the dust cover hanging in front of the fireplace and from the floor behind it she grabs a surgical mask and deliberately places it over her nose and mouth. Then she snaps on some rubber gloves.

Next, she picks up a large white plastic bottle and as she slowly unscrews the cap, she continues, "Time mesh distortion—as I was saying before you so rudely interrupted me—that is the endgame, you know. We opened up a fold in time way back in 1865, I know that for sure because I was there. But something went wrong. It has taken a bit longer than anticipated to get things back on track. But now we are there. Sadly, though, in spite of your undoubtedly playing your part—an important part at that—for you, it's too late. You won't get to witness it. You see, you had to go and kill Alves, didn't you? He should have had the honour of doing all this, not me. That was unforgivable. So cruel. To fry him in radiation."

She is now using both hands to empty the contents of the bottle all around the room. Castro by this time will have realised from the pungent, intoxicating smell that it is petrol.

"So I was hoping for something along those lines for you too. Sort of an eye for an eye type of thing. Biblical, if you like. I can't do the radiation thing right now so you will have to make do with this. But it'll do the trick, I am sure."

She holds up the now empty bottle for him to see and then throws it angrily across the floor. She approaches Castro around the table, violently grabs his long and unkempt hair in her fist and drags his head up, holding it there right in front of her own masked face.

"You know what? I've been looking forward to this moment."

She knows he can hear her words and that he will be able to understand her, but he cannot speak. The floor is hers.

"You have to admit, the map was a wonderful touch, though. I knew you would fall for it. You never could trust me, could you? The dust on the map that you so diligently wiped away with your hand was laced with an upgraded neuromuscular agent I have been working on for precisely this moment. It enters the bloodstream through the pores on your skin, through your hands in your case, and is pretty much instantaneous. It blocks the synaptic receptors in the brain and as you see it is really quite effective in stopping all muscular activity, but it doesn't stop your subconscious routines such as breathing or the beating of your heart. Ingenious, wouldn't you say? That way you will be fully awake as your skin melts right off your bones," Emma spits out the last words into Castro's face and then she bitterly slams his head back down onto the table.

She picks up a box of matches from off the mantlepiece. She walks over to the door, stopping on the way to push back Castro's hair carefully, so that he will have a clear view of her from his slumped over position as she pushes the matchbox open and removes a single match. Emma can see the terror in Castro's eyes and it comforts her.

"Betrayal is such an ugly, vicious thing," Emma says.

She strikes the match against the side of the box a couple of times before it flares into life. She holds up the lit match in her fingers so Castro can see it until it almost burns her fingers and then she drops it to the floor where it reacts immediately with the petrol, igniting the fumes in a bluish woosh spreading quickly across the floor and engulfing the room in flames in a matter of seconds. The curtains billow out in the heat and catch light, flames racing up the material and curling across the ceiling. She smiles in the same sardonic way Castro had done when he arrived earlier and she walks nonchalantly out of the house.

By the time she reaches the end of the lane and she turns onto the shortcut towards the Moss, she can see the house behind her burning furiously, flames now rising out of the windows on the upper floor too. She has no desire to watch it burn. This house has brought her only sorrow: Duncan had lost Jules; Moira Cawston had killed herself because of Gryphon; and now, as a siren from the fire brigade gets closer and closer, Emma knows that the flames will already have consumed Castro, he too is gone. Each additional loss multiplies the accumulated pain from the others.

As Emma approaches the Moss, she now feels, rearing up inside her all the psyches she has shared. All trying to be heard. Each and every moment she has lived through, all the way back to Duncan vies for her attention. She is losing control. All those experiences coexist in time, synchronised into a random collage thrown together into this miraculous but chaotic present.

Everyone she has ever cared about is gone. Even Castro. Only Lucie remains. As she strides across the Moss, Emma can feel Lucie's presence more than before. She has a gut feeling that Lucie must still be out there looking for her, edging ever closer. Emma understands that she has no memories of their life together before Alves met Lucie in Lisbon, but the love Emma feels for her friend is nonetheless real, she knows, even if she can only touch it in the most ephemeral of ways. But will that love be able to avoid yet more tragedy? Could

Emma even end up destroying what is now her only friend, too? Her mind is unclear, she feels so alone. Where are you Lucie?

XVIII
Inside

Bidston Moss—Present Day

When Lucie and Mason drove into Bidston well before sunrise, they had noticed a fire burning in a large house just outside the village, less than a mile from the Moss. Several fire engines were still dousing the last of the flames, the house already totally destroyed.

Even now, as the first glimmer of dawn spreads a dull grey light across the sky, from the parking bay where they are holed up at the far end of the massive and, with the exception of a few delivery trucks, empty car park next to the Bidston Moss shopping mall, they can still see thick black clouds of smoke belching out above the village into the overcast and blustery morning taking shape before their weary eyes. Down here though, they have seen no sign of any unusual activity, no police, no sirens, nobody hunting for a stolen ambulance.

From the moment they parked up here, Lucie has felt a gnawing unease in the pit of her stomach. Facing the brutal reality of Mason's father's death, is clearly reason enough to explain that away—the horrors of the past twenty-four hours ever-present in her mind. Somehow though, autopilot has kicked in and she is just about keeping her emotions in check, pushing any meaningful assimilation of all this back until she has time to handle it.

Mason too seems to be repressing any visible expression of his pain or grief but Lucie senses a more fundamental change has come over him. To have been reunited with his father after so long and then to have that source of such hope and joy snuffed out must have been a cruel blow indeed and has left him understandably scarred. His gentle and almost playful innocence has been burnt away like paint blowtorched from his eyes leaving just a gritty unfocused resolve.

As the daylight strengthens, they drag themselves out of the relative comfort of the ambulance, immediately noticing that the wind has picked up into a stiffish breeze. But what really grabs Lucie's attention is that no sooner has she taken a single step in the direction of the Moss, the nervous edginess she has been experiencing fires a shudder of anxiety up her spine, the hairs prickling on the back of her neck. Lucie opens the passenger door again, leans inside and takes Matt's gun from the glove compartment. She slips it into her belt in the small of her back under her jacket without Mason noticing. Given what had happened up at the ruins, she has no intention of being caught again with no protection and certainly not in such a disturbing place.

They head down a narrow passage at the very end of the car park flanked by huge wild gorse bushes. It leads behind the shopping mall onto the series of raised pathways which criss-cross the Moss itself or at least the sorry remnants of that place as still exist today. The Moss is not as Lucie had imagined at all, littered with all manner of discarded junk: car tyres, a broken bicycle with no wheels, a couple of old suitcases, a terminally ripped sofa with its guts strewn all around.

Rising just beyond the end of the car park and passing directly over the edge of the Moss is a busy flyover leading to the Wallasey tunnel approach a mile or so further on towards the Mersey, providing—even at this early hour—a constant background rumble of trucks and cars over the whole area. Under the flyover, Lucie and Mason make out a chain-link gate maybe fifty paces away which marks the entrance to the property where TransWorldX delivered Alves's gear.

Lucie had checked out the precise location of the place online back in London and she knows it covers a vast area. As the path rises a few feet, she can see it all laid out before her. First, an expanse of existing marshland with tall reeds growing out of stagnant waterlogged mudflats and beyond that, the Moss gives way to a series of abandoned docks which run as far as Morpeth in the distance where they merge into a newly built industrial park on the Birkenhead side of the Wallasey pool.

Back when Duncan was alive, this stretch of almost two miles of docks—the Great Float as it is known—must have been quite a sight, buzzing with life and noise: ships queuing, tying up, loading and unloading; longshoremen by the thousand; all manner of bustle and industry. But Lucie and Mason now see no evidence of anything going on at all here beyond the chain-link gate, no trucks, no vehicles on the entry road, and not a soul in view.

"Not exactly a hive of activity. Where is everyone?" Lucie mumbles to herself.

Mason barely grunts in response, his mind clearly elsewhere.

As they get nearer to the fence, Lucie feels her anxiety swelling to somewhere close to outright panic. Each step forward drives an ever-stronger sense of menace encroaching and spreading uncontrollably across her mind. She can't get her breath, she feels as if she is being smothered, fright choking the air out of her lungs.

She stops. Mason looks around from a few yards further up the path. Surely, he must in some way be sharing her distress but she can find no sympathy in his blank gaze. Lucie feels alone here, lost and utterly exposed. Involuntarily, she retreats a couple of steps.

"What's the matter?" asks Mason.

"I don't know. I can't explain it. But there is something truly frightening down here. Something…evil."

"Evil? Listen, you are in shock, that's all. It's hardly surprising. Your mind is just working out how to cope with all the appalling things that went down last night."

He doesn't get it at all. At that moment, Lucie realises just how little she actually knows of who Mason really is, of his true motivation in all this. He on the other hand, with his own unique and right now frankly disconcerting gift—if you can call it that—knows her inside out, quite literally.

How can she be sure that all his obsessing over her—and obsessing is certainly what it amounts to—is not merely a ploy, duping her into leading him straight to Emma? Hadn't he always insisted that Emma had to be stopped? Since their first connection that is what he had said, repeatedly. And what the hell did that mean? Stopped how exactly?

"I'll have you know that I am under no illusion as to what *went down* last night," Lucie makes it clear that she is none too thrilled at Mason's dismissive attitude. "I'm not crazy, you know. The fact you can't see it or feel it, doesn't mean it's not there, does it?"

"You need to calm down, push the fear into the background."

"Calm down? Right," Lucie fumes.

"There is nothing evil down here at all," Mason then even has the gall to snigger to himself, Lucie is sure. And that sort of comment certainly does nothing to help, actually raising her anxiety level, not lowering it.

What's more, Lucie is beginning to have real doubts over how far she can trust even herself to act in her and more importantly in Emma's best interest. She senses the edges of where her own free will ends and where potentially Mason's influence over her actions begins are becoming blurred. And then she realises annoyingly that Mason is probably picking up on these same thoughts. She can't get any privacy even in her own mind.

"I can't go on. Not that way at least."

Just raising her finger to point towards the gate triggers another surge of fear in her heart. The more she is conscious of it, the more that sense of dread builds inside her, drowning out every other emotion. At the same time, she sees Mason becoming more powerful and more controlling while she just shrinks away, becoming only weaker, more fragile. She is losing it completely. She turns away in despair and covers her face with her hands unable now to go either on, nor back.

"Hey, Lucie, it's OK," Mason is suddenly at her side finally understanding how bad things are for her. He grabs her arm and helps her retrace their steps back to the car park. As the Moss recedes into the background so Lucie's anxiety remarkably also fades.

Mason then leaves her next to the ambulance to do a quick reconnoitre of the perimeter of Emma's supposed hideout alone this time, thankfully. In the meantime, Lucie walks up to the other end of the strip where she feels positively elated in comparison to a few minutes earlier, although that basic sense of unease, even here, has not disappeared fully.

Despite it still being only 8:30 in the morning, the large out of town DIY stores and discount supermarkets seem to be doing a brisk trade with customers hurriedly wheeling trolley-loads of stuff back and forth to their vehicles. Everyone though seems keen on getting away from here just as quickly as they can.

What's more, Lucie notices that fewer and fewer cars have elected to park as far along in the car park as Lucie and Mason. The rows furthest from the Moss are already chock-a-block while the first two rows are still absolutely empty except of course for their ambulance.

Lucie goes into a dingy-looking supermarket with a mind to digging a bit deeper into her irrational panic attack. It is virtually empty.

"No-one goes anywhere near the Moss anymore," says the chatty cashier who seems grateful to have someone to talk to as Lucie buys a couple of bottles of water.

"They don't?" asks Lucie.

"It used to be a popular place for cyclists and walkers but a couple of months ago all that changed."

"What happened? Was there something that started it?"

"The only thing I can say is that I know it is dangerous down there. You can feel it all around. I even use a different route to get to work these days. It takes the best part of an hour instead of just a fifteen minute walk across the Moss but no way am I going anywhere near that place. It's creepy."

When Lucie comes back outside, so powerful has the wind become that she has to lean forward into it to keep her balance as she walks back to the ambulance. Standing by the rear doors, sheltering from what can only be described now as a gale, she recounts to Mason on his return what the cashier told her.

"I must have been wrong," Mason says.

"Hey, is that even possible?" Lucie jokes although at the same time she is trying to make a serious point.

Mason ignores her insinuation, "I've been thinking; it could be artificial."

"Artificial?"

"Yes, when I was locked up in Burnt Ash Lodge, I read a paper suggesting evidence of a link between low intensity electromagnetic fields emitted by certain types of geological storms and an increase in suicide incidence rates."

"Now you think I'm going to become suicidal. Please!"

"No, well…so long as you don't get too close to the source." Lucie can't work out if Mason is messing around or not.

"You're not exactly being very comforting, you know," she says.

Mason is certainly not laughing though, as he continues, "This could be some sort of man-made field thrown over a specific area. It's just the kind of revolutionary tech that would appeal to our friend Alves, wouldn't you say?"

"I only met him once, for lunch in Lisbon. I have no idea what gets him going."

"It's clear that the further back you are from the Moss, the less strength the field has, the less anxious you feel. Right? And the converse is likewise true. The closer you get, the stronger it gets. All done at a subliminal level targeting a specific emotional response: anxiety and fear. That will keep people away, stop them from becoming too inquisitive."

"You actually think this is something cool, don't you? Even though it is totally terrifying for me."

"Well, you have to admit it's a pretty neat solution. No need for security guards or anything cumbersome like walled blockades, or cameras. That would explain why there is no-one up this end of the car park, too."

"So how come you're not affected? You can't even feel it through me."

"I don't know."

"Probably another by-product of your brain rewiring," Lucie adds under her breath with a laugh.

"You might be right. That could have something to do with it."

"Really?" Lucie can't believe Mason is actually taking her cynical throwaway comment seriously.

"If you remember, my father said that his brain worked on the same wavelengths and patterns as Alves's. I guess there could be some sort of a natural blocking frequency built into my DNA for emotions that are man-made. If they're not genuine emotions, maybe that's why I can't feel them. Does that make any sense?"

"They feel genuine enough to me, I assure you."

Their discussion is brought to an abrupt halt as they both feel a sudden gust of wind which blows up into the air not just a mass of litter but also dirt, and even some small twigs broken off from the trees lining the car park in a mini-whirlwind.

Usually gusts by their very nature are short-lived bursts of stronger wind which then ease back to the underlying background wind speed. But this particular gust only seems to get stronger and stronger. People are finding it difficult to walk at all and several empty unattended trolleys are sent hurtling into the sides of the parked cars.

"What the hell?" Lucie has never seen anything like it. It looks more like something you see on television from the tornado belt in America, not a peaceful English weekend scene at all.

"I fear this is only going to get worse," Mason shouts above the ever louder roar of the wind. A high-sided delivery truck which has just unloaded its cargo is caught in a crosswind and topples over wrecking an expensive-looking SUV parked alongside.

"We are running out of time. Come on."

Mason jumps into the driver's side and fires up the engine. A less than enthusiastic Lucie climbs back in on the passenger side, aware that Mason must be planning on breaking into the Bidston Moss compound and she remembers only too clearly just how scared she was when she was still fifty feet from the perimeter fence.

She has absolutely zero desire to submit herself to an even more intense dose of that; becoming suicidal doesn't feel that off the cards. But her intuition tells her that the weird things happening here are all in some way connected to Emma. She can feel her so close now and she knows the only way to complete her journey to find her friend is to accompany Mason and to go along with whatever plan he may have.

The wind is hammering into the side of the ambulance, making the window on Lucie's side rattle chaotically, about to blow it straight off its flimsy-looking frame. Mason throws the ambulance into gear and accelerates around the car park and onto the access road towards the perimeter gate. Lucie wonders if the screech of metal on metal is actually the shearing away of the bolts holding the vehicle together and that the whole body of the ambulance could be ripped right off its chassis at any moment. Or maybe this is just that psychological anxiety field kicking in again.

Her panic multiplies exponentially the closer they get to the gate. But Mason has no intention of being stopped this time by Lucie's discomfort, or indeed by a chain-link metal gate. Lucie holds her head in her hands, too petrified to look, to even care what Mason is doing. She keeps her eyes tight shut letting out an anguished low moaning sound. Her heart she is sure actually stops for a few seconds, so appalling is this assault, so intense is her fear.

Then there is a deafening crash as the ambulance collides into the gate at speed, smashing the chains and ripping the gates clean off their hinges. One gate panel lurches up onto the bonnet and shatters the windscreen before flying over the roof of the ambulance.

Mason slams on the brakes and the ambulance screeches to a halt still dragging the remains of the second section of the gate lodged into the front bumper and across the passenger door. Lucie is thrown forward against her seatbelt and is severely winded. But as she gets her breath back she realises that her sense of anxiety has gone. She feels ecstatic; her relief far outweighing any concerns she may have as to what they might find in this place.

"Well, that should have got Emma's attention," Lucie quips chirpily.

Mason is already clambering out of the driver's side door, with a look of amazement etched across his face.

"My God! I have never seen anything like this, Lucie. It's amazing."

It is only then that Lucie realises that everything is quiet outside the ambulance. There is no wind at all. She too climbs out of the ambulance, navigating the piece of gate obstructing her door. She stands looking in awe back into the car park. Outside she can see trees bent over by the gales, all sorts of debris now being thrown around in the violent wind, while here only a matter of twenty metres inside the perimeter fence there is dead calm.

Looking upwards Lucie can see that there appears to be a milky, virtually transparent haze, covering the whole of Bidston Moss and several of the abandoned docks in a massive dome-like structure, which seems to be protecting the whole area from the gales. The dome must be close to a couple of miles in diameter at ground level.

"What is this place?" Lucie asks, hoping to get some sense of perspective in all this insanity.

"You remember those tracks you told me about in Lisbon, around the dome above the lab. Well, that has been taken to another level altogether here," Mason is in part answering Lucie while at the same time speculating on his own behalf. "The entire perimeter is most likely some sort of huge particle accelerator. Within its confines, the whole area is somehow kept stable, making sure it is not put under excessive stress. Really quite impressive. I guess this must be what Duncan has been working towards ever since his intervention over a hundred and fifty years ago."

"But why go to such lengths? What is the point of it all?" Lucie asks, but on that front Mason remains silent.

They can now see down the full length of the Moss to the docks with the abandoned warehouses and the disused cranes which line their wharfs. They follow the access road down a half a mile or so edging around the outer limits of the Moss until they reach the first of the buildings but they find no-one there at all.

"Emma is here somewhere. She has to be," Mason states, but clearly he too is perplexed.

They approach the only meaningfully sized buildings which could house the truckloads of equipment that were delivered here from Lisbon and elsewhere.

But they are just shells: roofs gone, walls crumbling. An old abandoned railway station is overgrown with weeds rising up to over six feet high between the cracked empty sidings and platforms. For the next hour or so, they look systematically through all the sheds and storage facilities but come up with nothing, just rubble and some ancient machinery, just deserted empty warehouses and putrid-looking docks. Nothing even remotely from the twenty-first century.

Lucie sits down disconsolately on one of the old rope mooring buttresses. Why hasn't Emma made an appearance? Surely, she must have seen them here. The water in the dock is dark and has traces of oil floating on the surface. The reflection in the water of the Moss on the far side is mirrored in the still black water. But something there draws her eye.

Something doesn't quite fit. She focuses more carefully remembering for a moment the mirror images she would look at in the greenhouse in the kitchen garden at Carsphairn Hall and then within the oil residue on the surface where the colours of the oil swirl, she starts to identify the broken outline of maybe a second miniature dome at the centre of the main structure but much smaller, directly under the apex. Oddly, when she looks out straight across the dock, the source of that reflected image is totally invisible.

"Hey Mason," Lucie shouts. "What do you make of this?"

Lucie feels some relief when Mason confirms her observation.

"I would never have seen that, for sure," he says praising her alertness.

"So how come I can make out that structure reflected in the water but nothing is visible to the naked eye?"

"There must be some sort of cloaking device which scrambles the image, probably something to do with the colours. From whatever angle you look at it, the colour temperature, the contrast, the shade and highlights must all be singled out and identified from the background you would see if this structure were not there and in real time they are replicated on its surface, rendering it invisible from whatever angle you happen to be looking at it. The presence of the oil slick must in some way cancel it out or slur that effect, so you can see some of it in the reflection. The technology behind this must be amazing. Let's go."

Mason is already heading off around the dock moving at a sharp clip. Lucie picks herself up and follows as quickly as she can.

It takes them several minutes to walk across the marshland on the other side of the dock but as they begin to approach where they calculate the inner replica dome must be, they begin to see the structure ahead of them. The cloak is not so effective from close quarters and from a couple of metres away it is pretty much fully visible. Its outer wall seems to be made of some gelatinous fluid which splits the light into a million colours not wholly unlike the oil slick on the dock.

It reminds Lucie of a bubble blown through a hoop of washing-up liquid but on a whole different scale, of course. It is maybe a hundred yards in diameter but still looks so fragile and delicate that it could burst by just touching it. As Mason approaches the bubble, he raises his hand to test its substance. His hand traverses the gel membrane, with no apparent resistance at all, fracturing the light into tiny multicoloured pixel-like fragments.

Once his hand is through, inside the bubble, these then reconstitute into the image of Mason's hand again while the fragmentation remains dazzling and hypnotic around his wrist. When he retracts his hand, there is no evidence of any residue from the gel or any moisture on his skin and no visible trace of his hand having been split into millions of pieces and reconstituted.

"That is so like Lisbon. Just before the explosion," Lucie states with a chilling cold tone.

"This must be the outer edge of Emma's containment field. It's the same as Kal encountered back in 1865 but bigger. At the centre of this bubble must be the exact spot where Duncan had his encounter with…whatever it was he came into contact with back then."

Lucie remembers with alarm all the disastrous consequences that ensued from Kal entering the containment field. She touches the gun still in her belt behind her, hidden under her jacket, as if it could offer some reassurance against unforeseen dangers to come. "Do you think Emma is in there now?" Lucie asks tentatively.

Mason ignores her. He walks forward and just as had happened with his hand, this time his whole body fragments and then reconstitutes itself on the other side of the containment field.

Lucie can still see him through the gelatinous surface of the field but as he takes a couple of steps beyond it his form starts to dissipate becoming quickly indistinguishable from the gel itself.

Lucie has no alternative other than to follow or lose contact with him altogether which she has no intention of doing. She takes a deep breath and steps into the gel. She feels a slight coldness on her skin and a distant tingling sensation across her vision but that is all. She can then immediately see Mason again some metres in front of her. He appears to be walking in slow motion, and even seems to be slowing down more the further he moves away from Lucie. She follows him forward.

The interior of the bubble seems transparent with just a film of translucent oil swirling across its surface which after a couple of paces becomes again invisible. Even from here at the heart of Emma's domain, Lucie can still see back all the way to the car park which now feels as though it belongs to another age, a different dimension, which might not be too far from the truth.

It is then that Lucie sees Emma, some fifty yards away, kneeling with her head lolling forward unnaturally. Lucie feels her heart skip a beat at finally seeing her friend again. She wants to rush forward to her but she can hardly lift her legs, something is slowing her movements. It is like she is dragging herself through half-dried concrete while in reality the marsh at this point only comes up to her knees and should not pose any real obstacle. She quickly realises the closer she gets to Emma the slower she seems able to advance the same as when Kal approached Duncan. Perhaps here too time could be moving at different speeds at different distances from the focal point of the bubble.

Then she notices that as she advances the terrain is also changing too, all of it. And not just here in the bubble, even outside on the horizon. Bidston Hill goes from being covered in silver birches and pine trees to a scorched and barren rock in a matter of what seems to be just a few minutes. Inside the bubble the wet marsh around Lucie's feet is drying out more and more with every laborious step she takes towards Emma.

Lucie tries to shout out to her friend but her words are swallowed up in the air in front of her mouth. She sees Mason who even after several minutes of effort is only just reaching Emma and has virtually come to a full stop. Lucie sees that Emma's eyes are closed. She looks serene but the way her head is falling forward is unnerving, making her almost unrecognisable to Lucie.

It takes Lucie several more minutes of hard slog to pull herself alongside Mason who has now stopped maybe five metres from Emma. The marsh has gone completely, the ground now a dusty rock. She can feel it, hot through her trainers. The air too is parched and the sky appears to have a dark red tinge like late dusk, not mid-morning.

Lucie cannot be sure if Mason is able to see her, or hear her here. He looks static, frozen.

"Is Emma OK?" she asks him.

At the precise moment Lucie speaks, Emma jerks open her eyes as though something in Lucie's words or perhaps just the sound of her voice has cut through to her, prompting her to come alive suddenly from a dormant state.

Emma rubs her eyes with excessive vigour as though they have been shut for an age and lifts her head peering curiously as if she is not quite able to make Lucie and Mason out through the hot dust-laden air.

Mason offers no answer to Lucie's question, he seems totally transfixed by Emma, staring intently at her.

"Lucie? Is that you?" Emma splutters in a half choke as though her voice has not been used for an age either.

"I let you go off to Lisbon on your own and just look what's become of you," Lucie jokes but her distress is clearly discernible in the quivering tone of her voice. Emma's stare now picks her out.

"Have you really come all this way just because of me?" she asks, seemingly with genuine surprise.

Lucie had somehow been hoping that the Emma she had seen in Lisbon may have been replaced by the one she knows and loves, the one that at seeing her would jump up and hug her to death, all that nonsense from Zac about Emma not being Emma anymore, relegated to some outlandish nightmare.

But while the words themselves seem authentic enough, Lucie is shocked at the stark lack of any shade of emotion, as if Emma's mind is not engaging with her heart, almost as if she were imitating her true self.

And then, as Emma takes in more of her surroundings, she becomes aware of Mason and her demeanour slides disturbingly into an even less familiar guise for Lucie. Emma slowly gets to her feet and scrutinises Mason with far more genuine interest than her life-long friend has warranted. In the blink of an eye, it is as though Lucie no longer exists.

"What have we got here, then?" Emma carefully stalks around Mason, and then adds with a sneer, "A new boyfriend?"

Lucie can feel the aggression bristle between Emma and Mason.

"Don't you see you are only going to compound this mess if you insist on going through with this?" Mason asks with a sudden depth of conviction, like he has unlocked the code to access Emma's own thought processes. Hardly surprising given what she knows of Mason, Lucie supposes. Then Mason adds in a more menacing tone, "Either you put a stop to this insane project once and for all or I will."

Emma laughs, "But he's so predictable, trotting out some feeble-minded threat. So disappointing."

"You understand exactly what I mean. You are already losing control of it."

"Am I now?" Emma ponders, clearly fascinated and yet, at the same time, perturbed by Mason.

Slowly, Emma steps right up to Mason, so close their faces are almost touching. But Mason doesn't flinch.

"You *are* different, aren't you?" Emma says with a puzzled look. "Do I know you?"

"Look around you," says Mason with cool-headed bluntness, "All of it was just a grotesque mistake." Lucie can see that Mason's attitude, his whole being is changing before her eyes. He seems so sure of himself, so much more confident about what he is saying.

"You're talking rubbish!" Emma shouts back at Mason. Lucie does a double-take, thoroughly shocked. Emma doesn't shout. Ever. Such an embittered and antagonistic pushiness is not in Emma's character at all. Lucie finds it deeply disturbing to see her friend like this.

Emma continues, "How can you say that? The whole point is that *without* this…" she spreads her arms and looks up to the heavens, embracing everything around them, "there would be nothing left on this planet. No life at all. Over the next few years these habitats will become commonplace, essential in fact."

"Ironic, wouldn't you say?" Mason butts in, more than comfortable to share the same aggressive energy which is evidently consuming Emma, "that all the devastation being unleashed on the world is all down to you, to what you are right now setting in motion."

"That is not true. The habitats offer a safety net, an ark, if you like—that is what they become known as. It's only down to them that humanity is kept alive at all for the next two hundred years until such a point where the time mesh technology can be developed and can offer us a chance to put things right."

"Put things right? You have to be kidding."

"Hang on. What the hell are you two talking about?" Lucie interjects, desperation seeping into her voice. Far from the reassurance she had expected on finally seeing Emma again, her friend's bizarre comments and behaviour and the ever-increasing hostility between Emma and Mason have sent Lucie's head spinning. "How can you say any of that nonsense about two hundred years from now?"

Once again Lucie's voice seems to resonate with Emma, who abruptly severs her private quarrel with Mason and walks briskly over to her friend. Here, at the very centre of Emma's containment field, time at least seems to be obeying the usual rules of physics. Or maybe Emma's awakening has stabilised just temporarily the volatile currents of time swirling around this place, Lucie cannot say. Affectionately, Emma puts her arm around Lucie's shoulder and guides her away from Mason a few paces, drawing her in.

"Look at this place," Emma says in a whisper, as if deliberately enticing Lucie into her confidence while she smiles sardonically in Mason's direction.

Emma then turns and points up towards Bidston Hill in the distance. Lucie sees the reddish sky outside the dome has intensified and darkened even over the few minutes Lucie and Mason have spent inside its protective shield.

Towering plumes of dark spiralling storm clouds lash across the barren landscape. The shopping mall is gone, Bidston Village looks abandoned and in ruins, the marshland of the Moss just an arid dust bowl.

"Outside, that is what it will be like here," Emma continues, "That is why we had to try something."

"Do you expect me to believe that…" Lucie hesitates, stepping away from Emma, "that *we*, in some way, are actually seeing into the future?"

"Not so much seeing as actually being a part of it. It's the place itself, this particular spot on Bidston Moss. Two different moments in time are being merged together, so we exist in both."

Lucie is lost for words. Emma's matter of fact explanation of the unexplainable makes Lucie realise that whoever this is before her, she certainly has nothing to do with the Emma that left for Lisbon only a couple of months ago.

Lucie and Mason are standing here communicating with someone whose origins may indeed lie outside of their own time, even though the words are being spoken by or through Emma.

"As you can see," Mason says kicking the ground, raising a cloud of bone-dry dust, "it hasn't worked. Your arks, your artificial habitats—whatever you want to call them—were never going to be the answer, were they? It's like putting a moth in a jam jar. It doesn't protect it. The moth will still suffocate. There is no life here."

Lucie looks all around outside the dome. Mason is right, she sees no sign of life anywhere: no trees, no plants, no animals, no people. She shivers.

"Don't worry," Emma says calmly to Lucie. "Here within the time mesh bubble we are safe, protected by the distortion itself."

"But it doesn't play out like that. You now know all too well where this leads."

"That is not true."

"You cannot lie to me!" screams Mason. "Don't you get it?"

A look of confused resignation appears on Emma's face. Lucie suddenly feels sorry for her friend. Mason seems even to be getting actually taller physically, and more in control of himself and those around him with every passing minute.

"Who are you?" Emma has snapped her focus back onto Mason, her deep frustration showing ever more clearly.

She abandons Lucie and walks over to him saying, "It's like you are snatching my thoughts before I even have the chance to finish thinking them for myself. How can you do that? I can't quite place you but somehow I do know you, don't I?"

"In a way, you do. We are both the product of a single moment in time. But our paths diverged. Until now, that is."

"Don't you just hate it when people refuse to answer a straight question," Emma spits out in exasperation, turning her back on Mason suddenly. She glares now at Lucie, a look of anger raging across her face. How could Emma have become so uncaring, her mood veering in an instant from tenderness to pure vitriol? "Who are you, I asked."

"My name is Mason Chambers," he answers.

"You don't say. Now there's a name," Emma is visibly stunned.

"I am directly descended from Duncan."

"Impossible," Emma rejects the idea out of hand. "Duncan had no kids. He couldn't."

"You're wrong about that too. Jules had a son who was born days after she landed in Australia. Duncan's son. He was my great, great grandfather."

Now Mason has Emma's undivided attention.

"You always had your doubts, didn't you? You always thought that was a possibility."

"There he goes again. With the mind games stuff. Lucie, is this guy for real?" Emma laughs uncomfortably.

Lucie tries to explain in a calm voice, "Mason has a photo taken just before Duncan's execution. In Newgate Prison."

"Jules really had a son?" Emma seems to drift off as if regressing into some other far off existence for a moment.

"Go on then," Mason jumps back onto the offensive. "Now you. Tell Lucie who *you* really are, why don't you?"

Emma ignores Mason completely.

After a moment Mason continues, "You can't, can you? Because you yourself don't even know. Well I can tell you. You are nobody. You are not even human. Strictly speaking you are not even alive. You are just a copy. A coded copy of some guy executed way back when."

Emma offers no comeback to Mason's attack. Her eyes flit around involuntarily, she seems only half in the moment, as though she is perhaps still having difficulty digesting who Mason is and that he is a direct descendent of hers.

"Well? Is Mason right?" Lucie asks sternly.

"Disappointing, for you to take the side of this freak. I'd keep well away from him if I were you, Lucie," Emma says defiantly, pointing an accusing finger at Mason, while failing to either confirm or indeed to refute Mason's allegation.

But there is a look in Emma's eye that Lucie recognises instantly. She had seen it so many times when they were kids; a momentary glint of sadness, tinged with embarrassment at being caught out, at her pretence of honesty being revealed as a sham but still not being able to accept it and much less confess to it. But in that glance, at that exact same moment, Lucie also knows that somewhere inside this shell at least some part of her friend still exists.

Emma stands back, smiles and takes a deep breath.

"This was our only chance, believe me," Emma explains. "You're right, Mason, life, even here, inside these sealed constructs, is dying. We had to try something. The original idea was sound enough. Opening a mesh distortion is like inflicting just the tiniest scratch on the surface of spacetime at a precise and pre-determined location. There is no risk of long-term damage being done to the mesh itself. It should have worked."

Mason then takes up the explanation. It is as though he is now putting into words the thoughts he is extracting directly from Emma's mind, making his own critical selection of what is most relevant. Emma seems to be no longer offering any resistance.

"But you were so wrong, weren't you?" Mason utters a despairing sigh and looks around at Lucie. "From the safety of their cushy habitats two hundred years into the future, they thought all their problems were being driven by climate change," Mason glares now back at Emma and says in a scathing tone, "You thought that by re-routing Duncan's brain, that with a single change to his DNA, just the *tiniest scratch*—as you call it—that you could reverse the catastrophe killing your world, that you could instil through Duncan some more sustainable technologies and miraculously everything would go back to normal. What could be simpler than that?"

"Duncan's surfacing was compromised," Emma states. "Kal and James breaking into the containment bubble corrupted the outcome. We had no choice."

"Oh, but you did. Give me a break. You *chose* to keep control of the process. You *chose* to prioritise the reopening of the time mesh distortion in Duncan's mind. You *chose* to carry on meddling with history. That was so short-sighted it beggars belief."

"You should count yourself lucky. Without that disruption caused by Kal and James you wouldn't even be here at all," Emma justifies. "We certainly didn't choose your creation, I can tell you that. The interruption in Duncan's surfacing must have avoided his love for Jules being stripped from his psyche. That was how it should have worked, you know. That way you would never have existed. Actually, you are only here thanks to me."

"Now you want to take credit for my existence. Such arrogance was always doomed to failure," Mason says in disbelief.

The storm clouds outside the artificial habitat have now thickened and merged into a continuous multi-layered mass rushing around the circumference in a horizontal torrent. But what is downright impossible, Lucie imagines, is that the direction of the wind at different altitudes above the ground sometimes flows clockwise while at others is anticlockwise, as if the wind itself is splitting into self-repelling channels. Those vicious forces effortlessly prise the roofs off any buildings they come across, flatten everything in their path and then pick up the debris and add it to the jet-stream causing the whole thing to accelerate even more.

Mason continues, "But now that you have reopened the time mesh distortion you've seen the full picture. *Now* you know, don't you? Climate change had nothing to do with it. It is your own project which is actually causing the downfall of the planet's own defence mechanisms. You have brought all this on yourselves."

Mason looks over at Lucie and explains, "Their original opening of the time mesh distortion back in 1865 imbedded into history an imbalance which should never have been there at all. An imbalance in time itself."

"What are you talking about, Mason?" Lucie asks.

"The universe trends towards increased disorder over time. Becomes ever more complex, ever more disparate. Entropy it's called. Dust accumulates on a shelf, paint gets chipped, potholes appear in the road, things break. Our bodies degenerate. We all die. That's just the natural consequence of time always moving in just one direction. They were right that it is possible to open two separate moments at the same time across a fault line in spacetime, but you can't change history. The more you try, the more that heightened chaos introduced from the future undermines the present, sparking incoherence and uncertainty. Now their upscaled reopening of that same distortion is going to rip time apart. Time is getting its own back on them."

"But how can anyone change history?" Lucie asks.

"That is the point. You can't," Mason asserts.

Emma calmly kneels down and closes her eyes as if adopting a position in meditation. After some seconds just breathing calmly, she replies to Lucie in a sombre, almost nostalgic tone.

"Time is like a waterfall, or more like a series of rapids, with some fast running channels and other slower more passive pools. That is the nature of the time mesh. I remember when I surfaced here. Right here, all those years ago. I could see the time mesh laid out in front of me. I was a part of it. It was so beautiful.

"Where the mesh came close to touching my hand," Emma reaches down extending her fingers, "it threw a flickered fusion of colours against my skin, it melted together with my being. It was truly majestic, awe-inspiring."

Lucie can easily imagine what Emma is saying. Strangely, she feels for the first time since she embarked on her search at one with her friend.

Emma continues, "There is no way to reverse it—Mason is right about that—the direction is fixed. But it is possible to lay down some markers, to obstruct the flow at a certain point. The water will still end up finding its way downstream but it will cause the flow to be subtly altered, and this can lead to consequential changes further on. It's like the butterfly effect, you know. Sometimes just an apparently insignificant obstruction leads to a massive effect, a much greater impact than could ever have been predicted. That is what we were trying to do."

Emma says no more. She bows her head until her chin is resting on her chest, her eyes remain closed.

"So that's your solution?" Mason breaks the intimacy of the moment for Lucie bringing her back to reality with a jolt. "To push on regardless, to persist in trying to change history again. Genius! While this time the whole of humanity hangs by a thread. You know inside, in your innermost thoughts, that it's throwing the whole basis of spacetime out of kilter. Time will cease to be reliable—we're already witnessing some of that pure chaos at first hand. Time will fluctuate uncontrollably and will end up breaking down altogether."

Lucie hears a cracking noise and looks up noticing for the first time several hairline fractures visible across the whole structure of the dome.

Mason continues with increasing urgency, "Your containment field could never hold back the scrambling of time you initiated. It is degrading right here before your eyes. This is your only chance to stop it. When it collapses, it will not be a mere explosion like in Lisbon; the gravitational imbalance will drag everything inside a new gaping black hole which will devour all it comes into contact with."

He mimics Emma's earlier gesture to the heavens and says, "Look around you. Look at where this is going, Emma. Open your eyes. Look, for God's sake!"

Emma stays immobile and silent, eyes still shut.

Lucie then notices that all around the perimeter of the dome lightning bolts fizz and crackle. It reminds Lucie of the moment just before the explosion in Lisbon when the wave reacted at its contact with the accelerator track. The containment field is buckling. It is clear the protective habitat will not be able to withstand the ever more powerful forces being exerted on it for much longer. More and more cracks are appearing and spreading quickly across its entire surface like ice breaking when you step too heavily on a frozen pond.

"I can't get through to her anymore," Mason says in defeat.

But Lucie knows—on some level at least—she is still in contact with Emma. She feels her presence. Lucie kneels down directly in front of Emma and says "I know you are still in there, Emma. Remember, when we ran for our lives from Carsphairn Hall you told me that when you first heard me being born, when you heard me cry that first time, you swore you would always be there for me. And you were. Always. Where is that friend of mine now?" Still Emma kneels unresponsive, apparently unmoved by Lucie's impassioned plea.

Lucie grabs Emma by the shoulders, shaking her and shouts, "So, is that it? Really, Emma?" Lucie looks at Emma's closed eyes in sorry disappointment as she continues dejectedly, "I can't believe you, of all people, are going along with this."

Emma suddenly lunges forward and almost without Lucie noticing she slips the gun out of the belt behind Lucie's back. Lucie has no time to react. Emma jumps to her feet and stands pointing the gun straight at Mason's head.

"Didn't see that coming though, did you?" Emma spits coldly at Mason.

"Oh, my God! Emma, what the hell are you doing?" Lucie cries out. How could Emma have known there was a gun tucked away in her belt, hidden from view at all times under her jacket?

She darts a glare at Mason with a sudden sense of foreboding. She is scared that in some way Mason could be orchestrating how this entire scene is playing out. Could he have deliberately planted the whereabouts of her gun directly into Emma's mind? But why on earth would he do such a thing?

"Or maybe the spanner in the works is you, Mason," Emma laughs a bit too loudly. She is bitter, almost mad, ranting, "Maybe you are the aberration and everything would have worked out just fine if you had never been born, had never been able to come barging in here and maybe if I kill you, everything will get back on track."

"Emma, please," begs Lucie. "No-one needs to die."

"I get the impression that your boyfriend here would disagree with you on that. He seems to think one of us must die. But who? That is the question."

"Mason, tell Emma that is not true."

Mason says nothing.

Then the true paradox of Emma and Mason meeting up here finally dawns on Lucie. In essence standing before her are two versions of the same being, but with distinct and frighteningly incompatible origins. Mason has evolved over generations in a more natural fashion—if you can call it that—while Emma was snatched, hi-jacked by some artificial future technology and then was passed from one host carrier to another over the same one hundred and fifty-eight years.

They may have the same roots but now, as they collide, they repel each other instinctively with such a powerful force Lucie realises that one will gain the upper hand, and one inevitably will end up being destroyed by the other.

She steps between Mason and Emma, directly into the line of fire.

"Get out of the way, Lucie," shouts Emma.

"Are you really going to kill me?" Lucie takes a step forward.

"Stop right there!"

"It's me…Lucie," she says taking another step.

"Look, Lucie. I am not your Emma. Mason was right. I will kill you. Have no doubt."

But Lucie knows that the words Emma is saying are a hoax. Her friend has no intention of killing her; she could never contemplate such a thing.

"I don't think so," Lucie says, now just a few paces from Emma.

Then Lucie realises that somehow the fake Emma is gone, too. The heartless and soulless veil which had smothered and disguised Emma ever since Lucie had found her in Lisbon has been lifted, revealing again her true self.

Maybe it was no more than Lucie's mere presence here, her unconditional support, her resistance to this madness, or maybe it was her having searched tirelessly for her, never giving up, having fought against all the odds and in the end having found her here; perhaps that had edged things in her favour and allowed Emma to reassert herself. Whatever the reason, whatever internal struggle Emma had faced alone, suddenly *her* Emma has now somehow taken back control.

"It has to be this way. Forgive me, Lucie."

Emma flips the gun around and points it at her own chest with her thumb on the trigger.

"No!" screams Lucie.

A gunshot rings out and Emma falls backwards onto the ground. There is a gaping wound in her chest, the bloodstain on her T-shirt spreading ever wider. Emma looks bewildered and frightened. She doesn't seem able to move at all, just lies on her back, blood oozing out from the wound.

Lucie falls to her knees in shock. She scrambles forwards towards Emma but just before she reaches her, she suddenly finds Mason has grabbed her arms from behind and is stopping her from advancing any further.

"Mason, let me go! What are you doing?"

"You can't touch her, Lucie."

"She is dying!"

"She will take over your mind so she can escape from here, while you die."

"You're crazy," Lucie struggles against Mason's vicelike grip but Emma remains just out of reach.

"I can't let that happen," Mason says coldly.

"Why? Emma, why?" Lucie asks, distraught.

Emma coughs; she is still alive, still conscious.

"I would never hurt you," she says in shock but still remarkably lucid and desperate to convince her friend. She coughs again. "I cannot leave here…I die whatever happens."

"She is lying, Lucie," Mason whispers into Lucie's ear. "Don't believe any of this."

Emma drifts away. She mumbles incoherently for some seconds and then is silent. Lucie is terrified that she has uttered her last words. But then, Emma screws up her eyes in sudden pain which perhaps allows her to refocus and she says, her voice now no more than a low deep whisper. "I still wonder who I am…I have memories…so many…but none of them are mine."

"Mason, I must go to her. You must let me…"

"I took so many lives…and their ghosts torment me…"

"She can't die like this, alone."

"So many stars…" Emma is struggling to breathe now. "I remember your voice…"

"Jesus Christ, Mason, please!" but Mason maintains his grip.

Emma is fading fast but in one last effort at contact with her friend, she manages to turn her head so she is looking straight at Lucie. She convulses, and coughs through a low rasping blood filled gasp, desperate to say one last thing, "Sorry, kid…I let you down again."

And the last traces of life fade behind Emma's eyes, dissipating into a vacant glaze. She is gone.

At that instant, a rush of wind pierces the bubble which immediately starts to disintegrate. Mason finally releases Lucie from his grip. Lucie crawls hopelessly over the hot earth until she is lying next to Emma. She touches Emma's face gently.

"Emma, I will always love you," she sobs uncontrollably. "Find peace, my friend."

Slivers of the structure which appear almost organic, a slimy, oily skin, peel away from its surface and once isolated shrivel and dry out in seconds into a fine dust. Then the circular multi-coloured containment wave contracts around

Mason and Lucie, with the corpse of Emma at its very centre. Lucie feels that she is being dragged down into the Moss itself. She is sure her own death is upon her. She can't breathe.

As she loses consciousness, a doubt flashes through her mind as to just how much of a role Mason may have played in Emma's death. He has prevailed undoubtedly. He has come out on top. He has survived. But the one thing Lucie knows above all else in that fleeting moment of lucidity is that she believed Emma completely, she knows her friend would never have betrayed her, would never have harmed her.

Some time later Lucie comes to, unable to recall exactly how she ended up here, or exactly where, or even when here is. The first thing she notices is the soft rain falling on her neck and a light breeze raising goosebumps on her skin. She is lying face down in the wet marsh. She splutters, air forcing itself back into her lungs. She opens her eyes and sees Mason lying next to her, also in the process of recovering consciousness. Who he truly is and who he will become is a mystery to Lucie, but she knows he is going to play a pivotal role in whatever this new tomorrow may bring.

The Moss has been restored, the trees on Bidston Hill are back. The shopping complex has been obliterated by the hurricane, but Bidston Village is largely unscathed, seemingly outside the immediate impact zone, although two hundred years in the future, that certainly hadn't looked the case. But that future is no longer Lucie's future. There is no evidence of the dome, nothing remains of any part of Emma's project. In fact, it may well have never existed at all.

Lucie is appalled and devastated that Emma has died and her sorrow and grief will last for whatever remains of her lifetime. But she then realises that while Emma may be gone, in the end, it was her friend who sacrificed everything, her life itself, to give Lucie, to give everyone, a second chance.

Acknowledgements

I would like to offer a debt of gratitude to the following for their works: *The Liverpool Underworld, Crime in the City 1750-1900* by Michael Macilwee; *The Gangs of Liverpool* also by Michael Macilwee; *Liverpool Gangs, Vice and Packet Rats, 19th Century Crime and Punishment* by Malcom Archibald and *Portrait of Wirral* by Kenneth Burnley.

I would like to thank Moira Young at Oxton Books at the Williamson Art Gallery for recommending the text *The history of The Hundred of Wirral* published in 1847 by William Williams Mortimer, an invaluable and inspiring source.

Can I also thank the staff at the Birkenhead Central Library and the Liverpool Central Library for their help in pointing me in the right direction to find multiple texts and maps.

Finally, and most importantly, I must thank my wife, Marcela, to whom I have dedicated this novel, for all those seemingly endless afternoons in lockdown, for her contributing so fundamentally to the development of the story and for sorting out so many plot issues. Without you this would never have happened.